Kingsley

Carolyn O'Neal

Cover Design by Mayapriya Long, BookWrights.com.

Author's Note: The USS Merrimack, the Civil War battleship, is spelled with a k on the end. For reasons unknown to the author, the k was left off when the Monitor-Merrimac Bridge Tunnel was named.

ISBN: 0996687807
ISBN-13: 978-0-9966878-0-5

For sweetest things turn sourest by their deeds;
Lilies that fester smell far worse than weeds.

-William Shakespeare

PART I

1 Kingsley

Gnats swarmed, and thick poison-ivy vines smothered the street signs. The thermometer on the dashboard registered one-hundred-and-one degrees. July in the dense, humid forests of eastern Virginia was like a jungle to thirteen-year-old Kingsley Smith. He dreaded getting out of Andrés Santos' air-conditioned Prius. He'd stink worse than the Sutherland stables. He didn't know why Andrés had to pick the hottest day of the year to search for dead fish and gay frogs in some backwoods stream near Williamsburg. Yes, Kingsley was worried about the fish dying, and yes, he was curious about the frogs turning gay. But those weren't the reasons he volunteered to help Andrés. He volunteered because of Amanda.

Amanda Santos Sutherland. She had told Kingsley years ago that her last name, Santos Sutherland, translated roughly into *Saint from the Southland* in Spanish and Scottish. She told him it reflected her parents' heritage and it was Spanish tradition to put the mother's maiden name at the end. Kingsley didn't know if that was true or not. Rich people could call themselves anything they wanted.

Amanda wasn't as beautiful as her mother but that didn't matter to Kingsley. Amanda was everything. Smart, rich, brave, and she was his best friend. Her long, black hair was pulled back in a messy ponytail and she always wore dirty riding boots, even when she was helping her priggish father search for fish and frogs in the muggy woods.

Kingsley was a nobody, just the overweight son of a missing dad and an

1

overbearing mom. He hunkered in the back seat of the car, next to a large box filled with work gloves, water-testing kits and empty bottles. He figured Andrés had brought the Prius to impress any eco-friends he might encounter, leaving his BMW back at the Sutherland mansion.

"How do you know if a frog has turned gay?" Kingsley asked, which made Amanda giggle. Kingsley felt a surge. Nothing was better than hearing Amanda laugh.

"They're not turning gay," Andrés said as he maneuvered the car down the gravel roads.

"Isn't that what we're looking for? Gay frogs?"

"No," Andrés said. "We're testing the water. Frog populations are being devastated by a host of man-made toxins. Petroleum, pesticides, and herbicides. Atrazine, for instance, is an herbicide popular among the large corn producers. I read a study that claimed atrazine emasculated 75 percent of exposed male frogs and turned 10 percent into females."

Kingsley fidgeted with his extra-large t-shirt, pulling it down over his lap.

"It parallels what's happening to alligator populations," Andrés said. "In some Florida lakes, alligator genitalia are one-third the size of what they used to be. Their reproduction rate is almost down to zero. Petroleum-based chemicals mimic estrogen and block testosterone, permanently damaging the development of male fetuses. Scientists have found abnormalities of their testis and smaller penis size."

Kingsley scowled. What sort of pervert measures alligator dicks for a living?

"How close are we, *Niña*?" Andrés asked. Andrés usually called Amanda *Niña*, which Kingsley discovered after a meandering and occasionally pornographic internet search meant girl in Spanish.

Amanda read aloud the directions from her phone. "Ten miles west of Williamsburg, near the Chickahominy Riverfront Park." She scrolled down. "It's called Methoataske Creek. That means *turtle laying eggs* in Shawnee."

Kingsley wasn't listening. He was studying the back of her slender, light-brown neck, wondering if she wore anything under her skimpy ocean blue tank top—the crisscross in the back suggested not—when she suddenly turned around to face him. "Maybe we'll find some turtles," she said.

Kingsley blushed and pulled his t-shirt to his knees. "Hope so," he mumbled.

He and Amanda had met when they were both ten years old, right after Kingsley's mother started taking care of Amanda's grandmother, Leslie Sutherland. They'd sit side by side in the back of Mrs. Sutherland's handicapped-accessible van, and he'd show her tricks his friend Billy Jackson had taught him. He'd turn his eyelids inside out, and Amanda would squeal. He'd roll his eyeballs up until only the whites showed, and Amanda would laugh. Now, almost four years later, Kingsley couldn't think of anything to say that wouldn't sound idiotic. He rubbed the back of his neck. Worrying about malformed alligator dicks and how to impress the girl he loved had given him a headache.

"Here we are," Andrés said as he pulled into an unpaved parking lot bordering a deep woods. He stopped the car and passed out gloves, giant black plastic garbage bags and heavy-duty shears. Andrés carried the box of empty bottles and water-test kits. "Follow me," he said to Kingsley and Amanda as he headed into the forest.

"What are you testing for?" Amanda asked as she and Kingsley followed.

"Bacteria, mercury, pesticides, lead, nitrates, BPA, DEHP." Andrés pushed aside low-hanging vines and waved away mosquitoes.

The humidity was relentless, and insects swarmed every inch of exposed skin. "We should have brought some OFF," Kingsley grumbled, swatting away clouds of insects.

Ahead, on the ground and tangled up with weeds, were several broken wooden boxes, each containing horizontal slats. "Looks like abandoned beehives," Andrés said. "Someone dumped them here."

Amanda ran ahead and pulled out one of the horizontal slats. It was filled with small, hexagonal-shaped cells. She pried the shriveled cap off one of the cells with her thumbnail uncovering the desiccated pupa inside. "Colony collapse disorder," she said, looking up at her father. "Right, Daddy? The workers disappear, leaving the queens and babies to starve."

"Looks like it, *Niña*," Andrés said. "That's why we need to test the water. Too much pollution and pesticide. It destroyed their immune system and left them vulnerable to parasites and disease."

"Einstein said that if the bees disappeared, man would soon follow," Amanda said.

"That's an urban legend," Andrés countered. "He never said that."

"Maybe it was Mr. Spock," Kingsley offered grimly. "I get those two confused."

They continued through the woods until Andrés came to a small, shoulder-high tree with feathery leaves. He broke off a leaf and handed it to Kingsley. "Take a sniff." It smelled like burnt peanut butter. "*Ailanthus altissima*," Andrés said. "Also known as the Tree-of-Heaven." He turned to Amanda, "*Niña*, go back to the car and bring me a couple of shovels. I want you two to dig it up."

"In this heat?" Kingsley shooed away sweat bees obsessively circling his head. "Why do we have to dig it up?"

"*Ailanthus altissima* is an invasive species, very nasty," Andrés said. "It doesn't provide anything edible for wildlife, no nuts or seeds, and it emits a poison that kills the roots of native trees."

Without saying a word, Amanda ran back to the car while Andrés headed deeper into the forest. Birds sang and squirrels chirped. Dragonflies zigzagged and butterflies floated. Something was constantly buzzing. Kingsley nervously looked around. He'd never gone camping. Never hiked in the woods before. Never climbed a tree. None of his guy friends had either. He hoped bears couldn't smell the sausage and eggs he'd eaten for breakfast. He didn't know what to do if he saw a bear. "Amanda," he called, trying to hide his fear. No one answered. "Amanda, where are you? Need any help?"

He heard a rustle and tensed. Amanda reappeared, carrying two shovels. "Here," she said, handing one of the shovels to Kingsley. She began digging around the small *ailanthus* tree but the roots were connected to a long series of other *ailanthus* trees, small and large, winding through the woods like prisoners on a chain gang. Amanda threw down her shovel and wiped the perspiration off her forehead. "There's a million of them. This is impossible."

Kingsley didn't give up. He cut the tangled roots with the shears, and then dug into the dirt, using his sizable bulk to bring up the stubborn roots. Amanda smiled. "You're good at this," she said. Kingsley grinned and kept pounding at the roots, sure he'd sweated away at least ten pounds by the time he'd dug up the tap root. He hoped so at least. Amanda pulled a water bottle from her backpack. "You've earned this," she said.

"Thanks," Kingsley said, breathing hard. He felt like a man, not just a pale, fat boy the bullies at his middle school had nicknamed *beluga whale*. He cocked his head, throwing back his wet bangs, and leaned on the shovel. "Maybe we could do this more often, you know, help your dad dig up killer trees."

Amanda laughed. "Killer trees, that's funny."

Kingsley held his shovel like a sword, ready to attack. Amanda pretended hers was a rifle. It felt like old times, the two of them, side-by-side.

Andrés reappeared from the woods, breathless. "*Niña*! Kingsley! Come and look at this!" He hurriedly led them through the woods, and the landscape changed.

Disposable diapers, plastic shampoo bottles, empty makeup compacts and everyday trash littered the ground. Cracked gallon jugs of bleach, open bottles of weed killer and rusted cans of pesticide leaked into the stream. Plastic grocery bags and partially deflated Mylar balloons, with still-bright *Get Well Soon* messages on them, billowed in the trees like misshapen heads. Methoataske Creek didn't smell like fresh water running over clean rocks, it smelled like rotten eggs and petroleum.

Amanda waved her arms in disgust. "People buy all this junk and then just throw it out. No one cares anymore."

"What's that awful stink?" Kingsley asked.

"Sewage," Andrés said. "Probably from a leaking septic tank or drain field. I don't think there're any sewage treatment plants nearby." He pushed aside a pile of leaves with his boot, uncovering old cans of motor oil. "Someone's been dumping here for a while, and it's a damn shame. One gallon of motor oil can contaminate a million gallons of fresh water." He knelt and took a handful of mud. Black oil ran between his fingers. "Neglect and abuse, the *real* horsemen of the apocalypse." He dropped the mud and wiped off his hands. He stood and jumped over the stream, using a large rock as a stepping stone, beckoning Amanda and Kingsley to follow. "Take a look at this." They hopped over the stream and squatted beside Andrés. On a pile of wet leaves was a small brown-and-yellow box turtle, about the size of Kingsley's closed fist. The turtle didn't move when Andrés picked him up. His head flopped to the side.

He never used the Sutherland pools, golf courses or stables. He was too fat to wear swimming trunks, didn't know how to play golf and was afraid of horses.

Kingsley slumped in one of the plush couches in the sizeable den of the Sutherland mansion, controller in hand, playing *Revenge of the Clones*. His mother stood in the arched entryway, hands on hips. "You've played video games all summer. You're gonna have an outside birthday party, and you're gonna have fun."

"I was outside all day yesterday with Amanda and Mr. Santos," Kingsley whined. "It was horrible. Hot and buggy. It gave me a headache."

Joyce rolled her eyes. "Excuses. Excuses. You're always getting headaches. You're having a pool party, and that's that."

Arguing with his mother was hopeless. Joyce Smith was an average woman with an average name. She wore her frizzy, brown hair in a tight bun, held in place by an army of bobby pins. Her uniform was the same every day: a flowered apron over a simple black skirt and white blouse. The only thing remarkable about twenty-nine year old Joyce Smith was her lazy, New Orleans accent and her sharp hazel eyes, and only her eyes hinted at the deep determination Kingsley knew lurked within.

Joyce plopped beside Kingsley on the couch. She leaned close, glancing around before whispering, "You think I enjoy wiping Mrs. Sutherland's flabby old behind? You think I wanna spend my days listening to fancy-pants Clare Santos bellyache 'cuz her diamond necklace don't match her diamond earrings? You think that's why we live here?" She took Kingsley's fleshy chin and looked him in the eyes. "I do this for you. So you can grow up around rich folk. That's the only way we'll learn how to get rich, too, by watching them. So stop complaining." She let go of his chin, stood up, and smoothed her apron. "It'll be fun, hon. I'll tell Enrique to saddle the horses. You can go on a trail ride."

"Trail ride!" Kingsley wailed. He threw down the controller. "I can't go on a trail ride. I'm not *spit-in-your-face-brave* like Amanda. Mom, this is *my* birthday," he said, "and I don't want to make a fool of myself in front of my friends."

"Stop whining," Joyce said. "You're as bad as your father. God, I hate whiney men."

Kingsley couldn't concentrate. He gave up on his video game and left the den. He wandered down the long hallway, passing portraits of Sutherland ancestors in ornate frames. He wandered to the wide front porch and leaned against one of the twelve marble pillars, sulking. His mother ruled Marlbank like a tyrant. No one would stand up to her. Not Floyd the chauffeur, or Latonya the cook, or Enrique the groom, and certainly not elderly Mrs. Sutherland, who hadn't spoken since her stroke. No one ever stood up to Joyce Smith. No one, that is, except Amanda.

Across the dirt road, the stable doors were open. Kingsley could hear stomping and snorting, like angry freight trains heavy-loaded with coal. Amanda had spoken of her sick stallion. Maybe she was at the stable. Kingsley hurried down the white marble steps, over the red brick driveway and across the road to the stable, hoping he could convince Amanda to tell his mother not to throw a big outdoor party.

Amanda, Andrés and Enrique were standing in a circle around a magnificent brown stallion lying on his side. A gray-haired man with a beard and a stethoscope was kneeling beside the animal, an open doctor's bag beside him. The horse weakly flicked his tail as the veterinarian listened to its chest. The other horses—all mares—snorted and stamped, as if they knew what was happening to their stallion and were mad as hell. Kingsley hovered at the entrance and beckoned to Amanda. She looked surprised to see him and trotted over.

"In all the years you've lived at Marlbank, I think this is the closest you've come to the horses," she said, only slightly exaggerating. Kingsley used to run around the empty paddock when he was younger and thinner but now steered clear of the stables.

Kingsley fidgeted nervously. "What's wrong?" he asked.

"They don't know yet," Amanda said. "The vet's still checking him over."

"So...," Kingsley hesitated, trying to think of what to say next. He kicked at the straw and dirt. "So..., what happened to that turtle? The one your father found?"

"The nature center euthanized him. He couldn't survive with that tumor."

"Gosh," Kingsley said. "That's sad."

"Yeah, I know," Amanda said. She glanced worriedly at the stallion. "I better get back."

Kingsley couldn't wait any longer. His words burst out of him. "Mom's ruining everything. She's turning my birthday into a pool party with horse rides. I told her all I wanted was pizza and video games, but she won't listen. Can you talk to her?"

Amanda affectionately punched him on the shoulder. "Is that why you came out to the stable? To ask me to talk to your mom?"

Kingsley nodded.

"Don't worry," Amanda said with a cocky grin. "I'll think of something."

Kingsley rubbed his shoulder and watched with anxious fascination as the veterinarian opened the horse's mouth.

"See how he's salivating?" the vet asked. "And how swollen his mouth is? Looks like arsenic poisoning."

"Arsenic?" Andrés said. He squatted beside the vet and looked up at Enrique. "Has anyone other than you groomed this animal?"

"No, sir," Enrique said. "I'd never…."

"Accidental poisoning isn't unheard of," the vet said. "Grooms used to give arsenic to horses to treat worms."

"No, sir!" Enrique repeated. "I'd never use anything on the horses that wasn't approved by Mrs. Santos."

Andrés snorted almost as loud as the mares. "She's not Mrs. Santos anymore." He winced and rubbed the back of his neck. Kingsley wondered if Andrés got headaches, too. "She's Miss Clare Sutherland. At least until she marries the senator."

Kingsley's ears perked up whenever anyone mentioned Clare's name. "Your mom's marrying Senator Steele?" he whispered to Amanda, alarmed at the thought of never again seeing Clare at the mansion.

She shrugged. "I hope not," she whispered. "I hate him."

"This isn't acute," the vet said. "This is chronic. He's been eating something laced with poison every day for a long time. It finally caught up with him."

Andrés tenderly stroked the stallion's neck, "Wouldn't arsenic kill him right away?"

"Not necessarily," the vet said. "Arsenic is a stimulant as well as a carcinogen. Before it was regulated, dealers would give horses small doses to make them more attractive to buyers. The horses look better for a while. Shiny coats. More pep. The long-term effects are deadly."

Andrés stood. "What about the mares? Why aren't they sick?"

The mares moved nervously in their stalls, twitching and whinnying. One stretched her neck out, flashing her teeth like a snarling wolf.

"That's the mystery," the vet said. He stood and dusted off his pants. "I've seen this before. Stallions get sick, and mares turn into four-legged she-devils. Last week I had to put down a prize stallion up near Richmond. Poor animal had a brain tumor as big is your fist. Their mares weren't sick, either. More agitated than usual, but not sick." The vet picked up his bag and headed to the first stall.

"A brain tumor?" Kingsley whispered to Amanda. "Isn't that what killed the turtle?"

Amanda nodded. "Daddy says it's a new disease. I hope the stallion doesn't have it. Daddy says that would mean it's moved up to mammals."

Andrés followed the vet to the stall. "Poultry farmers used to feed their flocks roxarsone, an arsenic-based additive. Maybe that got into the water supply."

The first mare reared. Enrique grabbed her halter. "Whoa, girl!"

"Hold her steady," the vet said. Enrique struggled to keep the mare calm as the vet positioned the syringe to take a blood sample. "Hold on tight," the vet demanded. The mare snorted and kicked the back of her stall. The vet finished taking the sample and turned to Andrés. "Just like the mares in Richmond. They all acted crazy, too." He headed to the next stall.

"Bisphenol A," Andrés said, as he doggedly trailed the vet. "Have you read the reports about BPA? It's added to plastics to make them flexible. It's everywhere. In water bottles and kids' toys. It coats the inside of cans. It's known to increase aggression in female rats and decrease testicle size in males. What if BPA mixed with the arsenic from poultry farms, mixed with petroleum from those damn Sutherland oil wells in the Atlantic, mixed with…?"

The vet moved to the next mare. "I'll let you know as soon as I have the test results." He entered the stall ahead of Andrés or Enrique. The mare snorted and reared, trapping the vet in a corner. "Whoa, girl," the vet said, holding out his hands. The mare's eyes blazed. She snorted and reared again, coming down hard. "Ahhhh!" the vet screamed. "My leg!" He crumpled to the floor.

Kingsley ran back to the safe, air-conditioned mansion as fast as he could.

If Amanda had tried to convince Joyce to cancel Kingsley's party, it didn't work. Kingsley's birthday began with a lot of sulking. He sat with Floyd, the chauffeur, in the rocking chairs on the high front porch of the Sutherland mansion, waiting for Joyce to unleash his public humiliation.

"Summer is hard on a fat boy," Kingsley said, feeling doomed. "Especially a fat boy who doesn't know how to ride or swim."

Floyd fanned himself with the morning newspaper. "I imagine so," he said. Floyd always wore long, navy-blue pants, a white shirt and a tie, ready to drive Mrs. Sutherland wherever she wanted to go, even though she hadn't gone anywhere other than church and doctor appointments since her stroke. Their rocking slowed when Enrique rounded the corner, muttering angrily and hauling a large plastic *Happy Birthday* banner across the manicured lawn. He stopped at the bottom of the tall marble steps, perspiration dripping, and called up to Floyd.

"I can't stand that woman. First I have to clean the pool, and now she wants me to hang this *pura paja* banner on the front of Mrs. Sutherland's *magnífico hacienda*. I'm a professional groom, hand-picked by *Señora* Santos. I'm not Joyce Smith's personal slave. It's not even *Señora* Sutherland's birthday." He glared at Kingsley.

"Don't cause trouble," Floyd said, calling down to Enrique. "Just do what she says."

"I don't take orders from *Señora* Sutherland's nurse."

Floyd returned to rocking and fanning himself with the newspaper. "Suit yourself," he said.

Kingsley agreed with Enrique. The banner was big, gaudy and unbearably embarrassing. He rubbed the back of his neck as he watched Enrique hang the banner between the banisters. The stress was making Kingsley's headaches worse; his head felt like a screw was twisting into the back of his skull.

Joyce marched out the front door, wiping her hands on her apron, and yelled at Enrique, "Not there, you fool!" She ran down the marble steps and grabbed the end of the banner. "Hang it *above* the porch, not beside it. Go get a ladder!"

Amanda joined Kingsley and Floyd on the front porch, taking a seat on the top marble step. Kingsley left his rocking chair and sat beside Amanda. The marble steps were scorching hot under the bright July sun, which only made Kingsley more miserable. "Why does Mom have to make such a big deal about everything?" He pulled at the bottom of his oversized t-shirt. "I don't even want a birthday party."

Amanda wasn't listening. She was too busy watching Enrique as he trotted down the red brick driveway and across the dirt road. He returned carrying a long ladder over his head, sweat highlighting his bare chest. He set up the ladder and began to string the banner across the front of the mansion. Joyce stood at the base of the ladder, yelling "higher," "lower" and "to the left."

Enrique was strong, tan and muscular. He had two samurai warriors tattooed on his back, one atop each shoulder. Their long swords crossed every time he flexed, which made Amanda squeal.

"Look! Look!" She grabbed Kingsley's arm. "Isn't he beautiful? Reminds me of a black panther gliding through a jungle."

"What do I remind you of?" Kingsley regretted asking the minute the words left his mouth. He could almost hear the taunts from the bullies at school, *Hey, beluga whale*! Kingsley felt more like a jellyfish than a panther. The wait for Amanda's reply was excruciating.

She smiled coyly. "A race car," she finally said.

"A what?"

"A race car. Like a Ferrari."

A Ferrari! She called me a Ferrari! Happiness swirled like dandelion seeds in a summer breeze. Kingsley hugged his knees and grinned from ear to ear.

At least until his mother started cursing.

"Son of a bitch!" Joyce yelled. She left Enrique teetering on the ladder and ran to her Dodge Charger parked in front of the mansion.

"What the...?" Enrique shouted, almost tumbling off the ladder.

Joyce rummaged through the glove compartment and ran back carrying a pistol—a Llama 32 caliber with a pearl handle. Kingsley knew that gun. He'd seen it before. It'd belonged to his grandfather back in New Orleans. Joyce aimed the pistol at the base of the ladder. Bam! She pulled the hammer back again, steadying the pistol with both hands. Bam! A third time. Bam! Three shots. Enrique swayed and Amanda ran down the white marble steps.

A curtain fell over Kingsley. Over what he could see, over what he could hear. But not over what he could smell. He remembered that smell. Sulfur and smoke, like something burning. He almost fainted, catching himself when he heard Amanda's angry voice. He blinked and shook his head, trying to regain his bearings, hoping no one noticed, and hurried down the steps to join Amanda and Joyce.

Joyce had shot a black snake. Shot its head clean off. "Are you insane?" Amanda shouted. "That snake wasn't hurting anyone!" She pointed at the ladder. "Enrique could have broken his neck! This is Grandmother's house, not yours! You work here, remember!"

Joyce blew smoke from the pistol like a gunslinger in an old western. "Snakes are evil. Killing 'em is a guaranteed ticket to heaven."

"That's the stupidest thing I've ever heard," Amanda said, hands on hips. Kingsley hid his grin. Only Amanda dared to talk to his mother like that.

"Don't you read the Bible?" Joyce asked.

"You mean that book that says you're not supposed to steal?" Amanda shot back.

Joyce's hazel eyes blazed, but she held her tongue. A familiar red convertible had just driven through the wrought-iron gate and was parking in front of the mansion. Out stepped a tall, handsome black man from the driver's side, and a beautiful blonde from the other side. Clare Santos was the most beautiful woman in the world as far as Kingsley was concerned. Blonde hair, blue eyes and peaches-and-cream skin. Clare wore tight, white pants and a fuzzy pink Sweet Briar College sweater. She looked like a double helping of peach ice cream without the stomach ache. Kingsley forgot about his birthday party. He forgot about the dead snake. His eyes were fixed on Clare. He forgot about everything—until he heard his mother cursing under her breath.

"Why the hell are *they* here?" Joyce huffed. She quickly took off her apron and smoothed her frizzy brown hair. She hurried out to greet the distinguished couple, hands extended. "Senator Steele! Mrs. Santos! What a wonderful surprise! Welcome!"

Kingsley was happy to see Clare, but confused. "Why'd you invite your mom and Senator Steele to my party?" he asked Amanda.

Amanda gave him a grin. "It's all part of my plan. They'll keep your mom so busy she won't have time to tell you to put on your swim trunks or ride a horse."

Kingsley was delighted. "Brilliant," he said. "But won't your dad be upset?"

Amanda's grin disappeared. "Probably," she said. "He has lots of reasons to hate the senator." She stared with dagger eyes at Clare and the senator, who were still talking with Joyce, "Causing Mom and Dad's divorce is just one of them. It really started when the government allowed oil companies to drill in the Atlantic and the Chesapeake Bay. Daddy blames the senator for the mess they made."

Kingsley didn't like listening to Amanda bad mouth beautiful Clare and the handsome senator, so he was glad when another car pulled up in front of the mansion—one much less impressive than the red convertible—and two boys hopped out: Dwayne Lee and Billy Jackson. Kingsley hustled the boys past Joyce, Clare and the senator, and up the marble steps. Amanda didn't join them.

"Doesn't she like video games?" Dwayne asked.

"No," Kingsley said, as the three boys piled onto the plush couch, pushing aside the mountain of birthday presents, most of them from Joyce. They grabbed the video game controllers. "She likes snakes."

The boys laughed.

The boys played inside all afternoon, unaware that outside Clare and the senator were running Joyce ragged, just as Amanda had planned.

"Joyce? Joyce?" Clare's melodic Virginia drawl echoed from the poolside gazebo, "We're out of Mai Tai's. And, if you don't mind, the senator prefers his extra sweet with a touch of mint. Joyce, be a love and mix up another batch."

"Joyce? Joyce?" Clare's voice echoed again. "Momma smells awful. She needs the toilet. And clean her up, while you're at it. She's ruining the atmosphere."

"Joyce? Joyce? Be a love and bring me my reading glasses. The senator is showing photos of his trip to the tar sands in Alberta. I've invested a bundle up there."

Hours had gone by before Joyce found the time to check on Kingsley and the other boys. She pointed at the afternoon sun streaming in through the den's bay window. "This is a pool party! Go outside."

"I can't," Dwayne said. "I get headaches. The sun makes them worse."

"I get headaches, too," Billy said. "Sometimes I throw up."

Kingsley gloated, never taking his eyes off the game. "I told you I didn't want a pool party, Mom."

Joyce stormed out. "What's wrong with boys these days?"

Latonya announced that lunch was ready and the video games were put on pause. The boys wolfed down burgers and grilled chicken and then quickly returned to their games. Two rounds of *Attack of the Red-Eyed Mutants* and it was time for dessert.

Joyce looked exhausted. Her frizzy hair poked out in every direction and her once-clean apron was wet and stained. "Bring out the cake!" she grumbled and Latonya brought it out. Joyce lit the candles.

Kingsley, Dwayne and Billy gathered around the table with Amanda and Joyce. Floyd, Enrique and Latonya stood behind them. Clare clung to the senator's arm, wearing a tight bikini and a flowered hat. Kingsley couldn't help glancing over at her every time he thought she wasn't looking. Her glow only slightly dimmed when Andrés arrived, wheeling the silent and slumped Mrs. Sutherland to the table.

"*Happy Birthday to you, Happy Birthday to you, Happy Birthday dear Kingsley…*" Everyone waited for Kingsley to blow out the candles. Clare pinched his chubby cheek. "Blow out the candles, you silly goose," she drawled.

Kingsley blew. The cake was cut and Kingsley was given the biggest piece.

Clare and Senator Steele declined any cake and returned to their lounge chairs by the pool. "When Amanda invited us," Clare said, lazily dipping her toes in the pool, "She promised John would meet dozens of important constituents, but I only see Momma's servants and these two little boys." She pointed to Billy and Dwayne, who were as enraptured by her beauty as Kingsley and were crushed when she called them *little*. "Amanda, why'd you tell me such a fib? Was it to get me under the same roof as your father?" She shot a glance at Andrés. "You know how much I abhor leeches."

Andrés flushed. "Can't you be a decent person for one minute? I know this isn't my home. I know Leslie isn't my mother. But if I move out, who'll raise Amanda? Certainly not you and your *senator*," he said, spitting out the word.

"Forgive me for wanting a real man in my life," Clare countered, reaching for the senator's strong arm. "I've never been with one before."

Andrés winced.

The senator may have been a cad, but he was still a politician. "Whoa, hold up there, Clare," he injected. "We're here to celebrate a birthday."

Andrés rubbed the back of his neck. "What's happened to you, Clare? Why have you become so cruel? You didn't use to be this way. We were happy. We had a good marriage." Andrés left the party and Amanda's eyes filled with tears. Kingsley knew why. Amanda loved her father and hated the senator for tearing her family apart.

The handsome senator tried to lighten the mood. "Whew, that was tense." He beckoned to Joyce. "You've been working all day. You need a break," he said. "Come and sit by the pool with Clare and me." Joyce was feeding Mrs. Sutherland bits of cake when he called. She looked startled by the request, and more than a little annoyed. She wiped her hands on her soiled apron, tried to smooth her untamable hair, and joined Senator Steele and Clare by the pool. He patted Joyce on the back. "This party is amazing," he said. "Clare raves about the way you take care of Leslie." The senator waved Kingsley over, too, and placed his free hand on Kingsley's shoulder. "And I hear you want to be a jet pilot when you're old enough."

Kingsley blushed and stammered, "Yeah, I, um...." Before Kingsley's father had disappeared, before he and his mother had moved to Virginia, and before he'd gotten fat, Kingsley had indeed wanted to become a Blue Angel jet pilot. He assumed that dream was dead.

"Then let's start right now," the senator said. "The first step to becoming a Blue Angel is to graduate in the top 10 percent of your class. That means work hard in school, get good grades and do all your homework. My job is to write your letter of recommendation to the United States Naval Academy in Annapolis."

Kingsley was stunned. "Recommendation? For me?"

"Of course!" the senator said.

Joyce clasped Senator Steele's hands, almost kissing them. "Thank you, thank you. His future means everything to me. I can't thank you enough." Kingsley was touched by his mother's joy. She seldom seemed proud of him anymore. Seeing her happy made him feel important.

"It won't be easy," the senator added. "He has to stay in school and stay out of trouble."

"He will," Joyce said. Kingsley wasn't so sure about the good grades but he relished being the center of attention.

Clare pulled out her smart phone and asked Senator Steele and Kingsley to squeeze together for a photo. "The future President of the United States with the future Blue Angel jet pilot." Senator Steele wrapped his arm around Kingsley and smiled. The bright flash worsened Kingsley's headache. He winced and his stomach churned, but he wasn't going to let that stop him from trying to impress Clare and the senator. "I know a lot about flying jets," he said. Kingsley had never been in a jet but he'd read about them on the Internet.

"Like what?" the senator asked, smiling.

Kingsley's left eye began to twitch. He rubbed it once and tried to ignore it. "If you're shot down and your parachute fails, guess what sort of tree you should aim for?"

"I've never given it much thought," the senator said. "Elm? Birch?"

Clare was watching. The boys were listening. His mother was beaming. Even Amanda was paying attention, although she still looked upset with Clare. "Neither," Kingsley said. "You aim for a tall tree with a single, undivided trunk. Little on top and thicker on bottom, like a triangle, so you can slide down. A conifer works best. A red spruce or a Norfolk Island pine. I read that on the Internet."

"Imagine that," Joyce said. "And here I thought pine trees weren't good for nothin'."

The senator applauded. "Bravo, Kingsley," he said. "I hope I'm never on a plane without a parachute but now I'll know what to do if that happens. You'll make a fine pilot. I just hope...."

Senator Steele's words faded. Kingsley could see him talking but his ears buzzed like he was in a tunnel. Suddenly, the senator disappeared. "What's going on?" Kingsley reached out his hands. "Mom! Mom! I can't see!"

He heard his mother's voice echoing in the distance. "Kingsley!"

Kingsley fell forward, his knees hitting a lounge chair. Joyce caught him before he hit the edge of the pool. Everything was black. Everything was silent. Kingsley couldn't see. He couldn't hear. All he could do was feel his mother's arms around him and the headache screwing deeper and deeper into the back of his skull.

3 The Dolphin Disease

Kingsley woke up worrying about his unopened birthday presents, at least until he opened his eyes. He wasn't at the mansion. He was in a room with white walls and beeping equipment. A man's baritone voice filled the room. "This isn't just India's problem or China's problem or the Middle East's problem. This is a worldwide epidemic . . . threatening America's present security and prosperous future...." The TV mounted on the wall was broadcasting the president speaking to a large crowd in front of the White House.

"Worldwide epidemic," Kingsley repeated. He closed his right eye, then his left. One eye worked, the other didn't. Joyce dozed in a chair next to him. "Mom?"

Joyce started and quickly stood up. She gently caressed his forehead. "How do you feel, hon?"

"My eye doesn't work."

"Which one?"

He pointed to his left eye.

Joyce bit her lip. "I'll tell the doctor."

He touched his head. "My headache's gone."

"They gave you medicine."

An intravenous bag hung next to his bed, with a tube connected to his arm, taped to his skin. A younger boy, probably four or five years old, was in the only other bed in the room. His eyes were closed, and he had a thick bandage around his head. A small, dark-haired woman sat beside the boy. She wore a colorful sari, like hundreds of butterflies, and purple earrings that dangled to her jaw line. She gave Kingsley a smile. "You're awake," she said. Kingsley had never heard an accent like hers before. Sort of British but she didn't look British. "Are you waiting for Dr. Barlow?"

"I guess," Joyce said. She didn't return the woman's smile.

"She's brilliant. An odd bird, but an excellent physician. Does he have headaches, too?"

Joyce eyed the woman suspiciously. "Maybe," she said. "No one's told me a damned thing. All they want from me is my signature and my money."

The woman gave Joyce a sympathetic smile. "My son was nineteen months when his headaches began. He'd curl up into a ball in the corner and hold his head."

"Where are you from?"

"Mumbai."

"Where?"

"India."

"India!" Joyce said. "And you came all this way to...."

"To see Dr. Barlow? Yes, we did. Our pediatric oncologist recommended we come here after all the conventional treatments failed. Chemo. Surgery. Radiation. His tumors kept growing."

"Tumors?" Joyce gasped.

The woman quickly covered her mouth. "I'm so sorry. I assume too much. Kindly accept my apology."

Kingsley tugged the bottom of his mother's blouse. "Just like the turtle and the stallion," he whispered. He spoke up to the woman in the sari, "Are the animals in your country getting sick, too?"

"Yes," the woman said, sadly. She stroked her little boy's forehead. "But only the males."

The woman in the sari was right. Dr. Joan Barlow was an odd bird. Puffy black hair with a thick, white streak running down the center, lots of eye makeup and colorful cat-eye glasses that made her look both smart and punkish. She smiled and pulled a chair next to Kingsley's bed. "All you need is an eye patch and a parrot," she said.

"Huh?"

"You want to be a pirate for Halloween, don't you?"

Kingsley cringed. "I'm too old for Halloween."

"You're still going to need both eyes and no more headaches, right?" Before Kingsley could answer, she shined a bright light into his eyes, both the eye that worked and the eye that didn't. "Tell me about your headaches. Where do they hurt?"

"In my head."

Dr. Barlow gave Kingsley a Cheshire Cat grin. "I mean what part of the head. In the front? On the side? In the back?

Kingsley rubbed the soft indent where his skull met the top of his neck. "Back here. It usually hurts just a little but today was different."

"Yesterday," Dr. Barlow said, as she felt the contours of his head.

"Yesterday?" Kingsley looked at his mother.

Joyce nodded. "Your birthday party was yesterday," she said.

Kingsley wondered how a whole day could pass without his notice. "What about my birthday presents? I haven't opened them yet?"

Dr. Barlow stared at him as if he was a bug-eyed goldfish in a tiny bowl. "What's the last thing you remember?"

Kingsley remembered playing video games with Billy and Dwayne. He remembered Clare's big blue eyes and tiny bikini. He remembered talking to the senator. "Jets. I remember talking about jets."

"Do you remember falling?"

"No."

"Do you remember losing your sight?"

Kingsley touched his face. He couldn't keep the panic out of his voice. "No."

Dr. Barlow moved her chair closer and spoke directly to Kingsley, looking him in the eye. "Kingsley, you have what's called secondary headaches. That means your headaches aren't like the kind you get from worrying about your homework or staying up too late. Secondary headaches are caused by specific conditions. In your case, they're caused by something inside your skull pressing against your brain. We know this because we took a picture of your head while you were asleep. This sounds scary but try not to worry. We're going to take good care of you."

She then asked Joyce to step out to the hallway with her. Kingsley reached for his mother's hand. "She'll be right back," Dr. Barlow said as she escorted Joyce out the door.

The president was still talking on the TV. "I understand the heartache of the parents and I have compassion for the children who can no longer associate with playmates and schoolmates. It is true that some medical sources say that this epidemic isn't communicated through air or bodily fluids, but no one in the medical community has come forth and unequivocally said that they know for a fact it is safe to be around such children. And until they do, I think we just have to do the best we can...."

Kingsley clutched the top of his sheet. He felt scared and very alone in the big white room. He cleared his throat, trying to draw the attention of the woman wearing the sari. "What's your little boy's name?"

"Adar," she said. "It means fire in Persian." Her voice was deep and soothing, like a warm bath on a cold night.

"My neighbor back in New Orleans had a Persian cat," Kingsley said. "His name was Snowball. The cat, I mean, not the neighbor. Don't you think Dr. Barlow looks like a cat?"

The woman chuckled. "It's those specs she wears."

"Yeah," Kingsley said. "And that white stripe in her hair makes her look like a skunk."

The woman laughed and covered her mouth with her scarf. "Excellent!" She walked to Kingsley's bed. "I should introduce myself. My name is Bapsi Cama." She offered her hand. Kingsley took it, noting how soft it was, very different from his mother's.

"My name is Kingsley."

"Good to meet you, Kingsley."

Dr. Barlow released Kingsley that afternoon, and a nurse wheeled him out of his room. Joyce walked beside the wheelchair. The nurse wheeled him to an elevator, which took him to the second floor. People stepped aside to let him pass. She wheeled him this way and that, over a crosswalk and to the parking garage. Kingsley's Aunt Mavis was waiting for them in Joyce's old Dodge Charger. Mavis and her twin sister, Maureen, alternated taking care of Mrs. Sutherland when Joyce wasn't working. With Mavis here, that meant Maureen was back in Yorktown at the Sutherland mansion. Kingsley was fine with that. Both of his aunts were nineteen years old. They had dropped out of high school at fifteen, the same age Joyce had dropped out when she became pregnant with Kingsley. Both had purple hair and colorful tattoos, and neither, as Joyce had said many times, had the sense God gave a gumball machine, but Kingsley liked Mavis better than Maureen and was glad to see her.

Joyce helped Kingsley into the back seat, and then settled in the front passenger seat beside her sister. "They want to put him on something called gene therapy," Joyce told Mavis.

"What's that?" Mavis asked.

Joyce shuffled through the stack of release forms, prescriptions, treatment schedules and contact information. "The doctor tried to explain it to me but I'm too damn stupid to understand." She found the sheet describing Kingsley's proposed treatment. "This is what it says. They take one of Kingsley's cells and stick a virus in it. Then they stick that cell back in his body."

"Sounds expensive," Mavis said as she started the engine.

Joyce sniffed hard. She rolled down the window and spat on the concrete floor of the parking garage. "Fucking hospital. When they asked me for my insurance card, I told them we were friends of Senator Steele and I forgot to bring it."

"What about next time, Joyce? How you going to pay when you can't get no insurance? You keep using the senator's name and people are gonna start asking questions about you. They're gonna find out what happened in New Orleans."

"Joyce Smith can't get insurance. Maybe I need to stop being Joyce Smith."

"Jesus, Joyce. You got yourself into a real mess," Mavis said. "No insurance, no social security." She lowered her voice. "Least not 'til the statute of limitations runs out on...."

"Shut up!" Joyce growled. "My son ain't ending up like some mummy from India with his head bandaged, you hear me. No one's ever taking my boy from me. Not the police, not his father and not some goddamn disease. No matter what I have to do."

Kingsley stared out the window. The streets were crowded. Some people wore white coats and hospital scrubs, while others were on crutches and in wheelchairs. He didn't recognize anybody. He read the road signs as they drove away from the medical center. *Lee Street. Jefferson Avenue.* Nothing looked familiar. "Where are we, Mom?" he asked.

"We're in Charlottesville," Joyce said.

"Where?"

"Charlottesville. It's west of Richmond."

Kingsley was confused. Charlottesville was in the middle of Virginia, hundreds of miles from Yorktown. "How'd I get here?" he asked.

"By helicopter. An ambulance took you to the hospital in Hampton, and they put you on a helicopter so you could see Dr. Barlow. She's a specialist. Best in the world, they say." Joyce reached around and stroked Kingsley's cheek. "Guess that means you're a very important person."

Kingsley wished he'd been awake for the helicopter ride. He'd always wanted to fly.

Kingsley didn't even want Amanda with him when he opened his birthday presents. He wanted to be alone. He sat on his narrow bed and tore away the wrapping. Clothes, books, toys, and more video games. He threw everything on the floor. He didn't want to play with any of it. Bad news had greeted Kingsley when he returned to the mansion. His two best friends were sick. Dwayne Lee had fainted during swim practice, and Billy Jackson had a headache so bad he threw up. Worse, two little boys in Billy's neighborhood had died. Died! One boy was seven, the other was only three. "I heard they had brain tumors," Billy told Kingsley. "Is that what you've got?"

"The doctor told me something's growing in my head," Kingsley said.

"Yep, that's a brain tumor," Billy confirmed. "I hope you don't die."

"Me, too." Kingsley rubbed the back of his head and wondered what the thing growing inside of him looked like. He tossed and turned all night. The next morning, Latonya was cooking bacon, eggs and pancakes, but nothing looked appealing, which was unusual for Kingsley. Eating was his only real skill. Floyd was drinking coffee and reading the morning newspaper, wearing his navy-blue pants, a white shirt and a tie, as usual. He was ready to chauffeur Mrs. Sutherland if she asked him, which she hadn't in a long, long time. She hadn't spoken since her stroke. Kingsley sat beside Floyd and picked at the bacon. Amanda came in, still in her pajamas, and wrapped her arms around Kingsley. "Welcome back," she said. "Everyone was worried about you."

Floyd looked up from his paper. "You look good," he said, "How are you feeling?"

Kingsley rubbed the back of his neck, "I don't know. Better, I think."

With that, Amanda ordered a special dinner. "Latonya, we need to celebrate tonight. Fix something special, like grilled swordfish with creole sauce, New Orleans style." She gave Kingsley a wink.

Latonya shook her head. "Wish I could," she said. She poured Floyd another cup of coffee and took the empty seat at the table. "I can't find fish anywhere. Haven't for days. Grocery stores are empty."

"No swordfish?" Amanda said. "Then let's have salmon. That's just as good."

"Don't you watch the news?" Latonya said, exasperated. "All the seafood departments are closed." She stood back up and went to the freezer. "We'll probably have chicken tonight, although, to tell you the truth, stores are running low on chicken, too." She pulled out a package of frozen chicken breasts and placed it in the refrigerator to thaw. "And beef is sky high. Mercy, I don't know what's happening. Pretty soon there won't be anything to eat."

Floyd showed Amanda the newspaper. "It's right here, in the headlines. "Ocean Yields Decimated." He read the article out loud:

Dr. Elizabeth Martin, a marine biologist with the San Diego Marine Research Center, is searching for the root causes of the epidemic that has resulted in the disappearance of sea life.

"Not all sea life has disappeared," Dr. Martin is quick to point out. "Only the sexually reproducing species." Dr. Martin explains that animals that reproduce via parthenogenesis (an asexual, self-cloning form of reproduction) are unaffected by the epidemic, as are plant and microscopic life. "Spontaneous parthenogenesis has been observed in several species of fish, from guppies to hammerhead sharks, but these species are also in crisis. I wouldn't expect hammerheads to survive the exodus of their food sources," Dr. Martin quips.

The pathology appears similar to colony collapse disorder, the name given over ten years ago to the syndrome that devastated the honeybee population. Hives had queens and eggs but the workers flew away and never came back. In the current aquatic epidemic, males die and disappear, leaving the females without mates. Outside stressors—air pollution, pesticides and herbicides—enhanced the honeybee's vulnerability. Similarly, fish are overwhelmed by a century of man-made toxins that have infiltrated the oceans. Plastics break down into microscopic pieces and are eaten by plankton. Small fish eat the plastic-laced plankton and pass it up the food chain. Combine this with decades of overfishing and current global warming trends, and disaster is inevitable.

Dr. Martin tells of a recent expedition to the coast of South Africa. "We captured two dolphins, a female and a male. The female was a healthy specimen. The male, however...."

Floyd stopped reading. He folded the newspaper and tucked it under his arm. "Any more bacon?" he asked Latonya.

Amanda frowned. "What happened to the dolphins?"

Floyd turned his chair away from Kingsley and Amanda. "Nothing happened to the dolphins," he sniffed. "You two go outside and play."

"I want to hear about the dolphins, too," Kingsley insisted.

Floyd threw the newspaper on the table. He wouldn't meet Kingsley's eyes. "Suit yourself." He left the kitchen.

Amanda picked up the newspaper and read the rest of the article:

"We captured two dolphins, a female and a male. The female was a healthy specimen. The male, however, had numerous life-threatening tumors. He died, of course." When asked to explain the reason behind the difference in the health of the male and female dolphins, Dr. Martin provided a basic lesson in DNA. "Females are protected by two large X chromosomes; males have one large X chromosome and one small Y chromosome. Y chromosomes have fewer genes and are more easily influenced by external factors [such as disease and toxins.]" Dr. Martin went on to explain that recent studies indicate...

Amanda looked up from the newspaper. "The turtle. The stallion. And now the oceans?" Her face was crushed with worry. "Is this why you had to go to the hospital?"

Kingsley felt like hitting something, but all he did was roll up the newspaper and throw it in the trashcan. "I'm sick of bad news."

Amanda stood up and declared, "We need advice from someone we can trust who knows medicine!" She nudged Kingsley's shoulder. "Come on, follow me." She led the way down the long hallway and out the front door.

Down the marble steps, across the red brick driveway, and past the stables, until they reached a well-worn path that meandered through the thick pine forest which separated Marlbank from the only other house in sight. "We need to talk to Dr. Jacobs," Amanda said. "He'll know what to do."

Retired epidemiologist Dr. Eugene Jacobs and his wife, Esther, were Mrs. Sutherland's oldest friends. Amanda pounded on the Jacobs's front door. "Dr. Jacobs! Are you in there? We have to talk to you."

Kingsley nervously twisted the bottom of his shirt. He looked back through the pine forest. He could see the huge white mansion glowing in the morning sun. "I think we should go back," Kingsley said. "What if he gives me a shot? I hate shots."

Dr. Jacobs opened the door in a flurry, his gray hair standing on end, his glasses askew. "Amanda!" he said, breathless. "What's wrong? Is Leslie all right?"

"Grandmother's fine," Amanda said. "It's Kingsley. He's sick."

"Kingsley!" Dr. Jacobs said, taken aback. He scowled at Kingsley. "I was napping!"

"It's important," Amanda said. "Who's the best doctor to see for the dolphin disease?"

"The *what* disease?"

"The dolphin disease. The one in the newspaper." Amanda told him about the dolphin with the tumors.

Dr. Jacobs' face softened. "Yes, I've read about that. Very strange. Affects only males. Some think it's a virus."

"That's why we need you," Amanda said. "Have you heard of Dr. Barlow in Charlottesville? That's who Kingsley went to see. This is important, Dr. Jacobs. Is she the best doctor in the whole world for the dolphin disease?"

Dr. Jacobs touched Kingsley's forehead, checking for a fever. "Please, come inside. I know a pathologist who might be able to help. You two can wait in the kitchen while I call him."

Kingsley and Amanda sat with Mrs. Jacobs in the kitchen while the doctor went upstairs to make the call. Mrs. Jacobs gave them each a piece of peach pie. "Those peaches better be from the Sutherland orchards," Amanda teased. Kingsley silently ate his pie as Amanda complained about her mother and the senator. "Clare called Daddy a leech in front of everybody. Everybody! Then Daddy moved out. He lives in an apartment in Hampton now."

Mrs. Jacobs gave a worried *tsk, tsk*. "Such a shame. I like your father. He's so active in the environmental movement." She offered Kingsley a second piece of pie, which he eagerly accepted, especially since he hadn't eaten any breakfast. "He worked so hard to prevent the oil wells in the Atlantic Ocean and the Chesapeake Bay. It's such a shame. All those spills. Things have changed so much since I was a girl."

"And that's not all," Amanda said. "Clare's marrying the senator and they're building a house in Chesapeake, at the Sutherland orchard. She doesn't care about me or Grandmother. All she cares about is the senator, and all he cares about are Grandmother's oil wells."

"Oh, Amanda, I'm so sorry. Is that why you started calling your mother Clare?" Mrs. Jacobs asked. "I noticed you don't call her Mom anymore."

Amanda's dark-brown eyes betrayed her hurt. "She doesn't love me. She's never loved me. I don't think she wants to be a mom." She sniffed and rubbed her nose. "Or at least, she doesn't want to be my mom. Daddy told me Clare's going to have a baby. The senator's baby. She and the senator aren't even married yet and she's having his baby. That's what Daddy says. Isn't that awful?"

The kitchen filled with stunned silence. Kingsley finally broke the quiet. "Does that mean she's coming back to the mansion?" Kingsley stirred at the thought of seeing beautiful Clare again. Looking into her blue eyes and sneaking a peek at how she fills her bikini.

"No, Kingsley," Amanda snapped. "Weren't you listening? She's not coming back. She's building a house at the Sutherland peach orchard with Senator Steele." She pursed her lips in disgust. "Guess I'm the only relative Grandmother has left. She hasn't heard from Uncle Jack in years."

"That might be a good thing," Mrs. Jacobs said. "Your Uncle Jack was quite a character."

Kingsley didn't want to hear any more gossip. He'd never met Amanda's Uncle Jack and was tired of hearing bad things about Clare. He left the kitchen and wandered into the living room. He ran his fingers along the tall bookcases and studied the framed photographs. One was of two women standing side-by-side, holding hands. Another was of a man and a woman, and two little boys. Kingsley picked up the photo of the family with the two little boys and wondered if the boys were sick. He replaced the photo and noticed something shiny. He pushed aside a knickknack and found a silver pendant the size of a quarter on a chain. Embedded on the pendant was a six-pointed star. He looked around. Mrs. Jacobs and Amanda were still in the kitchen. Dr. Jacobs was still upstairs, presumably contacting his pathologist friend. Kingsley traced the star with his finger, mesmerized by its symmetry and its shine. He could feel the struggle build inside him. He'd wanted to be a hero like Captain America when he was little. He still had a dream of becoming a Blue Angel jet pilot. He licked his lips. He'd never stolen anything before. Perspiration trickled down his forehead, and his breath became shallow.

He slipped the pendant into his pocket.

4 The Seer

Kingsley searched for a private spot in the Sutherland mansion to inspect his treasure. He found a dim corner of the library and sat on the floor beside a tall, cherry cupboard that smelled of tobacco and gunpowder. He pulled the pendant out of his pocket and traced the six-pointed star with his fingers. He pondered all he had learned about the dolphin disease. It caused brain tumors. Maybe the two boys in Billy's neighborhood who'd died had it. Maybe the stallion had it. None of the girls he knew had it. Not Amanda. Not his mother. Kingsley rubbed the pendant against his cheek, hoping it would give him good luck. Hoping it would cure him.

Unread books filled the library shelves and unappreciated paintings covered the walls. The closest was of a small boy running across a springtime landscape followed by a pack of hounds. No spelling tests marked with A+ or school photos taken every year since kindergarten hung on these walls, not like what his mother used to tack up all over their tiny apartment back in New Orleans. Across from the painting was a long poem in a gold frame. Kingsley started to read the poem.

They that have the pow'r to hurt, and will do none...

The door opened and a blade of light sliced through the dark. "Kingsley?" Amanda stood in silhouette, carrying a black-and-white composition notebook. "Are you in there?"

He quickly slipped the pendant back into his pocket. "Yeah."

"Why'd you run away from Dr. Jacobs' house? Why didn't you wait for me?"

Kingsley shrugged. "I had to go," he mumbled.

She walked toward his voice and sat with him beside the cherry cupboard. "My great-great-grandfather bought this from Robert E. Lee's estate."

"Bought what?"

"This cupboard," she said. "It's the most valuable thing in this house. That's what Daddy says. My great-great-grandfather went to Arlington after the Civil War. He bought it just before the government turned Lee's plantation into a cemetery." She leaned against Kingsley. "What are you doing?"

"Thinking."

"Me too. I've been thinking about that snake. The one your mom shot."

"The snake! I'm sick and you're worried about that snake?"

"It's all connected," Amanda said. "My father says the best measure of a person is how they treat animals. He told me never trust anyone who's cruel to animals." She bluntly added, "That's *one reason* why I don't trust your mom." The sad truth was that Kingsley didn't trust his mother, either. "Grandmother used to write poetry before her stroke. *Poetry gives life to ideals,* that's what she used to say."

Kingsley pointed to the long poem in the gold frame. "Did she write that?"

"Of course not," Amanda scoffed, "That's Shakespeare." She opened her black and white notebook, "I wrote a poem. Want to hear it?" Before Kingsley could answer, she started reading. "Black Snake by Amanda Santos Sutherland.

I do not blink.
I do not cry.
Shoot me,
poison me,
nail me to a tree.
I am small.
You are too big,
You are too blind
to see."

She closed her notebook. "The end. What do you think?"

"It doesn't rhyme," Kingsley said.

Amanda stood up in a huff. "You know nothing about poetry." She left Kingsley alone in the gloomy library.

August in eastern Virginia was just as hot and muggy as July. The only good thing was that there weren't as many bugs, which was strange. Last August Kingsley was constantly running into spider webs, and he was horrified when he found a big tick on the inside of his thigh. Kingsley sat in a rocking chair on the wide front porch of the Sutherland mansion, wearing shorts and a sweaty t-shirt, wishing he was inside playing video games. His mother had pulled the plug on his game console and threatened to throw it out the window if he didn't go outside. He sat with Floyd, who was wearing long pants, a white shirt and a tie, as always. Floyd was slicing an apple with a paring knife. He offered Kingsley a piece of apple.

Kingsley took the piece. "I start ninth grade in September. All the kids at school already think I'm a wimp. If word gets out about me fainting at my birthday party, I'll get beat up for sure."

"Bullies will do that."

Floyd had a deep vertical scar that bisected his dark face. Kingsley had been afraid of Floyd's scar the first time they met, but now they were comfortable friends. "Is that what happened to you?" Kingsley asked. "Did you get in a fight with a bully?"

Floyd nodded. "A knife fight." He swiped the paring knife above his scar.

Kingsley sat up in his chair. "Really?"

Floyd laughed, almost choking on a piece of apple. "No, not really." It took a minute for him to clear his throat. "I was born this way. I was teased about it when I was a boy, so I told everyone I was in a knife fight to look tough."

"Did that work? Did the bullies leave you alone?"

"Most times," Floyd said. "Guys'll back down if you give them half a reason."

"That's true." Kingsley knew he'd back down from a fight, but he wasn't so sure about Amanda or his mother. They were still arguing about the dead snake. "Amanda's the bravest person I know," he murmured. "Must be nice to be rich and brave."

Floyd nodded. "Yep, must be nice."

"And to live in a mansion and have a chauffeur," Kingsley added.

"I wasn't always a chauffeur, you know. I used to work at the Sutherland Shipyard. That was way back before your Momma started taking care of Mrs. Sutherland. Back when Mr. Sutherland was still alive."

"Did you like it?"

"Sometimes. Lots can go wrong building aircraft carriers. I almost—"

"You built aircraft carriers!" Kingsley interrupted. "Did any Blue Angel jets land on your aircraft carriers?"

"Once or twice," Floyd said. "I mostly worked in the office, bidding on Pentagon contracts. Drove me crazy. Every two years a new crop of congressmen would come in and change the rules. One year they'd worry about saving money, the next they'd worry about national defense. Too much politicking." He cut another piece of apple and handed it to Kingsley. "But I do miss those big ships. I was too old to learn welding and too loyal to fire, so Mr. Sutherland took me on as his chauffeur. Good thing, too, since he ended up selling the company."

"Is that how the Sutherlands got rich?"

"In a manner of speaking," Floyd said. "Their fortune started with the dawn of the ironclads."

"The what?"

"Iron battleships," Floyd said. "Amanda's great-great-grandfather started Sutherland Shipyard. His portrait hangs in the front hallway. Amanda's grandfather looked just like him, except for the whiskers."

Kingsley remembered the portrait. "White hair. Crazy sideburns."

Floyd finished the apple, holding the naked core delicately between his fingertips. "Cyrus was conscripted into the Confederate Navy about the same time the Union blockaded Hampton Roads Harbor."

"Conscripted?"

"Drafted," Floyd said. He stood and threw the apple core into the azalea bushes in the front yard and gave Kingsley a sheepish grin. "Don't tell your mother I did that." He returned to his rocking chair, and his voice turned somber. "When the Confederates captured the Navy Base in Portsmouth, the Union burned and sank all their ships. They didn't want their ships used against them. But that's exactly what happened.

"Cyrus Sutherland was part of the Confederate crew that raised and restored one of the sunken Union ships: the *USS Merrimack*. The Confederates welded four-inch thick metal armor to her hull and renamed her The *CSS Virginia*. The *Confederate States Ship Virginia*." Floyd glanced around and lowered his voice. "The Cock Sucker Ship *Virginia*, I like to call her. Ten guns, steam powered, and an impenetrable hull. The old girl had been through a lot but she came back fighting, harder and meaner than ever. She attacked the Union blockade and sank two of the Union's best ships, the *Cumberland* and the *Congress*."

Kingsley imagined the battle. Cannons booming, ships on fire, hand-to-hand combat. He shielded his eyes from the bright midday sun and looked south. Somewhere in the distance, the James River merged with the Elizabeth River and the Nansemond River, forming the Hampton Roads Harbor at the mouth of the Chesapeake Bay. The long Monitor-Merrimac Bridge-Tunnel, completed in 1992—eleven years before Kingsley was born—spanned the harbor and memorialized the famous naval battles.

"The *Virginia* destroyed five of the North's most powerful warships in two bloody days," Floyd said. "Lincoln declared the battle of Hampton Roads the Union's greatest calamity since Bull Run. They were scared, especially in Washington, D.C. The *Virginia* could speed up the Potomac, point her cannons at the White House, and hang Lincoln's head from her bowsprit. The Union had to find a way to defeat the South's warship. They came up with a brand-new design, an ironclad like no ship ever built. The *USS Monitor* looked more like a submarine than a warship. She had a metal hull and the first-ever rotating gun turret. Overnight, wooden fleets became obsolete. Iron warships were the world's first weapons of mass destruction, you might say. After the war, Cyrus started his own ship-building company."

"So the *Monitor* won?" Kingsley asked. "The Union's new ship beat the old *CSS Virginia*?"

"Not exactly," Floyd said. "But she did change the world."

Kingsley and Floyd were startled to see Amanda marching up the front steps. She was sweating under her heavy riding helmet, wearing her usual dirty riding boots, and she looked like she was itching for a fight. "Don't get in my way," she warned, arms waving. Dirt clods flew as she stomped into the mansion. Enrique followed Amanda, hat in hand. Kingsley and

Floyd gave each other a quick glance, and then scrambled out of their chairs, not wanting to miss the fireworks.

Joyce was sitting on the couch in the den, doing Mrs. Sutherland's nails. Mrs. Sutherland was hunched in her wheelchair, a blue blanket draped over her legs. "Boots," Joyce said, pointing the emery board at Amanda's dirty riding boots. Enrique slipped off his boots. Amanda left hers on.

"Who are those men looking at the mares?" Amanda demanded, hands on hips.

"They're men looking at the mares," Joyce said matter-of-factly. Mrs. Sutherland's sizable jewelry box was open and Joyce was wearing a pair of Mrs. Sutherland's dangling diamond earrings. They sparkled in the sunlight streaming in through the bay window. Joyce waved the emery board at Enrique. "Boy, you'd better get on back to the stable. Let them know you're a half-decent horseman. Maybe they'll give you a job."

"I better what?" Enrique asked. "I already have a job!"

Amanda pulled off her riding hat. Her long black hair fell about her face. "You're selling the mares, aren't you?"

"Not me. They're your grandmother's horses. She doesn't want them anymore." Joyce put down the emery board and opened a jar of hand cream. "And why should she? She can't ride them. Why should she keep a bunch of stinky horses?"

"For me. For my mother. For Uncle Jack."

Joyce let out a sarcastic snort. "Your mother? Oh, hon, don't tell me you're hanging on to that delusion. Your mother's not coming back. You know that. She's moving in with the senator." Joyce massaged Mrs. Sutherland's hands, gently rubbing the white cream into every crease, every pore, and every cuticle. "And tell me the last time anyone heard from your Uncle Jack?" She grabbed a bottle of ultra-pink nail polish, shook it vigorously, and applied polish to the curled fingernails of Mrs. Sutherland's left hand. She carefully outlined the edge of each nail then filled in the center. "He doesn't call. He doesn't write. Your grandmother doesn't even know if Jack's alive. What's wrong with your family? I'd be ashamed if I'd treated my mother the way your kin treats sweet Mrs. Sutherland."

"My grandfather built those stables," Amanda said. "He taught Clare and Jack how to ride. Grandmother would never sell the mares. You're a liar."

Kingsley gawked at Amanda, stunned by her daring. Even Mrs. Sutherland, soundless and stooped, looked up and fluttered her eyes. Kingsley was sure his mother would slap Amanda but Joyce didn't flinch. She just smiled and began polishing the fingernails of Mrs. Sutherland's right hand. "Sit down, hon. Sit down next to me." Amanda folded her arms and stood firm. "Come on," Joyce said, patting the couch beside her. "I won't bite." Amanda sat, arms folded. "Think about things for a moment," Joyce said. "Your father's moved to Hampton and your momma and the senator are building a house in Chesapeake. I bet you're hoping to go live with your father soon, right?"

Amanda loosened the fold of her arms. "Yes."

"And when you're gone, who'll ride those horses? Me? Your grandmother? Kingsley? You know we won't. Don't those mares deserve a full life? Don't they deserve someone who'll love them? Isn't that what we all want?"

Amanda murmured under her breath.

"Your stallion's dead, hon, and let me tell you, a bunch of mares without a stallion is a sorry sight."

"You don't know anything about horses," Amanda countered.

Joyce just smiled and stopped painting Mrs. Sutherland's fingernails. "A sorry sight indeed. I miss my Darryl every day of my life, and I know Mrs. Sutherland misses her husband, too."

The front door slammed open and Joyce's sister, Maureen—the sister Kingsley didn't like—shuffled lazily past Kingsley, ignoring him completely, and flopped on the couch beside Joyce, yawning, her purple hair slick and unwashed. Kingsley gawked at her. Her gruesome tattoos had multiplied during her days off, covering her neck and face, giving her the appearance of a psychotic kaleidoscope.

Joyce tenderly held Mrs. Sutherland's hands, careful of the freshly painted nails. She looked into the old woman's eyes. "Hon, I'm taking the evening off," she cooed. "Maureen's here to take care of you."

Mrs. Sutherland's eyes opened wide. She stared fearfully at Maureen and moaned as if she were in pain.

Joyce gently patted her knee and turned to Maureen. "Now listen to me, this is important. Mrs. Sutherland needs to be dressed and fed by eight a.m. tomorrow morning. She has an appointment with a lawyer to sell the mares.

Be sure she takes her arthritis medicine before she goes or she'll be hurting all day. Don't screw it up like you usually do."

"Whatever," Maureen said. She rolled her eyes and wheeled Mrs. Sutherland out of the den.

Joyce capped the polish, and placed it and the emery board into the pocket of her apron. "Time to go. I've got a big day tomorrow and have to get ready." She closed the jewelry box but didn't take off Mrs. Sutherland's dangling diamond earrings. She smiled at Amanda. "Pretty, aren't they? Your grandmother gave them to me. She thinks I'm an angel." Joyce stood and took off her apron, handing it to Amanda. "I'm so glad we had this little chat, *Mandy*." Amanda started to argue but Joyce cut her off. "Tomorrow, hon," she said. "Tomorrow's the day everything changes."

The next morning, Joyce, Mrs. Sutherland, and Kingsley headed to the lawyer's office in Norfolk to sell the mares. Kingsley was wearing new pants and a new shirt. Both were itchy and too small, especially the pants, which felt like barbed wire wrapped tight around his belly fat. He didn't know why he was forced to tag along. He'd rather have stayed at the mansion and played video games.

Joyce drove Mrs. Sutherland's van from Marlbank in Yorktown to the lawyer's office in Norfolk. She insisted on driving—over Floyd's protests. "I'm the chauffeur!" he said. Joyce ignored him. In downtown Norfolk, she searched for handicapped parking until she found a space on Colley Avenue. Joyce pushed Mrs. Sutherland's wheelchair over the crowded, bumpy sidewalks and Kingsley trotted behind. The air was hot and humid and full of auto exhaust. He couldn't wait to get inside air conditioning again.

When they arrived at the lawyer's office, the door was locked. Three people stood outside: two tall men in suits and ties, and a short buxom woman wearing a flowered skirt and a shimmering yellow blouse with big red buttons shaped like tulips. Perspiration pooled at her temples and stained her blouse. One of the men checked his phone as the other pounded on the office door.

"I don't understand," said the woman. "He's never late."

The man stopped pounding. "You work here?"

The woman nodded.

The man let out an irritated sigh and peered down his perfectly straight nose at Mrs. Sutherland. "You must be Leslie Sutherland," he said. "And you must be her nurse." He didn't look at Joyce, which annoyed Kingsley. His mother might not be as beautiful as Clare or as honorable as Amanda, but she was his mother and he loved her.

A cough came from the other side of the door, something banged, and a man cursed. The door swung open and the worst stench ever radiated from a handsomely dressed man standing just inside. "Please come in," the man offered his hand. "I'm Randolph Setter." The two tall men recoiled in disgust and Mr. Setter pulled back his hand. "Are you here for the sale of the Sutherland mares?"

"Yes, and we're in a hurry."

Mr. Setter barked at the woman in the yellow blouse, "Doris, bring everyone a beverage. Coffee? Tea? A cola for the young man?"

Doris scurried past the stinky Mr. Setter to a desk in the corner, grabbed a manila folder, handed it to Mr. Setter, and then scurried away again, presumably for the beverages. Mr. Setter turned to Mrs. Sutherland. He kneeled and took her thin, limp hand. "It's wonderful seeing you again, Leslie."

Joyce blanched. "You know Mrs. Sutherland?"

"Not exactly," Mr. Setter said, standing, "I met Mr. Sutherland when I was in law school. A pillar of the community. He spoke to my torts class about reforming—"

"Can we get on with it?" one of the men asked. "It smells like shit in here."

"Yes, I know." Mr. Setter led them to a small conference room. "I must apologize for that. I was deer hunting last night when I stepped onto a hollow log, in which, to my utmost mortification, a family of skunks had made their humble abode. I stumbled and was at once set upon by the scoundrels. I considered rescheduling today's appointment, but, as the French say, c'est la vie." He gestured dramatically to the chairs around a rectangular wooden table, "Please have a seat," and called down the hall, "Doris, where's the Sutherland file?" Doris yelled back that the file was in his hand. "Voilà! Ask and you shall receive!" He sat down with a flourish and opened the file. "Deer hunting at night is technically illegal, but only if you get caught." He gave Joyce a little wink. "I ended up skinning the skunks. I think I might mount the mother on the wall once she stops stinking."

Doris came in carrying a tray with a pot of coffee, a stack of Styrofoam cups, and a can of cola. Kingsley eagerly grabbed the cola, but none of the adults accepted her offer of coffee. Mr. Setter passed papers to the men and asked for identification. "Just to be clear, I'm handing out the sales contract for eleven Sutherland mares: Four Hanoverians, six warmbloods and one Holsteiner. If you would sign at the bottom, gentlemen, where it says purchaser." He passed a copy to Joyce. "And, Ms. Smith, if you would have Mrs. Sutherland sign where it says seller." The men signed their papers. Joyce wrapped her hand over Mrs. Sutherland's and together they signed Mrs. Sutherland's name. More papers were handed out, more signatures. One of the men gave Mr. Setter a check and left in a hurry, his chair scraping against the floor. The other man followed without even a goodbye.

"That was easy," Mr. Setter said. "Now to the distribution of the funds."

Kingsley sipped his cola. He was finally getting used to the stench.

"And the matter we discussed earlier?" Joyce asked, smiling coyly, ramping up her New Orleans drawl.

"Yes, yes." Mr. Setter handed Doris the check the men had given him and she scurried away. He hummed as he flipped through the rest of the paperwork. "I was about twenty-six or twenty-seven when I met Mr. Sutherland. Quite a striking man. Very handsome. I believe he had two children."

Joyce nodded. "A boy and a girl."

"The girl was gorgeous, as I remember. A blue-eyed angel with a charming touch of prepubescent chubbiness." He licked the corners of his mouth and returned to the papers. "The boy was a different story. Very rebellious. Isn't he in prison?"

"I can't say," Joyce said. "I've never met him."

"He was a wild one," Mr. Setter said. "Handsome, but troubled." Mr. Setter handed a stack of papers to Joyce. "Here you go, Ms. Smith, your new identity. Social security card, insurance card." He lingered on the photo on Joyce's new driver's license. "Twenty-nine years old, hmm, I wish I were twenty-nine again."

"What about Kingsley?" Joyce asked as she snatched the license from his fingers.

Mr. Setter waved his hand like a magician. "All taken care of. You'll receive a new birth certificate for Kingsley in the mail, and he's already on your insurance." Doris returned with two checks and gave them to Mr. Setter. She left and Mr. Setter handed the checks to Joyce. "Here you go," he said. "Mrs. Sutherland's check for the agreed upon amount, and your check. We'll call it a finder's fee."

"With my new name on it," Joyce said. She glanced at the checks then slipped both checks in her purse.

"Absolutely." Mr. Setter stood and escorted them to the front door. "I don't know what I'm going to do about the smell."

"Take a bath in tomato juice."

"I wish I had the time. I'm due in court in an hour." Mr. Setter opened the front door and shook Joyce's hand. "Call me the next time you need my services," he said, giving Joyce a wink, "I'd be happy to help you sell the rest of Mrs. Sutherland's holdings." He laughed. "In the meantime, nice to meet you, *Lily Fells*."

Kingsley mulled over what had just happened. "I don't like this, Mom. Why'd that smelly lawyer call you Lily Fells?"

"That's my new name, hon," Joyce said as she wheeled Mrs. Sutherland back to the van. "For when we go to Charlottesville to see Dr. Barlow. My name is Lily Fells and your name is Kingsley Fells, hear me? It's important you keep this straight."

Kingsley frowned. "This is because of what happened in New Orleans, isn't it? Because of what happened with Dad. That's why I have to lie to Dr. Barlow that my name is Kingsley Fells."

Joyce bit her lip as she loaded Mrs. Sutherland into the van and took the driver's seat, Kingsley sat beside her. She turned to Kingsley, her face flushed. "Your Daddy's dead and gone and can't do a thing for us now," she said, "so you listen to me." She paused and playfully tickled the fat under Kingsley's double chin. "Just do it, hon." She handed Kingsley her cell phone. "And do me a favor. Call Floyd. Tell him to meet us at the automobile dealership in Hampton, the big one on Aberdeen Road. Tell him to bring Latonya so one of them can drive Mrs. Sutherland's van back to the mansion. We're buying a new car, hon. I'm giving my old Charger to Mavis and Maureen."

41

When Joyce and Kingsley arrived at the automobile dealership, Floyd and Latonya were already there. Floyd had driven Mrs. Sutherland's glossy black limousine. "You do know that I'm Mrs. Sutherland's chauffeur, don't you?" Floyd said as Joyce handed him the keys to the van.

"You can drive me around anytime, Floyd," Joyce said with a coy grin. "I've always wanted a black chauffeur." Floyd sniffed and handed the keys to Latonya, who drove Mrs. Sutherland back to the mansion in the van.

Floyd stayed. "I'd like to see what kind of car your Momma buys," he said to Kingsley.

Joyce looked at a used BMW and almost bought it until Floyd opened the hood. "This car's been in a wreck," he said, pointing to a welded axle. "See there. Nothing but trouble. You want one of those new electric hybrids. My son-in-law says they're the best cars on the road."

Joyce took one of the new hybrids for a test drive, a royal blue Nissan Pegasus. Floyd sat beside her, Kingsley in the back. "Smooth," Floyd said. "She'll pay for herself in no time with all the gas money you'll save." The Pegasus was as sleek as a 1966 Mustang and could run sixty highway miles on one gallon of gas. When they returned to the dealership, Floyd waited with Kingsley while Joyce filled out the paperwork. Floyd ran his hand down the side of the new car. "Needs racing stripes."

Kingsley agreed. The Pegasus was the coolest car he'd ever seen.

Joyce returned with the keys, and Floyd headed to the limo. "Want to drive back to the mansion with me?" he asked Kingsley.

"No, thanks. I want to ride in Mom's new car."

Floyd tipped his hat. "Suit yourself."

Kingsley imagined himself driving the beautiful new car. He imagined one hand on the steering wheel and the other wrapped around Amanda. Maybe she'd lean her head on his shoulder. He grinned from ear-to-ear and lowered the window so he could feel the warm summer wind in his face. Joyce zoomed east on the interstate, all the way to Virginia Beach, to the smell of the Atlantic Ocean and the sound of the waves. They passed a row of high-rise hotels and a sagging amusement park stuffed with oversized people riding the Ferris wheel and roller-coaster. They rounded a corner and drove by a long white building with blue awnings. Joyce slowed the car. She seemed mesmerized. The building looked like it had been plucked off a postcard from another place, another era, as if it belonged on the Atlantic City boardwalk during the bootlegging twenties.

Kingsley was surprised when his mother made a U-turn at the next stoplight, returned to the white building, and pulled into the parking lot. "What are we doing here, Mom?" he asked. He read the sign in front of the building, *Edgar Cayce Foundation for Enlightenment and Research*.

Joyce stopped the car and stared at the building. "I feel like something's tugging at me, hon, telling me I should be here."

"What do you mean *something's tugging at you?*"

"I don't know, Kingsley. Something's telling me to go inside."

They got out of the car and Kingsley followed Joyce across a tile labyrinth with the yin-yang image of two dolphins in the center, and then walked up a flight of white, wooden steps. His mother had done a lot of questionable things in her life but he'd never known her to act so spooky. Inside, the building was fresh and cool, like a pine forest after an afternoon rain. Soothing music played over unseen loudspeakers. No one was at the reception desk. Joyce picked up a brochure and read it aloud:

The Sleeping Prophet

Edgar Cayce emphasized the spiritual nature of humankind, what he believed to be the truest part of ourselves. Although we possess physical bodies and mental attitudes, ultimately our deepest connection is to our spiritual nature. Spirit is the Life, Mind is the Builder, and the Physical is the Result. The impact of our choices will find expression in the physical, affecting ourselves, our relationships, and our world.

Joyce handed the pamphlet to Kingsley, who reread it, trying to understand. He'd never heard of this man and didn't know why he and Joyce were there. "Who's Edgar Cayce, Mom?"

"I don't know, hon," she said, looking around, searching for clues. "I don't know why I'm here or what I'm looking for. All I know is that it has something to do with you. I feel like these people are gonna tell me how to help you."

"Is Edgar Cayce going to cure my headaches?"

Joyce pointed to a large painting of a balding man wearing wire-rimmed glasses. Under the painting was an engraved plaque. "See there," she said, "That says he died in 1945."

Kingsley's confusion grew. "Then why are we here?"

A tall, slender woman suddenly appeared. Kingsley assumed she'd come from around the corner but he wasn't sure. She seemed to just materialize, like she was an angel or maybe a witch from *Harry Potter*. She had auburn hair and wore an ivory shirt with a simple, tan skirt. She headed straight toward Joyce, didn't waver or pause. She grabbed Joyce's arm and placed her other hand on Joyce's forehead. "Your daughter is the zenith that will change the world."

Joyce tried to pull away. "I don't have a daughter."

The woman held tight. Her high-pitched voice sounded like an alarm. "The Collapse is upon us. The years ahead are full of sorrow. Many will not survive the heartache, but you will." The woman released Joyce's arm, leaving indentations in her ruddy skin. "But you will," she repeated, and then disappeared around a corner.

Kingsley started to follow, but Joyce held him back. She shivered and rubbed her arm. "Let's get out of here."

5 Bapsi Cama

The humidity outside was so high that everything not air conditioned was constantly damp. Fortunately for Kingsley, he and his video games were inside, but he was frustrated by Amanda's lack of enthusiasm. He wanted to share with her the fun of killing mutants. He demonstrated the best controller sequences to use when a mutant was attacking alone or when they attacked as a group. "They're different, you see," Kingsley explained. "You can kill *one* mutant with a bastion rifle, see," he said, demonstrating a red-eyed mutant's head exploding, "but if a whole *army* attacks, you gotta go nuclear." Amanda never got the hang of it. She thought the mutants were cute, which infuriated Kingsley.

They were waiting for Joyce to get ready for Kingsley's next trip to Charlottesville to see Dr. Barlow. His mother was droning on and on, lecturing her sisters, Mavis and Maureen, about the importance of taking good care of Mrs. Sutherland.

"I won't be back until after dark," Joyce said, "That means you'll be alone with her all day and possibly all night, so don't screw up. Make sure Mrs. Sutherland stays healthy. Keep her clean and warm and well fed. Make sure she takes her arthritis medicine." Mavis was attentive, but Maureen rolled her eyes, as usual. Joyce snatched Maureen's chin, "If I find out you're taking her pain pills, you'll be on bedpan duty for the rest of your life."

Kingsley was worried. He hated his headaches, but he was more frightened of what Dr. Barlow might do to him. Would he have an operation? Would it hurt? Would he end up with a bandage around his head like the little boy in the bed next to him last time he was in the hospital? He could barely keep his mind on his video game. Amanda leaned against him, as if she knew what he was thinking. "Dr. Jacobs says Dr. Barlow is the best in the country for the dolphin disease, maybe in the world." Amanda pulled out her phone. "I found an interview with her online." Kingsley stopped his game, and Amanda played the video of Dr. Barlow talking to a reporter. Amanda turned up the sound.

"...scientists used to believe the substances surrounding DNA molecules were inconsequential," the reporter said. "They were wrong. With me today to explain the cause of The Collapse is Dr. Joan Barlow."

The camera turned to Dr. Barlow. "The Collapse?" she said, a dubious look on her face. "Is that what the news is calling the Y-Chromosome Linked Tumors Syndrome now?"

The reporter nodded. "Dr. Estella Jones from the CDC coined the phrase yesterday at a press conference. The Collapse is certainly easier to say."

"And more dramatic," Dr. Barlow said. "To understand the Y-Chromosome Linked Tumors Syndrome, you first must have some understanding of the epigenome."

"What is the epigenome?"

Dr. Barlow took off her glasses. "As you know, our genome contains the instructions for building all the parts of our body. But DNA is only half the story. Chemical tags cover our DNA to form a second layer of structure called the epigenome."

"How is the epigenome different from the genome?"

"Epi is the Latin prefix for *on* or *around*," Dr. Barlow said. "The epigenome shapes the physical structure of our genome, that is, our DNA." She paused for a moment. "Imagine a doctor wrapping a heavy bandage around your arm. If she wraps it tight, you can't move your arm. If she wraps it loose, you can. When the epigenome is tightly wrapped around our DNA, it turns our genes off. Relax the epigenome and the genes turn back on. Our DNA remains fixed but our epigenome is flexible."

"Are you saying changes in our epigenome caused The Collapse?" the reporter asked. "How can that happen? How can a disease affect males but not females?"

"There are many sex-linked diseases," Dr. Barlow said. "Hemophilia, for instance, is linked to the Y-chromosome, although it's inherited and thus not caused by external factors. Epigenenic tags, on the other hand, react to signals from the outside world. Diet, stress, toxins, and so forth. The first repeatable experiment supporting the theory that environmental factors can directly lead to epigenetic changes *and* that those changes can be passed from one generation to the next, occurred in 2008. That experiment involved a fungicide called vinclozolin. This fungicide was fed to pregnant rats. The male offspring had low sperm count, poor fertility, and an increase in several diseases including prostate and kidney disease. That this first generation had medical problems isn't surprising considering their mother's exposure. What was surprising was how transgenerational the effect was. Two generations later, the great grandchildren of the original exposed rats displayed the same problems: low sperm count and the other medical issues."

"So you don't agree with the current theory that The Collapse is caused by a virus?"

Dr. Barlow took a deep breath. "What I'm saying is that the Y-Chromosome Linked Tumors Syndrome is caused by more than just a virus. If it were exclusively a virus, we could isolate it. We could vaccinate against it."

"Do you believe The Collapse is caused by environmental factors such as pollution and climate change?"

Dr. Barlow cleaned her cat-eye glasses with the bottom of her white lab coat. "I hesitate to affirm such a controversial statement."

"But," the reporter pressed, "if we ban toxins, The Collapse should end."

Dr. Barlow shook her head. "That would be impossible. We can only test for toxins that have already been identified. This syndrome could be the result of a combination of two relatively innocuous substances that has created a third, unknown substance."

"Is there a cure?"

"The transformation of our epigenome took generations; it will most likely take generations to work its way out."

"But without men, we won't have generations."

Dr. Barlow gave the reporter a grim smile. "That's the heart of the matter, isn't it? Currently, all we can do is alleviate the symptoms, but there is hope for a cure. You might remember the stunning discovery right here in Charlottesville a few years ago, at the University of Virginia School of Medicine. A direct connection was found between the brain and the immune system. These neuro-immune vessels could explain why the tumors manifest so rapidly. My research with dogs suggests. . . "

Kingsley tried to understand. Was Dr. Barlow saying that men could disappear? "Did you understand any of that?" he asked Amanda.

"A little," Amanda said.

"What does it mean?"

"Remember when Daddy showed us all that garbage and we found that sick turtle? Remember what he said about a new disease?" Amanda asked. Kingsley nodded. "It means Daddy was right."

Kingsley wished Amanda had come with him on the three-and-a-half-hour drive to Charlottesville. An 18-wheeler had stopped on the interstate, slowing traffic. It didn't have a flat tire; it wasn't in a wreck. It'd just stopped in the right lane. The driver was slumped over his steering wheel, either dead or asleep, Kingsley couldn't tell. No police were there, no ambulance or EMT. Joyce had to creep around the truck at twenty miles per hour instead of the usual seventy.

In Charlottesville, they drove past blocks of new construction—empty of workmen—to get to the medical center. Joyce dodged pedestrians wearing hospital scrubs, and patients, mostly women and young boys, seemingly oblivious to oncoming traffic. "I guess if you're going to be hit by a car, in front of a hospital is a good place to do it," Joyce grumbled.

Kingsley remembered the parking garage from his last visit. Just like before, the six-story garage was narrow and packed. Joyce circled up, floor after floor, almost scraping a pick-up truck inching its way down. She finally found a parking spot on the top floor. "Eleven forty-five," she said. "We're late. We were supposed to check in fifteen minutes ago."

She grabbed Kingsley's hand and ran across the parking garage to the elevators. Kingsley worked to catch his breath. He was already nervous about seeing Dr. Barlow again and the running only made him feel worse.

His whole body ached. The elevator stopped at ground level and Joyce rushed Kingsley around the crowds of slow, sick people, and through the front doors. She took a number and found seats on a couch where they waited for the admissions clerk to call them.

Kingsley decided hospitals were strange places. People wore funny outfits and someone somewhere was always moaning or crying. He noticed a boy in a wheelchair with a bandage around his head. The boy's mother wore an African sundress and head wrap. The boy seemed to Kingsley like any other little black boy until he accidently rolled over Kingsley's foot and said pardon with a French accent. Kingsley asked the boy if he was from France.

"No," the boy answered, "I am from Gabon, Africa."

"Have you seen a lion?" Kingsley asked.

The boy shook his head. "No, they're all gone."

"Where'd they go?"

"The *Muuaji*," the boy said, pointing to the bandage around his head. "The Swahili call it the *Muuaji*. The Murderer. The disease killed most of the animals. The *mâle* die and the *femelle* can have no *bébé*."

Joyce gawked at the sick boy. "The same disease that causes headaches?"

"Yes, ma'am," came the answer, but not from the boy. Two big, strong men had just taken numbers and were looking for seats in the waiting area. "In humans it causes headaches. Maybe the animals get headaches, too. I don't know," one of the men said. He squeezed onto the couch beside Kingsley and introduced himself. "Ex-Marine by the name of Sam Hong," he said, shaking Kingsley's hand. He sported a buzz cut and a large tattoo lettered down his forearm, *Death Before Dishonor*. The other man found a seat in a nearby chair. He introduced himself as Walker Williams, also an ex-Marine. "I was a POW in Afghanistan until all my guards died and the women of the village let me out." He had Pisces and Aquarius tattooed on his hairy forearms, the fish on his right and the water bearer on his left.

Joyce wriggled anxiously in her seat. "What do you mean? Maybe animals get headaches, too?"

The ex-Marines didn't answer. Instead, much to Kingsley's shock, the one named Sam started crying and rubbing Kingsley's head like he was a puppy. "Poor boy," Sam said, leaning close and trying to hug Kingsley. "I'm sorry, boy, sorry we couldn't save you." Kingsley pulled away and left the couch. He wanted to get away from the blubbering ex-marine. He moved to another chair.

The other ex-Marine looked more angry than sad. He was carrying a large soda in a styrofoam cup with a plastic top and straw. "What's your name, son?" he asked.

"Kingsley."

"What's your last name?"

"Sm—," Kingsley hesitated. He almost told his real name. "Fells. My name is Kingsley Fells." He glanced at Joyce who gave him a little nod and a smile.

Walker raised his cup. "To Kingsley Fells, the last boy on earth."

Joyce's smile disappeared. "That's not funny."

"Not supposed to be," Walker said. He tossed his empty cup into the trash, slam-dunk style. "I joined the military eight years ago, mostly to piss off my father, but it's different now. The rest of the world is—"

"Dead," Sam said, wiping his nose with his forearm. "The Middle East. Africa. Asia. The streets are empty. I haven't seen a boy younger than fifteen since—"

"Did you see any girls?" Joyce asked.

"Girls? Oh, yeah, plenty of girls. A dime a dozen. Parents selling their daughters on street corners so they can send their sons to the United States for medical treatment. Sold to anyone. And I mean anyone." Sam closed his eyes and rubbed the back of his neck.

Walker leaned back in his chair, his hands behind his head and his boots on the magazine table. "As the poet said, *This is the way the world ends. Not with a bang but a whimper.*"

This disease didn't just cause headaches. It didn't just kill fish and turtles. It was all over the world. Kingsley barely heard the admissions clerk call his number. He barely felt Joyce pull him up from his chair. He was too shaken to listen when Joyce handed the clerk her new insurance card. "Fells. My son's name is Kingsley Fells. I just got married so we changed Kingsley's name to Fells. I threw away my old insurance card. Hope that's not a problem." The clerk smiled and asked for Kingsley's date of birth. She punched her computer, handed Joyce back her insurance card, and told

Joyce to take Kingsley to the eighth floor. Up in the elevator they went, where Joyce had to check in with another clerk, who also asked Kingsley's name and date of birth.

"And your name?"

Joyce licked her lips. "Lily Fells. My name is Lily Fells."

They waited in a plush lobby with large windows and a fancy statue in the corner that looked like a piece of wood with feathers on it. Kingsley walked to the window. Charlottesville was more hilly than Hampton. He could see the Blue Ridge Mountains in the distance.

A heavy-set nurse called Kingsley's name and led Joyce and Kingsley to a much smaller room. She asked Kingsley to step on a scale, which was embarrassing. She told him to take a seat and she proceeded to ask the same questions, name, date of birth, plus a few more. Medications, when his headaches began, and where it hurt. She placed a plastic bracelet around Kingsley's wrist with his new name on it. *Kingsley Fells*. She escorted Kingsley and Joyce to a semi-private room with a curtain drawn around the other bed. The nurse gave Kingsley a thin gown that tied in the back and told him to change in the bathroom.

Kingsley took off his jeans and his oversized sweatshirt, and threw them on the bathroom floor. He looked at himself in the mirror. Fat, pale, fourteen years old. He'd never ridden a horse, never swam in the ocean, and never kissed a girl. He didn't go out to see movies anymore because the seats were too small. His mother used to tell him that too much junk food and sitting around playing video games made him fat and caused his headaches. Kingsley used to believe her. He'd feel guilty when he snuck a 3 Musketeers bar or played an extra round of *Attack of the Mutants*. But as he looked at himself in the mirror, he decided his mother was wrong. He'd seen old movies with boys climbing trees and building forts, but none of the guys he knew were anything like that. No one played outside because the sun gave them headaches. No one played basketball because they were soon out of breath. No one wrestled or boxed because it was too exhausting. None of the boys, at least. The girls played sports, especially strong girls like Amanda. Kingsley stared at his chubby face. "Am I fat because of all the garbage in the water? Will my dick shrivel up like those alligators?"

He put on the hospital gown and trudged out of the bathroom, holding the back together so his boxers wouldn't show. He climbed in bed, and another nurse once again asked his name and his date of birth. She checked his answers against the plastic bracelet around his wrist.

Poles surrounded him, with bags and tubes attached to machines that seemed to beep for no apparent reason. Women were talking behind a curtain. One spoke with an accent. The curtain opened to reveal a sleeping boy Kingsley didn't recognize and two women. One he didn't know—the boy's mother, he presumed. He recognized the other. She'd worn a sari at her young son's bedside the last time Kingsley was in the hospital. This time she wasn't wearing a sari and the boy in the bed wasn't her son. She wore a white hospital smock with a nametag: *Dr. Bapsi Cama, Maternity.*

Bapsi smiled at Kingsley. "I know you! I never forget a face."

Joyce eyed Bapsi suspiciously. "How do you know Kingsley?"

"My son shared a room with him," Bapsi said. She tucked a stray hair into the black braid that circled her head like a tiara. "I was wearing a sari at the time and my hair was down. I looked quite different."

"Your son was seeing Dr. Barlow, too," said Joyce.

Bapsi paused. "Yes," she said. Her voice wavered. "Yes, he was." A moment of quiet passed, finally broken when Bapsi motioned to the boy in the other bed. "I'm visiting one of my young friends. He's seeing Dr. Barlow as well."

"And that gray liquid?" asked Joyce.

"That's the gene therapy. Dreadful looking, but fortunately you don't have to drink it." Bapsi closed the privacy curtain around the other boy and his mother.

Joyce fidgeted, nervously looking toward the door. "Can I ask a favor?"

"Do you need to step away?" Bapsi said.

"Yeah, um," Joyce hesitated. "I'm supposed to meet a real estate agent in the lobby in a few minutes. I thought we'd be done by now."

"I'd be delighted to stay until Dr. Barlow arrives," Bapsi said. As Joyce was about to leave, Bapsi asked a question. "I'm so sorry. I've forgotten your name."

"Lily Fells," Joyce said, without hesitation, as if she'd been Lily Fells all her life. "And my son's name is Kingsley Fells." She left the room.

Bapsi pulled up a chair beside Kingsley's bed. "So good to see you again, Kingsley. How have you been?"

"A boy downstairs said the lions in Africa are gone," Kingsley said. "And another man said all the animals are dying, which is terrible, except for the bugs. All the bugs dying is okay with me."

"I felt the same when I was young," Bapsi said. "I hated bugs, especially cockroaches." She shivered. "But I had no idea how important bugs were until they were all gone. Did you know that just about every fruit and vegetable needs them?"

Kingsley was about to tell Bapsi he was still okay with all the bugs dying because he didn't like vegetables when they were interrupted by a young woman wearing a lab coat knocking on the door. "Dr. Cama? May I speak to you for a moment?"

Bapsi waved her in with a smile. "Yes, please, come in."

"Dr. Barlow is on the phone with the CDC. They think they've found a virus."

Bapsi looked unconvinced. "A virus that attacks only males?"

The young woman nodded. "The CDC thinks females have a natural immunity. They compare it to the one percent of Caucasians who have natural immunity to HIV because they lack CCR5 receptors on the surface of their CD4 cells."

Kingsley tried to follow. He wished doctors would stop talking in code.

"Dr. Barlow won't be here for at least another thirty minutes," the young woman said. "Could you tell his mother?"

"Of course," Bapsi said.

After the woman left the room, Kingsley asked, "That lady was talking about me, wasn't she?"

Bapsi's face softened. "Have you spoken to your mother or Dr. Barlow about what causes your headaches?"

Kingsley wrinkled his brow. "Dr. Barlow says something's pressing against my brain."

"And do any of your friends have headaches?" Bapsi asked. "Have you spoken with them?"

Kingsley nodded. "Billy had headaches. He says two boys in his neighborhood died."

Bapsi took a deep breath. "So sad. So sad." The room was quiet, save for the beeping of the machines and the soft murmurs of the mother and son behind the curtain. Kingsley wondered if Bapsi was thinking about her own little boy.

"That woman was Dr. Carpenter," Bapsi said, breaking the silence. "She's working with the Center for Disease Control in Atlanta trying to find a cure for these headaches." She squeezed Kingsley's hand. "She and Dr. Barlow are just two of the many excellent doctors and scientists working on it."

Kingsley thought about this. When he was a boy, scientists had come to New Orleans after the *Deepwater Horizon* oil spills in the Gulf. They'd scrubbed gulls with soap, trying to clean away the oil, but the gulls were never the same. The gulls made nests but something had happened to their insides and they couldn't have babies.

"I forgot your little boy's name," he said.

Bapsi smiled and tenderly brushed a strand of hair away from Kingsley's eyes. "Adar. It means fire in Persian."

"He died. Didn't he?"

Bapsi's smile faded. "Would you like to see a picture of him?" Kingsley nodded. She pulled out her phone and shared her photos. The first was of a little boy with black hair and brown eyes, sitting atop the shoulders of a slight man, eating ice cream. "That's my husband, Jahan. I took these during the Bakrid festival in Mumbai."

"What festival?"

"Bakrid. It's a Muslim celebration of when Allah commanded Ibrahim to sacrifice his son Ishmael." Bapsi looked away and wiped her eyes before returning to the photos. "Jahan's hair was sticky all day." She pressed a button and a second photograph appeared. It was of Bapsi and two old men. Bapsi wore an emerald green sari. "This is my father and my uncle. We're standing in front of the fire temple."

"What's a fire temple?"

"It's similar to a church." She pointed to the white statues of somber bearded men embedded in the walls of the temple, all in profile. "Those are Persian guards." The land surrounding the temple was a study in contrast. On one side, tall buildings crowded shoulder to shoulder; on the other was a lush garden of timeless vines, gnarled trees and a few precious flowers.

Kingsley studied the temple. "Do you believe in Jesus?"

"I attended a Christian school in India," Bapsi said. "I know the Bible and respect the teachings of Jesus, but I'm not Christian. I'm Zoroastrian."

Kingsley pondered what that meant. "Do you believe in heaven? My grandmother's preacher used to say that believing in Jesus was all you needed to get into heaven, but what if you've done something bad?" Kingsley thought about the pendant he'd stolen from Dr. Jacobs, and his lower lip began to quiver. He puckered his mouth, trying not to cry. But he was genuinely afraid. If he was going to die, he wanted to go to heaven.

Bapsi stroked Kingsley's round, worried face. "The Parsee have a saying. *Manashni, Gavashni, Kunashni.* Good Thoughts, Good Words, Good Deeds. Follow that advice and the rest will take care of itself."

6 Jack

Dr. Barlow's hair was jet black and cut short, like a soldier's; no more white streak down the middle. Another doctor accompanied her. "This is Dr. Kim from Pediatric Neurology," she said, introducing the doctor to Kingsley and Joyce. Whereas Dr. Barlow looked like she'd be more at home in a Broadway production of *Cats* than in a hospital, Dr. Kim was the opposite: reserved and professional in appearance, with pale skin and extreme exhaustion in her eyes.

Dr. Kim turned on a large wall monitor. A black, white and gray image—like an underinflated basketball—appeared. She pointed to the bottom of the basketball. "As you can see here in this image of Kingsley's brain, Kingsley has a type of tumor known as a glioblastoma. Glial cells make up almost ninety percent of our brain. They provide scaffolding for neurons." She touched the monitor and the image changed to an illustration that looked like eggs in a frying pan surrounded by spindly spiders. "These larger cells are neurons, while the smaller cells are a particular type of glial cell known as astrocytes." She touched the screen again and the previous image reappeared. "Some glial cells produce chemicals that guide young neurons to make the correct connections. Others insulate neuronal processes and speed conduction. Without glial cells, the neurons don't function properly. Glioblastomas have always been more common in males than in females, but what we're finding in Kingsley's case is consistent with the Y-Chromosome Linked Tumor Syndrome already surfacing in Asia and

Africa."

"How did it get to America?" Joyce asked. "Did some diseased immigrant bring it here?"

Kingsley was embarrassed by his mother's comment about immigrants and grateful that Bapsi wasn't in his room. She'd left when Joyce returned.

Dr. Barlow shook her head. "We don't yet know the root causes."

Dr. Kim added, "A year ago, I would have told you that malignant glioblastomas were found only in older patients, never in children, but the Y-Chromosome Linked Tumor Syndrome has shattered all of our preconceptions about brain tumors, which is why finding the most effective treatment has been so elusive."

"I don't understand," Joyce said impatiently "What's so *elusive* about a boy getting headaches?"

"It's more than a simple headache," Dr. Kim snapped. She pulled a tissue from her pocket and wiped perspiration from her forehead. "I apologize; I've been on call for thirty-six hours." Panic seeped into her voice. "This syndrome is having a huge impact on hospital functions. We're being run ragged. And it's already affecting the food supply. I'm sure you've heard about seafood, but the syndrome is also affecting land animals. Farmers are finding these tumors in livestock. Bulls, boars, rams. Soon there won't be anything to eat or people to—"

"Dr. Kim!" Dr. Barlow interrupted. Dr. Kim turned away, wiping her eyes with the tissue. "Frankly, we've never seen anything like this syndrome," Dr. Barlow said to Joyce. "We're short staffed and everyone is exhausted."

Joyce pointed to the image on the screen. "And those," she asked, referring to the cluster of small pebbles in the base of the underinflated basketball. "What are those?"

"Additional, smaller cerebellar astrocytomas," Dr. Barlow said as she switched off the screen. "More tumors."

"More!" Joyce recoiled. "But this gene therapy stuff gets rid of them? Right? It'll cure my son, right?"

Dr. Kim pursed her lips. "Our main goal is to prevent more from growing."

Joyce looked back and forth from Dr. Kim to Dr. Barlow. "Aren't you taking them out? Aren't you going to operate?"

Dr. Barlow's voice softened. "Ms. Fells," she paused, gently taking Joyce's hand. "May I call you Lily?"

Joyce gave Dr. Barlow a wary "I guess so."

"Lily, when the Y-Chromosome Linked Tumor Syndrome was first discovered, the treatment was the same as the treatment for cancer. Chemotherapy, surgery, radiation. But these tumors have unique growth patterns. They manifest rapidly and can grow to the size of a marble in a matter of days. We've found that in this particular malaise, conventional therapies added to the trauma without…" She glanced at Kingsley. "That is to say, with these Y-Chromosome Linked Tumors, conventional therapies were counterproductive."

Computers buzzed. Nurses chatted in the hallway. A woman somewhere was wailing. Kingsley didn't understand all that Dr. Barlow and Dr. Kim were saying, but he knew it wasn't good. He licked his lips and gathered his courage. "Will it hurt? What you're going to do to me, I mean. Will it hurt?"

Dr. Barlow interlaced her fingers as if she was in prayer. "No, Kingsley, it doesn't hurt." Her fingers tightened and her knuckles turned white. "Any treatment that can change a gene's structure or function is considered gene therapy. This new malignancy is similar to cancer or autism in that it's caused by damaged or missing genes. What makes this disease different is that the damaged gene is specifically on the Y chromosome." She unlaced her fingers and adjusted her cat-eye glasses. "The last time Kingsley was here, I took a sample of his blood. I exposed that sample to a virus containing the genetic material necessary to repair Kingsley's Y chromosome. With your permission, our next step is to inject Kingsley with this material via the intravenous solution. We hope to change the genetic makeup of Kingsley's cells. As I mentioned before, I've seen some success with dogs."

"Dogs? You experiment on dogs?" Kingsley knew that Amanda wouldn't like that.

Dr. Barlow smiled. "These dogs are helping us find a cure." She patted Kingsley on his shoulder and shook Joyce's hand, and then she and Dr. Kim left.

A hospital administrator came in with forms for Joyce to sign. The administrator was a man, which was a nice change. Kingsley was tired of being around so many women. The administrator slowly reviewed every form and carefully explained that the gene therapy wasn't a guaranteed cure. "The Y-Chromosome Linked Tumor Syndrome is a new disease and gene therapy is an experimental treatment," he said. Kingsley didn't like hearing this. He wanted a guarantee. Joyce signed the papers and the administrator left. A nurse came in and injected gray fluid into Kingsley's IV. Drip, drip, drip, and it was over. Dr. Barlow was right, it didn't hurt. The nurse removed the IV and gave Joyce a prescription for pain pills that Kingsley should take every four hours for his headaches. She told Joyce to bring Kingsley back in two weeks. "Contact Dr. Barlow or Dr. Kim immediately if Kingsley feels nauseous or runs a fever," the nurse said.

Kingsley had several hours to think on the long drive back to Marlbank. He imagined Dr. Barlow wearing her usual white research coat and her cat-eye glasses while experimenting on dogs. What type of dogs? German shepherds? Dalmatians? Miniature poodles? Whatever the kind, if Kingsley were a dog, he wouldn't want a woman who looked like a cat experimenting on him.

Joyce phoned her sisters to check up on Mrs. Sutherland and was in an even fouler mood after she hung up. "Something's wrong," she grumbled. "Maureen says Mrs. Sutherland is fine but she sounded giddy, like she was drunk or high." Joyce lowered her window, letting hot and muggy air into the car. "She said Mavis was out shopping and didn't know where Floyd and Latonya were. I'll kill her if she's taken Mrs. Sutherland's meds again." She reached for Kingsley's hand. "It's been a hard day, hasn't it, hon?"

Kingsley didn't answer. All the complicated words Dr. Barlow and Dr. Kim had said came down to one thing: He could die. Just like Bapsi's little boy. He stared out the window at the dark clouds rolling in from the Atlantic. It was sunny when they left that morning but now a storm was coming.

"You're probably hungry," Joyce said, "We'll get dinner in Richmond. What would you like? Pizza? Burritos?"

"I don't care," he mumbled. He didn't want to talk to Joyce. He couldn't tell her how angry he felt. He didn't want to talk to anyone except Amanda. He'd ask her to go with him to the hospital next time.

"I wish I could get ahold of Mavis," Joyce said. "I don't trust Maureen. Marlbank could burn to the ground, and she wouldn't notice."

Kingsley didn't want to hear about Mavis or Maureen. He squeezed his eyes shut tight. "I don't want to be sick anymore! I don't want headaches! I don't want brain tumors. I don't want to die!"

"You're NOT going to die, hon," Joyce said. "Dr. Barlow knows what she's doing. You'll see. You'll be healthier than a red-tailed rooster in no time. I promise."

The drive-thru in Richmond had only French fries; no burgers or chicken nuggets. Joyce didn't argue. She ordered four large fries and two colas. They sat in the car and ate.

Then the rain began.

Thunder came in waves and the windshield wipers whipped back-and-forth. In no time, the streets were flooded and power lines were down. Joyce had to drive around a T-bone collision near Williamsburg. A little Honda had smashed into a long Lincoln. Joyce didn't stop. She slogged slowly through the storm all the way to Marlbank. "Mrs. Sutherland better be safe and dry, or my sisters are in for a world of hurt," she said.

The mansion was shrouded in thick rain. Outside lights barely illuminated Joyce's old Dodge Charger, the one she'd given to her sisters after she bought her new Pegasus. The limousine was there as was Mrs. Sutherland's handicap accessible van, but behind the van were two vehicles Kingsley had never seen before, a silver SUV and a pickup truck. The pickup was loaded with soaked hay and empty cages.

The front door of the mansion was wide open. Kingsley ran in first and flipped on the lights. The entryway floor was covered with wet leaves. Joyce closed the door behind her and called out to Mavis. No answer. She called out to Maureen. No answer. She cursed her sisters and told Kingsley to find them. Kingsley ran upstairs as Joyce hurried to Mrs. Sutherland's bedroom.

He gently knocked on Amanda's bedroom door. He heard her bed creak. "Amanda? Are you in there?" No answer. He slowly opened the door and was shocked. Not Amanda. Not Mavis or Maureen. Not a human being at all. A nanny goat stood atop Amanda's bed, chewing on Amanda's yellow comforter. The nanny goat bleated and Kingsley slammed the door.

Down the hallway Kingsley heard moaning coming from behind the bathroom door. "Amanda? Are you in there? Are you okay?" The moaning grew louder and crazier, like old women going mad. He cautiously opened the door and was assailed by a wall of black and white. He yelped and covered his head. A dozen or more black-and-white speckled hens ran over him, around him and between his legs.

Joyce called from downstairs. "Kingsley, did you find Mavis and Maureen?"

"No, Mom. Only chickens and a goat."

"What?"

"I found a goat on Amanda's bed and chickens in the bathroom."

"Oh, Lord. Tell me about it when I get back. I'm driving over to get Dr. Jacobs. Mrs. Sutherland's sick."

Empty medicine bottles littered the floor. He looked at the labels—Mrs. Sutherland's arthritis medicine. Kingsley didn't see any pills on the floor. He wondered if they'd been eaten by the chickens. Maybe, but it was more likely that Maureen had taken them, and he knew his mother would have a fit. He headed down the hallway to Clare and Andrés' bedroom. He grabbed the door knob and wondered what he'd find next. A cow? A couple of pigs? He swung open the door and was staggered by what he saw.

Five heads, three beards, colorful tattoos, ten arms and ten legs, all going every which way. Maureen, Mavis, and three strange men were on Clare and Andrés' king-size bed, naked. Two of the men were asleep. The third man raised his head and squinted at Kingsley.

"Who the hell are you?"

Kingsley slammed the door and ran downstairs. He ran out onto the wet front porch, desperate for his mother to return. Headlights glimmered in the dark rain. The Pegasus crept through the wrought iron gate and pulled up in front of the door. Joyce and Dr. Jacobs hurried out and up the marble steps, shaking umbrellas and raincoats. "I found Mavis and Maureen," Kingsley told his mother. "They're upstairs with—"

"Never mind that now," Joyce said, cutting him off. She hustled Dr. Jacobs to Mrs. Sutherland's bedroom. Kingsley followed. Mrs. Sutherland was in her bed, her eyes closed, covers pulled up to her neck. Dr. Jacobs checked her pulse as Joyce hovered nearby. "How could my own sisters be so stupid," she said. "The front door was wide open. She probably hasn't eaten since I left this morning. No wonder she's sick."

Dr. Jacobs pulled a stethoscope out of his bag and listened to Mrs.

Sutherland's chest.

"I found three men upstairs with Aunt Mavis and Aunt Maureen," Kingsley said. "And a goat and a bunch of chickens." Joyce stared at him as if he'd popped off his head and replaced it with a frying pan.

"Three men and a what?"

"She has pneumonia," Dr. Jacobs said, wrapping the stethoscope around his neck. "We need to get her to the hospital."

"I'll call 9-1-1," Joyce said. "I don't know how they'll get here in this storm. I was barely able to get you." Joyce left the bedroom to make the call.

Dr. Jacobs gently stroked Mrs. Sutherland's wispy white hair. "I should have checked on her earlier. I heard that awful music. I called Jack to complain but then the storm hit and—"

"Jack?"

Dr. Jacobs frowned. "Clare's brother." He pulled out a syringe and a vial of medicine from his medicine bag.

"Where's Amanda?" Kingsley asked. "What happened to Latonya and Floyd? Why aren't they here?"

"I don't know anything about Floyd and Latonya," Dr. Jacobs said. "But Amanda—" He stopped talking, and Kingsley soon saw why. One of the men from upstairs had sauntered into Mrs. Sutherland's room, wearing boxer shorts and nothing else. He took a seat in a hard-backed chair next to the door, legs askew, yawning. Dr. Jacobs scowled. "Amanda's with Andrés. She was—"

The half-naked man coughed and shifted in his chair.

Dr. Jacobs tapped the syringe and prepared Mrs. Sutherland's arm for the injection. "There was an incident with one of Jack's friends," he said. "Andrés took her to his apartment."

The half-naked man was blond like Clare and his eyes were the same sparkling blue. A deep cleft dotted the middle of his perfect chin, and his muscles had a definition even beyond Enrique's. He looked like a comic book superhero, missing only a cape and mask.

Joyce returned. "The ambulance is on the way. I'm going upstairs to find my sisters."

The man reached out as she passed, grabbing her arm. "We haven't been introduced."

Joyce startled. She hadn't seen the man when she came in. The lines on Dr. Jacobs' face deepened. "Joyce, this is Leslie's son, Jack."

"Jack Sutherland?" Joyce said. "You're Jack Sutherland?"

Jack nodded and rubbed his sculpted chest. "Six-foot-four, two-hundred pounds and ready when you are."

Joyce eyed Jack like he was a rotten piece of meat and pulled out of his grip. "I have to find my sisters," she said. She left the room and Jack slowly stood up.

"Guess I better find her sisters, too," he said with a roguish grin. He trailed Joyce. Kingsley started to follow, but Dr. Jacobs moved to stop him.

"Stay here with me, Kingsley," Dr. Jacobs said. "Stay away from those men. They're dangerous."

"Dangerous?" Kingsley repeated. "Then they might hurt Mom." He left Dr. Jacobs and ran up the stairs.

Joyce was in Amanda's room staring at the nanny goat. Jack was behind her. He grabbed Joyce and pushed her against the door jam. She pushed back. "Your mother thinks you're dead."

"Well I'm not, Joyce," Jack said. "Or is it Lily?"

Joyce froze.

"That's your name, isn't it?" he asked. "Lily Fells?"

Joyce pulled away and headed toward Clare and Andrés' bedroom.

Jack followed, taunting her with every step. "Lily Fells is all over the place. Mom's checkbook, bills of sale, contracts. Hell, it's probably on the deeds to the oil wells by now. You'll need to do a better job hiding your fraud if you want to stay out of prison."

"I'll keep that in mind," Joyce said, as she swung open Clare and Andrés' bedroom door. "Goddamit!" She yelled as she pulled Mavis and Maureen out of bed. "Get dressed! You may have killed Mrs. Sutherland!" One of the men still in bed hooted and slapped Maureen on her bare backside. Kingsley stood at the doorway. He turned away, embarrassed to look at his naked aunts.

Jack nodded to one of the two men in the bed, a hairy guy almost as muscular as Jack. The hairy guy pulled Mavis and Maureen back into bed, and Jack grabbed Joyce. Everything happened so fast. He pushed Kingsley out of the bedroom and then slammed the bedroom door in Kingsley's face. Kingsley blinked a couple of times, staring at the closed door. He tried the doorknob. Locked. Panic set in as he realized what was going on. His mother was locked in Clare and Andrés' old bedroom with three strange men. His skin went cold. "Mom! Mom!" He pounded on the door. "Leave my mother alone!"

7 Pancakes

Kingsley ran downstairs and called 9-1-1 again. No one answered. He left the address and a desperate message, "Help, my mother is being attacked!" He called Clare but she didn't answer, either. He left her a message, "Jack is here with two mean men. They're hurting Mom! Mrs. Sutherland is sick. Come as fast as you can." Kingsley ran back to Mrs. Sutherland's room. "You've got to do something," he said to Dr. Jacobs. "They're hurting Mom!"

Dr. Jacobs looked especially frail as he shook his head. "There's nothing I can do. The ambulance isn't coming, Kingsley. They just called and said they couldn't get through the storm." He began helping Mrs. Sutherland into her wheelchair. "I'm taking Leslie to my house. You should come with us. You'll be safer there."

"I'm not leaving Mom!" Kingsley insisted as Dr. Jacobs wheeled Mrs. Sutherland out of her room. "I don't care about the ambulance. I care about Mom. You have to do something!"

"I don't understand why Leslie's children treat her so badly," Dr. Jacobs said as he wheeled Mrs. Sutherland to the front door. Outside, the rain was still pouring. He paused wearily and faced Kingsley. "She was a wonderful mother. She gave them everything. Look at how they repay her. Clare neglects her and Jack abuses her. I tell you, Kingsley, much suffering befalls those who mistreat their mother, if not in this world then in the world to come."

Kingsley didn't want to hear anymore. Dr. Jacobs could figure out on his own how to get Mrs. Sutherland through the rain. Kingsley ran back upstairs and paced in front of the locked bedroom door. He didn't know what to do. The sounds coming from the other side enraged him. "Leave her alone!" he shouted. He pounded on the door. He pounded and pounded until he was exhausted and slumped to the floor. He was determined to stay there, outside the bedroom where Jack and his friends had imprisoned his mother, until the police arrived.

At sunrise, a loud groan came from the other side of the door and woke Kingsley. He jumped up, trying to orient himself, trying to remember why he was sleeping on the floor. The door opened and Jack Sutherland sauntered out, wearing a pair of blue jeans and nothing else. No shirt. No shoes. Kingsley scrambled to peek inside. The room was a mess. Torn sheets, knocked over furniture. Blood. Mavis and Maureen and the two other men were still asleep. Joyce was sitting on the side of the bed, buttoning her blouse. Her expression was flat, except for a deep furrow between her eyebrows. She barely looked at Kingsley. She opened Clare's closet, pulled out one of Clare's sweaters and wrapped it around her like a shroud. She flinched when Jack called to her from the hallway, "How about some pancakes, Lily?" She slowly stood and walked out of the bedroom like a zombie, not speaking to Kingsley. She followed Jack down the stairs. "And a fresh pot of coffee," Jack added.

Kingsley was furious. He snapped at Jack like a yipping terrier. "Latonya's the cook! You should ask her to fix your breakfast, not Mom!"

"Had to let her go," Jack said. "Floyd, too."

"Let them go? What'd you mean, you let them go?"

"Fired them both."

Kingsley's heart fell. He was counting on Floyd to help him and his mother escape the three men. "Floyd! You fired Floyd? Why?"

"Kept getting in my way," Jack said. "Seems to me there are plenty of people on the payroll already. Mavis, Maureen, Joyce...." He gave Joyce a devilish smile, "and Lily."

One of Jack's friends was from Alberta, Canada. The other had a strong accent and looked Middle Eastern. Kingsley guessed he was an Arab. Joyce cooked breakfast all morning. Fried eggs, pancakes and coffee. Every time

Joyce started to clean up, the men would order another batch and Joyce would have to begin cooking again. She cooked until the eggs were gone and the last of the pancakes were on the griddle. Mavis and Maureen finally came down to the kitchen, wearing panties and men's shirts. Nothing else. Mavis sat on the Arab's lap. Maureen sat on Jack's.

Joyce was flipping the final pancakes when the Canadian snuck up behind her and grabbed her hips. Joyce pushed him away, burning herself on the hot griddle. "Son of a bitch," she cursed. The Arab laughed so hard coffee came out of his nose. The coffee splattered on Mavis and she yelped and jumped off his lap. Kingsley snickered, which made the Canadian angry. He grabbed Kingsley's shirt.

"Don't laugh at him." He balled his fist, ready to punch Kingsley's terrified face.

Joyce grabbed the hot griddle, brandishing it like an axe. "Take your hands off my boy," she growled. Eye-to-eye they stood for a few tense seconds until Jack told the Canadian to sit down. He opened the cabinet above the refrigerator and pulled out a dusty bottle of whiskey. He poured three shots, and then tossed several medicine bottles on the table. Joyce grabbed one of the medicine bottles, shocked. "Mrs. Sutherland's arthritis pills." She picked up a second medicine bottle. "And Kingsley's headache medicine." She slammed the bottles down on the table, "Stealing medicine from an old woman and a sick boy? You're disgusting." Jack shrugged and the other two men laughed.

Kingsley snuck away to the den and called Dr. Jacobs. "Are the police coming?" he asked. "Did you call them?"

"I called them," Dr. Jacobs said, not sounding very confident. "They told me they'll send a squad car as soon as they could." Kingsley couldn't wait. His mother needed help now! He took a seat on the couch and stared at his video console. He wasn't even tempted to play. Killing mutants didn't seem as fun as it used to be. He called Floyd, hoping to convince him to return to the mansion. Thankfully, Floyd answered.

"Hello."

"Floyd, I need your help!"

"Kingsley! How are you, my boy? I hated leaving without telling you good-bye."

"Where are you?" Kingsley asked. "Dr. Jacobs said Amanda is with her dad. What happened?"

"Those three morons showed up, and all hell broke loose. Brought that goat and chickens and gave them the run of the house. Messed all over Mrs. Sutherland's antique rugs. Hoof marks on her hardwood floors. Latonya had a conniption fit. When she told those boys she didn't clean up after animals, that big fellow with the scruffy beard grabbed her and—"

"He almost hit me," Kingsley said. "But Mom stopped him."

"I believe it," Floyd said. "He's a mean one. He went after Latonya and that's when Amanda got hurt."

Kingsley felt like he'd been punched in the gut. "Amanda? Amanda's hurt? What happened?"

"You know how Amanda is," Floyd said. "She came between that big ex-con and Latonya, and he wrenched her arm right out of its socket. Poor little thing. I tell you, Kingsley, I was in a real fix. Mavis and Maureen weren't a lick of help, and Latonya high-tailed it out of there as soon as she could. I took Amanda to the hospital and called her father from the emergency room. She's with him now."

Kingsley clenched the phone, picturing the man attacking Amanda. He felt like hitting something. "Son-of-a-bitch! Did he break her arm?"

Floyd sighed. "Yeah, he did. I called Clare from the emergency room. She was in Chesapeake, at the Sutherland Orchard. I told her Jack was at the mansion with two other ex-cons. Is she there now? Is Senator Steele with her?"

"Clare? Here? No, she's not here. I haven't seen Clare since my birthday party."

"Good Lord," Floyd grunted. "I should've known Clare wouldn't take the time to protect her own mother—or yours—for that matter."

All Kingsley cared about at that moment was Amanda. He stopped thinking of himself. He even stopped worrying about his mother. He just wanted to see Amanda and make sure she was safe.

"Kingsley," Floyd said. "I'm moving to Lake Monticello. That's up near Charlottesville. I'm going to live with my daughter and her husband. The world's gone crazy and she needs me. She's expecting her first baby, a little girl, thank the Lord."

Kingsley was crushed. Floyd was the only good man Kingsley had left.

His father was long gone and Andrés had moved out. Dr. Jacobs was too old to help and now Floyd wasn't coming back. Kingsley had no one else to turn to. He was all alone.

"Kingsley," Floyd said. "Did you hear me?"

"Yes," he whispered, choking out the word.

"If those boys cause trouble, call the police," Floyd said. "I know that's not what your momma wants, but there are a lot worse things in this world than going to jail."

Kingsley swallowed hard, trying to clear his throat. He couldn't get any words out.

"Kingsley, I enjoyed our time together," Floyd said. "Call me the next time you're in Charlottesville for your medical treatment. Maybe you and your momma could stop by and meet my daughter. She's a fine woman, an engineer. I'm very proud of her. Her husband teaches at the University." A wave of jealousy hit Kingsley as he pictured Floyd with his happy family. "You're in my prayers, Kingsley," Floyd added. "I'm going to miss you."

Floyd hung up, and Kingsley felt numb. He punched paisley pillows until he was exhausted, then sat and stared out the bay window. How had his life unraveled so fast? Four years ago he lived in a small apartment in New Orleans with both his mother and his father. Now he was trapped in a cadaverous mansion in Yorktown, Virginia, with three criminals. Four criminals, if he included his mother.

The front lawn was covered with wet leaves and scattered limbs. The nanny goat was chewing on drenched azaleas and the chickens were scratching in the mud. Kingsley stared mindlessly at the water dripping from the oaks and poplars, until he saw a black and white police car drive through the front gate. He ran to the kitchen.

"Mom!"

Joyce was washing pots and pans. Jack and his friends were drinking whiskey.

"Mom, the police are here."

"Shit." Joyce wiped her hands on her apron. She started to leave the kitchen when Jack grabbed her by the wrist.

"What'cha gonna tell 'em, Lily?" he asked.

"Nothing!" Joyce snapped, trying to pull away. "If the roads are clear,

I'll take Mrs. Sutherland to the hospital."

Jack held firm and eyed Joyce up and down. "Be a good girl, Lily. Be a good girl and all your dreams will come true." He let go of her wrist, and she hurried out of the kitchen. Kingsley followed.

The dark circles under the police officer's eyes said everything. His uniform was wrinkled and his shoulders slumped. "Are you Joyce Smith?"

Joyce stood at the open doorway, nervously wringing the bottom of her apron. Kingsley hadn't seen her so anxious since they left New Orleans. "You poor man," she said. "You look dog-tired."

"Everybody's pulling double shifts," he said. "Half the force is out sick." He took off his cap and wiped his sweaty forehead. "Same with all the other city services. Fire. EMS. Hospitals look like refugee camps." He tucked his cap under his arm and checked his note pad. "Ma'am, we received a call from one of your neighbors, Dr. Eugene Jacobs, about an assault. Dr. Jacobs said I should speak with someone named Joyce Smith. Are you Joyce Smith?"

"Dr. Jacobs called the police?" Joyce licked her lips and smoothed her frizzy hair. "When I arrived last night, Mrs. Sutherland was ill so I contacted Dr. Jacobs. He's a family friend. Mrs. Sutherland has a bad cold. That's all." Joyce opened the entryway closet and pulled out a raincoat. "No one was assaulted," she said. "Good God almighty. There's nobody here but me and my boy."

"And Leslie Sutherland?"

"She's, um, she's actually at Dr. Jacobs' house. I was waiting for the storm to pass, and then I'm taking her to the hospital. We're leaving right now. For the hospital."

Joyce took several deep breaths as she slowly buttoned the raincoat. Kingsley could see the change in her face—the resolve. She was the mistress of the Sutherland estate. She put aside her fear and replaced it with her unbendable determination to survive. She stood straighter and stopped trembling. She smiled and moved close to the police officer, peeking at his note pad. "Oh, lookie there," she pointed to her name on the notepad. "There's your problem. Joyce Smith quit months ago. Moved to Texas, from what I heard. My name is Lily Fells."

"Lily Fells?" The officer frowned and checked his notes. "No one by the name of Joyce Smith works here anymore?"

"No, she left a while back. I'm taking care of Mrs. Sutherland now."

The officer closed his note pad. "Tell your neighbor to get his facts straight before he calls 9-1-1."

"He means well," Joyce said. "He's quite elderly. Easily confused. Plus, he's been sick. Something's going around."

"And it's getting worse," the police officer said. "If this keeps up—" He bowed his head and wiped the corners of his mouth. "Well, humans survived ebola. I guess we'll survive this too." The officer patted Kingsley on the shoulder. "Take care of that boy, Ms. Fells," he said.

Joyce accompanied the police officer to his car, slipping her arm flirtatiously around his. "Thank you so much for coming," she said. "Makes me feel safer having a strong man around." Once the officer was in his car, Joyce walked casually to her Pegasus. She waved as the police car drove out of the wrought iron gate, down the dirt road and out of sight. With the police gone, her smile disappeared. "I tell you Kingsley, I'm done putting up with Jack and those men." She opened the glove compartment of the Pegasus and began searching.

Kingsley couldn't understand what had just happened. Why his mother hadn't told the police about Jack. "We gotta get out of here, Mom. We should've followed the policeman."

"Where's my gun, goddamnit!" she said.

"Forget the gun, Mom. Let's go," he said, tugging on her sleeve.

Behind them, Jack stood at the doorway. "Looking for this?" he asked. He was twirling Joyce's pistol with the pearl handle around his trigger finger. "I know a crook when I spot one, Lily. Knew you wouldn't travel unarmed."

"I don't know what you're talking about," Joyce said. She smoothed back her frizzy brown hair. "We're going to pick up Mrs. Sutherland from Dr. Jacobs and then we're taking her to the hospital."

"You can go, but the boy stays with me," Jack said. "Just in case."

Kingsley didn't like be alone with Jack and the other men, but he didn't have a choice. While his mother was taking Mrs. Sutherland to the emergency room, Kingsley called Amanda. When she answered, he could hear a rumbling noise in the background, like heavy machinery. He told her what had happened since the Canadian had broken her arm. He told her about Jack firing Latonya and Floyd, but he didn't tell her that his mother had been trapped with Jack and those two other men all night. He didn't tell her about the awful sounds he'd heard coming from inside the bedroom.

Amanda was horrified to hear that Jack was still at the mansion. "I'm sorry my family is so messed up," she said. She had some news, too. "I'm at Clare's new house at the Sutherland Orchard," she said. "It's beautiful. It looks like a fancy farmhouse, something you'd see in a movie. Clare's putting in a special pool just for the baby. It's gonna have a fountain shaped like a giant mushroom. A man named Milton Gentry is building it. I met his daughter, Wanda. She drives the tractor. They're pushing down the peach trees to make room for the pool. I've never seen a girl on a tractor before."

That explained the rumbling noise. Kingsley was enraged. Is that why Clare didn't answer his call for help? Because of her new pool! It wasn't fair. Kingsley envied Clare's baby. Rich, good-looking and he'll have a mom and a dad. A Mom and a *Dad*. Kingsley rubbed the ache in the back of his head. It was getting worse by the minute. "I'm supposed to go for my second treatment the Wednesday before school starts." He glanced around and lowered his voice. "Want to come?

"If you go, I'll go," Amanda said. "Pick me up at my dad's apartment." That was the first good news Kingsley had had in a long, long time.

When Joyce returned, Kingsley hurried to the van to tell his mother the news from Amanda. He was especially eager to tell her that Amanda would go with them on his next gene therapy treatment, but Joyce cut him off. "Wal-Mart was a nightmare," she said. "I had to fight for the last carton of eggs. The women were acting crazy, like they're about to kill each other. It was insane." She opened the back of the van and handed Kingsley two small bags of groceries. "This is all I could find."

Jack appeared at the top of the steps. "That's why we brought those chickens and the goat," he said. "Eggs and meat."

Joyce harrumphed, unwilling to admit that might have been a good idea. She helped Mrs. Sutherland out of the van as Kingsley took the groceries to the kitchen. He didn't think to ask about Mrs. Sutherland. How she was or what the emergency room doctors did for her. All he could think about was unpacking the groceries. Three boxes of pancake mix, one bottle of Log Cabin syrup, one dozen eggs, two large bags of instant oatmeal, one box of powdered milk, two cases of beer, bleach, dishwasher tablets and Drano Kitchen Crystal Clog Remover. Nothing Kingsley liked. No ice cream. No candy. Not even any school supplies.

Joyce came in the kitchen and helped him put everything away. "I made another stop while I was out," she whispered to Kingsley. She glanced around before stashing the Drano under the sink. No one was in the kitchen except Joyce and Kingsley. "Went to see Mr. Setter. Remember him? He was that lawyer who smelled like a skunk." She gave Kingsley a quick wink. "Got it all set up, hon, after your next gene therapy treatment, we're moving out of here."

"Moving? Where? What about Amanda? We can't leave her. What about Mrs. Sutherland? Who's—" Kingsley wanted to ask more questions, but Jack came in looking for the beer. Both Joyce and Kingsley shut up.

For dinner, Joyce fixed a huge stack of pancakes for the men, but wouldn't let Kingsley have any. "The rest of us are having oatmeal."

"That's not fair," Kingsley whined.

Joyce waved her spatula at him. "These pancakes are for the men, not for you."

The next morning, all three men were nauseous and holding their stomachs. Jack showed Kingsley the inside of his mouth. "Looks like something is eating you from the inside out," Kingsley said. "Do you get headaches? Maybe you have the dolphin disease."

"No headaches," Jack's voice sounded hollow. He was trying not to let his tongue touch the raw places in his mouth. "Saud gets headaches but all I get are stomach aches and these goddamn sores."

"Maybe something's in the water," Kingsley offered. "I helped Andrés test the water near Williamsburg last month, and he found all sorts of bad stuff. Maybe that's why you're sick."

Joyce fixed pancakes for the men almost every day. She never let Kingsley or Mrs. Sutherland have any, and tried to keep her sisters out of them too. "They're for the men!"

Soon, Jack and his friends started drooling. Just a little at first, when they spoke, but it quickly progressed to a constant trickle. Maureen was far more attentive to them than she'd ever been to Mrs. Sutherland, especially after the men started vomiting blood. She cried and hugged them as if it was breaking her heart to see them suffer.

Life settled into a tense routine of pancakes and sickness. It seemed to Kingsley that everyone at the mansion was changing. The men were getting thinner while Joyce and her sisters were getting fatter, especially around the middle. Kingsley wondered how they could get bigger eating only oatmeal.

8 The Collapse

Late August meant the beginning of hurricane season. Storms rolled through Hampton Roads every evening, lightning playing hit and miss with the power lines. No power meant no air conditioning, no video games and worst of all, no refrigerator. Kingsley couldn't take much more. "Why are we putting up with this?" he raged at Joyce as she cleaned Jack's latest bout of bloody vomit off the bathroom floor. "Why won't you just call the police and tell them what happened? Jack should be in jail. Why can't we leave and go to a hotel? School starts soon and I gotta get ready."

"I ain't leaving Mrs. Sutherland," Joyce said as she scrubbed.

"Then take her with us!" Kingsley said.

Joyce threw the dirty rags in the bucket and snapped off her latex gloves. "We ain't going anywhere 'cept the medical center, you hear me? We ain't moving out 'til I'm good and ready. So stop pestering me." Joyce poured the dirty water into the toilet and washed her hands. "Now go change your clothes. I gotta take a quick shower. I'll be ready to go in twenty minutes."

Kingsley grumbled as he changed clothes, "At least the hospital will be air conditioned." He was angry with a lot of things, but mostly with his mother. Kingsley knew the real reason she wouldn't leave. Joyce was more afraid of the police than she was of Jack. Kingsley wished he was old enough to drive. If he could drive, he'd escape this awful place. He'd pick up Amanda and go somewhere safe without disease and without criminals.

But he couldn't do that. He had to go to his next gene-therapy treatment, which meant he had to listen to his mother lecture Mavis and Maureen about what to do with Mrs. Sutherland and the men while she was gone. "Take good care of Mrs. Sutherland. Take her to the emergency room if her pneumonia comes back. Not like the last time when you let those three morons in."

Kingsley hated Jack and the other two men. They broke Amanda's arm and hurt his mother in ways he didn't want to imagine, but he was still shocked by what Joyce said next. "No matter what happens to those men, no matter how much they moan and groan, even if they scream in agony, don't call an ambulance or even Dr. Jacobs. And, for God's sake, don't call the police."

Mavis paced back and forth across the brick driveway as Kingsley got into the Pegasus. "What if he dies?" she cried, "I love him."

"Who?"

"Saud," Mavis said. "He asked me to marry him."

"You're only nineteen! He's over thirty! If any of them die while I'm gone, drag their bodies to the stable and cover them with straw."

"I can't do that!"

"Yes, you can," Joyce said as she took the driver's seat. "Trust me, hon. Do what I say, and everything will be fine." She slammed the car door and started the engine.

Kingsley reminded Joyce about a hundred times to pick up Amanda at Andrés' apartment. "I gotta get some gas first," Joyce said. She pulled into a crowded gas station and immediately began cursing. "Worse than the goddamn Wal-Mart!" Drivers stood outside their cars and shouted at the lines of people in front of them to *HURRY UP*. Horns blared and a fistfight broke out when a motorcycle tried to cut in line. Everything about the situation was bizarre: The heat, the anger, the horns and especially the fact that all the drivers were women, even the ones coming to blows. Kingsley had never seen women physically fighting before. He didn't know whether to be scared or to laugh.

Joyce inched forward in line, finally reaching the pump. "Look at that. Up twenty dollars a gallon since July. We ought to get a discount, what with Mrs. Sutherland owning all those oil wells."

"Just pump the gas, Mom," Kingsley said. He leaned his head against the window. "We're going to be late again."

Amanda looked more beautiful than ever as she ran to the car. Long black hair, brown eyes, and skin the color of cinnamon sugar. Her arm was in a cast, but she was smiling. Something new stirred in Kingsley when he saw her. Something beyond what he'd felt for her before. He wanted to protect her and take care of her for the rest of his life.

Andrés, on the other hand, looked awful. Thin and brittle, like he'd crumble under the lightest touch. He stood at the entryway of his apartment, wearing a bathrobe and slippers, his hair shaggy, and his face unshaved. He waved goodbye as Amanda climbed into the back seat. Kingsley abandoned his mother in the front passenger seat to join her. "Your dad's sick, too?" Kingsley asked.

Amanda's smile disappeared. "He has headaches," she pointed to the back of her head, "the same place as yours."

"Is he throwing up? Does he have sores in his mouth?"

"No," Amanda said. "Nothing like that. Just headaches."

"Jack and his friends are throwing up all the time." Kingsley lowered his voice and nodded at his mother. "And Mom's different since Jack showed up, too," he whispered. "She's getting bigger around the middle even though there's hardly anything to eat."

Amanda studied Joyce. "Maybe she's pregnant?"

Kingsley blanched. "I hope not." He shivered every time he thought about his mother locked in Clare and Andrés' bedroom with Jack and those other men. Any child that came from that night would be disturbed and repulsive.

"Let's not talk about Jack or your mom anymore," Amanda said. "I'm looking forward to our trip to Charlottesville. That's my favorite name."

"What is?"

"Charlotte. When I have a daughter, I'm going to name her Charlotte." She drew close. "You have to get better so we can fix the planet. We can't count on the grownups to do it. They're too busy fighting each other."

Kingsley tried to listen, but she was so pretty and smelled so good. She wanted to go to college and study marine ecology so she could rebuild the oceans. "All we have to do is get rid of the plastics in the Pacific Ocean, the fertilizer in the Chesapeake Bay and shut down the oil wells. After that, we'll free all the fish from the aquariums and the oceans will be alive again." At that moment, with her so close, Kingsley would have agreed if she'd insisted the earth was as flat as a saucer and the moon was its teacup. Amanda pulled out her phone and started snapping photos. Smiling, frowning, and sticking out their tongues. When Joyce stopped at a stoplight, she turned and smiled, and Amanda was able to get a photo of the three of them. "That's a keeper," Amanda said.

Kingsley's right eye began to blur. Not now, he thought, not with Amanda sitting right next to me. He rubbed his eye. Amanda asked if he was okay and he nodded. "Yeah. I'm fine."

He leaned against the window and felt the car rumble. He'd thought he was getting better, but now he wasn't so sure. The vision in his right eye grew dimmer and his headache grew worse with each passing mile. He couldn't keep it a secret any longer. He told Amanda about his eye, and she told Joyce. That did it. Joyce hit the accelerator and the Pegasus flew west.

The lobby at the medical center was hot and crowded. It reeked of sweat and desperation. Joyce, Kingsley and Amanda had to squeeze through to take a number. They found a tiny spot in the corner to wait until the admissions desk could check them in. An elderly black man was crying and clutching a photo of an infant. "Nursing at his mother's breast one moment, rushed to the hospital the next." He wiped his nose and showed the photo to anyone who would look. "See here, my grandson. My only grandson. Not supposed to be that way. Babies going before old folk. It should've been me getting those brain tumors, not him."

Another woman joined in. She wore a headscarf and spoke with an accent. "A simple headache, that's all he had. A simple headache. I told him to stop complaining. Think of poor Ismail and his devoted father, Ibrahim. Think of their sacrifice. Pin-drop silence, that's what I want from you. The next thing I see, he's on the ground." She gestured to the floor. "How could I know? The last words I spoke to him were in anger." The woman wrapped her scarf over her face. "How could I know?"

An overwhelmed nurse's aide maneuvered through the crowd, handing out plastic cups of water. "I'm sorry this is taking so long," she said. "Half of our staff is out sick and the computers keep going down." She handed

Joyce a cup. "I've never seen anything like this. Boys are coming in from all over the world."

Kingsley started to tremble until Amanda took his hand. It felt soft and wonderful. Why did the best thing he'd ever felt have to happen at the scariest place in the world?

Two long, hot hours later, Kingsley's number was finally called and he was admitted. Once again, Kingsley's room was on the eighth floor, the same color walls, the same curtains, and the same computer, but instead of two beds for two boys, there were nine beds for nine boys. Ages ranged from toddlers to teenagers; the younger the boy, the sicker. Amanda gasped and pointed to the smallest child, a toddler still in diapers, and whispered, "Look at that little boy."

"Who?"

"Over there, the little one in the corner."

Kingsley was horrified. The boy's head was shaped like a pumpkin a month after Halloween. His skin was loose, like the back of Mrs. Sutherland's hands, with thick blue veins running over his forehead. "He can't have the same disease as me. I don't look anything like that."

"Maybe you're getting better," Amanda said.

The pumpkin-headed boy had a tube going into his nose, and his eyes seemed permanently half-closed.

Kingsley went to the bathroom and changed into a hospital gown. He looked in the mirror. His face was pale and his eyes were red. "Will that happen to me? Will I look like that soon?" He sat on the edge of the bathtub and cried. He didn't want Amanda to see him like this. He blew his nose and splashed water on his face and then returned to Amanda and Joyce, and climbed into bed. A nurse started his IV and told Joyce that Dr. Barlow would see them soon. While they waited, a friend came for a visit.

"Hello, Kingsley!" It was the Indian doctor, Bapsi Cama. She hugged Kingsley and he introduced Amanda. "So pleased to meet you," Bapsi said, warmly shaking Amanda's hand, as if they were the dearest of friends. Bapsi was about to give Joyce a hug—much to Joyce's trepidation—when Dr. Barlow arrived. The room quieted. All eyes were on Dr. Barlow as she examined each boy, beginning with the pumpkin-headed toddler. She spoke with the boy's mother and then moved to the next boy, and then the next.

Sometimes the mothers cried, sometimes they pleaded, and one kissed Dr. Barlow's hand. Kingsley was the last to be examined.

"My right eye's not working," he told Dr. Barlow.

Dr. Barlow frowned, "Wasn't it your left eye last time?"

Kingsley nodded. He felt he'd disappointed her. She looked sadder than the last time he was in the hospital, and her eyes had dark rings under them. The crease lines around her mouth angled downward, making her look like she hadn't smiled in weeks. She shined a light in his eyes, and then his ears, stopping when Amanda tapped her on her arm.

"What type of dogs do you use?" Amanda asked.

Dr. Barlow was taken aback by the interruption. "What?"

"Kingsley told me you experiment on dogs," Amanda said. Kingsley blushed. He should have known not to tell her about the dogs. She'd made such a fuss about the snake. "Where do you get your dogs? Are they from the pound? Do you experiment on abandoned animals?"

Dr. Barlow scrutinized Amanda as if she were a caged rat who'd just bit her finger. "They're not pound animals. They're clones."

"What kind of dog is that?"

Joyce snatched Amanda's good arm. "I'm sorry, Dr. Barlow, I shouldn't have brought her."

Bapsi intervened, softening Joyce's grip. "She *should* ask questions. Kingsley is her friend. Asking questions will help them process what is happening."

Dr. Barlow gave Bapsi an exasperated look, then pulled off her cat-eye glasses and addressed Amanda. "Cloning is a method of creating an identical copy of an individual. The nucleus of one cell from the individual to be cloned is inserted into an enucleated ovum. The ovum is then implanted into a female host where, if the implant is successful, it divides and grows into a fetus. As you already know, the Y-Chromosome Linked Tumors Syndrome is very specific and extremely deadly. There's no room for error in our research. We found a dog that manifests the syndrome quickly with the same symptoms we see in humans. Headaches, loss of vision. To test the efficacy of our gene therapy research, we've created thirty-five clones of the original dog. That is to say, thirty-five exact duplicates."

Bapsi shook her head. "Our abuse of the natural world is what initiated the syndrome."

Dr. Barlow jabbed her sharp glasses at Bapsi. "Your criticism of vivisection is almost as reckless as your speculations," she snapped. "The root cause of the tumors hasn't been determined."

Kingsley tried to shush Amanda but she wouldn't be silenced. "What if the puppy experiments don't work? Are you going to start cloning people?"

Dr. Barlow loomed over Amanda. "Cloning humans is illegal." She put on her cat-eye glasses and stormed out of the room.

Joyce rounded on Amanda. "This is why your father moved out! This is why your mother never visits Marlbank anymore! You're rude and arrogant, and you can't keep your big mouth shut." She hurried after Dr. Barlow, pleading for a moment of her time.

Amanda's eyes filled with tears. "I'm sorry."

Bapsi hugged Amanda. "Not at all, little one. Caring is what makes us human." Amanda gave Bapsi a weak smile.

When Joyce returned, she looked like a bull going after a matador's red cloak. "I want to say something, and I bet every mother in this room agrees with me." The others mothers listened. "That doctor," Joyce pointed to the door Dr. Barlow had just exited. "That doctor can butcher every dog on the planet. She can boil them alive for all I care, as long as she cures my son."

9 An Honorable Man

No laughter, no photos, no funny faces. Kingsley sat in the front passenger seat beside Joyce, while Amanda sat alone in the back. They drove past abandoned asphalt pavers, piles of untouched gravel, and lines of bright yellow *Men Working* signs without a man in sight. "It's getting worse," Amanda said, finally breaking the silence. "Men aren't showing up for work; either they're sick or their sons are sick."

Joyce gripped the steering wheel. "I don't want to hear any more talk from you, young lady, especially about anybody getting sick. Kingsley, hon, I've scheduled your next treatment in early September. And Amanda's NOT invited. I never—"

Kingsley didn't want to hear anymore. He switched on the radio and turned it up as loud as it would go:

... category two hurricane is twenty miles east of Cape Hatteras, and has a north by northwest trajectory. It's expected to make landfall in Virginia in the next few hours. Due to the current medical emergency, listeners are warned that police, fire, and ambulance services are severely limited. ...

Joyce banged the radio with the heel of her hand. "I'm sick of bad news." She pressed buttons until she found a country-music station playing Patsy Cline's *She's Got You*.

When they arrived at Andrés' apartment, Kingsley didn't want to say good-bye. He was afraid his mother would never let him see Amanda again. He gathered his courage and took Amanda's hand as they slowly walked to the apartment. When they reached her front door, he gave her hand an affectionate squeeze and smiled sadly. He didn't have to say a word.

"I know," Amanda said, softly. Kingsley's eyes filled with tears as she unlocked the door and called for her father. No one answered. They went inside and looked around. No one was there.

Kingsley poked his head out of the front door and called to his mother. "Andrés isn't here. We can't leave Amanda here alone."

"Yes, we can," Joyce called back.

"No, Mom! You heard the news. A hurricane's coming."

"What about Amanda's momma? Can't she come get her?"

This time it was Amanda who answered Joyce. "I can call her but she probably won't answer. She and the senator are busy with their new house at the Sutherland Orchard. I know the way, if you want to—"

Joyce loudly cursed Clare's laziness and yelled back to Amanda. "I ain't driving you to Chesapeake. I gotta check on Mrs. Sutherland. Leave a message for your folks to pick you up. And hurry up, I ain't waiting forever."

When they finally got back to the mansion, the pickup truck with the chicken cages was gone, but Jack's silver SUV was still parked behind Mrs. Sutherland's van. Kingsley, Joyce and Amanda were getting out of the Pegasus when the front door of the mansion banged open and Mavis flew down the marble steps—crying, sobbing, and waving her arms. Joyce leaned confidently against the Pegasus. "Did you bury them in the stable like I told you?"

"No!" Mavis sobbed. She could barely speak. "My husband. My husband."

"Don't tell me you married that idiot."

"No! I mean, yes. I wanted to marry Saud. That's why I took them to the emergency room."

"What! I told you to let them die."

"I had to." Mavis worked to catch her breath. She wiped her dripping nose. "But everything is awful now." She choked out the next word.

"Maureen!"

"Maureen?" Joyce grabbed Mavis's forearms. "Where's Maureen? Is she okay? Did those monsters hurt her?"

Mavis shook her head. "She's gone!"

"Gone where?"

Mavis took a deep breath and cried. "She stole my husband!"

"What are you talking about?"

"She stole Saud!"

Joyce relaxed. "So she and that idiot are gone? What about the other two? Jack and—"

But it wasn't Mavis who answered Joyce's question. "Frank went with them." Jack stood on the front porch, looking pale and gaunt, but very much alive. Kingsley could see the daggers in his eyes as he trotted down the marble staircase. "Welcome home," he said, reaching for Joyce. Joyce stepped back, but not fast enough. Jack grabbed her and slammed her against the Pegasus.

"Mom!" Kingsley tried to push Jack away. "Leave her alone!"

Jack wrenched Kingsley's arm around, pinning it behind him, and threw him on the ground. Amanda rushed to help Kingsley. "Stop it!" Amanda yelled. Jack leaned over Joyce, hitting her again and again.

"Leave her alone!" Kingsley yelled. He grabbed Jack from behind, "You're hurting her!"

Jack shoved Kingsley away and pulled a pistol out from the back of his jeans. The same pistol with the pearl handles that his mother had used to shoot the snake.

"Back off."

Kingsley froze. This wasn't a video game. He couldn't turn off the console and walk away. A real gun was pointed at him.

Jack yanked Joyce to her feet. "Maureen told me what you did. How you tried to poison us with those pancakes full of Drano." He pushed her up the marble steps. "I have a new respect for you, Lily Fells. I thought you were just a swindler. I didn't know you were capable of murder." Joyce stumbled, but she never cried or begged, as Jack dragged her into the mansion. "Get inside and fix dinner. We eat together from now on. If I die, everyone dies."

Kingsley had wanted to be a Blue Angel jet pilot when he was a boy.

He'd wanted to be a hero, like Captain America, and fight for justice and honesty. That meant protecting the people he loved, but he couldn't fight Jack. He followed Joyce into the kitchen and offered to help her fix dinner but Jack wouldn't let him. Jack ordered him to get out.

Kingsley shuffled down the hallway toward the front door. Being a hero also meant putting right the things he'd done wrong. He pulled the pendant from his pocket and rubbed the six pointed star. Being a hero meant telling the truth and accepting the consequences. He knew what he had to do, but he didn't want to do it alone "Will you go with me to Dr. Jacobs' house?" he asked Amanda.

"What for?"

"I have to give him something."

Pine trees cracked like bullwhips and their needles covered the ground. Dark clouds were moving in. Kingsley breathed hard, feeling weaker with every step. He doubled over when they reached Dr. Jacobs' front door, trying to catch his breath. "Are you all right?" Amanda asked.

"I feel dizzy," he said. Amanda rubbed his back until he was able to straighten. He rang the doorbell.

Dr. Jacobs was thinner than usual, with bloodshot eyes as if he hadn't slept in a month. "Come in," he said. The wind pushed them inside, and Dr. Jacobs quickly closed the door. "What are you two doing running around outside? Don't you know a hurricane is on its way!" He touched Kingsley's sweaty forehead. "You have a fever. I'll get my bag."

"No, don't go," Kingsley said. He glanced at Amanda and then slowly pulled the pendant out of his pocket. "I stole this off your bookcase."

Amanda gasped, "Kingsley!" Kingsley felt ashamed.

Dr. Jacobs took the pendant. He rubbed the raised surface. "It is quite lovely. Is that why you stole it?"

Kingsley shook his head. "No, I thought it would bring me good luck."

"Why would you think that?"

"Because you're old and rich," Kingsley said. He glanced at Amanda before adding, "I'll need a lot of luck if I want to get old and rich like you."

Dr. Jacobs' eyes moistened. "I am old." He glanced at the photographs on the bookshelf of his children and grandchildren. "And I am rich." He handed the pendant back to Kingsley. "You keep it." He placed his hand on Kingsley's shoulder. "It was very brave of you to come and tell me the truth, Kingsley. You're an honorable man."

All Joyce could find for dinner was the last can of chicken noodle soup and thawed, mushy biscuits from the freezer. The electricity was out and dinner wasn't dinner. It was a war zone. Curses flew as Jack threatened to beat Joyce to a pulp, and Joyce swore she'd cut Jack's throat if he touched her again. Mavis, Kingsley and Amanda were at the table, too, as was Mrs. Sutherland, sinking in her wheelchair, looking smaller than ever, like a featherless baby bird.

Jack waited for Kingsley to start eating the soup before he'd take a sip. "I don't think you'd poison your own son just to get to me."

Joyce gave Jack a look that made Kingsley shiver, like she'd plunge a knife in his chest if she could. She turned to Amanda. "When's your Daddy picking you up?"

"I don't know," Amanda said, worried. "I thought he'd be here already. I called again but he didn't answer. I don't know where he is."

"He's probably dead," Mavis said which earned a slap on the side of her head from Joyce. "Whaaa?" Mavis rubbed her ear. "You heard the news, men are dropping like flies." Kingsley knew something terrible must have happened for Andrés not to answer Amanda's calls.

"What about your momma?" Joyce asked. "Is she coming for you? Or is she too busy with the senator to give a damn about her daughter and her mother?"

Jack spit out his soup. "Senator? My sister dumped Andrés for a senator? Moving up, isn't she?" Amanda scowled. "Where does Clare live now?" Jack asked. "At the orchard, I'd wager. I'll have to pay her a visit soon."

Amanda tensed. She didn't look at her uncle, and Kingsley knew why. Amanda didn't want Jack Sutherland near her mother any more than Kingsley wanted him near his.

They finished their soup and Joyce picked up the empty bowls. "Help me clean up," she said to Amanda. "If you haven't heard from your father by nightfall, Kingsley and me will take you to your mother."

Jack leaned back in his chair. He placed the pistol on the table in front of him. "I'll take her," he said. Amanda blanched, terrified at the prospect of being alone in a car with her Uncle Jack. Kingsley wished he was brave enough to grab the gun. He wished he was strong enough to take Jack Sutherland by the throat and rip him to shreds.

But he wasn't.

He had to decide. Was he just a fat boy who dreamed of becoming a Blue Angel jet pilot or could he be a hero?

While Joyce was giving Mrs. Sutherland her evening bath and Jack was drinking the last of the beer, Kingsley snuck out the front door and peeked into each car, looking for keys left in the ignition. He checked the limo. None. He checked Jack's SUV. None. He checked his mother's Pegasus. None. He snuck back in the house to find Amanda, careful not to attract attention. "Come on," he whispered, and took her hand. He crept into his mother's bedroom and searched through her purse.

"What are you looking for?"

"Keys to the Pegasus. We're getting out of here." He found the keys and hurried Amanda out. It had started raining. The strong wind almost pushed them down the marble steps.

"Where are we going?"

"I'm taking you to your mom," Kingsley said. "The senator will know what to do about Jack."

"How are we getting there?"

"Mom's car."

"Who's driving?" Amanda asked as they sprinted through the rain to the Pegasus.

"Me," Kingsley said. He slid behind the steering wheel. Amanda climbed into the front passenger seat.

"But you can't drive!"

"It's better than Jack taking you."

"That's true," Amanda said. Tears filled her eyes. "But what about your mom. You can't leave her here alone."

"Yes, I can," Kingsley said. "I've asked her to leave a million times, but she won't go."

"I'm sorry you have to do this, Kingsley," Amanda said. "I'm sorry my family's so messed up."

Kingsley waved away her apology. "My family's messed up, too. We just have to get to your mom before the hurricane gets really bad."

Kingsley had never driven a car before but he'd watched his mother often enough. He put the quiet hybrid in gear and slowly crept down the red brick driveway. The howling wind drowned out the sound of the tires sloshing over the rain-soaked leaves and twigs as he drove through the wrought-iron gate. He snaked along the gravel county roads and over a tiny bridge that spanned one of the flooded tributaries of the York River, almost stalling in the muck. His last sliver of confidence vanished when the sun set and he hit the interstate.

Red taillights blazed for miles. Kingsley gripped the steering wheel. He wiped sweat from his eyes. He stayed focused on Amanda's directions until they passed a sign for the Monitor-Merrimac Bridge-Tunnel.

"I hate that tunnel," Amanda murmured.

Afraid to look right or left, Kingsley blinked frantically, working to keep his eyes on the red taillights ahead of him. "Don't they close the tunnel during hurricanes?" he asked.

"I don't know," Amanda said. She shivered and rubbed her arms. Ahead of them the mouth of the tunnel glowed against the dark abyss. "It's like driving into the belly of a monster. See the teeth?"

"What teeth?"

She pointed to sharp and jagged black triangles coming down like shadowy stalactites, turning the white concrete into an angry, hideous grin. "On the tunnel entrance. The black is from truck exhaust. Makes the tunnel look like it has teeth."

Windshield wipers slapped and Kingsley wiped away the dense fog building on the inside. A shiver of hot and cold rushed over him as they plunged into the tunnel. Bright lights hit him like a sledgehammer, worsening his headache. The narrow walls felt like a tomb locking him in. They drove down, down, down under the water. The stench of gasoline and burning motor oil made him queasy.

"Hope it doesn't spring a leak," Amanda said, biting her fingernails.

"Stop saying things like that!" Kingsley snapped. "No more monsters and no more leaks!" He rubbed his sweaty palms on the legs of his jeans as they inched behind countless cars and trucks. He could almost feel the thousands of pounds of water pressure above him, aching to get in. "Why are they so slow?" he said, gripping the steering wheel. The driver in the car in front of him pounded his dashboard and blasted his horn. It echoed loudly. Kingsley's ears popped as they rounded the deep bottom and the cars and trucks slowly inched back up. Kingsley followed the red taillights out of the bright tunnel onto the dark and crowded four-mile-long bridge that spanned the Hampton Roads harbor. Machine-gun hail pounded like shrapnel. Lightning hit the bridge railing and thunder boomed. Amanda screamed and covered her ears. The hail turned into a waterfall of rain, and the windshield wipers whizzed back and forth. *Whish! Whish! Whish! Whish!*

Barely half a mile onto the bridge, traffic came to a stop. Kingsley saw movement in the car ahead of them. The driver's door opened and a man staggered out. The man pulled a limp boy from the back seat. Diagonal rain pushed against the two of them, man and boy, as the man carried the boy to the edge of the bridge. "What's he doing?" Amanda said. The man stood at the edge, drenched, the boy in his arms. "Oh My God! He's going to jump!" Amanda pushed the car door open, struggling against the wind. She ran to the man. "Stop! Stop!"

"Amanda!" Kingsley yelled. "Get back in the car!" He wiped the windshield. He could see Amanda pleading with the man but couldn't hear her over the thunder and the pounding rain.

Kingsley hesitated, not knowing what to do. He was afraid of the hurricane. He was afraid of the lightning and thunder. But he was more afraid of losing Amanda. He got out of the car and slipped on the wet, oily bridge, cutting his hand. He scrambled to his feet. His head ached, and he didn't have his pain medicine. He could hear Amanda begging the man to move away from the edge.

The man climbed over the concrete barrier, the limp child still in his arms. "My son. My only son. I couldn't save him." Waves reached up and the man and the boy disappeared into the black harbor. Amanda screamed and lunged for the man. Kingsley grabbed her before she went over, too.

"They're gone," he shouted, holding her around her waist.

They hurried back to the car, soaked and trembling, blood dripping from Kingsley's injured hand. "Why would he do that?" she sobbed. "Why would he give up?"

Kingsley knew why. He felt like giving up, too. He understood hopelessness and the longing to turn back time. He leaned his head against the steering wheel, and waited for the hurricane to pass.

It was after midnight by the time the lightning moved north and the thunder hushed. No stars were in the sky, only the dull, waxing moon. Doors opened and stunned passengers snaked around the cars and trucks. Amanda lowered her window and called to a woman dressed in a business suit. "Have you seen the police? Do you know what's causing the hold up?"

The businesswoman shook her head. "Haven't got a clue." She pulled out her cellphone. "No signal, either. I'm going back to the tunnel. Maybe someone there can help. I have to get away from that nut on the Viper. Too many weird things are happening, and he's scaring the hell out of me."

Several yards away a man with dreadlocks stood on the hood of a small green car.

"The Lord has hardened your hearts! The destroyer has entered your houses! And there was a great cry in Egypt, for there was not a house where one was not dead."

Kingsley got out and scanned the mounting horror surrounding him. In the minivan in the next lane, a teenage girl was shaking a teenage boy slumped over the steering wheel. In front of the minivan, a truck driver opened the door of his cab and vomited.

The screaming prophet waved his arms to the heavens. *"And the Egyptians were urgent with the people, to send them out of the land in haste; for they said, 'We are all dead men.'"*

Amanda got out of the car and drew close. "I'm scared."

"Me, too," Kingsley choked, trying to hold back tears. "My head hurts and I forgot my medicine. Maybe this wasn't such a good idea."

"We've got to get out of here," Amanda said. She started to follow the businesswoman.

"Where are you going?" All Kingsley wanted at that moment was to curl up in the back seat and go to sleep.

"To the tunnel," Amanda said.

"You're going to walk?"

"Yes."

"That's crazy. The police'll be here soon."

"The police aren't coming, Kingsley," Amanda said. "Look around. Who do you see walking? Women! All the men are sick or dead. We're on our own, Kingsley. We have to get off this bridge. What if the hurricane returns? This could be the eye of the storm. It could get worse. We'll be safer in the tunnel."

Kingsley begrudgingly followed. "I thought you were afraid of tunnels."

"I'm more afraid of hurricanes."

They weaved between the stalled cars and eighteen-wheelers until Kingsley couldn't walk any further. He doubled over and threw up. He fell against the huge rear tire of an eighteen-wheeler and wiped his mouth with his sleeve. On the side of the truck was a picture of a twelve-foot-tall smiling cow wearing a straw bonnet. Amanda helped Kingsley up. "Let's make a game of it," she said. "We'll count the steps. One, two, three," Amanda encouraged. "Four, five, six. We'll be there soon, Kingsley. Then we'll get your medicine." Kingsley dragged his feet. Every step was a burden. "Thirty-one, thirty-two, thirty-three."

"I want to die," Kingsley said. Memories mixed with visions. He didn't know where he was. He forgot why he was walking.

"We'll get your medicine soon," Amanda said.

"No," Kingsley said. "No, you don't understand. I keep seeing my father. Bleeding all over the carpet. I can't go back. I can't live with Mom. Not after what she did." He stumbled and started to cry. "I'll never be a Blue Angel."

"Keep counting," Amanda said. "We'll be there soon." They walked with sullen and spiritless crowds of women, children, and a few broken old men, all headed toward the bright yellow glow of the tunnel. "Fifty-six, fifty-seven. Look, Kingsley, see those lights? We're almost there."

"I'm thirsty," Kingsley said.

"Look, Kingsley." Ahead of them was a soft-drink truck. Amanda banged on the door, "Hey, Mister! Open up, we're dying out here!" She gave Kingsley a thumbs-up, and then climbed up to peer into the cab. "Aaaah!" She screamed and jumped back, covering her mouth.

A black woman wearing green scrubs came over to help. She climbed up and peered in the window. "He's been dead for a while," she said. "Rigor mortis has begun." She stepped down from the truck, hands on hips. "Where's highway patrol? Hasn't anyone noticed the tunnel's blocked?" She waved her arms at the overhead camera hanging from a streetlight. "Hey, you, in the camera. We're here. Send help!"

"Do you think they know we're here?" Amanda asked.

The woman shrugged. "Who knows?" She opened the cab and grabbed the dead driver's keys. Then she unlocked the back and handed out plastic bottles of soda. Amanda grabbed one for Kingsley before the crowd swept in.

"Here, drink this," She helped him sip the warm fizz. It tasted terrible.

Women and children descended on the truck like vultures, pushing each other aside. Soon the truck was picked clean, nothing left except hundreds of empty plastic bottles littering the bridge and the stiff corpse of the dead driver.

The sound of running motors and the high-pitched screams of frightened girls echoed against the walls of the tunnel. Kingsley covered his nose with the edge of his shirt. "Why don't they turn off their engines?" He moved slowly, leaning against the tunnel wall as he walked. His vision blurred and his legs wobbled. He fell to the oily floor.

"Kingsley!" Amanda yelled.

Kingsley saw his father. "Dad?"

"It's me, Amanda."

"The bait looks alive," Kingsley said. His fingers twitched.

"Try to stand up," Amanda said. She pulled him to his feet. "We have to get through the tunnel."

Kingsley took a few steps until the pain in his head pushed him back down. He stared up at the ceiling and remembered Floyd's description of the sea battles between the Confederate Ship Virginia and the Union ships she sank. Cannon balls firing, ships burning, and dead men floating with their faces turned down. His eyes went dark. Kingsley could hear Amanda calling his name. He felt his head in her lap and her hand on his forehead. He reached up and touched her soft face. "I choose you," he said. "From now on, I choose you."

The pain drifted away.

PART II

10 Heaven and Hell

April 15, 2010. Eight years earlier. The southern Louisiana coastline was full of life. Pelicans flew overhead in formation, and snowy egrets tended their fuzzy chicks in the gnarled live oak trees. Curious gulls waddled along the wooden dock, eyeing Kingsley and waiting patiently for him to toss them a piece of squid. Kingsley's job was baiting hooks and he was good at it. "Rigging is all about making the bait look alive," Kingsley told the men and women watching him. He pulled a small gray squid from the bait bucket and placed it on the grungy prep table. "That's what my dad says." Kingsley loved being the center of attention, especially when pretty wives accompanied their rich husbands.

"How old are you?" one of the pretty wives asked.

"Six," Kingsley said, with a slight whistle through missing front teeth. "But I'll be seven in July."

"You're adorable," the woman cooed.

Kingsley beamed. "I've fished with Dad since I was three years old, but I'm not fishing forever. When I grow up, I'm gonna fly jets."

"Jets!" The rich man who'd booked the charter took off his New York Yankees baseball cap and ran thick fingers through his silver hair. "Son, you're just what this country needs, a boy with ambition who's not afraid to get his hands dirty."

Kingsley loved helping his father prepare for a fishing trip in the Gulf of Mexico. He loved the smell of salt water and fresh bait. He carefully picked up a two-inch-long hook from the prep table and dazzled his audience with his dexterity. "First thing I do is punch this hook all the way through this here squid's head." He struggled with the sharp hook, mostly for show, until it poked through the squishy head of the small invertebrate. The pretty wife cringed. Kingsley strung the leader through the squid's mantle and finished the rigging. After he'd baited a half-dozen hooks, he threw them into a large cooler. His father, Darryl Smith, loaded the cooler onto his boat. Darryl called to his passengers. It was time to go. He helped each passenger, one-by-one, up the gangway.

Kingsley didn't go with them. He stood with Joyce and waved good-bye as Darryl maneuvered the boat away from the dock and around the buoys. Gulls flew overhead, keeping pace. One of the passengers tossed a piece of bread in the air, and a gull swooped to catch it.

Joyce shooed away a particularly aggressive gull stalking Kingsley for leftovers. "Get away from my boy!" she fussed. They waited until the boat was beyond the horizon. Joyce took Kingsley's hand and walked down the dock, heading to their small house a few blocks away. "Good God Almighty, you stink," Joyce said. "I don't know why Dad gets you to string those ugly fish."

"They're squid, Mom."

"Squid? Is that what they are?" she teased, squeezing his hand affectionately. "You must be the smartest boy in the whole wide world knowing such things. But you ain't stringing bait all your life. I got big plans for you, hon. You're gonna be somebody when you grow up."

"I know, Mom," Kingsley said. "I'm joining the Navy, and I'm gonna be a Blue Angel jet pilot."

"That's right, hon. Now, listen up. Get a bath as soon as we get home, and I'll get dinner ready."

"Yes, Ma'am."

Kingsley made soap bubbles in the tub until the warm water turned cold. The smell of Cajun fried shrimp spooned over red rice and beans called him to dinner. He gobbled his dinner and then rushed to the TV. Captain America was on. Joyce sat beside him and cheered every time the Captain beat the bad guys. At eight o'clock, Kingsley put on his pajamas and climbed into bed without arguing. He was tired and wanted to get up early to welcome his father home from his fishing charter. Joyce came into his bedroom and read a story. This was Kingsley's favorite time of day, even better than helping his father bait the hooks. Joyce cuddled in bed with him and read a new book they'd just gotten from the library, a fable about a king who had everything but wasn't willing to share with nature. One day the king saw bluebirds eating a few cherries from the trees in his garden. He became enraged! The king ordered his royal guards to kill all the birds. The guards aimed their arrows and shot down the birds, one after another, until there were none. The next year, the trees didn't have any fruit at all. The king was perplexed. *Why are there no cherries?* He asked his wisest counselor. *The bugs ate all the cherries*, the counselor replied, *because there were no birds to eat the bugs.*

"That was dumb," Kingsley said. "I'd never hurt a bird."

"I know you wouldn't, hon," Joyce said. She kissed his head and turned off his light. Kingsley fell into a peaceful, happy sleep.

He woke at sunrise and waited anxiously by the front door for his father. Darryl arrived with swordfish steaks, a wallet full of cash, and kisses for everyone. He picked Joyce up and swung her around. She laughed like a schoolgirl. Kingsley begged to be swung, too, and Darryl obliged. "I'll take you out on the boat next Sunday," Darryl said. "Maybe let you take the helm."

Kingsley was ecstatic. "It'll be just like flying a jet."

That evening, Joyce prepared blackened swordfish with creole meuniere and key-lime pie. Kingsley's life was perfect.

April 20, 2010. 9:45 p.m. The offshore drilling rig, *Deepwater Horizon*, exploded in the Gulf of Mexico, killing eleven people and leaking oil for eighty-seven days.

Darryl, Joyce and Kingsley walked solemnly to the beach, hand in hand. No tourists were sunbathing. No fishermen were trying their luck on shore. Newly posted signs warned, *DANGER! KEEP OUT OF THE WATER.* They made their way to a makeshift tent erected near a line of rescue squad trucks. Serious-looking men and women wearing Hazmat suits were scurrying about, some putting up more signs, while others were collecting samples of seaweed and marsh grass and putting them in small plastic bags.

"What are they doing, Dad?" Kingsley asked.

"I don't know, son," Darryl said. Smoke billowed in the distance. "But I'm sure it ain't good."

A van pulled up and a woman jumped out. She was holding a black bird. She handed the black bird to one of the men in a Hazmat suit. He ran to the tent and began scrubbing the bird in sudsy water. The black bird wasn't black at all. It was a gull.

Kingsley followed the man to the tent, Darryl and Joyce not far behind. "It's supposed to be white," Kingsley said, shocked. Kingsley looked up at his mother. "Someone hurt a bird, Mom, just like the selfish king in the story."

Joyce returned Kingsley's concern. "It's 'cuz of that damn oil spill, hon."

A few moments later, the man in the Hazmat suit shook his head. The gull was dead. Kingsley was horrified. "Who'd hurt a seagull?" he asked, tears in his eyes. Joyce tried to comfort him, but all Kingsley could do was plead with the man in the Hazmat suit. "It's supposed to be white. It's supposed fly behind my Dad's fishing boat."

The man in the Hazmat suit looked more angry than upset. "There are worse things in this world than death," he said. He pulled off his thick gloves and threw them on the table, "and what's happening right now in the Gulf is one of them."

Oil flowed for eighty-seven days, leaking two-hundred-million gallons into the Gulf and destroying the lives of fishermen, their families and untold wildlife.

October, 2013. Three years later. Hardee's was full at nine o'clock on a school night, the dinner crowd lingering and the late-night rummagers just arriving. Ten-year-old Kingsley Smith filled his extra-large cup with a combination of cola and orange soda as Darryl carried their food on a tray. Darryl stumbled as he took a booth near the window and Kingsley could smell the alcohol on his father's breath. They unwrapped their Monster Thickburgers, and Darryl counted: "Three. Two. One." Kingsley finished his burger, his fries, and most of his drink before Darryl was half way through his burger.

Darryl swirled a couple of fries in ketchup. "I got a new joke for you," he said. Kingsley grinned. He loved his father's jokes. Darryl popped the fries in his mouth. "So, Jesus was walking around the desert, followed by a bunch of guys saying '*ten*.'"

"Ten?"

"Folks gathered around from all over, trying to figure out who this man was and why a bunch of shabby looking fellows were following him, saying '*ten*.' Someone asked one of the shabby followers, *Why do you keep repeating the word ten?*' The disciple pointed to Jesus. *That's what he told us to do! Get behind me, Satan.*"

"Get behind me, say ten!" Kingsley laughed. "That's a good one, Dad." He grabbed a handful of Darryl's fries and sucked them into his mouth like spaghetti. Outside, scrawny gulls fought over scraps in the parking lot.

"Remember when I owned that fishing boat?" Darryl asked.

"Uh huh."

"Marlin, snapper, swordfish. They were beautiful, especially just before I pulled them out of the water. Shimmered like jewels."

"Yeah, I remember," Kingsley said.

Darryl leaned back in his seat. "I went to the dock this morning, when you were in school. The marshes are all gone. The oil killed everything. Remember those baby egrets we used to watch? Poof," Darryl waved his hands like a magician, "Disappeared." He sniffed and used a napkin to blow his nose. He threw it on the tray. "Wouldn't want to live there even if the fucking bank gave our house back to us for free. Whole place stinks like death."

Kingsley played with the packets of salt, pouring them on the table like sand as he listened. They stayed at Hardee's long after their meal was finished, waiting for Darryl to feel sober enough to walk to the public-housing apartment they now called home.

Sirens filled the New Orleans night, and the smell of smoke from the St. Charles refinery filled the air. Darryl and Kingsley walked the broken sidewalk past the old Dauphin Hospital where Joyce worked cleaning rooms. It looked like a prison more than a hospital, with dark red brick and narrow windows that lit the night sky like eyes on a jack-o'lantern. Kingsley didn't like thinking about his mother washing bedpans and wiping up vomit, but that wasn't the worst thing she did at the hospital.

Joyce changed after the *Deepwater Horizon* drilling rig exploded in the

Gulf of Mexico. After Darryl lost his fishing boat, they were forced to move out of their little house on the beach. The bills piled up and Joyce took a job cleaning hospital rooms. Debt collectors came and Darryl's drinking escalated. He couldn't hold down a job. That's when Joyce started stealing. At first she stole only cash from the patients when no one was looking, but she quickly learned that the real money came from stealing medicine. "It's easy," she boasted to Darryl, "I sneak into the storage cabinets while the nurses are boo-hooing about all the oil-covered seagulls on TV."

Kingsley found a box full of medicine and medical supplies under his parents' bed. Pills, bandages, gauze, capped hypodermic needles, vials of liquid he couldn't pronounce, pads, face masks, stethoscopes and blood-pressure monitors. Darryl hated it, but whenever he objected, all Joyce had to do was say, "Somebody's got to earn a living around here," and Darryl went for the bottle.

A dirty young man with thinning hair and slumped shoulders was sitting in the hallway of the public-housing complex, his back against the wall. Darryl and Kingsley hurried past him. When they reached the front door of their unit, Darryl quickly unlocked the door. He quickly relocked it behind them. Kingsley threw his school backpack beside the TV. He didn't open it; didn't check his homework. Instead, he turned on his X-Box and played *Total Annihilation.*

Darryl pulled a bottle out of a kitchen cabinet and drank, not bothering to get a glass. He called to Kingsley. "Go to bed. Your mother'll be home soon." He wiped his mouth and leaned against the counter. "God knows what she'll do when I tell her I'm leaving and taking you with me."

Kingsley paused his game. "Leaving? Where're we going, Dad?"

"We've moving in with my folks. Just you and me. That's my plan, at least." Darryl took another swallow. "This has been a long time coming. Stealing. Lying. Selling drugs. Police'll be busting down our door any minute." He capped the bottle, but didn't put it away. "Now go get ready for bed and don't forget to brush your teeth."

Bedsprings creaked as Joyce slipped into Kingsley's warm bed. He knew her smell. Perspiration, antiseptic, and lavender body lotion. He was too old for a story, but not too old for a kiss on the cheek and a whispered *I Love*

You. Joyce slipped out of his bed as quietly as she'd slipped in. Kingsley had almost fallen back to sleep when he heard arguing coming from the living room. He clutched his Captain America action hero and climbed out of bed. He cracked his bedroom door just wide enough to see.

Darryl was holding something in his hand. "You didn't get this out of no goddamn storage cabinet! You stole it from a patient, didn't you? Right out of his room!"

"Maybe if I wasn't married to an out-of-work, mush-mouth fisherman-turned-welfare slug, I wouldn't have to steal," Joyce snapped. She pried open his hand and pulled out a medicine vial. "God, I hate whiny men."

"You should be in jail," Darryl said. "Stealing from a sick person. You're disgusting."

"You think I want to live in this dump for the rest of my life?" Joyce said. "You think I want my Kingsley going to that shit hole of a public school? I'm sick being poor and I'm sick of New Orleans. I hate all the low-life trash I have to put up with around here. I grew up with trash; I don't want my son living that way."

Kingsley was about to close the door when he heard his father's voice, louder and angrier than before. "We're leaving. Kingsley and me. We're moving out first thing in the morning."

Joyce flew into a rage. "You ain't taking my boy!"

Outside a dog howled. The old man who lived in the unit next door yelled at them to shut up. Kingsley held his breath. All he could see were two shadows struggling. He heard curses and grunts. He jumped at the sound of a loud *BANG*. His heart raced. He heard footfalls. Someone was coming. He ran to his bed and hid under the covers. Joyce flipped on his bedroom light and opened his closets. "Get up, Kingsley. We gotta go." She grabbed fistfuls of his clothes and ran out.

Kingsley followed his mother to the living room, leaving his Captain America action figure behind. He stepped on one of his green Army men, bending the rifle and hurting his foot. He smelled sulfur and smoke, like something was burning. Darryl was on the floor in front of the TV, a red pool soaking the matted beige carpet. Kingsley rushed to his side. "Dad!" He looked up at Joyce. "What happened to Dad?"

Joyce was shoving Kingsley's clothes into a black plastic bag. "Somebody shot him," she said. She stuffed coats from the hall closet in another bag, and then threw Kingsley's shoes at his feet. "Put on your shoes. Hurry up. We gotta get out of New Orleans before someone calls the police." Joyce pulled Kingsley's school photos off the walls and stuffed them in with the coats.

Darryl raised his head and mouthed something Kingsley couldn't understand.

"What, Dad? What did you say?" Kingsley turned to Joyce. "Call a doctor, Mom. Call 9-1-1. We gotta help Dad!"

Joyce stuffed Kingsley's school backpack with a few of the toy jets and Legos scattered around the TV, but stopped when she noticed Kingsley was still in bare feet. "Get your shoes on! Hurry!" Kingsley reluctantly slid into his sneakers. "Hurry, Kingsley!" Joyce forced the backpack into his arms. "Come on, we gotta go!" She grabbed the black plastic bags in one hand and Kingsley's hand in the other and rushed out the door, stepping over the dirty, slump-shouldered young man in the hallway.

The young man crawled to his feet and stumbled after her. "Joyce, Joyce, I got money."

The next door opened and the old man, holding a fluffy white cat, yelled out, "I heard the argument. I heard the gunshot."

"Mind your own goddamn business," Joyce growled.

"I already called the police," the old man said.

Kingsley struggled against Joyce's grip. "We gotta go back! We gotta help Dad!" Joyce held tight. She hustled Kingsley to the parking lot.

The slumped-shouldered young man followed. "Got any Percocet, Joyce? I need it bad. Brought cash-money." He offered her a wad of bills.

Joyce took the bills and handed the addict the keys to her apartment. "You'll find everything you want in a box under my bed. Take it all." She loaded Kingsley and the black plastic bags into the back seat of their Dodge Charger.

"Why'd you do that, Mom?" Kingsley asked. "Why'd you give that man the keys to our home? Dad needs a doctor."

"Police'll think it was a robbery." She started the engine and pulled out of the parking lot. "We'll find a new home up north. Delaware or New York. The North is full of lonely and desperate people, hon, and the rich are as lonely and desperate as we are."

"We gotta go back!" Kingsley said. "We gotta take Dad to a doctor!"

"It's too late, hon," Joyce said. "There's nothing a doctor can do for him."

"What are you talking about?"

"He's dead, hon."

The black plastic bags loomed around Kingsley like oil-covered ghosts, trembling every time the car hit a bump. "He's not dead. He's just hurt. How do you know he's dead?"

"I know he's dead 'cause I saw him get shot, hon."

"Who shot Dad?"

Oncoming headlights illuminated Joyce's face. She glanced at him in the rearview mirror before she went dark again. "A stranger shot your daddy," she said. "A black man."

"A black man?"

"He looked like that movie star you're always talking about."

"A movie star shot Dad?"

"Yeah, hon," Joyce said. "Now don't you go telling anyone about what happened here, and for God's sake, don't ask any more questions."

Amanda was crying. Strangers had gathered. A woman in a white smock pushed on his chest and breathed into his mouth. Kingsley didn't feel anything. His headache was gone. He wandered through the crowd until he heard screaming. The crowd faded, and Joyce was holding him, rocking back and forth, back and forth. Her eyes were red. She rummaged through his pockets and found the pendant Dr. Jacobs had given him. She held the pendant to her heart.

Kingsley wandered through the darkness until he saw a bright light. Memories floated like soap bubbles in the bathtub. He touched the memories. It was like touching a horse's nose, sometimes they were soft and warm, and sometimes they bit and kicked.

Joyce cried and begged for Kingsley to come back to her. But he didn't return. He didn't want to be Joyce's son anymore.

"No," he said. "I decide. I decide where I go and when."

11 Charlotte

Charlotte Sutherland knelt beside the valve box and plunged her gloved hand into the deep dank hole, completely unafraid of encountering a black-widow spider or awakening a hibernating snake. Mud and thick roots encased the water pipe. She dug away the mud and hacked at the roots with a sharp-edged trowel. She cleaned the rusted threads with a wire brush, and then bathed the pipe with lubricant. She stood and reinserted the T-bar wrench. "Come on," she said through gritted teeth. "Turn, damn you." Half an inch. Stop. Another half-inch. Stop. The sound of water flowing grew louder, like mallets on a kettle drum, as the passageway grew smaller and the pressure increased. She'd twisted the handles of the waist-high T-bar wrench until the valve closed.

An old woman shuffled out of a nearby three-story house, wearing slippers and a faded housecoat. A pair of bifocals hung from a chain around her neck. She gawked at Charlotte. "The city told me my water would be off ten 'til noon. It's eleven-thirty now."

"They should have told you eleven 'til one," Charlotte said, not looking up from her work.

"One! I'm having people over for Bible Study at one. We're reading the Acts of the Apostles." The woman shaded her eyes from the late-morning sun. "Do you know Acts of the Apostles?"

"No, ma'am."

The woman dropped her hand. "Neither do I. Never got past Luke.

Don't know if I should serve hot tea or hard liquor. Is there a lot of killing in Acts?"

Charlotte shook her head. "I don't know."

"Any sex?"

Charlotte chuckled as she pulled a shiny black pipe out of her tool bag. "I don't think so."

"I only read the Bible for the sex and violence," the woman said. She wrinkled her nose. "What's that awful smell?"

Charlotte motioned to a pickup truck pulling a trailer, a backhoe parked beside it, and a pile of freshly turned dirt. "Patched that sewer line this morning. Someone complained about raw sewage backing up in their bathroom."

"Dottie told me her upstairs toilet ran all weekend," the woman said. "'Course she can't hear a lick so it could have run for months. Is that what caused the backup?"

"Probably," Charlotte said. She pulled a rag out of the back pocket of her coveralls and wiped her hands. "That and roots in the line."

"If you're finished with the sewer, what are you working on now?"

"I'm installing a backflow preventer and pressure reducer," Charlotte said, as she screwed the black pipe onto the water line.

"Backflow preventer and pressure reducer," the woman repeated. The corner of her mouth twitched. "That's what I need. Something to prevent backflow and reduce pressure."

"Keeps the water supply safe and protects the pipes. This will take me about half an hour. I'll be done before one." Charlotte shifted her weight and leaned against a large boxwood shrub.

"Watch it there, girl!" the woman said. "My husband planted that when we were newlyweds."

Charlotte gave a curt nod, her eyes glued on her work. "I'll be careful."

The woman tugged on her bifocals. "Twenty, thirty, forty. The Collapse was forty years ago, right?"

"Yes, ma'am."

"Chester died thirty years ago. Only the good die young, I guess." She put on her glasses and her face softened with recognition. "Goodness, you look just like Amanda Santos."

Charlotte was startled. She immediately stopped working and looked up at the woman. "You knew my mother."

"Oh, yes," the woman said. "I knew her. Mercy, you're a spitting image."

"I'm her clone."

"Clone?" The woman wrinkled her nose as if the stench from the sewer had suddenly gotten worse. "The old biddies at Bible Study talk about cloning all the time." She shook her head. "Babies without sex. Wouldn't wish that on my worst enemy."

Charlotte stood and faced the woman. "How did you know my mother? What was she like?"

"We went to St. Andrew's Academy together. I guess Amanda told you about St. Andrews."

Charlotte solemnly shook her head. "No, she never told me about St. Andrews."

"After St. Andrew's, I didn't see Amanda for years," the woman continued. "We reconnected during the Gasoline Riots of 2025. That was the worst winter I can remember. No food, no electricity, no water. The world had fallen apart and we were looking for someone to blame. We were in our early twenties and mad as hell. We spent the night together in the Portsmouth jail and were happy to have warm beds and a few pieces of stale bread. Did she tell you that?"

"No," Charlotte said. "She didn't tell me."

"My word, you look just like her. Except your hair's shorter. Amanda always kept her hair long. You've got her dark eyes and skin. From the Santos side of the family, no doubt. You sure didn't get that deep tan from the Sutherlands." She pointed to Charlotte's protruding belly. "You're pregnant?"

"Yes," Charlotte said. She smiled and rubbed her stomach.

"Your clone, I presume?"

Charlotte nodded.

The woman roughly snapped a leaf off the overgrown boxwood. "Just don't kill my plant." As she turned to leave, Charlotte asked another question.

"When you knew my mother, was she happy?"

The woman gave a sad chuckle. "Everyone was happy before The Collapse." She went back to her house.

Charlotte finished before one o'clock. She packed her supplies and threw them in the back of the pickup. She drove the backhoe onto the trailer and secured it.

The sky held onto the cold steel of late March. The trees were bare, and the bright snow of February had turned into mud. Only the evergreens broke the monotony of gray and brown. Charlotte drove the pickup and trailer to a small public park facing the Hampton Roads Harbor. She sat on a bench and ate her lunch of pita and brown rice. Across the harbor were scores of rusting battleships, aircraft carriers, and patrol boats, anchored and untouched for decades. She threw a piece of pita into the water. Nothing nibbled on it from the depth. Nothing flew down from the sky. She finished her lunch and drove north. Her next assignment was another sewer leak somewhere between Williamsburg and Yorktown. Charlotte didn't go to the leak. Not right away, at least. She took a detour. She drove to Marlbank.

The road was full of potholes. Manicured pastures had turned into forests. Charlotte parked outside the wrought-iron fence and stood at the front gate, her fingers wrapped around the tarnished brass roses and copper thistles. Weeds pushed asunder the red brick driveway like displaced baby teeth. Overgrown shrubbery enshrouded the mansion. No birds pecked in the tall grass, no squirrels scampered in the thick trees, no horses trotted around the paddock. Charlotte pressed her face against the fence. "We used to own that, *Niña*. My mother grew up there," she spoke to her unborn baby. She didn't walk to the quiet front porch. She didn't sit on the moldy rocking chairs. She didn't tap on the beveled glass. She got back in the truck and headed to the leaking cesspool.

Charlotte worked until sundown. She drove the pickup and trailer to a sprawling, mostly empty apartment complex in Hampton. The parking lot was little more than buckled asphalt mangled by overgrown tree roots. She threw her mud-encrusted boots in the back of the pickup, and then she peeled out of her smelly coveralls, hooking them on the rear view mirror. None of her neighbors took notice as she walked across the parking lot wearing only her oversized undershirt, panties and dirty socks. Even if they had, nothing would have come of it. Charlotte had never known a time when she couldn't dress as she pleased and walk freely, day or night, without fear of man or beast. She'd never heard a wolf whistle or a mosquito buzz. Not live, at least. She'd seen movies, read books. She knew about men and animals but they were no more real to her than dinosaurs.

Charlotte climbed the stairs to her second-story apartment and tried the door. Locked. "Nanna," she leaned her dirty forehead against the door. "Open up."

"Who is it?"

"John Wayne," Charlotte said.

Two deadbolts clicked and an old woman peeked out. She wore a tattered robe and threadbare slippers. Long gone were her hourglass figure and her peaches-and-cream complexion. Both had turned brittle and dusty gray. Clare Sutherland didn't live with Senator Steele at the Sutherland Orchards. Both the senator and the orchards were gone. She now lived with her granddaughter, Charlotte, in their small, two-bedroom apartment in Hampton. Across the street was a long-abandoned automobile dealership that thirteen years earlier had been converted into a fundamentalist church.

Charlotte pushed the door open and trudged toward the bathroom. "I don't know why you lock that door. Who's going to come in? Old Lady Hinkle across the hall?"

"You've never been robbed," Clare said, as Charlotte stripped off her dirty underwear and socks. "I have proof."

"Proof of what?" Charlotte asked, as she threw her dirty clothes in the hamper.

"Joyce Smith," Clare said. "She's alive."

Charlotte started the shower. "Water down the whiskey again, Nanna?"

"This time is different. I spoke with Randolph Setter's granddaughter."

"Who's Randolph Setter?" Charlotte called from behind the shower curtain.

"He was Joyce's lawyer. The one who'd helped Joyce change her name and steal father's oil wells. I spoke with his granddaughter. She's a lawyer, too. I sent her a photo of father's Robert E. Lee cupboard. The one bought after the Civil War. I took that photo for the insurance company right after father's funeral. Thank God I still had it. She's interested in helping me find Joyce."

"Why would she help us?" Charlotte called as she washed her hair.

"I didn't ask," Clare said. "Maybe she wants to redeem her grandfather's reputation. Maybe she's sorry for what he did to us. My father was a very important man. He owned the shipyard. He was—"

"Does she know Joyce's new name?" Charlotte asked, as she stepped out of the shower and worked a towel over her pregnant belly, under her full breasts, and between her legs. "Isn't that why you couldn't find Joyce forty years ago? Because you didn't know her new name?"

Clare pursed her lips. "Amanda knew it." She lowered her head, not meeting Charlotte's eyes. "I don't know why she never told me. Because of that boy, I suppose."

Charlotte ran the towel over her short hair, then hung it on the rack and headed to the kitchen, completely naked. "How do you know this attorney isn't a shyster like her grandfather?"

"Because I have nothing left to steal," Clare said, as she followed Charlotte to the kitchen. "You don't know what it was like. Amanda was stuck in that tunnel. I was in Chesapeake, at the orchard. I couldn't get to her. John hired a helicopter to fly us to the mansion, but it was too late, Momma was dead. Everything was gone. Joyce stole everything. Well, almost everything." Clare pointed to a long poem in a gold frame that looked out of place among the shabby furniture. "She left that Shakespeare poem Momma calligraphied before her stroke." Clare bitterly began to recite the poem: *They that have the pow'r to hurt—*

Charlotte interrupted. "Every time you tell the story, it's something different. The last time you told me Joyce met you at the tunnel entrance and took you and my mother back to the mansion. The time before that you said some black nurse drove my mother home. What am I supposed to believe, Nanna? You don't even know where your mother's buried."

"Everything was so confusing," Clare cried, "It's because of The Collapse. I don't know what happened to Momma or my horses or anything. Joyce was gone and everyone else was dead. Who could I ask?"

Charlotte rummaged through the refrigerator and pulled out a carton of rice milk. "Has she actually seen Joyce? The shyster's granddaughter. Has she actually talked to her? Does she know where she lives?"

"She's seen the cupboard—"

"Leave it alone, Nanna."

On the stove was a simmering pot of corn chowder. Charlotte ladled a bowlful. "If Joyce is still alive, she'd be an old woman by now.' Charlotte sat at the small kitchen table with her chowder, spoon and carton of rice milk.

Clare brought a loaf of dense rye bread to the table. "She's younger than I am. Barely in her sixties. Besides, this isn't about me. It's about you and the baby."

Charlotte quickly downed the chowder and handed the bowl to Clare for a refill. She started on the bread. "Nanna, I have a good job. I'm going to have a baby soon. I don't care about Joyce." She wolfed down the second bowl of chowder as fast as the first, then leaned back and scratched her round belly. She took a deep breath and let out an exhausted burp. "I don't care about Marlbank or the oil wells or what happened to your mother." She looked away, adding bitterly, "I don't even care what happened to mine."

Clare's eyes watered.

Charlotte groaned. "Don't do that. Don't make me feel guilty. I support this household. I work all the time. And I'm tired." Charlotte pushed herself up from the table. "I'm going to bed."

It was still dark when Charlotte got up the next morning. She ate cold oatmeal and peeked inside the bagged lunch Clare had packed for her. Leftover rye bread with corn syrup. She sighed and walked down the narrow front steps of her apartment building. A city bus had just pulled up in front of the complex, and a woman wearing a nurse's smock had just gotten off. She was walking up the steps as Charlotte was walking down. She greeted Charlotte with a weary: "How's your grandmother?"

Charlotte shrugged. "Still crazy."

The neighbor smiled and continued up the stairs. "It's tough getting old."

Charlotte drove the truck south on Interstate 664, pulling the trailer with the backhoe behind her. She worked for *Gentry and Daughters Plumbing and Excavation* in Chesapeake, Virginia. She had to check in and pick up her new assignment. Hers was the only vehicle on the dilapidated Monitor-Merrimac Bridge-Tunnel. Ceiling tiles littered the floor of the tunnel and most of the overhead lights were out. After the tunnel, Charlotte stopped in the middle of the four-mile bridge. She turned off the motor and watched the sun blossom over the Atlantic. "Imagine what it looked like before The Collapse, *Niña*. Fish and birds and boats full of handsome men." She kneaded a knot in her lower back. "Enough daydreaming. Got to get to work."

Charlotte parked beside a well-drilling rig. She unloaded the backhoe and headed to a large garage filled with well-worn tools, pipes and motors. Charlotte was crossing off *Algonquian Ave. sewer leak/water line upgrade* from the jobs list when the door swung open and in came Wanda Gentry, a ruddy woman in her fifties wearing faded coveralls and sporting a friendly swagger. Wanda grinned sheepishly at Charlotte. "Clare called me this morning. Most likely right after you left."

Charlotte dropped the marker on the workbench. "You're kidding?"

Wanda pulled off her John Deere cap and a thin gray braid fell down her back. "Told me about that lawyer who claims to know Joyce. Went on and on about how she's going get her fortune back. About how you and the baby will live in the lap of luxury once she gets the mansion and her pop's oil wells back. I told her it was a fool's errand, but you know how she gets."

"Oh, I know," Charlotte said. "She's single-minded about finding Joyce." Charlotte tapped her forefinger on the next item on the jobs list. "I'd like to handle this one. *Install a gray-water irrigation system.* That recycles wastewater from baths and showers, right?"

Wanda nodded. "It's for a farm in southern Chesapeake, close to the North Carolina border. The owner's a good friend of mine. She's bought an old apple orchard, and I wish her well. All that reaching and bending to fertilize each blossom, whew, it's a lot of work."

"Nanna talks about the Sutherland peach orchard all the time. Makes it sound like paradise."

"Oh, I remember the peach orchard," Wanda said. "I helped my father tear it down after he built Clare's house." Wanda gave a bitter chuckle. "She wanted to put in a baby pool."

Charlotte nodded. "Nanna's told me about your father. Sounded like he was a good man,"

"He was." Wanda pursed her lips. "Um, there's something else," Wanda said. "But you're not going to like it."

"What?"

"Clare set up a meeting with that lawyer this Friday afternoon," Wanda said. "She wants to borrow the truck, and she wants you to drive her."

Charlotte groaned. "Oh, Nanna."

"I told her you shouldn't be driving all the way to Charlottesville less than a month before your due date. Thought that would throw her off the scent, but she said if you shouldn't be driving to Charlottesville then you shouldn't be digging up leaky drain fields in Williamsburg, either. She had me there so I told her it was okay to take the truck."

Charlotte let out a long sigh. "Thanks. I guess."

Charlotte completed the gray-water installation the next day and returned just before sundown. She unhooked the trailer and moved the truck close to the garage so she could vacuum the truck's upholstery, preparing it for the two-hundred-mile trip to the lawyer's office the next morning. Clare would fidget and complain the whole way if she had to sit on a dirty seat.

Charlotte was returning the vacuum when Wanda came in. "Got some bad news," Wanda said. "Can't let you use the truck tomorrow."

Charlotte crammed the vacuum into the crowded closet and turned to Wanda. "I don't know if I'm happy or sad to hear that. What happened?"

"Main break in Norfolk." Wanda picked up a dirty pressure gauge from the workbench. She pulled a rag out of her back pocket and began cleaning the gauge. "Downtown, near the Jones Institute. Caused a huge sinkhole on Colley Avenue. Sarah's already there. I'm heading out in a few minutes. I'll need the truck all weekend to tow the backhoe back and forth."

"You'll need me out there too," Charlotte said. "I'll tell Nanna to cancel her appointment with that lawyer."

"Appreciate that," Wanda said. She returned the cleaned pressure gauge to its proper slot and leaned against the workbench. "I wish you could have met my father."

Charlotte gave a little nod, "Me too."

"Pop was a good man," Wanda said. "Taught me how to dig wells and repair engines, but you already know that. He knew your family long before Clare married that senator. Knew her when she was still married to your grandfather, Andrés Santos."

Charlotte shook her head. "Nanna never mentioned that."

"Yep, he did some volunteer work for Andrés. Helped him with one of his environmental projects, I think, something about returning oyster shells to the Chesapeake Bay."

"I didn't know that," Charlotte said.

"Pop tried to help Clare find Joyce. He contacted the police but they were too busy dealing with The Collapse. Then Pop got sick." Wanda began straightening the workbench, returning wrenches to their proper place and collecting stray screws and washers. "Clare's wasting her time, if you ask me. She ought to forget about it. Let the past stay in the past."

Charlotte didn't answer. She tapped the next item on the jobs list. "Repair deep well submersible pump. I can take care of that tonight." She picked up the broken pump and began taking it apart.

Wanda stopped her. "It's not the motor. The pump's got a bad check valve. Motor pushes the water up, but it doesn't stay up. As soon as the motor stops, the water slides back down into the ground."

Charlotte rummaged through the supplies until she found a replacement valve. "Nanna only has one picture of Joyce and it's forty years old," Charlotte said as she worked. "She emailed it everywhere. To hospitals, to lawyers, to the police. Never heard back. Not even from the police."

"The police were too busy dealing with all the dead men to worry about the whereabouts of a swindler," Wanda said. "It's like that pump you're working on. Everything's humming along fine, water's going where it's supposed to go, but let that check valve break and the water starts going wherever it pleases. So it sinks right back into the well because that's what water does. It doesn't want to come out of a faucet just to wind up as somebody's piss."

Wanda moved close. "Joyce was tired of being everybody's piss. Clare knows that. Pop told me how Clare treated her family. Her husband, her mother, hell, even her daughter." Charlotte tensed at the mention of Amanda. "Clare didn't care about anybody except herself. That's the real reason the Sutherlands lost their fortune. The Collapse hit, Joyce saw an opportunity, and she took it."

12 Red Eyes

"Forty years!" Clare crumpled on the threadbare floral loveseat, the largest piece of furniture in the sparse living room. "I've searched for Joyce for forty years, and now Wanda says *NO!*"

Charlotte stood over Clare, hands on hips. "Just call the lawyer and reschedule."

"Reschedule for when? After the baby is born? Do you think you'll want to leave your daughter to drive me to Charlottesville? You think I'm crazy, don't you? You and Wanda. I know you talk about me. *Crazy old Clare, she thinks she can get her mansion back.*"

Charlotte yawned and rubbed her back. "I'm exhausted, Nanna. I don't want to argue." She plopped heavily next to Clare and placed her hand on Clare's bone-thin shoulder. "I know this is important to you. It's important to me too."

"No, it's not," Clare moaned. "You're not like me. You won't ignore your daughter when she needs you the most." She balled her hands into tight fists and banged them against her forehead. "I have to do this. Have to. Please. I can't bring Amanda back but I can bring Joyce to justice."

Charlotte reluctantly gave in. "I'll call Wanda and tell her I'm taking Friday off, but we'll have to get up early to catch the bus to Charlottesville."

Clare trembled with every step down the narrow staircase. Charlotte followed, carrying Clare's battered suede suitcase. Inside the suitcase, Clare had packed a hodgepodge of papers to give to the lawyer, including Amanda's black-and-white composition notebook, plus two bag lunches for the long bus trips to Charlottesville and back. She hadn't packed any clothes since they weren't spending the night. The sun was barely peeking over the horizon when they reached the bus stop. Clare frowned at the plastic bench, "Dirty," she mumbled, brushing at the faded graffiti. "What time is it?"

"Six-fifteen," Charlotte said. She took a seat, still holding Clare's suede suitcase. "Bus arrives at six-twenty."

Clare pulled a faded lace handkerchief from her purse and placed it on the bench beside Charlotte. She sat on the handkerchief and took the suitcase out of Charlotte's arms, holding it tight against her chest like a shield. Across the street, the front windows of the abandoned automobile-dealership-turned-fundamentalist church sparkled in the morning light. "I wish a giant earthquake had caused The Collapse. Then it would be God's fault."

"That would've destroyed the infrastructure. Roads, bridges, tunnels."

"Tunnels," Clare shivered. She patted Charlotte's leg. "My ever-practical granddaughter, Amanda didn't have a practical bone in her body." She closed her eyes. "Or maybe she did and I wasn't paying attention."

Charlotte stood up and stared down the empty street.

"Amanda was trapped in the tunnel," said Clare.

"You're just going to upset yourself talking about this."

"Joyce's son was with her. I can't remember his name." Clare covered her ears. "Oh, God. Oh, God."

"Nanna, don't."

"So much death." Clare squeezed her eyes shut. "I should have listened to Andrés. He saw what was happening." She rocked forward, as if she were about to throw up. "I had a baby boy, did I tell you that? His name was John, after his father. John Steele, Jr. He didn't live a week."

"The bus will be here soon," Charlotte said.

"The tunnel. The tunnel. I can still smell the stench of all those dead men." Clare rocked back and forth. "I can still hear the screaming."

The bus arrived, and a neighbor wearing a nurse's smock got off. "Nanna, we have to go," Charlotte said. Clare didn't move. The bus driver called to Charlotte, saying she couldn't wait. Charlotte took the suitcase out of Clare's white-knuckled grip and kneeled beside her. "Nanna?"

Clare's lips trembled. "It's my fault," she whispered. "It's all my fault."

The bus driver called out impatiently, "Are you getting on, or aren't you? I have a schedule to keep."

Charlotte looked from Clare to the waiting bus. She stood and asked the neighbor to take Clare back to her apartment. "She'll be all right once she's inside," Charlotte said. She helped Clare stand and gave her a hug. "It's okay, Nanna. You stay here. I'll find out what happened to Joyce, I promise."

The bus stopped three more times: Hampton, Newport News and Williamsburg, each time taking on a passenger or two. Without exception, every passenger paused when they saw Charlotte, shocked to have a pregnant young woman in their midst. Some asked to touch Charlotte's belly, others just stared. One old woman became hysterical, and the driver had to stop and remove her from the bus. Young women were rare enough, but a pregnant young woman was a melancholy remembrance of the past and a hopeful portent of the future.

Charlotte opened Clare's battered suitcase and pulled out Amanda's old black-and-white composition notebook. The pages were yellowed, the edges frayed. The first entries were covered with flowers and hearts, and drawings of horses with flowing manes.

Happy Birthday to me, Happy Birthday to me, Happy Birthday, dear Amanda, Happy Birthday to me. I am ten years old today. Daddy gave me a new riding helmet. Grandmother gave me a new coat and breeches. She said I could ride the stallion. Mom invited Dr. Jacobs' grandsons to my party. It was fun.

Charlotte flipped through the pages.

Grandmother had another stroke so Mom hired a woman named Joyce Smith to take care of her. She talks funny. She says 'ain't' instead of 'isn't.' She has a son named Kingsley. He likes Skittles and Captain America.

The bus pulled into the Richmond station and Charlotte got off. She ate her packed lunch: a crunchy barley-and-oatmeal patty. She ate Clare's lunch, too, and licked the crumbs off the brown paper. She walked past dusty vending machines to the water fountain. The water was cloudy. She let it run until it cleared before she took a long drink. She checked the schedule; the bus was late. She settled on a bench and returned to the notebook.

Joyce's two sisters work at the mansion now. I think they're on drugs. One of them is nice but the other is really mean. Mavis is the nice one. She reads romance novels all the time. Grandmother is afraid of the mean one. So am I. I wish Clare was here. I hardly see her anymore. She's always with the senator. I wish she would fire Joyce and her sisters, except then I wouldn't have Kingsley.

A photograph fell out of the notebook. It was of Amanda when she was a young teen. She was smiling. Beside her was a fat boy with a goofy grin. In the background was a woman with frizzy brown hair. Charlotte turned the photo over. *Amanda, Kingsley and Joyce.* Charlotte tenderly stroked the image of Amanda before returning the photo to the notebook. She flipped through the pages.

Life is unbearable. I heard that the last man in Virginia died last night. He killed himself with a gun, just like Daddy. Women are all alone now. I'll be twenty-four years old in September and I desperately want a baby. I'm going to the Jones Institute to try artificial insemination. Bringing a baby into this world is insane, but I have to try. Otherwise I might as well die, too.

Charlotte flipped to the final entry in the notebook to a poem entitled, "Amanda's Lament."

How can I miss what I have never known?
I hear his art, feel his music, and taste his tender touch.
But I am Lot.
My lover turned to salt, my land destroyed.
By peace. And war. And want and need.
By endless miles of oil and earth alloyed.
My world is muted sameness,
No passions feed my soul.
What squandered shadows do I cast
In fractured daybreak, longing for the past?

The bus arrived and Charlotte put away the notebook. She took a window seat, and the monotonous brown and gray Virginia landscape blurred by, punctuated only by evergreens and an occasional daffodil. No animals. No birds. Not even a dead raccoon picked at by turkey vultures.

Someone tapped Charlotte's shoulder. "When are you due?" Charlotte looked up. An attractive pregnant woman with olive skin and a gently arched nose was standing in the aisle.

Charlotte's mouth opened in shock. "You're pregnant!" She suddenly winced and rubbed the small of her back.

"Are you nauseous?" the woman asked, hovering over Charlotte. "Should I tell the driver to pull over?"

"No," Charlotte said. "Just a backache. I've had it for a few days."

The young woman nodded and rubbed her left side. "Mine's in my hips, just above my leg joint. Dr. Fells warned me that I might not have a typical pregnancy." She pointed to the empty seat beside Charlotte. "May I?"

"Yes, please." Charlotte moved her suitcase, and the young woman sat.

"Are you seeing Dr. Fells, too?" the young woman asked.

"Who?"

"Ray Fells. At the medical center in Charlottesville. Her real name is *Rachel* but I've heard she prefers *Ray*. The only place I see other pregnant women is in Dr. Fells' office. Isn't that where you're going?"

"Actually I'm going to—"

"Amazing woman. I'm one of her first human trials, I'm proud to say." The young woman thumped her round belly.

"I'm not—"

The young woman held up her hand. "Yes, I know what you've heard, and it's all true. Dr. Fells can be very temperamental, but genius must be allowed. After all, she's changing the world. She's—" The young woman suddenly gasped and stood up from her seat. "Look! Look! There!" She leaned over Charlotte as windows flew open and hands reached out. The bus rolled to a stop and filled with excitement. "Beside the road! She made them!"

A herd of white-tail deer were grazing on the side of the road. Does and fawns, no bucks. Charlotte was too stunned to speak. She'd never seen anything so beautiful. She finally regained her voice and stammered, breathlessly, "How...how did they clone so many?"

"They're not clones," the young woman said. "They're genetically engineered. Dr. Fells made them. She's a genius. Look at their eyes. They're red. Everything from now on will have red eyes."

"Red eyes? What do you mean? Why will everything have red eyes?"

The bus driver ordered passengers back to their seats.

"We'll talk later," the young woman said with a superior grin. She returned to her original seat and the bus picked up speed. It pulled into the Charlottesville station twenty minutes later. Charlotte asked the driver for directions to Linda Setter's office, the attorney who'd contacted Clare. "Not too far. Just follow the signs to the public library. Ms. Setter's office is next door."

Charlotte followed the signs, passing a statue of the early American explorers Lewis and Clark and their Shoshone guide, Sacagawea. An old woman with matted hair sat under the statue, her hand held out to Charlotte. "It's my fault," she mumbled. "It's all my fault."

"You sound like Nanna," Charlotte said. She gave the old woman a dollar.

Piles of dusty, disorganized books dating back to when Linda Setter's grandfather worked for Joyce were stacked from floor to ceiling. A framed skunk skin hung on the wall. Linda Setter was as disheveled as her office. Painfully thin with sallow skin and messy hair, she wore a misbuttoned shirt and a gray skirt. On her desk was a plate of crumbly muffins. "Take as many as you want," Linda said, pushing away the muffins. "One of my clients brought them in. I have celiac disease so I can't eat wheat, which means there's almost nothing for me to eat. In the old days, sufferers lived off meat, fruit and vegetables. All I can eat is rice and corn."

Charlotte gratefully took a muffin. "My grandmother used to own a peach orchard," she said, wolfing down the muffin.

Linda pursed her thin lips. "Beyond comprehension, isn't it? All the food they had back then. No wonder everyone was fat," she said, mournfully glancing at the muffins. She frowned and leaned forward in her chair. "Where is your grandmother? I thought she was coming."

Charlotte wiped her mouth, "So did I. She has phobias and couldn't get on the bus. They seem to get worse every year."

Linda nodded knowingly. "Her generation has trouble functioning in our brave new world. Tell me, Charlotte, what does your grandmother hope to accomplish?"

"Justice," Charlotte said. "My grandmother blames Joyce for the fall of the Sutherlands." She finished the muffin and asked for another.

"Of course," Linda handed her the plate.

Charlotte balanced the plate on her lap and ate a second muffin and then a third, crumbs falling on her denim jumper. "She wants the mansion and oil wells back, and she wants Joyce to go to jail," Charlotte said. She brushed crumbs off her pregnant belly. "Sorry, I'm hungry all the time. Eating for two."

Linda gave Charlotte a patronizing smile. "Your grandmother's message said Joyce Smith worked for your family."

Charlotte nodded; her mouth full of muffin. "She took care of Nanna's mother, Leslie Sutherland." She swallowed and wiped her mouth. "Could I have a drink of water?"

Linda stiffened. "Of course," she left her office and returned with a glass of murky water.

Charlotte examined the water and took a hesitant sip. She drained the glass in one huge gulp and smacked her lips. "There's a lot of iron in this water, manganese, too. Are you on city water?" Linda nodded. Charlotte placed the glass on Linda's desk. "A good sequestering agent would clear that up," Charlotte said with a burp. "Excuse me." She burped again. "Sorry. Joyce was some sort of nurse. Nanna's fuzzy about the details."

"The alleged crime occurred decades ago," Linda said. "That's a long time. What else does your grandmother remember?"

Charlotte opened her suitcase. "Nanna has some papers she wanted me to give you, including a photo of Joyce when she worked for her family." She pulled out the photograph of Amanda, Joyce and Kingsley, and handed it to Linda.

Linda studied the photo for a quiet moment, and then returned it to Charlotte. "Anything else?"

"Joyce handled all the finances for the Sutherland estate. Paid the bills, did the shopping. She decided who worked at the mansion and how much they were paid. Cooks, chauffeurs, stable grooms. She had her own little kingdom. She'd write the checks and give them to my great-grandmother to sign. Same with the contracts. Nanna said Leslie would sign whatever Joyce put in front of her."

"Who gave Joyce this authority?"

Charlotte looked down and brushed more crumbs off her belly. "I don't know. Nanna, I suppose."

"Do you have copies of the contracts Leslie Sutherland signed when she was under Joyce's care?"

"Only one." Charlotte rummaged through her papers. "For the sale of eleven mares." She handed Linda the contract. "Nanna says Joyce built a wall around Leslie. No one could get in and figure out what was going on."

Linda studied the contract. "This appears to be a legitimate contract." She placed the contract face-down on her desk and folded her hands over it. "Tell me how Leslie died."

Charlotte shifted in her seat. "I wish Nanna was here. Sometimes she says Joyce left Leslie trapped in her wheelchair to die of thirst. Other times she says Joyce pushed her off the belvedere." Linda gasped. "Once she told me Joyce shot Leslie, and another time she said Leslie wasn't even at the mansion when The Collapse started, that Joyce took Leslie with her when she left."

"Where is Leslie buried?"

Charlotte shook her head. "I don't know. That sounds crazy, but all I have is Nanna's word." Linda jotted down notes. "Do you know where Joyce lives?" Charlotte asked. "Couldn't we just call the police?"

Linda put aside her notepad and leaned back in her chair. "There are a few problems. Virginia has a statute of limitation on fraud that has long expired."

"What about murder? What about Nanna's claims that Joyce murdered Leslie?"

"There's no proof of murder," Linda said. "And even if there were, crimes committed during the first years of The Collapse are seldom prosecuted. Records from that time are unreliable and, frankly, with so much death, trying to prove the murder of one elderly woman would be fruitless."

Charlotte gritted her teeth. "So this was a complete waste of time."

"Not necessarily. You could—" Linda hesitated. "I mean, I might be able to put you in contact with Joyce." Once again she studied the contract for the eleven mares. "My mother is in her upper fifties, so she was alive when my grandfather was practicing law." She looked up at Charlotte. "I showed her the photograph your grandmother sent me, the one of the antique cupboard. She thinks she's seen it."

Charlotte scooted forward in her chair. "Does she know where it is?"

Linda nodded. "At the medical center, but don't get your hopes up. Your claim of ownership is tenuous. Forty years is a long time. Like I said, things change."

Charlotte suddenly buckled in her chair and let out a loud groan.

Linda rushed over. "Are you all right? Do you need a doctor?"

"I don't know," Charlotte said. "I might be in labor."

13 An Old Friend

Linda Setter escorted Charlotte to the trolley stop in front of the public library, holding her arm all the while to make sure she didn't fall. "The trolley is free and will take you to the medical center. I'll call ahead and have someone meet you at admissions," Linda said.

"Can't you come with me?"

Linda tensed. "No, um, I'd rather not. I'm not the most popular person at the medical center."

Charlotte frowned. "Why?"

"Don't worry about it," Linda said. "My mother works the admissions desk. She's a pistol, but she'll take care of you." The trolley arrived and Charlotte climbed aboard. Linda told the driver to drop Charlotte off at the front entrance of the medical center. "One last thing," Linda said, "Sometimes it's better to let the past stay in the past."

"I've heard that advice before," Charlotte said. Linda waved goodbye as Charlotte found a seat and the trolley jolted forward. An elderly passenger sitting near her smiled and gently touched Charlotte's forearm. "So good to see a young person," she said. The trolley weaved around an abandoned construction site. A tall, rusted crane was engulfed by thick vines of wild grape, supple honeysuckle and hairy poison ivy. Young trees pushed the crane's bucket toward the sky, and a faded plastic fence encircled the site. The trolley passed a university with white pillars and a tall statue of Thomas Jefferson. It paused beside a quiet athletic field to take on a passenger. Outside, one lone woman walked the track. The trolley started up again, and minutes later arrived at the medical center. The driver pointed to the front door. "Admissions is in the lobby."

The wiry, gray-haired admissions clerk had a striking resemblance to Linda Setter, only older. She was busy admitting a patient when Charlotte arrived. Behind her desk, an open door led to a well-appointed lecture hall where a dozen or so women listened to an attractive blonde wearing a white lab coat, standing at a podium. Her voice drifted into the lobby.

"No installments. No bartering," the blonde told her audience. "Full payment must be received before each implant. If you can't afford the procedure or can afford only one implant, you should leave now. There is a one-in-four chance of a successful pregnancy with each implant—25 percent—and the odds aren't cumulative. They don't improve with each subsequent try.

"But funds alone won't secure an implant. Originals must be available for medical examination. If you intend to carry someone else's clone, both you and the original must undergo medical screening. We do not accept cells from deceased originals, so don't try to dig up Queen Elizabeth or Catherine the Great." A small rustle of laughter filled the room as the blonde added one last point. "And, obviously, no males."

Charlotte didn't notice the admissions clerk staring at her and drumming her fingers. The clerk cleared her throat loudly and snapped out a very impatient, "Next!"

"I'm sorry," Charlotte said as she handed the clerk her insurance card.

"Should be," the clerk said. "What's your name?"

"Charlotte Sutherland."

"Date of birth?"

"August 12th, 2033."

The clerk sniffed her disapproval. "Twenty-four years old and already pregnant? You must be rich." Before Charlotte could answer that she wasn't rich at all, the clerk barked the next question. "Who's your doctor?"

"I think I'm in labor."

"Congratulations. Who's your doctor?"

"I'm from out of town."

"So you don't have a doctor," the clerk said in a sour tone. "Getting pregnant must be easy where you come from."

"I *do* have a doctor. She's in Norfolk. I'm not due for two weeks!"

"Got that wrong, didn't you?"

"I had to meet with an attorney."

"I know," the clerk said. "She called me."

On the other side of the lobby, the elevator door opened and a small, hunched doctor with a severe limp came out. She wore her long gray hair like a braided tiara, and her skin was the color of lightly brewed tea. She hobbled to the admissions desk. "Are you Charlotte Sutherland?" she asked. The older woman's voice was deep and soothing.

Charlotte nodded, "yes."

"Splendid!" the old woman said. "Linda Setter called me." She took Charlotte's calloused hands in both of hers, as if they were the best of friends. "My name is Dr. Cama, but you shall call me Bapsi." She tapped her bony knuckles on the admissions desk. "Did you hear that, Betty? This young lady is one of Linda's clients." Bapsi turned back to Charlotte. "Linda is Betty's daughter. Delightful girl and a fine solicitor; she just started her own practice last year."

"Pain in the neck," Betty grumbled, as she returned Charlotte's insurance card. "Too much like my father, not enough like me. I don't know how she can be my clone and end up a lawyer like him."

"Oof," Bapsi waved her hand dismissively. "Linda is a dear girl. So smart. So attractive. No wonder you wear such a lovely smile."

Betty scowled, "You think this is a smile on my face?!" She gestured to the open door of the lecture hall and at the blonde stepping down from the podium. "Dr. Fells is back. You have no idea what I have to put up with. The way she treats—"

"I'm so sorry, Betty," Bapsi said. "But I do have to rush." She grabbed Charlotte's suitcase and herded Charlotte toward the elevator. She called back to Betty over her shoulder, "Please let me take you out to lunch tomorrow, Betty. I want to hear all about Linda's new practice."

"I'll be lucky if I have time to go anywhere tomorrow with Dr. Fells around," Betty answered. "Chief Holland is back too, of course. Can't have one without the other. If you knew half of what…."

Betty's complaining faded as Charlotte and Bapsi reached the elevator. Bapsi entwined her arm around Charlotte's muscular bicep, "Sugar sweetens the bitterest tea," she said with a smile.

Charlotte glanced back at the blonde in the lecture hall. "Was that Dr.

Fells talking to those women?"

Bapsi raised her eyebrows. "You've heard of Ray Fells? Linda told me you were a plumber from Hampton."

"I talked to one of her patients on the bus," Charlotte said. "You won't believe what I saw. I can barely believe it and I was there."

Bapsi gave a knowing smile. "Tell me!"

"Deer," Charlotte said, and Bapsi laughed with delight. "An entire herd. They were the most beautiful things I've ever seen."

"And they all had red eyes, didn't they?" Bapsi said as she pressed the 'up' button to call the elevator.

Charlotte nodded. "How did you know?"

"They're—" Bapsi's answer was interrupted by a loud alarm. Piercing. Insistent. It rattled the hospital windows.

"What's wrong?" Charlotte asked. "Is there a fire?" A bulky security guard bolted past them, locked the front doors, and pulled out her nightstick. "What's going on?" Charlotte asked, clutching her belly and the baby inside. "Why is she locking the doors?"

A tall black woman strode confidently out of the lecture hall. She had high cheekbones and wore a tailored suit. She reached behind the admissions desk and the alarm stopped. Her voice was strong and calm. "Attention, please. I need everyone to clear the lobby. You can wait in the cafeteria or the gift shop." She called to the bulky guard standing at the front door, "Keep those doors locked until the police arrive." She gestured to Bapsi and Charlotte. "Step away from the elevators, Dr. Cama."

Bapsi didn't move. "My patient is in labor."

"She'll have to wait in the gift shop until I give the all clear."

Bapsi reluctantly obeyed. "That's Odelle Holland," she whispered as she escorted Charlotte away from the elevators. "She's in charge of hospital security. I delivered her thirty-nine years ago next November. Six pounds, twelve ounces. Perfect Apgar score. She's not a clone, you know. You can tell by her age. Anyone over thirty isn't a clone. They're either conceived naturally or through artificial insemination." Bapsi glanced around before adding, "She was natural. I knew her parents."

Two more guards arrived, both carrying nightsticks, neither wearing a gun. The two guards and Chief Holland waited by the elevators. One of the elevators dinged and the door opened. Inside stood a ragged white woman holding an infant; her dress was faded and her sandals were broken. The woman sank to the floor when she saw the guards, the infant still in her arms. She scooted into a corner and started to cry. "My baby! My baby!"

Odelle stepped inside and carefully pried the infant out of her arms.

The woman's cries turned into slobbering shrieks. "No! No! You can't take my baby!" She struggled against the two guards dragging her out of the elevator. The bulky guard unlocked the front doors and the two guards pushed and pulled the shrieking woman out of the hospital and into a waiting police car.

Odelle returned to the admissions desk. In clipped words, she announced that everyone could resume their activities. She headed back to the elevators, as did Bapsi and Charlotte.

"Poor thing," Bapsi said. "She probably couldn't afford the cost of a pregnancy."

"Or didn't qualify," Odelle said, still holding the infant. "The baby's real mother's waiting for me in the nursery." They entered the elevator, and just as Odelle hit the button for the fourth floor, the infant spat viscous white slime all over the lapel of her tailored suit. "Ugh!" Odelle grimaced and held the baby at arm's length.

Bapsi offered to take the drooling baby, and Odelle gladly accepted. She pulled a tissue out of her pocket to clean her lapel. "Thank God Ray already has a daughter," Odelle said. "Child care definitely isn't in my repertoire."

Charlotte cooed at the baby and touched her tiny arm. "What happened?" she asked.

Odelle finished cleaning her lapel before answering. "The city has only eight uniformed police officers and two patrol cars," she said. "Usually that's more than enough. Loitering and panhandling are the most common complaints, with the occasional robbery. Nothing like the old days, from what I hear." Bapsi nodded in agreement. "Murder and rape hardly exist. But kidnapping is another matter entirely. The most frequently committed major crime in the country and the most despised. And it's getting worse. Last year we had seventeen attempts in twelve months. This was the tenth *attempt* this year and it's only March." The baby began to bubble and Odelle quickly moved to the opposite corner of the elevator.

"That was the tenth kidnapping this year?" Charlotte asked, alarmed.

"Tenth attempt," Odelle emphasized. Her voice filled the elevator, and she stood taller. "No child has been kidnapped from this hospital since I've been in charge of security."

"Betty tells me you and Dr. Fells were on holiday," Bapsi said. "I was so glad to hear that you two could get away. Both of you work so hard. Where did you go?"

"The B&B at Sugar Hollow."

"Anniversary?"

Odelle smiled. "Something like that."

The elevator stopped at the fourth floor, and Bapsi handed the baby back to Odelle. She turned right, toward the nursery, holding the dripping baby at arm's length, while Bapsi turned left, toward maternity.

Bapsi led Charlotte to a pleasant room with a bed, sofa and private bathroom. A nurse came in with a hospital gown, and Charlotte stripped out of her denim maternity jumper right there in front of Bapsi. She'd never had reason to be shy and didn't bother going into the bathroom to change. "Would you like to make a phone call? Is there anyone we should contact?" Bapsi asked after Charlotte slipped on the hospital gown. She patted the bed. "Mother? Wife?"

Charlotte stretched out on the bed. "I live with my grandmother," she yawned. "I'll call her later."

"Who's your doctor?" Bapsi asked, as she felt Charlotte's abdomen.

"Dr. Miles-Johnson," Charlotte said, yawning and stretching her arms overhead. "At the Jones Institute in Norfolk."

"And you've seen her regularly for prenatal care?"

"Uh huh," Charlotte murmured, closing her eyes.

"Excellent!" Bapsi finished the exam and covered Charlotte with a blanket. "You're carrying low. Did your doctor tell you that?"

"Uh uh," Charlotte grunted.

Bapsi made a few notes in Charlotte's chart. "You look so familiar, Charlotte. I wonder if I've met your mother." No answer. Charlotte was falling asleep.

Charlotte woke early the next morning and immediately buzzed the nurse. When the nurse arrived, Charlotte sat up. "My back hurts," she said.

"That's not unusual," the nurse said. She examined Charlotte. "Five centimeters. I'll tell Dr. Cama."

The nurse left and Charlotte slipped on her shoes. She wandered out of her room and down the quiet halls of the maternity ward, all the while kneading her fist into her lower back. A voice called from the next room.

"Hey! Didn't I talk to you on the bus?" It was the pregnant woman who'd told Charlotte about the deer with red eyes. "Are you in labor, too?" the woman asked.

"Yeah," Charlotte said, rubbing her back, "and it's a bitch. I'm not due for two weeks."

"I'm being induced. Dr. Fells says I'll be a mother before midnight." The woman beckoned Charlotte to the chair beside her bed. Charlotte came in and took the seat. "My name is Arielle." She offered Charlotte her hand.

"Charlotte." She shook Arielle's hand. "I'm glad you saw me. I wanted to ask you about those deer we saw on the bus. Why do they have red eyes? Aren't they clones?"

"Not clones," Arielle said. "And not artificial insemination either. They're genetically engineered. Dr. Fells figured it out. She's a genius. Beyond a genius. A miracle worker."

An orderly brought in breakfast: A spoonful of oatmeal and a cup of peppermint tea with a few brown sugar cubes on the side. Arielle balked at the sparse breakfast. "That's all?"

"Dr. Fells' orders," the orderly said. "No solid food until after the baby is born. It's just a precaution, in case you need anesthesia."

Arielle rolled her eyes as the orderly left the room. "Stupid rules." She crushed the sugar cubes into her tea and took a sip. "The deer are only the beginning," she said. "Dr. Fells is bringing back several species of mammals and birds. Sheep, seagulls, some rodents, cows. I've heard rumors that she has a menagerie on the tenth floor. Other universities are using her model to bring back fish and reptiles, even insects. Want to know the most amazing part of it? They can reproduce without doctors. No artificial insemination. No cloning. No medical intervention at all."

"On their own?" Charlotte asked. "Did Dr. Fells cure The Collapse? Did she bring back males?"

"God, no," Arielle said with a laugh. "Dr. Fells believes the effort to bring back males is a waste of intellectual resources. She genetically engineered the deer to reproduce via parthenogenesis, but that's only half the story. What's truly amazing is the way they achieve genetic diversity.

That's essential if you want to avoid the problems associated with cloning."

"Par-then-o—"

"Parthenogenesis," Arielle said. "It's a form of asexual reproduction. Males aren't involved. Some animals are naturally parthenogenetic. A few species of fish and reptiles, for instance. Earthworms are hermaphroditic, which isn't exactly the same but that's why they survived The Collapse. Thank God Dr. Fells didn't turn everyone into a hermaphrodite!" she giggled. "Can you imagine? I'd rather my daughter have red eyes than be half male and half female."

"Your daughter?"

Arielle proudly rubbed her belly. "The first of her kind. She won't have to go through doctors to get pregnant, like you and me." Arielle finished her breakfast and wiped her mouth with the top of the sheet. "Cloning isn't sustainable, you know. It causes too many problems."

"What sort of problems?"

"Clones lack genetic diversity, making them highly susceptible to disease. A virus that kills one can kill them all. Plus, there's the issue of birth defects, especially with clones of clones."

"But, I'm a clone," said Charlotte.

"I know. So am I. First generation clones are usually fine, but second and third generations have problems. They've seen it in animals. They don't live as long as the original."

Charlotte's shoulders sagged. "My baby is a second-generation clone."

"That's what motivated Dr. Fells. She's an original, but her daughter's a clone. Like I told you, she's a genius. She's changing the world."

Charlotte left Arielle and shuffled back to her room. She slumped on the edge of her bed, and cheerlessly ate the breakfast the orderly had left for her. It was just like Arielle's: oatmeal and peppermint tea. Once finished, she walked to the window, rubbing her belly. "I just want you to be healthy, Niña." She left her room again, and wandered the fourth floor, away from maternity. She heard babies crying and instinct drove her to follow their sound. She found the nursery, and stood outside, tapping on the glass windows, smiling at the infants. Each one was wrapped in a yellow blanket. Each one was a clone of her mother. Charlotte stared at the infants until her legs tired. She wandered down the hall until she found Bapsi Cama's office. She knocked on the open door. "Dr. Cama?"

Bapsi was stretched out on a long purple couch, eyes closed and feet propped atop a black pillow. She started when she heard Charlotte. "Come in! Come in!" She struggled to her feet and slipped on her shoes. "Please forgive me for not coming to see you earlier. The night nurse called hours ago. I'm afraid I fell asleep." She welcomed Charlotte into her office. "How do you feel?"

"My back hurts, but mostly I'm starving. All I had for breakfast was a spoonful of oatmeal. Yesterday, I only had muffins for dinner. The orderly said we couldn't have more because of, um," Charlotte paused. "I can't remember."

"Oof!" Bapsi said dismissively. "Silly hospital policy. No wonder you're hungry. A light breakfast is fine during labor. Would you join me for a bite?"

"Yes!" Charlotte said, "Definitely!" Bapsi heated a pot of rice and dal on a small, well-worn cooktop. "Smells wonderful," Charlotte enthused.

"Yes, it does," Bapsi said, as she divided the mixture into two small bowls and handed one bowl and a spoon to Charlotte. "I was able to find a bit of turmeric and garlic to liven it up." She took the other bowl and invited Charlotte to sit on the couch. "In India," Bapsi said, "we used to celebrate children's birthdays with rice and dal, and then bathe them in milk and sprinkle rose petals on their heads. This was supposed to give the child a luxurious life." She turned the kettle on. "Tea and conversation, better than all the medicine in the world. I make my own tea. Dried mint and peelings from my navel orange tree." She sat on the couch next to Charlotte. "How are you getting along?"

A shadow crossed Charlotte's face. "I'm worried about my baby. Whether she'll be healthy."

Bapsi scoffed. "Of course she'll be healthy!"

"She's the clone of a clone," Charlotte said. "She might not live as long as—"

Bapsi took Charlotte's hand. "You're a strong and beautiful young woman. I've delivered more babies than hairs on my head. Don't worry. Your daughter will be fine."

Charlotte relaxed and ate her rice and dal.

An oil portrait of a Tibetan girl hung on the north wall above an overflowing filing cabinet. The girl wore a pink shirt and a pensive smile, with long strings of red beads wrapped around her small body and a gold earring dangling from her left ear.

Photographs hung above the purple couch. The first was of a row of eight dead tigers laid side by side. Two men with shotguns stood behind the tigers. One man was English, the other Indian. Behind them, men in turbans sat atop elephants. "That man," Bapsi pointed to the Indian man holding the shotgun, "that's my great-grandfather. He was a banker before the Partition. Hobnobbed with English aristocracy." She stroked the image of the tigers in the photo. "I'm appalled that anyone could slaughter such magnificent creatures."

The next photo was of a small man standing in front of a boulder. "That's my father," Bapsi said. A winged image was carved into the boulder. "And that's a Zoroastrian angel." The angel's bearded face was in profile, and his wings had three tiers of feathers. "Zoroastrians were driven out of Iran a thousand years ago and sought sanctuary in India. There's a legend that the king of India told them they could not stay. He presented the Persian refugees with a cup of milk filled to the brim. The cup was used to illustrate that India was full and could not accommodate the Iranian refugees. One of the Zoroastrian priests added a bit of sugar to the milk, promising the king that the Zoroastrians would only sweeten India; they would displace no one."

The kettle whistled and Bapsi poured boiling water into her teapot. "I wish I had honey. My uncle raised bees when I was a girl. I do have sorghum molasses. Would you like a little in your tea?"

"Sure," Charlotte said. Bapsi poured the tea, adding a spoonful of molasses to each cup. "I think I should go home," Charlotte said. "Nothing's happening as far as the baby goes. I haven't had any contractions."

"Oh, yes, you have," Bapsi said, smiling. "Those backaches are contractions. You were four centimeters dilated when I examined you last night and five centimeters this morning. Like I said before, I've delivered more babies than hairs on my head. Trust me, you'll have your daughter late tonight or early tomorrow morning."

Bapsi sat beside Charlotte and sipped her tea. When they'd finished, she took Charlotte's bowl and cup and set them on her desk. Bapsi beckoned

Charlotte to stand. "Come. Walk with me," she said, intertwining her arm with Charlotte's. They strolled down the hallway, passing the nursery, heading to maternity. "This is what I think you should do," Bapsi said, "Get dressed and go outside. It's a beautiful Saturday morning. The clean air should move along the birthing process. Take a walk. Ride the trolley. Come back at lunchtime and I'll examine you again."

"That sounds great," Charlotte said. "You don't think it'll hurt the baby, do you?"

"Of course not," Bapsi said. "She'll be fine."

Charlotte eagerly changed into her maternity jumper and hurried out of the medical center. The fresh air was invigorating. In the distance, the Blue Ridge Mountains hinted at the rebirth of spring with ribbons of redbud blooms. Charlotte rode the trolley around the university, past the white pillars and the statue of Thomas Jefferson, and to the athletic field, but this time the field wasn't empty. The stands were filled with fans cheering a heated game of soccer. Teenage girls in ponytails flew across the field.

Charlotte had to search for a place to sit in the crowded bleachers. She found a spot behind a heavy-set redhead and a chatty Asian, and settled in to enjoy the game. The scoreboard said three to zero. One team wore blue and gold, and the other wore red and black. A sweaty referee struggled to keep up. The goalie for the blue-and-gold team was a powerful redhead with curly hair and a broad smile, just like the woman sitting in front of Charlotte. But the goalie wasn't the center of attention—that belonged to a beautiful blonde forward on the blue-and-gold team.

The blonde sprinted across the field, barreling through the red-and-black midfield and evading their defenders. The red-and-black goalie ran to stop her, but couldn't even slow her down. The blonde plowed into the goalie, knocking her asunder, and then kicked the ball so hard it almost tore a hole in the back of the net. A whistle blew and the referee came running. The ref gave the blonde a yellow card and the stands erupted. Boos at the ref and chants of "Abby! Abby! Abby!"

"You can sure tell she's Ray Fells' daughter," the Asian woman said, laughing. "No doubt about that!"

Charlotte wanted to join the conversation. "Dr. Fells has a daughter?"

The heavy-set redhead turned and nodded. "Almost makes Dr. Fells seem human, doesn't it?"

"Shhh," the Asian woman cautioned. She motioned to the top of the bleachers where Dr. Fells was seated. The Asian woman lowered her voice. "Didn't you see her sneak in at halftime? I guess that's why Abby's acting up. She's a completely different person when her mother's not around. She can actually be quite sweet."

Alone, on the highest row of the bleachers, Dr. Fells sat working on her computer, occasionally glancing at the game.

"Abby can be well behaved, especially when Sandy's around," The Asian woman said, "Otherwise she's too much like her mom."

"She is Dr. Fells' clone, after all," the heavy-set redhead said. "For better or worse, our daughters are younger versions of ourselves."

The redheaded goalie made a dramatic save, and the crowd jumped up and cheered, almost drowning out Charlotte's loud groan, "Ahhhh!" Charlotte buckled over, clutching her belly.

"Are you hurt?" the Asian woman asked. "What's wrong?"

"Contraction!"

"What?" The Asian woman jumped up, flustered. She looked at the top of the bleachers and screamed, "Dr. Fells! Dr. Fells! She's in labor! We need you!"

Ray Fells closed her computer and ran down to Charlotte. She kneeled and felt her abdomen. "Help me get her to my car," Ray said. The women helped Charlotte stand and walk down the bleachers.

"Thank you, thank you," Charlotte said repeatedly, holding her belly.

They loaded her into the front passenger seat of a sleek maroon sedan. Ray jumped behind the wheel, revved the engine, and screeched out of the parking lot. She swerved around a deep sinkhole and passed the slow-moving trolley.

Charlotte gripped the door handle every time the sedan took a tight curve. "Thank you for driving me to the hospital."

"What the hell were you doing at that soccer game?"

"Dr. Cama suggested it."

"Stupid old fool."

"She said it would move the labor along."

"She should be fired," Ray said. She pulled up to the emergency room and grabbed a wheelchair. She barked at the first nurse she saw. "Tell Dr.

Cama to get her lazy ass off her couch and meet me in maternity." She helped Charlotte out of the car and into the wheelchair, and then rushed her to the elevator and hit the button for the fourth floor. She leaned against the wall of the elevator and took a deep breath.

"I don't really need a wheelchair," Charlotte said. "The contraction's passed."

Ray scowled down at Charlotte. "You can have that baby in the gutter for all I care." The elevator doors opened on the fourth floor, and Bapsi and two nurses greeted them. Ray ordered the nurses to take Charlotte to her room. Then she turned on Bapsi like a rabid wolf. The entire corridor could hear her rage. "What the hell is wrong with you? Are you senile? Telling a woman in labor to go watch a high school soccer game? She doesn't know the city! What if she'd gotten lost?"

"She's not going to deliver for hours," Bapsi said.

"This isn't like the old days when you were young, Dr. Cama. We don't have so many babies that we can just throw them away."

Bapsi flinched. "Ray, please, listen to me. I told her the fresh air and exercise would move her labor along, and that's exactly what happened."

"Maybe it's time for you to retire," Ray growled.

Back in her room, Charlotte changed into her hospital gown. Bapsi's hands trembled as she examined Charlotte. When she finally spoke, her voice wavered. "You're up to seven centimeters."

"I enjoyed seeing the soccer game," Charlotte said. "I think going outside was good for me."

Bapsi finished the exam and patted Charlotte gently on her knee. "Thank you for saying that." She pulled a tissue from her pocket and blotted perspiration from her nose and forehead. "I have the greatest respect for Dr. Fells. The greatest respect in the world, but sometimes she quite frightens me."

14 Her Face Not Forgotten

Charlotte called Clare to tell her she would be staying another night. She didn't tell her she was in the hospital. "And I didn't tell her I'm in labor," Charlotte told Bapsi after she'd hung up. "She'd have a panic attack. She's afraid all the time. Practically paralyzed. If anything happened to me or the baby—"

"Tell her the truth," Bapsi said. A small amount of confidence had returned to her voice. She entered her notes in Charlotte's chart. "Tell her you're bringing home a healthy baby girl in a day or two." She finished her charting and headed to the door. "You should rest. I'll be back in half-a-sec."

After Bapsi left, Charlotte struggled out of bed and walked to the large window. Outside, the medical-center grounds were quiet. Tiny springtime leaves were popping out on the azaleas and dogwoods. A few medical personnel and patients meandered about the grounds. Bicycles filled the bike rack, and one or two cars and trucks came and went. Nothing special. At least not until a shiny, black limousine turned the corner and parked just below Charlotte's window. A woman wearing a chauffeur's jacket stepped out and opened the back passenger door. Out came two women, as different from one another as a boulder is from a boll weevil.

The first woman was massive. Almost seven feet tall with shoulders as wide as a door, she had bronze skin and a square jaw. The second woman was difficult to pin down. She was pale but animated. Her face looked

135

youthful yet she carried herself like a woman in her sixties. Her dangling diamond earrings cast sparkling prisms on the polished limo as she joked with the chauffeur, affectionately rubbing the driver's back, before heading to the front door. Doctors approached her with handshakes and smiles and she greeted them warmly, like a well-heeled politician talking to constituents. She and her huge companion entered the medical center. A few minutes later, voices filled the hallway outside Charlotte's room.

"I'm taking care of one of your daughter's patients," Bapsi's voice echoed. "I expect her to deliver tonight."

"Is she pregnant with one of those awful rotifer babies?" a second voice asked. "What a horrible name. *Rotifer baby.* Imagine she'll be mighty upset when she figures out a rotifer ain't nothing but a weird bug. Bad enough not having any men around, now Rachel's gone and created a world of freaks." The woman grunted derisively. "She changed the world all right. She's made it worse."

Bapsi stopped outside Charlotte's doorway, the jeweled woman beside her. The massive, square-jawed companion stood silently behind them. "Your daughter is a brilliant scientist and an exceptional physician," Bapsi said. "Her accomplishments with animals are miraculous."

"Maybe so," the woman said as she tugged on one of her dangling diamond earrings. "But she ain't why I'm here." As Bapsi entered Charlotte's room, the woman stared at Charlotte with intense hazel eyes, searching Charlotte's face and scrutinized her belly. She might have stayed there all day had Bapsi not politely, but insistently, closed the door.

"Ohh! Ohh!" Charlotte said, knotting the sheets in her hands. "Contraction! Harder than the last one." Bapsi calmly talked Charlotte through the pain, encouraging her to breathe slowly until the contraction passed. She dabbed perspiration from Charlotte's forehead with a cool washcloth. Slowly, Charlotte's tension eased. She turned to face Bapsi. "Why is cloning a dead person illegal?" Charlotte asked. "Wouldn't that be healthier than cloning clones? Arielle said first-generation clones don't have problems, only second and third generation."

Bapsi gave a startled laugh and affectionately reached for Charlotte's arm. "So many questions!" She checked the time. "We have about twenty minutes until your next contraction." She settled into the chair beside

Charlotte's bed. "Where to start? From what I understand, cloning humans is more difficult than cloning other animals. The nuclei in the cells of primates tend to tear when they're removed. That's what I've heard, um—," she hesitated. "I've never participated in any animal experiments. Saving one life doesn't justify the suffering of another." She paused for Charlotte's protests. When none came, she continued. "As for human beings, both science and the government had to wrestle with all the biological, ethical and spiritual issues surrounding cloning humans." Bapsi squinted at Charlotte. "Are you sure you want to talk about this? Wouldn't you rather relax?"

Charlotte shook her head. "I feel better talking."

An orderly brought in a bucket of ice, placed a few of the ice cubes in a cup, and handed the cup to Charlotte. "This will help cool you down," she said. Charlotte thanked her and sucked on an ice cube. The orderly left the room.

"Let's start with the most definitive issue first," Bapsi said. "Biological. When a cell divides, its chromosomes split into two. At the end of each chromosome is an enzyme called telomerase. Telomerase prevents chromosomes from shortening when they divide, similar to how the stiff tip of a shoelace prevents unraveling. Over time, telomerase weakens and chromosomes grow shorter. As appealing as cloning a saint like Mother Theresa or a Nobel Prize winning physicist like Marie Curie may sound, cloning an aged individual with shortened or damaged chromosomes isn't a good idea.

"Ethically, the fear is that women will choose to clone only certain types of individuals. We don't want a world filled only with saints and scientists any more than we'd want a world filled only with beauty queens. We want a diverse community."

Bapsi leaned back in her chair. "Now spiritually, that's another matter. Our bodies are vessels for our souls. For as long as we live, our soul stays with us. Your soul is whole and intact within you. My soul is whole and intact in me. I don't know if your baby has a soul yet, but once she's born a soul will find her and she will become a person separate from you, as it should be."

"I'm not religious," Charlotte said.

"Not to worry," Bapsi said. "This is just my personal theory. If a dead person is cloned, their original soul wants to return to their original body, even a cloned body. It's a perfect fit, like slipping into a favorite pair of shoes. But there's the problem. Their memories would be a perfect fit, too. What I mean to say is that their memories wouldn't fade."

Charlotte's skepticism showed on her face.

"I know it sounds preposterous," Bapsi said, "but I've seen it happen. I delivered a girl—oof—she must be close to twelve years old by now. She was a clone of her dead grandmother, a great artist. Everyone thought, *this is what we need, an artist to lift our spirits*, but they were wrong. The child possesses all of her grandmother's memories. They never faded."

"Why is that bad?" Charlotte asked.

Bapsi shook her head. "This child remembers everything her grandmother endured, the death of her husband, the death of her sons, even her own death. You said your grandmother is paralyzed with fear?"

Charlotte nodded. "Nanna was supposed to come with me but was too afraid to get on the bus."

"And she's a grown woman," Bapsi said. "Imagine those memories thrust upon a child. Actually, Dr. Fells is the one who criminalized the cloning of dead people. She and Security Chief Holland went to Washington to push through the legislation."

Bapsi gave Charlotte a wry smile and lowered her voice. "I shouldn't gossip, and especially not about Dr. Fells, but I want to tell you this one thing." She closed her eyes and clasped her hands. "I can almost hear my dear father's reprimand: *Remember the woman whose tongue was plucked out for gossiping,* he would say, quoting the Sacred Book of Arda Viraf." Bapsi opened her eyes and moved close.

"Dr. Fells went to Washington D.C. because of her mother, Lily Fells." Bapsi pointed to the door. "You saw her. She was standing at the doorway when I came in. I've known Lily for decades. I wouldn't be here without Lily. The Fells Foundation rebuilt this hospital after The Collapse. The Foundation is dedicated to finding a cure. Lily tried twice to bring back her dead son. Twice!"

Bapsi wiped her eyes with a tissue. "I don't know how she endured it. I lost my sweet little Adar once; I can't imagine losing your son again and again. Lily hired surrogates to carry his clones. One woman was local, the other from West Virginia. I delivered the first boy, the one born to the local woman. Poor little thing suffered terribly. I heard about the second birth through hospital gossip. I don't condone what Lily did, but I can't blame her for trying. He was a delightful boy."

"You met him?"

Bapsi nodded. "Yes, he and I formed a little friendship. I would visit him when he came in for—" Bapsi's eyes widened and she slowly pointed at Charlotte's face. "That's where I've seen you before. Your mother. I never forget a face. Your mother and Lily's son were friends."

15 Lily Fells

Charlotte quickly sat up in bed. "You knew my mother?"

"I believe so," Bapsi said, "What was her name?"

"Amanda," Charlotte said. "How old was she when you knew her? What was she like?"

"She was young. A teenager, I think. Very pretty," Bapsi said. "But what I remember most is her spunk. She stood up to Dr. Joan Barlow, which is no small feat. She asked about the dogs in Joan's lab. She was concerned about their care." Bapsi paused. "I have a thought. Lily might still be in the building. Would you like to speak with her?"

"Yes, definitely!" Charlotte enthused. "This may be my only chance."

Bapsi checked the time. "Three o'clock. I'll see if I can get a message to her." A nurse came in to tell Bapsi that Arielle needed her. Bapsi patted Charlotte's knee. "I'll return as soon as I can. Until then, Vondra will stay with you."

Nurse Vondra Douglas looked like a woman who took no guff. She stood at the foot of Charlotte's bed, hands on hips. "Did Dr. Cama talk to you about pain relief?" she asked after Bapsi had left.

"No," Charlotte said. "We talked about why it's illegal to clone dead people."

Nurse Douglas rolled her eyes. "Oh, for heaven's sake! Did she tell you all her crazy notions about souls hopping from one person to another?" Charlotte nodded, and Nurse Douglas groaned. She plopped heavily into the chair beside Charlotte's bed and rubbed her legs. "Lord, this has been a long day."

"Dr. Cama said she knew a girl who was born with her grandmother's memories."

Nurse Douglas snorted noisily. "Dr. Cama's got a few screws loose, if you ask me. The closest thing to that transferring of memories business I've ever heard was when Dr. Fells gave a lecture about it. Lord, that was boring, I half fell asleep, but I do recall her saying cells have memories. I'd believe Dr. Fells' scientific explanation before I'd believe Dr. Cama's soul-hopping nonsense."

Nurse Douglas slapped her thighs and stood up. "Enough of that foolishness." She checked Charlotte's vitals and told her about her pain-relief options: drugs, epidural, Lamaze. She asked if Charlotte would like a massage to help relax. Charlotte nodded, and Nurse Douglas kneaded the muscles around Charlotte's neck, working out tension and soreness. "Now, there's a story for you," Nurse Douglas said, as she moved to Charlotte's arms and hands. "The real reason Dr. Fells pushed for the law to ban cloning dead people. It isn't dead women Dr. Fells doesn't want cloned. It's dead men. She hates men. Of course she's never met a man, but I guess she's read about them in history books."

"In high school, my history teacher told us the country is better now than before The Collapse. Less wars and crime," offered Charlotte.

Nurse Douglas scoffed as she moved to massage Charlotte's legs and feet. "I don't know about that. People still have a talent for messing up everything." She finished the massage and washed her hands. "Listen to me, gossiping like a school girl. I'm almost as bad as Dr. Cama." She studied Charlotte's chart. "So, how's your pain on a scale of one to ten? Do you want anything before your next contraction?"

"No," Charlotte said. "They're not that bad."

"Good," Nurse Douglas said. "But tell us before the contractions become too painful." She sat down in the chair again and talked about taking care of a newborn, about breast-feeding and diaper changing.

"When can I take her home?" Charlotte asked.

"As soon as Dr. Cama gives the okay," Nurse Douglas said.

Charlotte grimaced and balled her fists. "Another contraction. It hurts!!"

Nurse Douglas tried to talk Charlotte through the contraction, but it wasn't enough. She hit the intercom. "Dr. Cama, Ms. Sutherland's going to need something for the pain."

Moments later, Bapsi rushed in and gave Charlotte an analgesic. "You'll feel better in half-a-sec," she said, her face flushed. She turned to Nurse Douglas. "Vondra, I need you to help me with Arielle." She took Charlotte's hand and spoke quickly. "Charlotte, listen to me. One of the orderlies found Lily Fells. She'll be here in a few minutes. Do you still wish to speak with her? I could ask Lily to come back tomorrow if you don't want to see her now."

"I don't know," Charlotte said. She rubbed her forehead. Her hair was a sweaty mat. "She's Dr. Fells' mother, right?"

Bapsi nodded, "Indeed she is, but don't worry, she's nothing like Dr. Fells. They couldn't be more opposite."

"I look so horrible." She squeezed Bapsi's hand and took a deep breath. "Yes, please. Ask her to come. This may be my only chance. I want to go back to Hampton as soon as I can. Tomorrow, I hope."

"I'll leave the door open for her," Bapsi said. "I'll return before your next contraction. Vondra, please come with me."

Bapsi and Nurse Douglas hurried out of the room. Charlotte could hear them talking. "Arielle's having a difficult time. I need someone to…." Their voices faded.

Now alone in her room, Charlotte gripped the top of her sheets, balling her fists. "I wish I'd never come here. I should have listened to Wanda. I just want to go home." She was close to tears when there was a knock on her door. Charlotte sat up. "Come in," she said, her voice shaky.

The woman at the door was dressed in a black skirt and ivory blouse. Her hair was dark brown and stylish. Her high heels clicked on the linoleum as she calmly entered Charlotte's room. Her face was smooth, her makeup perfect. Only the muddled spots on her hands betrayed her age.

"Hello, my name is Lily Fells."

"Thank you for coming," Charlotte said. "I, um, I saw a herd of deer on my way here. The ones with the red eyes."

"Those deer are my daughter's monstrosities. She's an MD, a PhD, and a bunch of other initials I can't remember to save my soul." She strolled around the room nonchalantly, running her fingers over the flat surfaces as

142

if she were checking for dust, stopping at the foot of Charlotte's bed.

"Dr. Cama said you wanted to talk to me. That I may have known your mother." Charlotte invited the woman to sit in the chair beside the bed, but the woman didn't take it. Instead, she sat on the couch against the wall. "Come on over here, hon," she said, patting the couch. Charlotte had to struggle to get out of bed. She held her belly as she waddled to the couch. "Now," the woman said once Charlotte was sitting beside her, "Tell me your Momma's name."

"Amanda Santos Sutherland," Charlotte said, carefully enunciating each word. "Dr. Cama says she was a friend of your son's."

The woman's eyes narrowed. "Amanda? Hmm? I do recall a girl named Amanda. She may have gone to school with my boy. He attended the finest private school in Williamsburg, of course, St. Andrews Academy."

"That's where my mother went to school," Charlotte said, excited. "How old was she when you knew her? What was she like?"

"It was a long time ago, I barely remember—"

"Anything, please, tell me anything."

The woman touched the corner of her mouth, careful not to smudge her lipstick. "Amanda was very athletic. She and my son rode horses together. Show horses. And they were on the swim team together, as I recall. He was a better swimmer, of course, but she was very good."

"So she was happy?" Charlotte asked. "When you knew her, she was happy?"

"She was happy when she was with my boy. In fact, the only person I can recall making her unhappy was her mother."

Charlotte took a sharp breath. "Nanna?"

"But that's a long story." The woman reached out, her hand hovering over Charlotte's oversized belly. "May I?"

Charlotte hesitated. "Well, um—"

The woman didn't wait for an answer. She rubbed Charlotte's stomach like it was a magic crystal ball. "Beautiful child. Such a beautiful child," she murmured, as if she were in a trance. The woman abruptly stood up from the couch. "What am I thinking? You should be in bed." She helped Charlotte back to bed and stood beside her, hands folded. "I heard you came all the way from Hampton. Is there anything you need?"

"I didn't bring anything for the baby," Charlotte said, settling into bed.

"No diapers. No clothes. Not even a blanket."

"The hospital will take care of all of that. What about you? How are you getting home?"

"Same way I got here, by bus."

"Oh no," the woman said. "You can't take a new baby on that dirty bus. What if it broke down?" She called to her huge companion, who had been waiting outside the door the whole time. "Phoebe Ann, go tell Alfred she's driving this young lady to Hampton tomorrow." The huge woman grunted and prowled away.

"No, that's too much trouble!" Charlotte said.

"Don't be silly; she's happy to do it. Alfred's not her real name, you know. Some jobs just shouldn't be done by a woman." She smoothed Charlotte's sheets and gently tucked her in. "I still call police officers *he*. Guess that's why I don't get along too good with Odelle. Always thinking she's a man." She made a guttural sound in the back of her throat like she was about to spit. "One more thing for me and Rachel to argue about."

She appeared deep in thought as she studied Charlotte. "I better go now," she finally said. "Let you get on with birthing that baby." Emotions flooded her face as she moved away from the bed—joy, concern, and anxious anticipation. "Oh, and by the way, I've taken care of your hospital bill so you won't have to worry about a thing when you're back in Hampton."

"You don't have to do that," Charlotte said. "I have money."

The woman dismissed her protests with a wave. "It's nothing. And don't forget, Alfred will take you home once you're discharged."

Charlotte's eyes filled with tears. "I can't tell you what this means to me. I was supposed to have the baby in Norfolk. Nanna was supposed to be with me. Nothing's gone as planned. Thank you. Thank you so very much."

"Plans," the woman said as she twirled one of her dangling diamond earrings. "Plans are funny things."

Charlotte's labor continued through the night. Either Bapsi or Nurse Douglas was with her during the night, and both were with her at the end. "Breathe. Breathe. Push. Push," Bapsi said. Nurse Douglas held her hand and wiped her forehead. Charlotte's room glowed red, orange, and gold. The rising sun streamed in through her window. Daybreak.

And the baby was born.

PART III

16 Tigers

Cold grabbed him. A blue ball suctioned wet slime from his nose and mouth. He tried to push the ball away but his arms merely flailed. Cold washed more slime from his face and his body, and placed him on a hard table, which he didn't like at all. Bright lights hurt his eyes. Monstrous shadows hovered above him. He blinked, trying to focus. He blinked again and a familiar face emerged from the fog. Bapsi Cama. She looked terrible. Wrinkled and old, like Rogue from the X-Men had sucked the life force out of her. Her voice was as loud as thunder. "Call Chief Holland," she said. "Wake her up, if you have to. Don't tell anyone else."

Another voice thundered back. "What if Dr. Fells answers?"

"She's going to find out sooner or later," Bapsi said.

"Stop yelling!" Kingsley shouted.

Bapsi wrapped a yellow blanket around him but it was way too tight. Kingsley couldn't move his arms and hands. He wanted to cover his ears and his eyes. Everything was too loud and too bright. "My arms are stuck!" he yelled. "I can't move!" But Bapsi didn't loosen the blanket; instead, she carried him through the air, which was quite a shock.

The next time Kingsley blinked, he saw the one person he most wanted to see. "Amanda! You're here!" But she looked different. Older and her hair was short. She looked more like a grown-up woman than a teenager.

Kingsley had a million questions. "Are we still in Hampton? Or is this the medical center in Charlottesville? I see Dr. Cama but where's Dr.

147

Barlow? Where's Mom? How'd we get out of the tunnel? Why do you look older? Why does Dr. Cama look so awful? Why'd you cut your hair?" He asked but Amanda didn't answer. All she did was smile and stroke his face.

Bapsi slumped in the chair beside the bed. She held her forehead with both hands, as if it weighed a hundred pounds. "Have you ever read *The Jungle Book*?" she asked, not looking up. "It's the story of a boy who battles a tiger named Shere Khan. Everyone rejoiced when the tiger died." Her voice cracked, and she rubbed her eyes with the palms of her hands.

Charlotte nuzzled Kingsley's bald head. "Isn't she perfect?"

"She?" Kingsley said. "Amanda, why are you calling me *she*?"

"I love the cute little sounds she makes," Charlotte said.

This infuriated Kingsley. "I don't make *cute little sounds*!"

Bapsi's eyes were red. "I took Adar to the zoo in Mumbai when he was two years old," she said. "I wanted him to see a real tiger before they all disappeared. I wish I hadn't. The zoo was a disgrace. All the animals were sick. They only had one poor, pathetic tiger left, and he was old and filthy. Nothing like the magnificent animals in my great-grandfather's photo. His fur was matted and he had sores all over his body from spending every moment of his miserable life in a cage." She pulled a tissue from her pocket and wiped her eyes. "We'd do anything to see a real live tiger again. Pay any price to hear him roar, to watch him roam and rule the jungle. We mourn their disappearance the way a mother mourns the death of her child."

Charlotte stopped nuzzling Kingsley. "You're scaring me, Dr. Cama. Is something wrong with my baby?"

The rising sun illuminated Bapsi's face like candles on an antique Persian rug. She rubbed her thin, boney hands together as if she were kneading worry beads. "Stories tell us of the extremes. Like the tale of the vengeful and lame Shere Khan. They only tell us the bad. Reality is much deeper."

"What are you saying?" Charlotte asked.

"Your child is a gift from another era. Like a tiger found alive in a long forgotten jungle."

"I don't understand," Charlotte said. Kingsley felt the same way. Why was Bapsi so sad?

"Your baby is a boy."

Charlotte gasped.

Kingsley howled, "Of course I'm a boy!"

"That's impossible!" Charlotte said.

"You didn't know?" Bapsi asked.

"She's my clone!" Charlotte said. "How can she be a boy?"

"Maybe your doctor found a frozen embryo and switched—"

"Without telling me?" Charlotte carefully peeled away Kingsley's blanket, which he didn't like at all.

"Stop. Stop," Kingsley said. He tried to push away her hands but his arms wouldn't cooperate. "Amanda, what are you doing?"

Charlotte's face paled. "No, no, please, not a boy," she moaned and clutched Kingsley against her chest, rocking him back and forth. He could hear her heartbeat. He could feel her breath on the top of his head. *What was going on?*

Bapsi wrapped her arms around Charlotte's shoulders. "Whatever happens," she whispered, "regardless of how he came to be, your son will need your love as much as a daughter."

It must be the drugs. That's what Kingsley decided. All the gene-therapy treatment and pain pills Dr. Barlow had given him for his headaches had messed with his brain. He was like those prescription-drug addicts back in New Orleans, the ones who'd buy stolen Percocet from his mother. *That's some weird shit*, they'd say. *Thought I was a bird flying through the Andes, man.*

"All I need is a good night's sleep," Kingsley said. He closed his eyes. "That's what Floyd used to say. Everything looks better after a good night's sleep." It had to be a drug-induced hallucination, or maybe just a nightmare. Bapsi hadn't turned into an old woman. Amanda hadn't grown up overnight and cut her hair. She didn't cry when Bapsi told her he was a boy.

Kingsley slept soundly until he was woken by someone placing him on a high table under a bright lamp. Strangers unwrapped his blanket, and once again he was cold and naked in front of everyone. He couldn't see with the light in his eyes but he could feel someone pressing his stomach and thumping his chest. They stuck something in his ears and pricked his heel with a needle. "That hurts!" Kingsley wailed. "Where's Amanda? Where's my mom?" No one answered. Kingsley kicked his foot until he was rewrapped in his blanket and placed in Charlotte's arms.

"What's your assessment?" Bapsi asked.

"His color is good," the stranger said. Kingsley's eyes slowly focused and he could see that the stranger was a woman wearing a white coat. "Pulse and breathing are strong. Six pounds, two ounces. I'm giving him an Apgar score of eight."

"That's good," Charlotte said. "Right? That's good, isn't it?"

A harsh voice came from the hall. "Your immune system has temporarily suppressed his tumor growth." Everyone turned. A blonde in a lab coat stood at the doorway. Kingsley blinked, forcing his newborn eyes to focus. He couldn't see her, but her voice scared him. "He won't survive. He has the same Y-Chromosome Linked Tumor Syndrome that killed every male in the last forty years. Better if you don't get attached."

Kingsley's lower lip quivered. The woman came closer. With every step she took, Kingsley's fear grew. As she came into view, his fear was replaced by shocked amazement. Blonde hair and peaches-and-cream skin like Clare Sutherland but she had Joyce's sharp hazel eyes. The perfect mixture of Sutherland and Smith. She stood beside Charlotte's bed and Kingsley read her nametag: *Dr. Ray Fells, Director of Genetic Research and Reproduction.*

The stranger who'd pricked Kingsley's heel nervously grabbed his blood samples and headed toward the door, not making eye contact with Ray. "We'll know more after the lab reports come in," she said and quickly left the room.

Ray stared at Kingsley like he was a bowl of rotten food that she couldn't decide whether to study or throw in the garbage. Bapsi, on the other hand, treated him like she treated everyone, with kindness and love. She bent down and kissed his forehead. "Be happy, little one," she said. She took Charlotte's hand. "I have to go. I've been on duty since yesterday morning. I must get some sleep."

Then Bapsi turned and squared her hunched shoulders the best she could, facing Ray. She roughly snatched Ray's forearm. "Dr. Fells, please come with me," she snapped. She pulled Ray out into the hallway. Kingsley couldn't see her but he could hear her. "You may speak to me anyway you see fit," Bapsi scolded, "but you may not speak to one of my patients in that manner!" Kingsley grinned, picturing little old Bapsi Cama shaking her boney finger in the harsh doctor's face.

The nurse closed the door, muting the argument. "Did you intend to breast feed your baby?"

Kingsley looked around. He didn't see any babies. "What baby?" he asked. As usual, everyone ignored his question. "Amanda, I'm talking to you!" he said. She still didn't answer and it hurt his feelings.

"I'd hoped so," Charlotte said. "But I haven't been around babies very much."

"Let me help you," the nurse said. Kingsley blushed as the nurse helped Charlotte lower her hospital gown. Not only did Kingsley think that Amanda was half naked in front of him, but her breasts were huge, each one as big as the moon. And they were leaking.

"Are they supposed to do that?" he asked. He'd only seen naked women online and their breasts didn't leak. He tried to turn away, but the nurse wouldn't let him. She grabbed one huge breast and shoved it into Kingsley's mouth, covering his face. He gagged and pulled away. "Stop! I can't breathe!" he yelled. The nursed tried again, and he started to cry. He hated crying in front of Amanda, but it was all he could do. They wouldn't listen to him, and they wouldn't answer his questions. His crying must have worked because the nurse gave up and Charlotte covered herself. The nurse left and returned moments later with a bottle, which for some reason Kingsley couldn't understand, he knew how to drink!

Kingsley was beginning to realize he wasn't the same fourteen-year-old boy. He wasn't in the hospital for his gene-therapy treatment. Amanda hadn't become an adult overnight. Maybe she wasn't even Amanda. Everyone around her called her Charlotte. Even Bapsi called her Charlotte. This wasn't a dream. It wasn't a drug-induced nightmare. It was real, and the worst of it was that no one seemed to understand a word he said. He looked at his hands. They were tiny and he couldn't unclench his fists. What's wrong with me?

He finished his bottle, and then something happened that absolutely convinced him he wasn't the same. He pooped in his pants. Kingsley hadn't pooped his pants before, not that he could remember. He'd peed in his pants once in his grandmother's church when the preacher started sermonizing about Noah's flood and Kingsley couldn't hold it in anymore, but that was a long time ago.

The nurse took off his diaper and lifted his feet over his head. Kingsley was horrified. Black poop stuck to him like tar. And if that wasn't bad enough, when the nurse cleaned off the poop and Kingsley saw his privates, he was shocked. It was worse than what Andrés had said about the alligators. Everything was red and staggeringly out of proportion. Some parts were too small and others were too big. Kingsley closed his eyes. It was all too much. He howled as loud as he could. The nurse returned him to Charlotte, who tried to comfort him, but it was no use. He cried and cried until he couldn't cry anymore. He took a deep breath, about to start crying again, when he heard a knock on the door and the one voice who could tell him what was going on.

"May I come in?"

"Mom! Mom!" Kingsley yelled. "Where am I? How did I get out of the tunnel? What's going on? Why am I so small? Why are my—"

But just like everyone else, Joyce didn't answer any of Kingsley's questions. She stood at the doorway, her diamond earrings dangling and her huge companion behind her.

Charlotte enthusiastically waved her in. "Ms. Fells, come in, come in! I had my baby!"

"Lily," she said. "Call me Lily."

As Joyce came closer, Kingsley could see how much she'd changed. Her voice sounded the same but she looked different. She wasn't the same twenty-nine-year-old Joyce Smith he'd left with Jack Sutherland at Marlbank when he and Amanda escaped. Her face was smooth like plastic wrap over a bowl. Her brown hair wasn't frizzy anymore, it wasn't even brown. More of a dirty blonde. Her clothes were all wrong, too, like something a rich woman would wear. Even her makeup was different. Kingsley didn't like any of it. And he certainly didn't like seeing her wearing Mrs. Sutherland's diamond earrings.

Joyce was carrying a large basket. She set it on the table next to Charlotte. "How's my favorite patient?" she said.

"I'm fine," Charlotte said. "It was a long night but I—"

"I meant the boy."

Charlotte startled. "You heard I had a boy?"

Joyce smiled and twisted one of the earrings. "Not much gets past me. Tell me, how is my sweet little darling?"

"They're waiting on the results of his blood tests," Charlotte said. "But he seems healthy."

Joyce flushed bright red, her hand to her heart. She fell into the chair beside Charlotte's bed, and tears filled her eyes. "Healthy," she said, her voice little more than a whisper. "He's healthy."

"Are you all right?" Charlotte asked. "You look like you're about to faint."

Joyce took a breath and looked up at Charlotte. "Tell you the truth, hon, I'm feeling better than I've felt in a long, long time."

The basket Joyce brought was covered with a towel embroidered with a trio of rabbits chasing each other in a never-ending triangle. Joyce whisked off the towel. "Ta da!" In the basket were an assortment of breads and muffins, and a small jar of rare peach preserves.

"Peaches!" Charlotte grabbed the jar. "Where'd you find—"

"Look in the envelope."

Intermixed with the muffins was a long envelope. Charlotte opened it and found enough cash to buy a car. "Oh, Ms. Fells, this is too much!" She tried to hand the envelope back to Joyce. "I can't take this."

Joyce waved aside the money and fixed her eyes on Kingsley. She lifted Kingsley out of Charlotte's arms, without asking permission. She turned her back on Charlotte and walked away, nuzzling Kingsley's warm, round head, her breath tickling his skin. "I've missed you so much."

Memories overwhelmed him. Memories of lavender body lotion and Cajun spiced shrimp hopping around in the fry pan like they were alive. Memories of holding her hand as they waited for the school bus. Of watching her tack his drawings of jets and his A+ reports on the walls of their little house by the dock. Of sandwich kisses, Joyce on one side and his father on the other. But Kingsley also remembered the night they left New Orleans. His mother told him a movie star had shot his father. Kingsley knew that wasn't true. She'd pushed him into their beat-up Dodge Charger for the long drive to Virginia, to the Sutherland mansion, and to Amanda.

Joyce was almost to the door when Charlotte climbed out of bed and tried to take Kingsley from Joyce's arms. "I need to feed him," she insisted. Joyce wouldn't budge. "He's hungry," Charlotte added. Joyce still wouldn't let him go. Charlotte's agitation grew. "Please, Ms. Fells, don't make me call the nurse."

Joyce reluctantly handed Kingsley back to Charlotte. She lingered, watching Charlotte cradle him. "I'll come by later," she said. Kingsley could hear the longing in her voice. He felt it too. He was torn. He knew she loved him but he also knew the bad things she'd done. Charlotte tried again to return the envelope but Joyce shook her head. "I've got all the money I'll ever need." Her eyes stayed on Kingsley until she left the room.

Strange voices woke Kingsley. He looked around. He didn't see Charlotte anywhere. He wasn't in her room. He was someplace else. Someplace noisy. Telephones rang and computers buzzed, and beside his crib, a nurse was talking to a tall black woman. Kingsley squinted to read the tall woman's nametag: *Security Chief Odelle Holland.*

Ray Fells was with them, staring intensely at Kingsley, which made him squirm. He didn't like being scrutinized as if he were a laboratory rat, especially by Dr. Fells.

"Are you going to arrest her?" the nurse asked Odelle.

Odelle shook her head. "Not until the baby dies, if at all." She wrinkled her brow. "She really didn't know she was carrying a boy?"

"Dr. Cama is sure of it," the nurse said.

"How can you not know what's growing inside your body?" Odelle asked. She flicked a piece of lint off her tailored suit. "Has anyone talked to Ms. Sutherland's doctor? The one in Hampton, I mean."

The nurse nodded. "Dr. Miles-Johnson. She's in Norfolk, actually. At the Jones Institute. She's as baffled as we are."

"Did she perform the implant?" Odelle asked. "This Dr. Miles-Johnson, did she implant the boy's embryo into Ms. Sutherland?"

"She sent Charlotte's records. They confirm she implanted what she thought was Charlotte's clone. She didn't think it necessary to check the gender of the fetus. She couldn't tell me who cloned the boy."

"Or wouldn't." Odelle said with a sigh. "Nothing's ever easy, is it?" She reached out and straightened a wayward strand of Ray's blonde hair. Ray didn't object, quite the opposite; her intense glower at Kingsley softened.

"So, let me get this straight," Odelle said. "It appears that some unknown doctor in Norfolk surreptitiously cloned a dead boy then, allegedly, tricked Dr. Miles-Johnson into implanting this illegally created embryo into an unsuspecting twenty-four-year-old plumber from Hampton. Is that right? Is that what you're telling me?" The nurse nodded, and Odelle sighed again.

Kingsley was sure they were talking about him, and he was sure it wasn't good. He studied Odelle's dark face. She was a strong woman and taller than Ray by several inches. Her voice was clear and commanding.

Odelle noticed Kingsley studying her. "He's looking at me. I'm no doctor but he seems pretty alert. What if he doesn't have the tumors?"

"We'll know soon," the nurse said. "The lab's sending the results as soon as they come in. Dr. Cama asked me to call her before you did anything."

"Before I did anything?"

The nurse nodded. "Dr. Cama wants to talk to you before you decide what to do with Charlotte or the baby."

"You can tell Dr. Cama I've already decided," Odelle said. "I talked with the District Attorney, and we agreed that Dr. Cama may discharge Ms. Sutherland, but the baby's not leaving the hospital until I know who he is, who cloned him, and how his embryo ended up in Ms. Sutherland. I'm putting a twenty-four-hour guard on the boy. No one is allowed to see him without my permission." Odelle added one final instruction. "And don't tell anyone about the boy. I want to keep this quiet. No one sees his chart other than you, me, Dr. Fells, and Dr. Cama."

"The only other nurse who knows is Vondra Douglas. She helped Dr. Cama deliver him. I'll make sure she gets the message."

Odelle turned to Ray. "How long do these boys usually live?" Ray didn't answer. Her gaze had softened, but she was still staring at Kingsley. Odelle gently placed her hand on Ray's slender shoulder. "Please tell me Lily didn't have anything to do with this."

Ray looked up into Odelle's dark-brown eyes. "I love you."

Odelle scowled. "That doesn't answer my question."

"A few days," Ray said. "A week at most."

Odelle motioned to a hefty woman wearing a security-guard's uniform. "No one other than hospital personnel is allowed on this ward or in Ms. Sutherland's room. No visitors and definitely no press."

Kingsley played the conversation between Ray and Odelle over in his head. They'd spoken so freely in front of him, as if they'd thought he couldn't understand their words. When the nurse returned him to Charlotte's room, Charlotte had showered and was dressed in her denim jumper, now too big for her. Kingsley tried to warn her. "They want to take me away from you!" he said. "They might arrest you!" Charlotte cooed and patted his back. "They're putting a guard outside your room!" he said. "We need to get out of here now!" Charlotte didn't respond. She sat on the couch and gave him a bottle. Kingsley felt so frustrated. He couldn't understand why she was so calm.

An Asian teenager in a pink-and-white hospital smock arrived with Charlotte's lunch: corn chowder, rice cakes and peppermint tea. She placed the tray on the table beside the couch. Her face lit up when she saw Charlotte. "Hey, you were at my soccer game," the girl said. "You sat behind my mom and Sandy's mom and started screaming."

Before Charlotte could answer, the teen started talking again. "I'm a junior volunteer. They used to call us candy stripers, or candy strippers, as Abby says. She's a junior volunteer, too. And so is Sandy. They're on my soccer team. They were playing when you came to the game. Sandy's the best goalie ever. She's why we won states last year. She's helping the baby with the red eyes. Sandy is, not Abby. Abby's volunteering because she has to. She's in trouble with her mom, as usual. Abby's a great forward but she's always getting in trouble. Yellow-carded, you know. Have you seen that baby with the red eyes? Absolutely creepy. Looks like a Martian. Don't you think that's what a Martian would look like?" The girl shivered. "Do you need me to cut up your food?"

Charlotte sipped her soup. "No, thanks."

"Do you want something else to drink? I could bring you a cup of ice if you want cold tea instead of hot."

"No thank you."

"I know how to give shampoos without using water," the girl said. "Do you need a shampoo?" Charlotte told her she'd just taken a shower. "How about a foot massage?" Once again, Charlotte said no. She didn't want a massage.

"Have you seen the bathrooms downstairs?" the girl asked. "The men's rooms, I mean. They still have those weird vertical toilets. I'd say those toilets reeked but I kind of like the idea of having someone different around. Don't you get bored being around girls all the time? I know I do."

Charlotte smiled at Kingsley. "I guess so," she said.

Kingsley thought about what the girl said. No men. He hadn't seen any guys in the hospital. No male doctors, nurses or orderlies. Even the security officers were women.

"Wouldn't you love to see a penis?" the girl asked. "Not just on the Internet or on a statue. A real one. I'd like to see a real one someday." Kingsley was shocked that the girl would ask such a question and scared that Charlotte would tell her about his. But Charlotte never got the chance. The girl talked nonstop, barely taking a breath. "Such a funny word. Penis. It should have a better name. More regal. More majestic, like, um, I don't know. *Lion stick*, maybe. What do you think?"

Charlotte gawked at the girl. "I have no idea—"

The girl meandered to the window. "Abby says they should tear down that statue of Lewis and Clark near the bus station. Have you seen it? The one with Lewis and Clark acting like they discovered America or something, with Sacagawea cowering behind them. Makes Abby mad. She says Sacagawea did all the work and that statue barely shows her. Abby says they should tear down all the men statues and replace them with statues of women. Sandy told Abby they can't rewrite history, but Abby said men did it all the time. *To the victor goes the spoils*, that's what Abby says. My mom says lots of places never—" The girl suddenly stopped talking but didn't stop making noise. She squealed so loud it hurt Kingsley's ears.

"Did you see that? A bird! A bird!"

Charlotte rushed to the window, still holding Kingsley. A large white bird with bright-red eyes was perched on a tree.

"Come on," the girl said, beckoning Charlotte, "We've got to tell Sandy!" She hurried out the door. Charlotte stayed by the window, gawking at the bird. Kingsley wanted to go with the funny girl. He kicked his feet until Charlotte left the window and followed the girl. He was so happy! Charlotte understood him!

The security guard followed them to Arielle's room. Kingsley had almost forgotten what Odelle had said about arresting Charlotte until he saw the gruff-looking guard.

A large red-haired teenager was sitting on the couch, holding a sleeping infant. Arielle wasn't with her. She was in bed, on her side, facing the empty wall, facing away from her baby.

"Sandy! Sandy!" the Asian girl said to the redhead.

"Shhh!" Sandy said.

"I saw a bird!" The girl rushed to the window and pulled open the curtains. The room filled with bright-afternoon sunlight, and Arielle buried her head under her pillow.

Everyone except Arielle hurried to the window—Sandy, Charlotte and the security guard. All marveled at the large white bird with bright-red eyes, everyone except Kingsley. *What's the big deal? It's just a seagull.* The gull spread her wings, and everyone gasped as it flew to the top floor of the medical center and into an open window. That did surprise Kingsley. Gulls usually didn't fly into hospitals.

A nurse came in and fussed at the Asian girl. "Nikki! You're supposed to be helping the orderlies serve lunch, not staring out the window." She took the sleeping baby from Sandy's arms.

"Wait!" Sandy said. "Dr. Cama said I could—"

"Dr. Cama's not here." The nurse placed the infant in the bassinet beside Arielle's bed and ordered Nikki and Sandy to go help the orderlies. The girls left, still enthusing about the gull. Kingsley was sorry to see them go.

The nurse turned to Charlotte. "You can visit for ten minutes. That's all. Then go straight back to your room. Don't leave the ward." She motioned to the security guard to wait outside Arielle's door, and then left.

Charlotte held Kingsley close as she quietly approached Arielle, who was still buried under her pillows. "How are you feeling?" Charlotte asked tentatively. Arielle didn't answer. Charlotte took a seat in the chair beside Arielle's bed. "Did you see that bird? It was beautiful. White and gray, and it had red eyes."

Arielle flinched at the mention of red eyes. "I wonder what real birds would think if they saw it," she mumbled.

Kingsley studied the newborn in the crib. She was pale and had a streak of thick black hair that stood out like an unruly Mohawk. She looked like a normal baby—until she woke and opened her eyes. The effect was startling. Just as Nikki had described, her eyes were bright red. She looked like a being from another planet. Kingsley stared at her and she stared back at him. He couldn't decide if he wanted to make friends or run away.

"I didn't think I'd feel this way," Arielle said, rolling over, facing Charlotte. "She's an entirely new species."

"You've got the blues," Charlotte said, "that's all. Your baby is beautiful. Look at all that hair! See my baby? Bald. Completely bald. I just hope he has hair before—" Charlotte tensed, immediately correcting her mistake, "before *she* goes to school."

Arielle quickly sat up. "So it's you! I heard the nurse telling the security guard that someone had a boy. You know cloning a dead person is illegal, don't you?"

"I didn't clone him!"

"Then why'd they post the guard? I heard them say they're not going to arrest you until after he dies."

Charlotte looked ready to punch someone. "First off, I'm sick of people acting like I did something wrong. I was supposed to have a girl. I paid my doctor to clone me. Me! Charlotte Santos Sutherland, daughter of Amanda Santos Sutherland. I didn't work my butt off pulling pumps in the middle of winter to clone some boy I don't even know!"

Kingsley reeled at these revelations. "How could you be Amanda's daughter?" he asked. "Amanda's my age. She can't be your mom!" Charlotte didn't answer. All she did was pat him on the back, which he found increasingly aggravating.

Arielle eyed Charlotte with a newfound awe.

"Second," Charlotte said, "he's my baby and he's not going to die. And I will damn well beat the crap out of anyone who says otherwise."

"Jesus, Charlotte," Arielle said, "I was just telling you what I heard. Whatever happens, you're in trouble. If he dies, you'll go to jail for cloning a dead person, and if he lives, it'll be even worse. People don't want men back. They're afraid of them."

"Afraid?" Charlotte brushed her lips across the top of Kingsley's head. "I think it'll be great having men back."

"Why? We don't need them anymore," Arielle said. "Women have adapted to a world without men." Arielle glanced at her red-eyed baby and winced. "I know my life's not perfect, but at least I don't have to worry about rape or war."

Charlotte rolled her eyes. "Rape and war. That's what everyone says. What about all the good men did?" She pointed out the window. "Thomas Jefferson wrote the Constitution. He founded the University of Virginia. He was a man. Doesn't the good outweigh the bad?"

Arielle shrugged. "Maybe, but I'm not the person you have to worry about. Dr. Fells has a lot to lose if men come back. Her entire career would be ruined."

"That's her problem," Charlotte snapped. She abruptly stood up. "It's time for me to go. I'm taking my baby home." She left Arielle's room and stopped by the nurses' station. "I'm ready to go home now," she told the nurse on duty.

The nurse hesitated. "That's up to Dr. Cama."

"Then call Dr. Cama!" Charlotte marched back to her room, the security guard close behind.

Kingsley was still preoccupied with the conversation between Charlotte and Arielle. "Baby? What baby?" The only baby he'd seen was the one with the red eyes. "Why did you say you had a baby?" he asked Charlotte. As usual, she didn't answer.

When Charlotte arrived at her room, someone was already there. Bapsi was hurriedly packing Charlotte's old tweed suitcase.

"You have to go," Bapsi whispered. "Today. Now. Don't check out. Don't pay the bill. Just take your baby and get out of here." Bapsi closed the suitcase and handed it to Charlotte. She also handed Charlotte a yellow diaper bag. "I've packed bottles and diapers for several days. If you think you're being followed, get off the bus and take a different route home."

"Why? What's going on?"

"Did you notice that security guard?"

"Yes," Charlotte said. "I assumed she was here to keep us safe."

Bapsi shook her head. "She's here to make sure your baby doesn't leave the hospital. I talked to Dr. Barlow's research assistant. She's all aflutter about getting a real live boy."

"I don't understand."

"Joan thinks she can cure him."

"Who?"

"Dr. Joan Barlow," Bapsi said. "She's been working on a cure for The Collapse for forty years."

"Isn't that a good thing?"

"She's never cured anyone, not even her dogs," Bapsi said. "I've seen this before. The boys die horrible deaths, just to be butchered like lambs at Bakrid and stuffed in her freezer next to all of her sacrificed dogs. Live or die, he should be with you. Not here. Not in a hospital. And certainly not another experiment in Dr. Barlow's laboratory." She glanced at the doorway. "I've asked Vondra to distract the guard. Once the guard's gone, we'll slip out."

They watched and waited as Nurse Douglas approached the guard. She talked to the guard for a moment and convinced the guard to leave her post. Nurse Douglas gave Bapsi a little wink as she led the guard away.

"This is it," Bapsi whispered. "Remember. Don't tell anyone he's a boy. If he lives, raise him in the country, away from prying eyes. Somewhere he can grow up as nature intended. If not, bury him where no one will find him." Charlotte carried Kingsley and the diaper bag. Bapsi carried Charlotte's suitcase. "You're a good mother and a good woman, Charlotte. You should raise him. Not anyone else."

17 The White Dungeon

Kingsley couldn't see Dr. Barlow, but he recognized her voice. She sounded tired, "Let me have the boy," she said. "I can cure him."

As Charlotte peeked out of her room, Kingsley peeked out too. Five women were standing at the nurses' station: Ray, Odelle, two security guards and an old woman with frazzled white hair like Albert Einstein, wearing kitty-cat glasses: Dr. Joan Barlow.

"I read your last report," Ray said to Dr. Barlow. "You hypothesize that the microenvironment of the tumors facilitates their resistance to gene therapy. Isn't that obvious? And what about your much heralded link between the brain and the immune system? That research began before The Collapse."

"If I have seen further it is by standing on the shoulders of giants," Dr. Barlow replied.

Ray reacted as if she smelled something foul. "That wasn't a compliment. Are you incapable of an original thought? It's been forty years with no discernible progress. The reasons are clear. Neither your laboratory nor the entire medical community can address all the factors that caused The Collapse. You're wasting your time and the hospital's resources trying to bring back men."

Kingsley squirmed in Charlotte's arms. "What are we waiting for? We've got to go!"

"Shh," Bapsi cautioned.

Dr. Barlow cleaned her glasses with the bottom of her lab coat. She wasn't as easily intimidated by Dr. Fells as the other doctors and nurses. "So I should just give up? Is that what you're saying, Rachel? I should just step aside and let you recreate the world as you see fit?"

Ray stiffened. "I would prefer it if you addressed me as *Doctor Fells*. And yes, you should just give up, as you say."

At one end of the hall, Dr. Barlow and the others congregated by the nurses' station, beyond that were the elevators and the nursery. At the other end was the stairwell. "We can't use the elevators," Bapsi whispered. "And I can't walk down four flights of stairs." Bapsi handed Charlotte the suitcase. "You'll have to go alone. Take the trolley to the bus station. Vondra's on duty until midnight. She'll cover for you as long as she can. With luck, you'll be home before anyone notices you're gone."

Charlotte tiptoed out of her room and toward the stairs, holding Kingsley against her shoulder. Propped up, he could clearly see Ray and Dr. Barlow. His agitation grew as he listened to what they were saying.

"Healing the environment was never our goal," Dr. Barlow said. The bags under her eyes were bluish gray and her skin was waxy and pale. Kingsley thought she looked like a vampire.

Ray crossed her arms in triumph. "A species that cannot reproduce without medical intervention is doomed. The only option is to fundamentally alter the nature of life on earth." She paused. "Correction. Not alter. Restore. Life began as a single sex organism and now that nature has eliminated the Y-chromosome mutation, the Rotifer Project will restore—"

"Nirvana?" Dr. Barlow injected. "Paradise? As the daughter of Lily Fells, you of all people should know that women are capable of as much mayhem as men."

"I was going to say, restore the natural balance," Ray said. She turned away, almost seeing Charlotte and Kingsley, when Dr. Barlow grabbed her arm.

"Have you seen the canine teeth of apes? Baboons? Chimpanzees? They're elongated. Quite vicious looking."

"I'm not creating primates for your lab."

"But not in humans," Dr. Barlow said. "Our canines aren't significantly longer than any of our other teeth. Somewhere in our evolutionary past, females chose males with shorter canines. They chose gentler, less aggressive mates. So you see, it's up to women if we want men to change."

"I don't want men to change," Ray said. "I don't want them at all."

Kingsley had heard enough. He was both angry and confused. "The daughter of Lily Fells?!" he asked. "Mom has a daughter?!" He suddenly remembered the prophecy from the mysterious woman at the Edgar Cayce Foundation: *Your daughter is the zenith that will change the world.* "You're changing the world and I don't like it!"

"Shh," Charlotte whispered, rubbing Kingsley's back. "Please don't cry."

"I'm not crying," Kingsley insisted. "I'm mad!"

One of the guards turned her head, looking for the noise. She spotted Charlotte and Kingsley near the stairs and started toward them.

"Will someone please answer me?!" Kingsley said. "What does she mean? Why doesn't she want men at all?"

His questions echoed in the stairwell and Kingsley had a revelation. His words didn't sound like words. They sounded like a baby's cry.

"Hold up, there," the guard called. She started to run. Odelle quickly followed.

Charlotte dropped her suitcase and diaper bag. She held Kingsley tight. "You're not taking my baby!"

"You can leave," Odelle said, "but the boy stays." Another guard arrived and together they struggled to take Kingsley.

"No!" Charlotte said. She wouldn't give up without a fight. She balled her fist and downed the first guard with a fierce right cross. Charlotte was strong, but Odelle was experienced. Odelle grabbed the downed guard's nightstick, held it crossways, and backed Charlotte into a corner.

"I'm not leaving without my baby!" Charlotte pushed against the nightstick. The downed guard jumped to her feet and pulled Kingsley out of Charlotte's arms. She handed Kingsley to Ray, and then grabbed Charlotte's right arm while the other guard grabbed her left. They dragged Charlotte to the elevator. "I have a lawyer!" Charlotte yelled. "I'll go to the police! I'll tell them I had a boy, and you stole him from me! He came out of me! I'm his mother. He's mine!"

Heads popped out of neighboring rooms, watching the upheaval. Bapsi tried to intervene, "She's his mother! Let her go," she said, pulling vainly on one of the guard's arms. When that didn't work, Bapsi pleaded with Odelle.

"You can't do this. Please."

Kingsley couldn't believe what was happening. He was in the arms of Ray Fells, the woman who hated men, and two security guards were hauling Charlotte away. The elevator doors closed and Charlotte disappeared. "No!" Kingsley wailed. "Bring her back!"

Bapsi hounded Odelle, begging her to change her mind. "This is wrong. Please, he belongs with his mother!"

"That's the crux of the matter, isn't it?" Odelle said, twisting the nightstick in her hands. "We don't know who his mother is."

Bapsi's eyes blazed. "I've known you since the day you were born, and I've never been so ashamed. You may know the law, but you don't know right from wrong. How dare you take a baby from his mother!"

Odelle winced. "Dr. Cama, you have to understand my position—"

"Give me the boy," Dr. Barlow interrupted, sidling close to Ray. She clawed at Kingsley's blanket. "I can cure him." In the arms of Ray Fells while Dr. Barlow salivated over him like a mangy hyena, Kingsley felt like he was in the middle of a tug of war between Lord Voldemort and Count Dracula.

Odelle stepped between Ray and Dr. Barlow. "I don't know if the boy should be given to you or not. That's for the Board to decide. All I know is that someone has created an illegal clone, and I'm taking him into protective custody until the police can figure out what's going on, and who's going to jail. Until then, no one sees him without my approval." She turned to Ray and her eyes narrowed. "Not even Lily."

Kingsley felt unmoored without Charlotte. He didn't know what to think or who to trust. He was afraid for her and for himself. At least he still had Bapsi. She stayed in the nursery, rocking him and giving him a bottle. "Appalling," she said "Absolutely appalling. What sort of ogre takes a baby from his mother? I don't care what Odelle says. I promise you, little one, someday, somehow, I'll return you to your mother."

Kingsley looked at his tiny fists stationed on either side of his bottle. Useless. That's all he was. Useless. He couldn't unclench his hands. He couldn't speak. He couldn't do anything except eat, cry and poop.

And sleep.

Kingsley wasn't in the nursery when he woke. Bapsi wasn't holding him.

He was under a blue sky dotted with puffy white clouds. He flexed his legs, hoping to feel grass between his toes. Hoping this was all a bad dream and Amanda was stretched out beside him. He took a deep breath.

Something was wrong. The clouds weren't moving. The air had the lifeless smell of rubbing alcohol and ammonia. Kingsley wasn't outside. He was in a small room with white walls, no windows and a taunting façade of a blue sky painted on the ceiling. Long mechanical arms hovered like a dentist's drill. Computer monitors hung from the wall. A woman he didn't recognize was peering into a huge microscope. She wore a white lab coat and her hair was pulled into a severe bun. He asked her where he was but she didn't answer. She didn't pick him up or rub his back. She didn't offer him a bottle or check his diaper.

Dr. Barlow came in, but her presence didn't comfort Kingsley, either. Quite the opposite.

"Now I know where I am," Kingsley said, terrified. "I'm in your laboratory."

Strange machines whirled test tubes round and round, and the muffled barking of Dr. Barlow's cloned dogs penetrated the walls. Kingsley clenched every muscle in his body, afraid he was Dr. Barlow's newest research subject.

Dr. Barlow picked him up with bony, gnarled hands and Kingsley was afraid she'd drop him. She placed him on a high table and shined a bright light into his eyes. The light hurt. He squinted and tried to push it away but couldn't control his arms. She pricked his heel with a sharp needle, and squeezed his blood onto a glass slide. Kingsley kicked and cried, trying to stop the torment.

Dr. Barlow gave the slide to the woman at the microscope. They talked in a code Kingsley couldn't understand, about cells and DNA, proteins and epigenetic markers. Kingsley wished Amanda was with him. She understood science better than he did, and she was much braver.

A strange machine with long octopus arms was next to the table. Dr. Barlow passed one of the octopus arms over Kingsley's head and neck. It didn't hurt but it frightened him. She picked him up and carried him to another room with another strange machine that looked like a giant doughnut. She placed him on a cold slab and strapped down his body and his head. She gave him a shot that hurt and left the room.

"Don't leave me alone in here!" Kingsley cried. The giant doughnut began to hum. The slab began to move. Kingsley screamed. "Get me out of here!"

Kingsley shut his eyes tight and pretended he was somewhere else. He pretended he was sitting on the front steps of the Sutherland mansion. Amanda was beside him. It was sunny and birds were singing in the blooming dogwoods. Amanda was smiling and telling him everything would be all right. He tried to take her hand, but she wasn't real. *Where are you, Amanda?*

The machine stopped, and Dr. Barlow returned. She unstrapped Kingsley and carried him back to the white room with the huge microscope. She didn't talk to him. She didn't coo or kiss him or tell him she loved him, like Charlotte would have. Once again, she placed him on the high table and pulled a white mask up over her nose and mouth. Kingsley shivered uncontrollably.

He heard a familiar voice outside the door. "I'm going inside and you can't stop me!" It was Bapsi Cama. He was rescued! The door flew open and Bapsi hobbled in, pushing past the guard stationed in the hallway.

Kingsley cried out when he saw her. "Help me!"

Bapsi faced Dr. Barlow, two old women, one with thick gray hair, the other with white wisps, "What is he doing here?" Bapsi demanded. "Why isn't he in the nursery?"

Dr. Barlow pulled down her mask. "The Board decided this was the best place for him."

"That's ridiculous," Bapsi said. "This is definitely NOT the best place for him. I've seen how you and Fadia treat those dogs. Isn't that dreadful enough without torturing this dear little boy? Can't you run your tests without him? Without using those poor dogs, for that matter."

Dr. Barlow sighed and took off her glasses. "This is a very old argument, Dr. Cama. We're curing The Collapse. The Board understands that, why can't you? My dogs are engineered to rapidly manifest the Y-Chromosome Linked Tumor Syndrome. We test new drug regimens on some, surgery on others, then we euthanize—"

"Does every innocent creature left on the planet have to die so humans can live? Can't you grow the tumors in a petri dish or use plants for your tests?"

"Plants!" Dr. Barlow laughed, mockingly. She beckoned Bapsi to the large monitor on the wall. "Come, Dr. Cama. Come see what a miracle looks like." She turned on the monitor. "Amazing, isn't it?"

Bapsi was silent for several minutes as she studied the image on the monitor. Kingsley studied the image too but it was meaningless to him. An oval filled with gray mush. When Bapsi did speak, her words were little more than a whisper. "Is this him?"

Dr. Barlow nodded. "We just did a CT scan."

Bapsi stroked the image. "I don't see any tumors. Has nature cured herself? Can this boy survive?" Dr. Barlow gave a noncommittal shrug. Bapsi picked up Kingsley, tears in her eyes. She held him close and whispered so low that only he could hear. "Tigers."

Kingsley was sure Bapsi would rescue him from Dr. Barlow's cold, white dungeon, but that didn't happen. Strangers fed him and cleaned him. "I don't want to be here," he said. "I want Charlotte." But they didn't take him to Charlotte. Time lost all meaning. Was it day or night? When he wasn't eating or sleeping, he was on Dr. Barlow's table or strapped down in the room with the scary donut machine. Boredom punctuated by terror. No one talked to him or kissed his head. No one held him close and told him how much she loved him.

The woman at the microscope who assisted Dr. Barlow had a nametag: *Fadia Barzan, Research Assistant.* She placed him on the high table and felt his head. She pulled off his sock and pricked his heel for what Kingsley guessed was the hundredth time. Maybe they were vampires. Maybe that's why they needed so much of his blood. He glanced at Dr. Barlow. She was very pale, and the room didn't have any mirrors or windows. Maybe she was supernatural.

"What Dr. Cama said about nature healing herself," Fadia said. "Do you think that's true? Is that why he's still alive?"

Dr. Barlow shook her head. "We are why he's alive. We saved the boy's life."

Fadia stopped examining Kingsley. She went to the door and closed it securely. "But we didn't," she whispered. "We created his embryo the same way we created all the other boys and they all died."

"I've fought The Collapse for over forty years, and now I have a healthy boy," Dr. Barlow said. "What more proof is needed?"

"An experiment is only a success if it can be repeated. Can we clone another healthy boy?"

Dr. Barlow didn't answer. She had a dreamy look in her eyes. "I deserve the Nobel Prize for medicine," she said.

Fadia smeared Kingsley's blood on a slide and went to the microscope. "I could go to jail for this."

"Don't be absurd," Dr. Barlow said.

"I'm the one who switched the embryos," Fadia whispered. "I'm the one who gave that doctor in Norfolk the cash to implant the boy."

"You were merely the courier," Dr. Barlow said. "It was Lily's money."

Kingsley tried to figure out what they were talking about. Did Dr. Barlow turn him into a baby? Is that why he couldn't walk or talk? Why? And why would his mother pay her to do it?

"Couldn't Ms. Fells have hired another surrogate to carry the boy?" Fadia asked. "She has the money. Why trick that poor Sutherland woman to carry him?"

"She has her reasons," Dr. Barlow said.

Fadia wasn't satisfied. "Cloning a dead person is bad enough but what we did was fraud. The Sutherland woman thought she was having a baby girl." Fadia slapped her hand on the table. "It's not fair. If he lives I can't tell anyone that we cured The Collapse because I'll go to jail. And if he dies, all that risk was for nothing."

Dr. Barlow gazed at Fadia over her cat-eye glasses. "You were well paid. That's more than most medical researchers get. If you wanted fame, you should have gone into show business."

Kingsley could hear dogs whimpering and remembered what Dr. Barlow said about her experiments. Drugs and surgery and death. He felt like whimpering, too. He began to wish he had the tumors. He'd rather die now than live the rest of his life trapped in Dr. Barlow's laboratory like those dogs. He was sure his life was over when the door swung open, but this time it wasn't Bapsi. It was the woman he feared the most, the woman who hated men.

It was Ray Fells.

She marched in and pulled Kingsley off the high table, whisking him out of the white room. Dr. Barlow sputtered after her. "You can't take him!

The Board won't stand for this! You'll lose your position. You'll lose your tenure. You'll lose your license."

The security guard followed Ray and Kingsley to the elevators. Ray stopped just before getting on and turned on Dr. Barlow. "I know too many of your secrets to be frightened by your threats, Joan," Ray said. "Go to the Board, if you want. Go to the police. Your involvement in this fiasco would interest them far more than mine."

Dr. Barlow backed away.

18 The Gull

Kingsley didn't know if he was going from bad to worse. In the elevator, he floated in Ray's arms up to the top floor of the medical center. What would he see next? Another dungeon? Another torture chamber?

The elevator doors opened and Kingsley was engulfed in the aroma of fresh hay and the sound of bleats, moos and chirps. He had entered the realm of the Rotifer Project. A state-of-the-art Noah's Ark, except this time the animals weren't in pairs. Ray walked to the end of the hall, and walked through the last door on the right. The guard followed, stationing herself outside.

Ray flipped on the light. On a handsome wooden desk was a computer, a stack of empty petri dishes and photos of Odelle and a pretty blonde teenager holding a soccer ball. Ray's walls were decorated with precise rows of impressive diplomas and randomly scattered photographs of wildlife: Deer grazing, dolphins leaping, and geese flying in V formation. The windows were open and unscreened. Kingsley could see real clouds moving in the breeze. Real clouds, not just paintings on the ceiling. Fresh, moist air from a morning rain shower filled the room.

On the right side of Ray's desk was an inviting crib with soft padding and warm blankets. No more cold metal tables. On the left was a large cage, and inside the cage was a gull. Maybe the same gull Kingsley had seen outside Charlotte's window, although it looked much bigger in person than it did in the tree, bigger than Kingsley in fact. It had a sharp yellow beak and glowing red eyes. The gull cocked her head sideways, intently watching Ray and Kingsley.

Someone else was in Ray's office. Someone neither Ray nor Kingsley noticed. A bony woman was crouching behind a dark cupboard. Kingsley instantly recognized the cupboard. It was from Mrs. Sutherland's library. Amanda had told him it once belonged to Robert E. Lee.

"What the hell are you doing in my office?" Ray snapped at the crouched woman.

The woman's knees cracked as she stood. "My, um, my daughter," she stammered. "Dr. Fells, my daughter's a lawyer. Did you know that?" Ray stared at her, as unblinking as the gull. "Well, um, no," perspiration glistened on the woman's cheeks, "you probably didn't know that." She nervously wiped her hands on her hospital smock, and Kingsley read her nametag: *Betty Setter, Admissions Clerk*. "She wants to know, um... Actually, it's for one of her clients." Betty pointed at the cupboard. "Where did you get that?"

Good question, Kingsley thought. He wanted to know how Mrs. Sutherland's antique cherry cupboard ended up in Dr. Fells' office. It belonged at Marlbank.

"None of your business!" Ray snapped. "Now get out of my office before I call security."

Betty scurried out and Kingsley was disappointed.

The gull's bright-red eyes followed every movement as Ray placed Kingsley in his new crib. The gull had white breast feathers, huge gray wings and a curved beak that could snap Kingsley's arm in two if she'd wanted. Kingsley scrunched up his face and began to cry, but Ray didn't ignore him like Dr. Barlow had. She didn't prick his heel, or place him atop a cold metal table. She picked him up and cradled him tenderly. She even gave him a warm bottle.

Kingsley felt very conflicted about Ray Fells. She said she was Lily Fells' daughter, which meant she was his sister. That seemed impossible. But here she was, cradling him in her arms. He didn't know if she hated him or loved him, if she was the villain of his story or the hero.

After he ate, Ray returned him to his warm crib. The gull was still watching him. Kingsley stuck out his tongue. The bird ruffled her feathers and turned her head. Kingsley felt a small triumph. At least he could still intimidate a bird. He fell asleep.

He woke to the sound of silverware tapping against ceramic plates and Ray and Odelle talking. He looked around. The window was still open, and it was still light outside. The gull was in her cage, and Ray and Odelle were eating what Kingsley guessed was lunch—beets and brown rice. Ray seemed uninterested in her food. She stabbed mindlessly at the beets. Dark red juice pooled at the bottom of her plate and droplets stained her white lab coat.

Odelle grimaced when the red juice hit her white lab coat. "Are you okay?" she asked.

"Why wouldn't I be?"

Odelle winced as Ray stabbed at her food. "I'm just glad I'm not one of those beets."

Kingsley didn't like Odelle—she'd ordered Charlotte thrown out of the hospital—but he did respect her. Odelle was in charge of security. Ray probably wouldn't toss him out the window or feed him to her gull while Odelle was around. "Is this about Barlow or your mother?" Odelle asked.

"Both. Neither," Ray said. "Does it matter? They're practically the same person."

"What's that supposed to mean?"

Ray put her plate on her desk and walked to the open window. No birds sang in the trees. No gnats landed on her lunch. Kingsley began to wonder if he was still in Virginia.

"Abby wants to use my brand-new Pegasus to drive her friends to some male-worshiping concert in Richmond," Ray said. "I should tell her no, but I don't want another argument. I get enough of those from Mother."

Odelle joined Ray at the window. "Abby's your daughter so of course she's strong willed," she said. "Strong willed and brilliant, just like her mother. But that's not what you're worried about." She caressed Ray's shoulders. "You're nothing like Lily. You don't have a dishonest bone in your body. Believe me, sometimes I wish you did. You're brutally honest even when it hurts. Check that. Especially when it hurts." Ray smiled and took Odelle's hand. They stood together at the window for a few moments. "Since Ms. Sutherland's arrival, you've been secretive and evasive," Odelle said. "And I don't like it. So let me ask you again. Is this about Joan Barlow and Lily?"

Ray let go of Odelle's hand and returned to her desk. "Barlow and my mother have worked together for so long they're more like evil twins than scientist and benefactor. Neither can see that human civilization has adapted to this post-Collapse world. Neither sees the beauty in the new normal. There hasn't been a war since before The Collapse. Jails are almost empty. Our air's clearer, our water's cleaner. My new Pegasus is a perfect example. Doesn't use gasoline at all, doesn't need anything from Mother's oil wells." She gazed at Kingsley, her face inscrutable. "My first Rotifer Project infant was born the same day he was, but Mother barely notices. All she does is criticize. That child represents a physiological leap in what humans can accomplish as a species. And not just in reproduction; that child will be able to survive the harshest conditions. Extreme drought, toxic environments, exposure to radiation. Her metabolic activities have the ability to come to a reversible standstill and...."

As Ray extolled the benefits of the Rotifer Project, something astonishing happened, astonishing to Kingsley, at least. The gull opened her cage door with her beak, flew over Ray's desk, over Kingsley's crib, and perched on the handle of the closed office door. She used her large feet to turn the knob. Kingsley had never seen anything like it. The bird opened the door and flew out. Neither Ray nor Odelle seemed alarmed by the bird's escape. Kingsley didn't know which was more remarkable, the resourceful bird or the fact that Ray and Odelle weren't surprised by the bird's actions. Moments later, the gull flew back in and returned to her cage, preening herself as if nothing odd had occurred.

While Kingsley was watching the gull, Odelle had returned to her chair. She inspected Ray's plate and delicately poked one of Ray's beets with her fork. "Remember the last time we played chess?" she asked as she ate the tender beet.

"Vividly," Ray replied. "You won."

"In chess, it's not the smartest person who wins; it's the person who makes the fewest mistakes."

"Are you saying I'm the smartest?" Ray said with uncharacteristic coyness.

"Stop fishing for compliments," Odelle said. "It's beneath you. My sources tell me the Board is going to close Barlow's lab, and it's because of the boy. The Board is angry that this unknown doctor in Norfolk has apparently cured The Collapse instead of Barlow. And if the boy dies, it only reinforces the fact that Barlow's lab has accomplished nothing. Either way, you win."

Ray leaned back in her padded office chair and intertwined her hands behind her head. "That's the best news I've had in years," she said, grinning at the ceiling. "I almost feel sorry for Barlow. And for Mother. She poured a fortune into Barlow's lab, and now the Board is shutting it down."

Odelle didn't join Ray in her revelry. "Who else knows about the Sutherland boy?"

"Dr. Cama, of course. Nurse Douglas, Dr. Barlow, Fadia Barzan, a few orderlies, your staff, the Board—"

"Practically the entire planet," Odelle said with a groan. "A boy is big news, even a sick boy. I've spoken to Charlotte Sutherland's obstetrician in Norfolk. She denies all responsibility and knowledge of how this happened." Odelle's mouth twitched. "Obviously she's not entirely forthcoming."

"This isn't the first male cloned since the ban," Ray said. "Were charges filed against the hospitals in those cases?"

"Not against the hospitals, only against the doctors." Odelle stood and carefully smoothed the wrinkles from her tailored suit. Then she leaned down and kissed the top of Ray's blonde head. "We both know who's behind this. I just don't want you to get hurt."

After Odelle had left, Ray stood by Kingsley's bassinette and scowled down at him, making Kingsley squirm. It was bad enough having the scary gull looking like she'd tear him apart, now he had it on both sides. But Ray didn't tear him apart. Quite the opposite, she gently picked him up and walked out of her office. The security guard followed.

The wide hallway was filled with welcoming sunshine from large windows and skylights. Ray patted Kingsley's back as she passed technicians and orderlies. Some smiled, others avoided her eyes. She opened an unmarked door and went inside a large room. The guard stationed herself outside the door.

Kingsley's nose twitched at the earthy aromas of hay and manure. A large pen held two black-faced lambs, cuddling together, asleep. Ray took a seat on the floor beside the pen. She leaned against the wall, still holding Kingsley. One of the lambs opened its bright-red eyes and walked over to her. She ran her fingers through the lamb's curly coat. "I wanted to tell Odelle the truth," she said. "But I can't betray my own mother. Every day of my life, I've heard only one thing: *Bring back my son. Bring back my Kingsley.* You're all she cares about. You're why she rebuilt this hospital. You're why she sent me to medical school and funded Barlow's insane experiments. You were always so important to her, so much more important than me."

19 Memories of Amanda

The aroma of hay carried Kingsley back to Mrs. Sutherland's stable. He was ten years old, chasing Amanda around the paddock, pretending to be a cowboy, Amanda pretending to be a pony. He could feel the wind on his face as he ran. He and his mother had just escaped New Orleans, and Joyce was desperate for work. She'd applied for the position as Mrs. Sutherland's live-in caretaker and Kingsley had gone with her. The interview was over and Joyce and Clare were leaning on the paddock fence, watching Kingsley and Amanda run and romp. "Kingsley, time to go," Joyce called. Kingsley and Amanda came running, and Joyce helped Kingsley climb over the fence. She turned to Amanda. "Thank you, Mandy, for showing Kingsley around."

Ten-year-old Amanda stood up straight, looked Joyce in the eye, and proudly announced, "My name isn't Mandy. My name is Amanda Santos Sutherland." She pointed to her backside. "My initials are A.S.S. And don't you forget it!"

Clare laughed and Kingsley started to giggle, until he saw the color rise in his mother's face. "Spirited," Joyce said through a gritted smile. "I love that in a girl."

The memory felt so real. Kingsley could smell Joyce's lavender body lotion. He could hear her voice. He did hear her voice! Kingsley startled out of his reverie.

"What are you doing sitting on the floor with my boy?" Joyce was standing at the doorway, her massive, mute companion behind her.

"Speak of the devil, and there she is," Ray said.

Joyce harrumphed and rolled into the room like a queen. She pulled Kingsley out of Ray's arms. "Your secretary wouldn't tell me where you were, so I reckoned you were up here with your menagerie of freaks." She snuggled Kingsley. "My baby, my sweet Kingsley."

"You can't take him to prison with you, Mother," Ray said. "Odelle won't let him leave the building, and she certainly won't give him to you."

"Joan and I were very discreet," Joyce said. "If Odelle causes too much trouble, I'll sic Phoebe Ann on her." Joyce laughed. Ray didn't. Kingsley appraised the silent giant waiting by the door and hoped his mother was kidding. "It may take a day or two before I can bring my sweet boy home, but I can wait. Hell, I waited forty years."

Kingsley was angry. Joyce had paid Dr. Barlow to turn him into a baby and now he couldn't walk or talk. He didn't know how or why, but he was sure she'd used Mrs. Sutherland's money to do it. "You're going to be in a lot of trouble when Amanda hears about this!"

Joyce rocked him in her arms. "There, there, hon. See what you did, Rachel, you made him cry."

"You only call me Rachel when you compare me to my father."

Joyce sighed. "This is why raising boys is easier than girls. I have more arguments with you in a day than I had with Kingsley his entire life."

"That's not true!" Kingsley said. "You're always fussing at me."

Joyce kissed the top of his head and then shifted him to her hip. She rubbed her neck and shoulder. "I've had a crick ever since that Sutherland girl came to town. Phoebe Ann, come over here and hold Kingsley for me. My bra strap's too tight. It's eatin' into me."

The mountainous woman looked as frightened as Kingsley did by the request. He'd never seen anyone like Phoebe Ann, not even in a video game. Square-faced, hawk-nosed, jet-black hair in a blunt cut, and as big as a buffalo. Kingsley could feel her hot breath as she nervously wrapped her enormous hands around his small chest. She held him away from her, like a pot of boiling water. He felt her sweat through his thin yellow blanket. He wanted to call out for someone to save him but was afraid Phoebe Ann would drop him. Or worse, crush him.

Joyce adjusted her bra strap. "Digs into my shoulder somethin' awful," she said. "Haven't owned a decent bra since before The Collapse." She took Kingsley back in her arms and gave Phoebe Ann a cheeky grin. "You're so lucky, Phoebe Ann, being so flat-chested." Phoebe Ann grunted and backed away as if Kingsley was a bomb about to explode.

Joyce gestured at the lambs. "What's in that pen? Goats? You know I hate goats."

"They're not goats, Mother."

"Your father brought a goat with him the first time I met him. God, what a monster he was. His death was the only good thing to come out of The Collapse."

"They're lambs," Ray said.

"Lambs?" Joyce said. "I thought you weren't going to create any livestock, only wild animals."

"The Board insisted. They wouldn't continue to fund the Rotifer Project unless I brought back domesticated animals. I disagree with their decision. I didn't create animals just so they could be abused." Ray eyed Joyce. "I suspect you had something to do with that decision."

Joyce smacked her lips. "Leg of lamb with mint jelly, I can almost taste it now." The lambs bleated, as if they knew what Joyce had in mind.

"I've lived my entire life without it."

"You've lived without a lot of things, hon," Joyce said. "Nothing like a good piece of meat."

Ray stood and brushed hay from her pants. "Why are you doing this? It's pointless and cruel, not to mention illegal. You can't keep paying Barlow to create infants just to watch them die."

"He's not going to die."

"He'll die," Ray said. "One way or another." She left the room, leaving Joyce, Kingsley and massive Phoebe Ann alone with the bleating lambs.

The security guard came in and ordered Joyce to take Kingsley to Ray's office. Joyce smiled sweetly and Kingsley knew what she was thinking. Phoebe Ann could easily overpower the guard, and Joyce could take him anywhere in the world. The guard nervously pulled out her cell phone but Joyce stopped her. "Put that away," she said. "You don't have to call Odelle every time I sneeze. I'm taking him back to Rachel's office."

Ray was sitting at her desk when Joyce arrived with Kingsley. Phoebe Ann and the security guard stayed in the hallway. "Would it kill you to say something nice to me once in a while?" Joyce snapped. She gave Ray's cheek a hard pinch. "And wear a bit of rouge, for Heaven's sake."

"Stop it." Ray pushed Joyce's hand away. "I have work to do."

"I can't believe you're my kin." Joyce picked up the framed photo of the pretty young blonde with a soccer ball. "At least Abby cares about how she looks," Joyce said. "But not you. No makeup, haircut like some 1990s gigolo, living with that big, black security guard. Good God Almighty, what has the world come to?"

"I don't know what you have against Odelle," Ray said. "Other than the fact that she knows you're a crook."

Joyce returned the photo to Ray's desk and sauntered to the gull's cage. Kingsley was still in her arms. "Filthy animals," she said, wrinkling her nose. "Nothing but scavengers. Used to eat our garbage back in New Orleans. The ones that weren't covered in oil, that is." She spun the bird's cage. The gull squawked angrily and flapped her wings.

Ray sprang from her desk and stopped the spinning. "What's wrong with you? Why are you so cruel?"

"Why couldn't you make something more colorful, like a peacock?"

"Only male peacocks are colorful."

"That's why we need to bring back men."

Ray shook her head and returned to her work.

"You asked me why I'm doing this," Joyce said. "I never told you about my trip to Virginia Beach. It was after my last baby Kingsley died." She left the cage and sat on the edge of Ray's desk, knocking over several photos. "Phoebe Ann went with me. I'd seen a psychic before, I never told you about that, either. Saw her before you were born and everything she said came true."

"You and Barlow should be in prison," Ray said, straightening the photos.

"Is that your new mantra? *You and Barlow should be in prison?* At least it's better than your old one. *I'm jealous of my dead brother.*" The pink in Ray's cheeks validated that Joyce had hit a very old wound.

Kingsley listened carefully. He wondered who Ray's dead brother was.

"The psychic told me Kingsley's soul didn't want any of those other surrogates," Joyce continued. "Not that girl from West Virginia. Not the Shifflet woman from the Valley. She said his soul never even entered their bodies."

"*Soul?*" Kingsley asked. "Why are you talking about my *soul?* And what's a surrogate?"

"There, there," Joyce cooed. "Don't worry, hon, that nasty seagull's not going to bother you. The psychic told me Kingsley wouldn't return until I'd done right by the Sutherlands. And that's what I'm doing."

"You paid for this advice?" Ray asked.

Joyce looked ready to smack Ray. "Don't talk to me like that! I survived The Collapse when most of the world was falling apart. Not only survived, I thrived. Sent you to medical school when everybody else was scrambling to put food on their table. So you listen to me, Rachel Fells, I gave Charlotte money, I paid her hospital bills, and I'm fixin' to pay for her to have another baby. What more do I have to do?"

"Foolish," Ray said.

Joyce held Kingsley high like a trophy. "And here he is. See how he looks at me. He knows I'm his mother."

Ray stood, took Kingsley out of Joyce's arms and returned him to his crib. "There are reasons why cloning the dead is illegal, Mother. All the money you've thrown at Barlow is wasted."

Joyce followed Ray to Kingsley's crib and gently tucked the yellow blanket around him. "You've never loved a child."

"I have a daughter," Ray said.

"You have a clone. It's not the same. And if that wasn't bad enough, now you've created a world of red-eyed monsters."

Was constant arguing the curse of mothers and daughters? Kingsley remembered how Clare used to fuss at Amanda, even on the first day he met them. Clare was interviewing Joyce for the position of taking care of Mrs. Sutherland. Amanda ran in wearing dirty riding boots, as usual, and her black hair pulled into a halfhearted ponytail. She grabbed Clare's iced tea and mud streaked down the side of the glass onto the polished dining room table. She tried to climb onto Clare's lap but Clare pushed her off.

"You're dirty," Clare said. She straightened Amanda's wayward ponytail. "Stand still." She pulled out a tangled scrunchie and a few strands of long black hair.

"Ouch, that hurts!"

"It wouldn't hurt if you'd brush it once in a while."

"Why?" Amanda asked, "So boys will look at me the same way they look at you?"

Clare blushed and impatiently pulled out another tangle. "This is my daughter, Amanda. She takes after her father."

In no time Kingsley and Amanda were best friends, sitting side by side on the marble front steps of the mansion, trading Skittles, Kingsley's favorite candy. "Purple for your green?"

"Yellow for your red?"

Trades were made and Amanda tossed a half-dozen purple Skittles into her mouth. She showed Kingsley her purple tongue. He stuck a green Skittle on his front tooth and Amanda laughed.

Kingsley longed to see Amanda again and to hear her laugh. Moreover, he needed Amanda. She was smart and could help him understand what was happening.

"Tell me one thing," Ray asked Joyce. "How did you lure the Sutherland girl to Charlottesville? It certainly was convenient that she had her baby here, at the medical center, instead of in Hampton."

"Here?" Joyce scoffed. "You think I wanted her to have Kingsley here? She was supposed to have him in Norfolk. It was all arranged. I'd have my baby boy without all of the nonsense I'm dealing with now. It's because of that damned attorney, Setter's granddaughter. I couldn't believe my eyes when—"

"You didn't bring the Sutherland girl here?"

"Of course not!" Joyce said. "With Odelle watching my every move? The switch was all arranged. They'd give Charlotte a baby girl, and I'd have my boy."

"Give her a girl! Are you telling me you'd kidnap a baby girl and give her to Charlotte?" Ray turned back to her work. "I can't listen to this."

"Kidnap? Of course not. Girls are easy to buy if you have the money; The Collapse didn't change that. Charlotte wouldn't have realized the girl wasn't her clone for months, maybe even years." Joyce took a breath. "What I was about to say, before you got all high and mighty on me, was that I couldn't believe my eyes when I saw Charlotte. Dark hair! I expected her to be blonde and beautiful, like Clare. Why would anyone clone

Amanda? She wasn't nothing but a spoiled brat." Joyce put her hand on her hip, mocking Amanda's swagger. "*My name is Amanda Santos Sutherland, A.S.S., and don't you forget it.* Good God Almighty, I'd never let Kingsley be raised by that girl's clone."

Kingsley fumed. "Don't you dare make fun of Amanda."

"Oh, baby," Joyce cooed. She hovered beside Kingsley's crib, patting his stomach.

"Don't touch me!" he said, trying to squirm out of her reach.

"Oh, look at him, Rachel," Joyce said. "You made him cry."

"I thought you hated Clare," Ray said.

"I did," Joyce said. "Clare was almost as much of a monster as your father. She treated poor old Mrs. Sutherland like dirt, and then had the gall to blame me for Mrs. Sutherland's death. I'm not the one who neglected her! I'm not the one who abused her! Her own children did that. I was the only person with her when she died. Me. Not Clare. Not Jack. I brought her with me when I went searching for Kingsley. Mrs. Sutherland died peacefully in the van. Not surrounded by strangers in a stinking tunnel." Joyce's voice broke. She gripped the rails of Kingsley's crib. "I never hated Clare more than I hated her that day. All she did was scream at me over her momma's money and her father's oil wells. Never said a word about my Kingsley. Not a word of comfort. Never apologized for what her insane brother done to me."

Joyce squeezed her eyes shut, and Kingsley tried to piece together what must have happened. His mother had found him in the tunnel, and then, for some reason, Dr. Barlow turned him into a baby.

A flash of sympathy crossed Ray's face, but disappeared as soon as Joyce opened her eyes. "I don't care," Ray said.

Joyce brushed away her tears. "I don't hate Clare anymore. She got what she deserved. Especially after Amanda did what she did. You know how she died, don't you?"

"Amanda?" Kingsley said. "Something happened to Amanda?" He strained to hear every word. "What happened to Amanda?"

"She jumped off the Monitor-Merrimac Bridge," Joyce said as casually as if she were telling Ray about her new dress, a smug grin on her face, "or so I heard." Kingsley's throat tightened. His body tensed. Even Ray looked up from her work. Joyce clapped her hands. "Splat! Right into the Hampton

Roads harbor. I reckon Clare made quite a scene when they found Amanda's bloated body washed up on the beach, all covered in seaweed." Joyce chuckled as if this was the funniest thing she'd ever said.

Kingsley held his breath. He remembered the man holding his son during the hurricane. He'd stood at the edge of the bridge, and a giant wave rose up and grabbed them both, father and son. Is that what happened to Amanda? Did she fight against the wave, desperately trying to swim? Kingsley exhaled more sorrow than his heart could endure. It's all my fault. If I'd been there. If I'd treated her better. If I'd told her how much I loved her, this wouldn't have happened. She'd still be alive.

Joyce instantly noticed the change in Kingsley. "Something's wrong! He's not breathing."

"I'm surprised he's lived this long," Ray said.

Joyce snatched a fistful of Ray's blonde hair. "He's not breathing! You're a doctor, help him!"

Time stopped for Kingsley. He didn't care. His tiny body crumpled. His skin paled. Someone pumped his chest. He didn't cry. Someone stuck him with a needle. He didn't squirm. He'd lost too much. He didn't want to live anymore.

He was barely aware of Bapsi holding him. "You miss your mum, don't you?" she said. He wasn't in Ray's office. He was in the nursery, in Bapsi's arms, rocking in the rocking chair. Bapsi tickled Kingsley's mouth with a baby bottle, trying to get him to eat. "She went to the police, but I'm sorry to say, they sided with the hospital. Betty tells me that Linda is petitioning the Governor on your mum's behalf, but you'll be an old man by the time the women in Richmond decide what to do."

Kingsley turned away from the bottle. He didn't want to eat. How could he eat? His mind was flooded with images of Amanda at the bottom of the ocean. Her body bloated. Her beautiful face destroyed.

Bapsi held Kingsley close as she cradled him in her arms. "Well, I'm not going to let you suffer alone. I'm taking you to your mum, just like I promised. I don't care if they arrest me. I'm not leaving you in this cold-hearted hospital for one more day."

Kingsley wished Bapsi would just go away. He didn't want his mother. Not after what she'd said about Amanda. She called Amanda a brat and was joyful about Amanda's death. Kingsley felt very certain that he never wanted to see Joyce again.

"This time, I have a plan," Bapsi whispered, "And I have help."

Kingsley didn't care about Bapsi's plan. He didn't care that outside the nursery, an orderly was talking to the two guards stationed by the door. One of the guards followed the orderly to the elevators and disappeared. "Good, good," Bapsi said, watching through the glass window. "One down, one to go." Moments later Nurse Douglas came around the corner and spoke to the second guard. The second guard refused to budge. Nurse Douglas shook her finger in the guard's face, arguing with her.

"Come on, come on," Bapsi said, quietly wishing the guard to leave. "Charlotte is waiting."

Charlotte! Kingsley perked up. Bapsi wasn't taking him to Joyce. She was taking him to *Charlotte*! That changed everything.

The second guard popped her head into the nursery. "I have to go to security to check on an incident report," the guard told the nurse. "Nurse Douglas claims I reported that she was asleep on duty and wants my head for it. Will you be all right 'til I return?"

"Dr. Cama and I can hold down the fort," the nurse said. "Good luck. Tell Chief Holland to send someone to replace you if things don't work out."

"Will do," the guard said. She and Nurse Douglas left the nursery and stepped into a second elevator.

"Here we go," Bapsi whispered. She stood up from the rocking chair and called to the nurses' station. "He's still not eating. I'm taking him for a little walk, just to the stairs and back. Maybe that will help."

The nurse hesitated. "Wait until security arrives."

"Oh, Ellie," Bapsi persisted. "I'm just taking him to the stairs and back. What do you think I'm going to do, run away with him? At my age, I can barely walk."

The nurse smiled and relented. "Just to the stairs and back," she said.

Kingsley's heart raced. Baspsi causally walked out of the nursery, but once she was out, she pulled a tissue out of her pocket and wiped perspiration from her temples. "Your mum's waiting for me in the lobby. If we hurry, she can make the four o'clock bus. No one will know you're gone until it's too late."

She was careful of her bad hip as she limped toward the stairs. Kingsley wondered how she'd make it down four flights when he saw Sandy, the red-headed soccer goalie and junior volunteer. She was waiting for Bapsi at the stairwell, wearing her blue-and-gold soccer uniform with her tube socks rolled down and dirty cleats. Bapsi quietly handed Kingsley to the teenager. "If anyone asks, tell them I gave you the baby, which is the truth," Bapsi whispered. "If anyone gets in trouble for this, it should be me." She kissed Kingsley's forehead. "Have a good life, Little One. Don't make the same mistakes we did. *The souls suspended head downwards in hell are the souls of those who bring corruption to water.*" Bapsi gave Sandy an embarrassed smile. "That's from the sacred Book of Arda Viraf." She touched Sandy's muscular forearm and told her she'd meet them at the bottom of the stairs.

20 Escape

Sandy was big and bulky, and didn't look like a superhero at all. She wasn't sleek and beautiful like Storm from the X-Men comics. Her hair was the color of pumpkin pie. Freckles covered most of her face and she had a cockeyed grin. But to Kingsley, she was better than all the superheroes combined. He felt safe in her strong arms as she whisked him down the stairs, three steps at a time. When Sandy reached the ground floor, they waited for Bapsi to arrive and tell them what to do next.

The lobby was packed. The line to the admissions desk coiled like a snake, winding all the way to the gift shop and back again. Dresses and well-worn dungarees, high heels and thick-soled cowboy boots, and every hairstyle imaginable—long, short, buzz cuts, ponytails and some neatly tucked into small white caps. The noise hurt Kingsley's ears, but that didn't matter. He couldn't wait to see Charlotte.

Kingsley heard a familiar, high-pitched voice. It was Nikki, the chatty Asian teenage volunteer who'd screamed when she saw the gull outside Charlotte's window. She was sitting on the floor with her computer on her lap, near the front doors. She was talking nonstop to a pretty blonde teenager. Kingsley had seen the blonde before in the photos on Ray's desk. She looked a lot like Ray. Actually she looked exactly like Ray except younger, and Kingsley wondered if she was Ray's daughter. Both wore the same blue-and-gold soccer uniforms as Sandy. The blonde was juggling a soccer ball on her knee, annoying the women around her.

187

Nikki closed her computer and shoved it into her backpack. She stood and worked through the crowd, making her way to the men's room. She dramatically opened the men's room door with a grand swoosh and batted her eyes. "I have always depended on the kindness of strangers," she said and sauntered in.

Kingsley probably would have been happy to see Nikki again if he hadn't been so desperate to see Charlotte. He strained to see every face, hear every word. He listened to nearby conversations. "If The Collapse is over, I want to clone my uncle," one woman told her neighbor. She opened her purse and pulled out a wrinkled plastic bag containing several off-white squares. "My grandmother saved his baby teeth. They should be able to clone him from this, don't you think?"

On the other side of the lobby, the elevator *dinged* and the doors opened. Bapsi hobbled out. She waded through the crowds of women toward the front door, conspicuously carrying a large, yellow diaper bag. Someone would call her name and she'd stop to talk, glancing nervously in Kingsley's direction. Another woman would ask a question and she'd stop again. Everyone knew dear old Dr. Cama. Everyone was her friend. Kingsley guessed that was why Sandy risked so much to help him.

Watching Bapsi was nerve-wracking. Kingsley wanted her to hurry up, but he knew to stay quiet. Making any sound would ruin everything. Bapsi finally reached the front entrance, and that's when Kingsley saw Charlotte. She looked beautiful, like Amanda all grown up. She was wearing her bulky maternity jumper—now too big for her—and carrying her tweed suitcase. Bapsi whispered in Charlotte's ear, and Charlotte smiled. She started toward him, pushing through the crowd.

Nikki came out of the men's room and worked her way to Sandy and Kingsley. "What's going on? Why are you holding that baby?"

"It's a favor for Dr. Cama," Sandy said.

"What sort of favor? Is she—?"

"Shhh, Nikki, you've got to be quiet!"

Nikki lowered her voice. "Is this a game? Is that a real baby? Why are all these women here?" Sandy shushed her again.

Kingsley saw Charlotte's head peeking above the mass of women, and then she sank back down again, like a bobbing buoy on the ocean. He was nervous. Afraid something would ruin their reunion, afraid Nikki's questions would attract attention. Charlotte surfaced again, and her smile grew with every step. Sandy smiled when she saw Charlotte. "Is that your Mom?" she whispered.

Kingsley kicked his feet with excitement. He knew Charlotte wasn't Amanda. Amanda was dead, but she was the closest to Amanda he would ever have. Charlotte swept Kingsley out of Sandy's arms and kissed his round, bald head. She held him close and Kingsley nuzzled Charlotte's chest. His heart melted and his stomach growled. He hadn't eaten since he was in Ray's office and he was hungry.

Bapsi was still holding the diaper bag. She hustled Charlotte toward the front door. "We have to hurry. The four o'clock bus leaves in twenty minutes." Charlotte held Kingsley close and followed Bapsi, squeezing through the lines of women. They were halfway to the entrance when the alarm blared.

Three guards ran into the lobby with Odelle right behind them.

"Attention!" Odelle yelled over the screeching alarm. "You must clear the lobby. You can wait in the cafeteria or—" The startled crowd drowned out her voice. Odelle called to Betty at the admissions desk. "Turn off the alarm!"

"What?" Betty yelled back. She gave Bapsi a worried glance.

"Turn off the alarm!" Odelle repeated, louder.

Betty sank behind her desk for a moment then came back up. "The switch is jammed. I can't turn it off."

Odelle looked disgusted. She pushed her way through the ready-to-stampede crowd to the admissions desk and turned off the alarm. She ordered one of her guards to lock the front doors and the other two to search for the baby.

Kingsley clenched his mouth shut, afraid they'd be found if he started to cry.

Bapsi led Charlotte back to the stairs. "You can't go out the front," she whispered. She looked around, frantically searching for another exit. She clutched the yellow diaper bag tight against her chest. "I need to find another way—"

A new voice behind Bapsi offered a solution. A voice Kingsley hadn't heard before. "I know what to do."

Abby Fells wasn't just Ray's seventeen-year-old daughter, she was her clone: Same blonde hair, same strong hazel eyes. She stood behind Bapsi, holding her soccer ball under one arm. "There's an elevated walkway to the parking garage on the second floor. I've got a car. I can take you all the way to Hampton."

Charlotte didn't hesitate. "Let's go." She started up the stairs, Kingsley in one arm, her tweed suitcase in the other.

Abby jogged beside Charlotte and took the suitcase. "I'll carry that, you carry the baby." She dashed ahead, up the stairs two at a time. Sandy joined them, running beside Charlotte. Nikki followed at Sandy's heels.

"Where are we going?" Nikki asked, excited. No one took the time to answer.

The two guards searching the lobby spotted Charlotte holding Kingsley. "There she is!" The guards pushed through the crowd.

Bapsi tried to slow them. "Just the person I was looking for," she said to the first guard. "Could you kindly help me move the couch in my office?"

The first guard was polite but unstoppable. "Not today, Dr. Cama." She blew her whistle and ran up the stairs.

Bapsi seized the second guard's arm. "Please! Let her go."

The second guard wasn't as polite as the first. She roughly shoved Bapsi against the wall and ran after Charlotte. Angry gasps rippled through the crowd as the elderly doctor teetered precariously, clutching her bad hip, and then crumbled to the floor.

Kingsley couldn't see what happened to Bapsi after that. He didn't know whether the crowd rushed to Bapsi's aid or trampled her underfoot. He thought about the first time he met Bapsi Cama. He'd collapsed at his birthday party and was flown to the medical center. He remembered Bapsi's purple sari and her dying son, and how she stayed with him when he was afraid. When he saw her again in this strange, new world, aged and stooped, she was the woman who rescued him from despair. "One day," he said, "when I'm big and strong, I'll come back and rescue you."

Charlotte followed Abby down an empty hallway to a door marked *Exit to 2nd floor parking garage*, the two guards close behind. Abby pushed open the door and cool air hit them. They were outside, on an elevated walkway that separated the medical center from the parking garage. Below the walkway, security guards swarmed, rolling out heavy barrels to block the exits. A police siren shrieked in the distance. Kingsley couldn't hold in his panic. "They're coming," he wailed, "they're coming!!"

Sandy stopped in the middle of the walkway and stood her ground. She yelled to Abby. "I'll block security. You keep going." She crouched like a goalie. Wide stance, arms spread, as the two guards ran toward her. Charlotte and Nikki kept running but Abby slowed, looking back and forth from Sandy to Charlotte. "Save the baby, Abby," Sandy said. "If you can't do it, nobody can." She wiped perspiration from her face and gave Abby an affectionate wink. "Just like the P-K's at last year's tourney."

The first guard charged, but Sandy was as unmovable as a mamma bear. She stopped the guard with one strong swipe.

Nikki cheered. "Good job, Keeper!"

The second guard slipped around Sandy.

"Nikki!" Abby yelled. She tossed Charlotte's tweed suitcase to Nikki along with the car keys. "Start the engine. Mom's car can outrun anything the police can afford." She turned to face the guard who'd gotten past Sandy.

Nikki hesitated. "What? Me? I don't even know what's going on!"

"I'll catch up," Abby said. "Run, Nikki, run."

Nikki ran and Charlotte followed. Kingsley watched from Charlotte's shoulder.

The guard pulled out her nightstick. "Step aside, Abby. You don't want to embarrass your mother, do you?" That did it. Abby's eyes blazed. She dropped her soccer ball and reared her right leg. POW! The ball hit square into the guard's face. "My nose!" the guard yelled. "She broke my nose!"

Kingsley didn't know why Abby was helping him and at that moment, he didn't care. Charlotte scrambled into the back seat of Ray's sleek maroon Pegasus, Kingsley firmly in her lap. It still had its new car smell. Nikki nervously started the engine, grumbling nonstop that she didn't know how to drive. But she didn't have to grumble for long. Abby jumped in, red-faced and breathing heavily. Nikki gratefully scooted over to the passenger seat and Abby took the wheel. "Your mom's going to be so mad at you," Nikki said.

"She's always mad at me." Abby hit the accelerator and the Pegasus roared, spiraling down the parking garage, squealing around corners, and speeding past the 5 mph sign. "Sandy wants me to save the baby and that's what I'm going to do."

"She didn't tell you to break that guard's nose," Nikki said. "She didn't tell you to steal your mom's car." The Pegasus scraped against a square concrete pillar and Nikki covered her ears. "You're wrecking the car!"

The gates to the parking garage were down, and heavy barrels blocked the exits. Abby circled the first floor, searching for a way out.

"We're trapped!" Kingsley cried. "I can't go back!"

The guards were hurriedly barricading the back entrances when something white and gray rocketed out of a tenth-story window. A bird! It was Ray's smart gull. Kingsley watched in amazement as the gull screeched across the sky and dive-bombed the guards moving the last barrels. The guards ducked and ran, covering their heads, leaving one entrance unblocked. If he hadn't seen it, he wouldn't have believed it.

Abby revved the Pegasus and smashed through the entrance gate. She jerked the steering wheel hard to the right, almost flipping the car. Sirens screamed in the distance.

"Hurry! Hurry!" Kingsley wailed.

"I hear the police," Charlotte said.

"I can't hear anything!" Nikki said, eyeing Kingsley. "Can't you shut her up?"

"The police are right behind us," Abby said. Red lights flashed as the Pegasus sped down Jefferson Park Avenue toward the interstate. "There's the sign for I-64."

"Go east," Charlotte said. "To Hampton."

Nikki gasped. "Hampton! We're going to Hampton? That's a million miles away!"

The Pegasus jumped on the interstate and the police car shrank in the distance. "We're losing them," Abby said. "But we're still not safe. Mom has a satellite tracker. We'll have to dump this car and—"

"And steal another one?" Nikki asked. "I don't want to go to prison!"

"No one's going to prison," Charlotte said. "Pull over."

"What?"

"Pull over. I know something about cars."

"Are you postpartum or something?" Nikki asked. "The cops'll find us."

"No, they won't," Charlotte said. "Pull over, and I can disconnect the satellite feed."

Abby pulled off at the next exit, and Charlotte jumped out. She raised the hood and leaned over the engine. Kingsley had never seen a woman mechanic before. A moment later, Charlotte slammed the hood and got back in, wiping her hands on her baggy maternity jumper. "They won't find us now. Just stay off the interstate."

"Sweet," Nikki said. She turned around, extending her hand to Charlotte. "I'm Nikki Shao."

Charlotte shook her hand. "Charlotte Sutherland."

Nikki nodded at the blonde. "This is Abby Fells."

"Fells? Like Dr. Fells? Like Lily Fells?"

Abby blanched. "You know my grandmother?"

Charlotte nodded.

Abby glanced at the mirror, nervously smoothing her hair. "Yeah, well, good for you."

"What's going on?" Nikki asked. "Why are they chasing you?"

Charlotte hesitated. Kingsley saw the suspicion in her eyes. He felt it too, especially around Ray Fells' daughter. "They wouldn't give me my baby," Charlotte said. "She, um, she wouldn't eat, and Dr. Cama said it was because—"

"It doesn't matter," Abby said, cutting her off. "It'll be dark in a couple of hours. We need to find someplace safe where we can figure out how to get you to Hampton without the police or Chief Holland finding us."

Charlotte searched the floor of the car. "Oh no! The diaper bag. Dr. Cama packed milk bottles and diapers. I need them. My baby will starve without it."

"We can't go back to the medical center," Abby said.

Nikki pulled her laptop out of her backpack. "Where are we?"

Abby leaned close, studying Nikki's computer screen. "Just east of Lake Monticello."

"Should we try for Richmond?"

Abby shook her head. "No, they'll expect that. We should stay south." She thought for a moment. "Bring up directions to Fork Union." Nikki loaded the directions, and Abby smiled. She punched Nikki on the shoulder. "You're not totally worthless after all."

Abby turned to Charlotte. "We're going to Fork Union," she said as Nikki rubbed her shoulder. "They have a farmer's market. We can buy food there. Hopefully we can find baby bottles and something you can use for a diaper. Our soccer coach owns a campsite along the James River. It has everything else we'll need for the night. Tents, sleeping bags. We'll camp tonight and figure out the best way to get to Hampton without attracting attention."

"As long as we're back by Monday," Nikki said, as Abby started the engine. She turned to Charlotte. "I have to get at least a B+ in geometry if I want to go with Abby and Sandy to see Phillips-Head Screwdrivers. Heard of them?"

Charlotte shook her head. "No."

"Best band ever! Absolute best. Me, Abby and Sandy are going over spring break. They put on a fantastic show. They play on a high stage, surrounded by four huge screens showing all-male bands. They're so beautiful, the men I mean. Duke Ellington, Elvis, U2. All the greatest and—"

"Shut up, Nikki," Abby said. "No one wants to listen to your idiotic fantasies."

Nikki stuck her tongue out at Abby and returned to her computer. Something she saw made her panic. "NO! This reeks! This totally reeks!"

"What?" Charlotte asked. "What's wrong? Are we being followed? Have they found us? What's the matter?"

Nikki sighed dramatically and closed her computer. "This is officially the worst day ever." She leaned her head against the window. "I forgot my geometry homework."

21 Fork Union

Kingsley was sure they were driving in circles. They'd passed the same red barn twice and more than once had driven the wrong way on Route 53.

"Go EAST!" Charlotte said. "Look at the sun. You're driving west!"

Abby U-turned at an abandoned apple orchard, and Kingsley's empty stomach ached. Charlotte struggled to feed him. She did exactly what the nurse had told her to do. She shoved her bulging breast into his little face.

"I can't breathe!" Kingsley howled. He needed food but he needed air even more.

Nikki plugged her ears and scowled. Everything in the back seat was soaked wet with milk: Charlotte's jumper, Kingsley's blanket, and the once-spotless upholstery of Ray's new Pegasus. "Maybe she's sick of boobs," Nikki said. "I sure wouldn't want that thing shoved in my face."

"That's not helpful," Charlotte said.

The roads worsened the further they traveled into the countryside. "Stupid trees!" Abby said as she swerved around an opportunistic *ailanthus* tree growing in the broken asphalt. Tree-of-Heaven was what Andrés had called them when he told Kingsley and Amanda to dig one up. Most of the trees Kingsley could see were either *ailanthus* or pine. They pushed out the old oak and hickory forests. He didn't see any birds in the sky or dead animals on the highway, which Kingsley thought was strange. There were always a few dead raccoons and squirrels on the side of the interstate when he went for his gene-therapy treatment.

Abby hit a deep rut and Kingsley pooped in his diaper. Maybe it was just a fart. Either way, it smelled awful.

"What a stink!" Nikki said. Kingsley wasn't happy about the situation either.

"I'm sorry," Charlotte said. "I need to change him but I don't have any diapers."

Nikki lowered her window and cool air swirled through the car. They drove past empty shopping centers and vine-covered billboards. The car bucked again, rumbling over another rut. "Do you have to hit every pothole?" Nikki fussed.

Abby cursed as she swerved around another *ailanthus* tree. "Yes, Nikki, I have to hit every damn one."

"Roads aren't maintained beyond the cities," Charlotte said. "Only the interstate. You take your life in your hands if you drive over a bridge. Tunnels are even worse."

"How come you know so much about cars and bridges?" Nikki asked.

"It's my job," Charlotte said. "I'm a water operator."

"What?"

"Like a plumber. I drill wells, repair pumps, clean septic tanks. Things like that. Sometimes I work on cars."

Nikki stared at Charlotte, dumbfounded. "When our upstairs toilet stopped up, we just didn't use it anymore."

"We're almost at Fork Union," Abby said. "We'll pick up food and water before we head to Coach's campsite."

"And diapers," Charlotte added.

"Yeah," Nikki wrinkled her nose. "We know."

Springtime in a small Virginia town used to mean song birds looking for mates and gray squirrels searching for buried food. Not anymore. As the Pegasus rolled into the small town of Fork Union, no old men sat on park benches playing checkers. No children played in front yards. No robins searched for worms, no cardinals nested in the trees, no dogs barked in the distance. It was nothing like what Kingsley expected to see on a sunny late afternoon. Just crumbling sidewalks and abandoned buildings without even the dignity of a for-sale sign in front. Everything was as silent as the grave, everything except Nikki.

"This place is a dump! Look at those buildings! They're falling apart. Did you see the park we just passed? Nothing but weeds! How's anyone supposed to play soccer in all those weeds? This place reeks. It's like living in the Stone Age."

"Hampton is almost as empty," Charlotte said. "Our roads are terrible, too."

"But you know all about roads," Nikki said. "Why can't you fix them?"

Charlotte shook her head. "The problem isn't knowing how to fix them, the problem is getting the materials. Petroleum to make asphalt, limestone to make cement. There just aren't enough women in mining and manufacturing. My grandmother barely knows how to change a light bulb, forget trying to teach her how to make one." She leaned forward and tapped Abby on the shoulder. "Are you sure there's a farmer's market here? This town looks deserted."

Before Abby could answer, Nikki asked more questions. "And that's another thing, why aren't there more people in the world? What about cryogenics? What happened to all those frozen embryos from before The Collapse? And all the frozen eggs and sperm? I read about it on the Internet. There used to be huge sperm banks all over the country. Why aren't there—"

"Nikki, don't you know anything?" Abby said. "Cryogenics uses liquid nitrogen and has to be refreshed every six months. When The Collapse hit, people barely had electricity and water. They didn't have time to worry about making liquid nitrogen for frozen sperm and embryos."

"So what happened to them?"

"They thawed and rotted." Abby slowed the car. "We live in a bubble, Nik. Our moms are doctors so we have cars and homes and a place to go to school."

"And animals," Charlotte said. "I couldn't believe my eyes when I saw those deer and that seagull."

"Oh, that bird!" Nikki said. "Did you see how it swooped down on those guards? Was it really trying to help us escape?"

Abby looked in the rearview mirror. She puckered her lips and pinched her cheeks. "Mom's animals aren't like animals before The Collapse." She slowed in front of a wooded campus and parked next to two tall pillars holding a metal arch. She read aloud the historical marker. "*Fork Union*

Military Academy. Coeducational until 1919 when the trustees transformed it into an all-male academy."

"Coeducational?"

"It used to have female and male students, but changed to an all-boy school," Abby said as she got out of the car. She slammed the door. "Talk about backing the wrong horse."

Charlotte was in too much of a rush to stop and read the sign. Kingsley's diaper was leaking, which for Kingsley was not only uncomfortable, but was also embarrassing. Charlotte carried Kingsley to a small house with a red roof and a wide front porch. The girls followed. An old woman in a rocking chair was weaving baskets out of dried corn husks. She wore a long skirt, and her gray hair was tucked neatly into a lacy white cap. She smiled when she saw the girls. Her smile turned into a silent gasp when she saw Kingsley. Charlotte called up to her. "Do you know where I can buy diapers?" The old woman didn't answer. She stared slack-jawed at Kingsley. "I heard there's a farmer's market," Charlotte added. "I need a bottle and something for my baby to drink."

The old woman raised a thin, bony finger and pointed to the far end of the campus, her voice barely above a whisper. "Down the road a piece, past the barracks."

"Thanks," Charlotte said. She waved to the girls. "Come on."

They'd barely left the old woman when Nikki saw a small cannon mounted atop an elevated platform. "Look at that!" She bolted away.

English ivy smothered the cannon's wheels and carriage. A disintegrated bird's nest was lodged in its muzzle. Abby ran after Nikki, quickly overtaking her, reaching the cannon first. Kingsley wished he could run, too. He used to love playing on the cannons at the Yorktown battlefield.

"We don't have time for this," Charlotte snapped. "I have to find diapers."

Nikki climbed up the cannon and sat astride the barrel. She hugged the cold metal. "Imagine how gorgeous they all were, marching in their pressed uniforms, carrying flags and bayoneted rifles. I'd do anything to see them."

"This cannon's from World War One," Abby said. She kneeled beside a large stone pallet engraved with the names of the Fork Union cadets who'd died in war. "Some sort of memorial."

Charlotte called out to the girls. "Stay there if you want, I'm going to find the farmer's market." She marched through the tall, uncut grass, to the first brick building.

Abby followed, but Nikki lingered. "Come on, Nik," Abby said.

Nikki climbed down from the cannon. She knelt beside the engraved names of the long dead cadets and brushed away dust and debris. She touched her lips and blew them a kiss goodbye, then ran to catch up with Abby and Charlotte. "Sometimes I think I'm going to tear in two," she moaned. "I miss them so bad."

"You've never even met a man," Abby said. "Why do you constantly obsess over them?"

"Easy for you to say, you're in love with Sandy," Nikki said, and Abby blushed. "But what about me? What am I supposed to do?" She dragged behind, her head bent. "I'm sixteen-years-old, and my life is already ruined. It's not fair."

Kingsley agreed. It wasn't fair. He'd been stuck for hours with a dirty diaper and an empty stomach, and all he could do was cry.

When they reached the first building, the brick walls were covered with thick vines. Charlotte spat on the grimy window and rubbed a peephole. Inside, textbooks were left open on the desks next to faded plastic pens and corroded calculators. Laminated posters of rockets and missiles and a yellowed map of the world covered the walls. The chairs and desks were covered with dust and a whiteboard had *Graph these: $x - 2y + z = 4$; $10x - 4y - 5z = 20$; $2x + 6y + 3z = 18$* written on it.

"Algebra," Abby said.

"Weird," Nikki said.

"I don't see anything I can use for a diaper," Charlotte said. She pushed away from the window. "Let's go."

"It's like the boys just vanished," Nikki whispered. She wrapped her arm around Abby's waist and Abby draped hers over Nikki's shoulder. "Their books were still open, like they thought they were coming back. Didn't anyone see The Collapse coming?" The girls left the building and followed Charlotte.

"Some did," Charlotte said as they walked past a row of barracks toward the center of the campus. "My boss's father owned a construction company. He taught my boss how to drill wells and drive a backhoe when she was a girl. He even changed the handles on some of his tools so they'd fit her hands. Nanna told me lots of men tried to—"

Charlotte quieted when five old women wearing long dresses and lacy white caps approached. The woman they had talked to on the front porch was with them, carrying a basket full of unshelled English peas and a loaf of bread. She offered the basket to Charlotte as the other four women quietly gawked at Kingsley and smiled. "New mothers need fruits and vegetables," the old woman said.

Charlotte eyed the basket. "Fruits and vegetables?"

Nikki snatched a handful of the pea pods and popped them in her mouth. "Go on," she nudged Charlotte. "You must be starving." Nikki shared her peas with Abby.

The old woman smiled and once again offered Charlotte the basket.

"Thank you," Charlotte said. She tore off a large piece of the bread and shared the rest with Nikki and Abby. She nibbled the bread and her eyes lit up. "This is delicious!" She wolfed down the rest and licked the crumbs off her fingers. "I've never tasted anything like it."

"Pumpkin," the old woman said. "I grew it by hand. Planted the seeds and pollinated the flowers. I harvested three pumpkins last fall. A lot of work but worth the effort to see you enjoy it." She touched Kingsley's cheek and her eyes softened. "I haven't seen a baby since before the bad times. My son was a cadet. He'd just been accepted into West Point when he died."

"I'm looking for diapers and a baby bottle," Charlotte said.

"Try the flea market in Hamilton Hall," the woman said. She pointed to a tall stone building in the center of the campus. Charlotte thanked her and headed toward the flea market. The old women watched her go, their eyes moist.

"Why is it easier to grow peas than pumpkins?" Nikki asked, as she and Abby followed Charlotte.

"Peas can be self-pollinating," Abby said.

"What?"

"Self-pollinating. It's a lot like cloning, but it also has the same problems, especially after a few generations. Not enough genetic diversity. Peas are healthier with animal pollinators. Bugs, birds and bats."

"And people," Nikki said.

"Yeah, and people," Abby said. "Some plants are abiotic, that means they don't need animals to help them reproduce. Their pollen is moved by wind or water. Corn and wheat are abiotic, which is why almost everything we eat is made of wheat or corn." She pointed to the ubiquitous pines that surrounded the military academy. "Most evergreens are abiotic. They produce tons of pollen, which is carried on the wind."

Nikki sniffed and scratched her nose. "That explains a lot."

A woman wearing faded jeans hovered over an open fire pit, stirring soup in a large Dutch oven. Another was cutting cornbread into squares. There were a few early spring vegetables for sale: collards, kale, and more English peas, but no fruit, honey, meat or cheese. Charlotte bypassed the food and hurried to Hamilton Hall, Kingsley squirming constantly in her arms. His empty stomach ached and the dirty diaper burned his skin. Charlotte searched the flea market until she found a toy vendor. She begged the vendor to sell the diapers off her baby dolls. The vendor wouldn't take Charlotte's money. She happily gave the diapers and a toy baby bottle to Charlotte, free of charge.

Charlotte ran out of the flea market, clutching Kingsley. She hurried past the brick buildings and barracks, searching for a private place to change his diaper. She settled on a quiet spot behind the cannon. She sat on the grass and unwrapped Kingsley's blanket. She glanced around one last time before she pulled off his diaper, making sure no one would see that he was a boy. Cool air soothed Kingsley's red rash but Charlotte didn't have a washcloth to clean him. She had to wipe him on the grass, which stung. She quickly put one of the clean baby doll diapers on him.

Kingsley's bottom wasn't wet but his stomach still ached. He was hungry and thirsty. Charlotte didn't try to nurse him, not after her failed attempt in the backseat of the Pegasus. She expressed milk and filled the toy bottle, and gave it to Kingsley.

It was horrible. The old nipple disintegrated in his mouth. Charlotte frantically dug the bits of rubber out of his mouth as Kingsley coughed and spat. He flailed his hands and feet, gasping for breath. "I'm going to die!" he cried. "I'm going to die! Just like I died in the tunnel!"

Kingsley stopped crying. He stopped flailing. "Just like I died in the tunnel?" Memories rushed in. Gasoline. Crying women. Raging headache. Kingsley held his breath. He remembered the pain drifting away. He remembered watching fourteen-year-old Kingsley Smith's head lying motionless in Amanda's lap. He held his breath until he couldn't hold it anymore, and then he let out a scream that racked his tiny body to the core.

"I'm dead! I'm dead! I'm dead, and I've gone to hell. Fire and brimstone! That's why my skin burns! That's why my stomach aches! I've stolen, I've fibbed, and now I'm in hell."

Charlotte sobbed. She rocked him back and forth. "I don't know what to do. My baby, my poor baby." Her tears rained on Kingsley's head.

Neither Kingsley nor Charlotte noticed the cooling shadow. Neither noticed the stranger walking through the tall grass toward them. She wore an ivory shirt with a simple, tan skirt and carried a large knapsack. Her hair was gray with a recollection of auburn, her voice calm and soft. "Sure is making a fuss, isn't he?"

Charlotte startled. "She!" Charlotte sobbed. "My baby's a girl!"

The woman sat in the grass beside Charlotte. "Don't worry, I can keep a secret." She rubbed Charlotte's back like a favorite aunt. "You're trying too hard. You've got to relax. Take a deep breath." Charlotte gulped air with short, staccato breaths. "No, no, *Breathe*," she said, melodically. "In and out, in and out." Charlotte sniffed and swallowed, and finally took a deep breath. "That's a good start," the woman said. She tossed aside the bottle with the disintegrating nipple. "First let's get rid of that thing. You need to learn how to breastfeed."

"I can't. I'm no good at it."

"Give it a try."

Charlotte wiped her tears and once again did what the nurse at the medical center had taught her. She smashed her full, leaking breast into Kingsley's tiny face.

Kingsley hated it. He was convinced he was in hell, and being suffocated by Amanda's lookalike was part of his punishment.

The woman winced. "Pull back, pull back. You're feeding him, not smothering him." She opened her knapsack and pulled out two pillows. She placed one pillow behind Charlotte's back. "Lean against the cannon wheel," she said. "There, now doesn't that feel more relaxed?" She placed the other pillow underneath Kingsley so he was a bit higher on Charlotte's lap. "Taking care of a baby is exhausting."

Charlotte flushed and her tears returned. "All my life I've dreamed of having a baby, but it wasn't supposed to be like this. Nanna was supposed to come with me. My mother was supposed to be alive to help me."

"I know," the woman whispered. "Our mothers are supposed to be with us forever." She showed Charlotte how to cradle Kingsley's head in the crook of one arm, while her other hand guided her breast. "Good, good," the woman said. "Let his chin lead the way."

Kingsley was afraid. He turned his head and cried. Charlotte was crying too, but the woman wouldn't let her give up. She gently placed her hand on the back of Kingsley's head and guided him. "Once he's latched on, his nose should be barely touching your breast. Not squished into you." She showed Charlotte how to hold her breast so Kingsley could breathe as he ate.

It worked like magic. Kingsley's terror drained away as the warm milk filled his stomach. He released the rage he'd felt moments before. He relaxed in her arms, finally getting the peace of mind he needed almost as much as the milk.

"Breastfeeding shouldn't hurt," the woman said. "If it hurts, break the suction and try again."

Charlotte couldn't keep her eyes off him. "It doesn't hurt."

"He needs a bath," the woman said. "You can use one of the sinks in the first barracks. No one will bother you. But there's a problem. The academy hasn't had water in years. Marcy has to tote water from the river to make her soup, which is a darn nuisance. You'll have to fix their pump, but that should be easy for you."

Charlotte looked up at the woman, startled. "How'd you know I was a plumber? Do you know Dr. Cama? Did she send you?"

The woman didn't answer. "Good thing you came this way. Lucky for you and lucky for the town." The woman stood up and brushed the grass off her skirt. "The pump house is around back, next to the maintenance garage. And don't worry about people finding out he's a boy. Like I said, I can keep a secret."

When Kingsley woke, his stomach was full and Nikki was holding him. They were in a dim, weatherworn shack with one open door, no windows, and one glaring light bulb shining overhead. Charlotte was studying blueprints. Abby wasn't with them. Charlotte carefully rolled up the brittle blueprints and placed them on a dusty shelf. "This is pretty typical of pump houses," she told Nikki as she stripped and twisted two wires, and then used a wrench to tighten a bolt. "Some better, some worse. Lots of the potholes you see are from busted water pipes under the asphalt." She pointed at two metal tubes that looked like torpedoes. "Those are the pumps." She finished with the bolt and flipped a switch. The pumps made a loud noise and then slowly settled into a steady rhythm. Charlotte took Kingsley from Nikki. "Let's go see if they work."

Abby was lolling on a bench near the front of the campus, the knapsack with the pillows beside her. "Did you fix their water?" she asked.

"I hope so," Charlotte said. She found an outside spigot. Vendors gathered to watch. Charlotte turned the handle. Nothing came out. They waited. A minute later there came a loud gurgling sound, and then a strong stream of pitch-black fluid shot out.

Everyone jumped back. "Ugh!"

"Let it run for a while," Charlotte said. "It'll clear up. You need to get a plumber out here at least once a year to maintain the system, or you'll be out of water again."

"There are no plumbers," one of the vendors said. "No electricians either. Amazed we got power."

"Me, too," Charlotte said. She took Abby and Nikki aside. "I need to give my baby a bath," she whispered. "Don't let anyone follow me." She grabbed the knapsack.

As Charlotte carried Kingsley to the barracks, one of the elderly vendors tapped Nikki on her shoulder. "I used to work here. I taught statistics."

Another spoke up. "I bred Arabian horses. Owned a stable just east of Bremo Bluff."

"I was a writer," a third woman said.

"Of what?" Nikki asked.

"Fiction."

Nikki rolled her eyes. "No wonder there's no water. Put the three of you together and you couldn't dig your way out of a shallow grave."

Charlotte found an unlocked door and wandered down an empty hallway, her footsteps leaving a muddy trail in the dust. She passed a glass display cabinet filled with sports trophies and faded photos of young men.

She located the boys' locker room. Musty jerseys and shorts were still hanging from the lockers. Charlotte parked the knapsack beside one of the sinks and turned on a faucet. Black fluid sputtered. Charlotte let it run for several minutes until it cleared. She tasted the water and smacked her lips. She found a dusty glass, rinsed it out, and then drank and drank and drank. Kingsley had never seen anyone so thirsty. She filled a sink and made sure they were alone before unwrapping Kingsley's blanket and taking off his diaper.

The water was shockingly cold. Kingsley cried until he saw a crying baby looking at him in the mirror over the sink. The baby was small, bald and had hazel eyes. Cute. Round but not fat.

Charlotte used one of the jerseys to dry him, and then put his diaper back on. She wrapped Kingsley in another jersey and laid him gently on the soft knapsack. He was chilly but his stomach was full and his bottom didn't hurt. Charlotte took off her jumper and underwear and washed them in the sink, washing out the dried milk, and then she washed Kingsley's smelly baby blanket. She stood at the sink, naked except for her shoes. Kingsley thought it strange that she could walk around naked but he had to be covered, especially since they were at a boys' military academy. She wrung out the clothes the best she could, and found a dry sweatshirt and shorts to slip on. She carried Kingsley and her clean, damp clothes back to Abby and Nikki.

The girls were agitated. "We have to get out of here," Abby grumbled. The vendors and the elderly women wearing long dresses and white caps were with them, but no one was talking about the fresh water or the running faucets. They didn't react when Charlotte arrived with Kingsley, both clean and wearing Fork Union jerseys. Everyone was looking up.

A large gull with red eyes was circling overhead. The vendors twittered like excited schoolgirls when the bird swooped down and perched atop one of the pillars.

"Do you think it's lost?" Nikki whispered.

"No," Abby said. "It's following us."

22 Camping Along the James

The bridge was covered with Virginia creeper, honeysuckle and poison ivy. Cracks etched like lightning across its concrete walls. Small trees were embedded in its asphalt. Water rushed under it. "That's the James River," Abby said. "But I don't remember it being this high last fall."

The James River stretches across the state, from the Appalachian Mountains to the Chesapeake Bay. It merges with the Elizabeth River and the Nansemond River to form the harbor called Hampton Roads. Kingsley didn't know much about the James River, but he knew a lot about the Hampton Roads harbor. The Civil War battle between the Monitor and the Merrimack took place in the harbor. The Monitor-Merrimac Bridge Tunnel spanned the harbor. Amanda had died in the harbor.

Nikki nervously picked at her fingernails as they all got out of the car. "Did Coach drive over this when she took us camping?"

"No," Abby said. "We didn't drive, remember? We canoed from Scottsville, but the river was a lot calmer then." She tore vines away from a sign. "Built in 2005." She turned to Charlotte. "How long does concrete last?"

"A long time, but it has to be maintained. Roots can tear apart concrete just like they tear apart asphalt."

"Maybe there's another way across," Nikki said.

Abby shook her head. "Not unless we go back to the interstate."

Charlotte handed Kingsley to Nikki. "Only one way to find out."

Charlotte started across the bridge. The going was slow. Too slow. Kingsley wanted to jump out of Nikki's arms every time Charlotte stopped to pick at broken pieces of concrete. When she finally reached the other side, she gave the thumbs up and jogged back. "Steel girders underneath the asphalt. Whoever built this thing knew what they were doing."

They climbed back into the car, and Abby drove across the bridge. Nikki checked her computer as they passed rows of abandoned doublewides. They came to a dusty, unmarked intersection. "I think we go left," Nikki said. Abby turned onto a dirt road and rumbled into the darkening forest. Kingsley fell asleep in Charlotte's arms.

New springtime leaves silhouetted against the moonlit sky. Thick evergreens cast shadow puppets in the breeze. Kingsley woke to the muffled roar of the James River in the distance. He could feel warmth from a crackling fire. He could smell its smoke. He was in a basket, a pillow under him, and a beach towel over him like a blanket. Above him floated a full moon and one magnificent star.

"That's not a star," he heard Abby say, as if she knew what he was thinking. "They're planets. Jupiter and Venus. They're in conjunction, that's why they're so bright."

He squirmed in his basket. "What's going on?" he asked and was immediately whisked into Charlotte's lap. Charlotte and the two girls were sitting in low wicker chairs, arranged in a semicircle around a campfire and a steaming pot of soup. Kingsley guessed they'd bought the soup at the farmers market. Charlotte wrapped a sleeping bag around herself and Kingsley. Abby sat next to Charlotte, a frayed quilt covering her legs. Nikki shared Abby's quilt, her computer in her lap. Light from the moon and the campfire illuminated a small storage shed with a wobbly table in front of it. Beside the shed was a large tent. Beyond the tent was Ray's Pegasus, parked in the dirt.

"I wrote a story about the Military Academy," Nikki said. "I call it The Cadets." She crossed her legs and most of the quilt went with her. A brief tug-of-war with Abby ensued until they settled on half the quilt each and Nikki began to read.

"The girl was barely sixteen-years-old and terribly nervous about visiting the all-boys military academy. She'd heard about all the gorgeous cadets who lived there and was anxious to meet them, but afraid it would be the end of her virginity."

Abby rolled her eyes, "Here we go again."

"The boys were amazing. Seventeen-year-old sex machines."

Abby winced. "Sex machines? Really, Nikki?"

"I'll take out sex machines." Nikki tapped the screen. "The girl followed the boys into an algebra classroom but the teacher wasn't there yet." Nikki looked up at Abby and Charlotte. "Like the classroom we saw at Fork Union, remember?"

"Of course we remember," Abby said. "We're not imbeciles." She threw aside her half of the quilt and stirred the soup. She gingerly took a taste. "Hand me those bowls, Nik."

Nikki handed Abby three bowls, and Abby passed around the soup. Diced potatoes floating in watery liquid. It looked pretty skimpy to Kingsley—no chicken, no bacon, no beef.

"The girl was incredibly beautiful. The boys didn't have a chance. They felt faint, overwhelmed by her beautiful skin and beautiful hair."

"Use a different word," Abby said, as she passed around cornbread. "You already told us she's beautiful."

Kingsley liked Nikki even though she talked too much. She was skinny and silly and reminded him of Billy Jackson, even though Billy was a black boy and Nikki was an Asian girl. But most of all, he liked Nikki because she wanted boys back. Abby was different. She was Ray Fells' daughter and didn't talk about boys at all. Kingsley didn't know why she'd helped him escape the medical center. He had no reason not to trust her, but occasionally, when she rolled her eyes or said something sassy, she reminded him of Amanda.

"The girl modestly took a seat next to a handsome boy with a buzz haircut. His mouth watered at the thought of her naked body. He breathed in her scent, and she breathed in his scent. They both sniffed the air, breathing in each other's scent. He stunk of damp oak and musk and she—"

"Stunk!" Abby said. "How do you know what boys smell like? Or musk, for that matter?"

Nikki stuck her tongue out at Abby, which caused Kingsley to laugh for the first time since he had been with Amanda. It felt good.

"An officer entered the room, and the girl almost fainted. He was gorgeous. Muscles like barbells and hair as thick as molasses."

Abby gagged. "Molasses hair? That's disgusting!"

"Stop criticizing me!" Nikki snapped. "I'm trying to be creative." Nikki sniffed and continued her story. "The officer ordered the cadets out of the classroom. He took the girl's delicate hand. On the wall was a map of the Americas. He pushed her against the map. The curves of the continents mirrored the curves of her luscious breasts and shapely hips."

"Luscious breasts and shapely hips? I thought this was supposed to be about you!"

"Shut up, Abby!" Nikki hid under the quilt, her voice muffled. "I bare my soul, and all you do is make fun."

Abby tugged the quilt away from Nikki's face. "I'm sorry, Nik." She playfully took Nikki's right hand. "Come on, introduce Charlotte to Sheila."

"Sheila?" Charlotte asked.

"Sheila has lunch with us every day at school," Abby said. "She's Nikki's hand. Nik draws a mouth and two eyes on it and calls her Sheila. Didn't you sign Sheila up for soccer tryouts?"

Nikki sat up in her chair. "Yeah, I did. Coach Liz kept yelling 'Sheila,' 'Sheila.' It was so funny." Nikki balled her fist and *Shelia* gave Kingsley a kiss, which made Kingsley laugh for the second time that day.

Kingsley felt warm and lazy in Charlotte's lap. His stomach was full, his diaper dry and he was surrounded by friends and family.

"I don't know what would have happened if you hadn't helped us," Charlotte said to Abby and Nikki, "Dr. Cama told me they wanted to experiment on—" Charlotte paused, as if weighing whether to tell them the truth that Kingsley was a boy. Kingsley was anxious to see how Nikki would react but he was nervous about telling Abby. She was a mystery, and Kingsley had a feeling Abby knew more about him than she let on. Kingsley was both disappointed and relieved when Charlotte said, "—her."

"Thank Sandy and Dr. Cama," Abby said. "They're why I helped you." As she nestled another log into the glowing campfire, a pendant on a silver chain dangled from her neck. Kingsley was stunned. He recognized the pendant. He'd stolen it from Dr. Jacobs, thinking it would give him good luck. He'd tried to give it back, but Dr. Jacobs said he could keep it. The pendant was in Kingsley's pocket when he died in the tunnel.

"That's beautiful," Charlotte said. "Are you Jewish?"

"No," Abby shook her head. "My grandmother gave it to me."

Nikki sat up in her chair, grinning. "You wouldn't believe Abby's grandmother, not in a million years. If you think Dr. Fells is power mad, just wait 'til you meet Lily Fells."

Kingsley listened carefully, wanting to hear every word. He hoped they'd explain how penniless Joyce Smith became rich and powerful Lily Fells.

"I've met Ms. Fells," Charlotte said. "She brought me a basket of gifts. She was very kind."

"Kind? Are you kidding? She wants to rule the world. Tell her, Abby. Tell Charlotte about your grandmother."

Abby poked the fire with a stick. "There's not much to tell. She moved here after her son died. She told everyone she was Jewish because—"

Nikki jumped in. "It's really a funny story, almost as good as the one I wrote about the cadets." She scooted her chair closer to Charlotte. "Lily grew up in New Orleans, see. She was poor and the city was a mess. Oil spills galore and lots of crime. Murders and robberies. That was before The Collapse, of course. Lily got pregnant when she was a teenager by some loser and...."

Kingsley flushed. "Loser! My father wasn't a loser! He was a good man!"

"...she had a boy. He's dead now, of course."

Kingsley reeled. Hearing his life and death voiced so casually was brutal.

"And if that wasn't bad enough, then Lily moved to Virginia and was raped."

Charlotte recoiled. "Raped?" she said. "That's horrible."

Kingsley felt a rush of rage at Jack Sutherland. And a rush of guilt at himself. He shouldn't have left his mother alone with Jack. He should have rescued both Amanda and his mother when he had the chance.

"Isn't that right, Abby?" Nikki asked. "That's what you told me. Your grandmother was raped. That's why your mom hates men, because she was conceived because of a rape." Abby stirred the fire and murmured an unheard answer.

Charlotte pulled the sleeping bag she'd shared with Kingsley around them like an invisible cloak. "I've never met anyone who was actually attacked by a man."

"The problem is that Dr. Fells looks more like the rapist than she looks like Lily," Nikki said. "Blonde and stuff. Kind of creepy, when you think about it. Your kid looking like your rapist."

"It's more than that," Abby said, still stirring the fire. "Grandmother talks constantly about her dead son. How wonderful he was. How sweet he was. Mom says Grandmother loved him more than she loves us."

Kingsley felt a lump in his throat. He loved Charlotte and wanted to stay with her, but hearing Abby talk about Joyce tore at his heart. He knew the bad she'd done. She shot his father and stole from Mrs. Sutherland, but she was his mother.

"So far this isn't a very funny story," Charlotte said. "Is that why Ms. Fells told everyone she was Jewish? Because she was raped?"

"Huh?" Nikki said. "Oh, I don't know why she claimed to be Jewish. Abby, tell Charlotte about your mom's bat mitzvah."

"Her what?" Charlotte asked.

Abby returned to her chair and confiscated half of Nikki's quilt. "A bat mitzvah is a coming-of-age ceremony. Grandmother thought telling everyone she was Jewish would make her look classy. She hired a rabbinical student to teach Mom Hebrew." Abby smiled up at the moon. "You should hear Mom tell the story. She's so dry. Once the ceremony was over, the guests filed into the social hall to wait for the rabbi to bless the bread and wine. Of course, Grandmother had never actually attended a bat mitzvah before so she's slinging back the wine, one glass after another, until she realizes no one else was drinking."

"Half-snockered," Nikki added.

Abby rubbed Dr. Jacobs' pendant between her forefinger and thumb, just as Kingsley used to do. It shimmered in the firelight. "No one at the synagogue was fooled. They all knew Grandmother wasn't Jewish. I guess after The Collapse, after so much tragedy, who cares? Mom is different from Grandmother. Mom wants to make the world a better place. That's why she created the Rotifer Project. Grandmother just wants what she wants."

The sound of a snapping twig drew everyone's attention.

"What was that?" Charlotte asked. "Is someone out there?"

No one answered.

Abby stood and took a few steps toward the sound. The woods were black, not even the bright moon and stars could penetrate the darkness.

"Probably just one of Mom's deer."

"Too bad Farty Ann's not here," Nikki said. "We could've had roasted deer meat for dinner instead of that watery soup."

"Venison," Abby said.

"Who's Farty Ann?" Charlotte asked.

"Grandmother's bodyguard," Abby said. "Grandmother calls her Phoebe Ann after Annie Oakley. No one knows her real name."

"Who's Annie Oakley?"

Abby returned to her seat. "Annie Oakley was a sharpshooter in the wild west. Phoebe Ann Mosey was Annie Oakley's real name. It's kind of a joke. Like, you know, Phoebe Ann is Grandmother's sharpshooter."

"She's really creepy," Nikki said. "Doesn't talk, only grunts. Probably can't read or write, either." Nikki lowered her voice and leaned close, her face illuminated by the fire. "She carries an old, smelly pouch made out of some animal skin wherever she goes. Know what's in it?"

Charlotte shook her head. Kingsley shook his, too, but no one noticed.

"Knives," Nikki's voice was eerie. "She carries around hunting knives and sharpens them every day. Like it's some sort of religious ritual." Nikki gave a little shudder. Kingsley shuddered too. He remembered when Phoebe Ann held him. The woman was a cross between a linebacker and a Sasquatch—scary enough without the knives.

Abby broke the tension. "Mom wants to run genetic tests on her," she said. "She thinks Phoebe Ann has a Y-chromosome somewhere in the mix."

"Why does your grandmother need a bodyguard?" Charlotte asked. Kingsley had wondered, too. He'd been curious about that since the first time he saw the giant.

Abby hesitated. "Um, she just, um, she worries a lot." She didn't meet Charlotte's eyes.

Nikki changed the subject. "Who were those women at Fork Union wearing the little white bonnets?" she asked.

"Old-order Mennonites," Abby said. "Grandmother says half the state would have starved if not for the Mennonite farmers in the Shenandoah Valley. I don't understand why they don't have daughters. They should be the richest people in the state. Grandmother said she once traded a pearl necklace for a sack of cornmeal."

"They probably gave their food away," Charlotte said. "Like the woman who gave us the pumpkin bread and peas."

Nikki smugly shook her head. "It's not about money. Cloning is a sin."

"Nikki, you're a clone!"

"Yeah, I know, but the Pope condemned it. 'Course he's dead now, so who cares? If a tree falls in the forest and nobody hears it, who gives a shit? But I bet that's why those Mennonite women don't have children. I just wish they'd bring back men."

"You wouldn't if you paid attention in history class," Abby said.

"I can tell you why men should be brought back in three words," Nikki said. "Jesus Christ, William Shakespeare and Hugh Grant."

"That's seven words," Abby said.

"Who's Hugh Grant?" Charlotte asked.

"He was gorgeous," Nikki said. "I'll show you a picture." She tapped her computer screen.

Abby was unyielding. "I'll see your three and raise you one more. Hitler, Stalin, Ted Bundy and Jack the Ripper. And answer me this, what do all four of them have in common? They all killed women."

Charlotte pulled Kingsley close. "Don't listen to her, *Niño*," she whispered. "I want you back." Kingsley felt her caress and knew he was safe and loved.

Nikki never got the chance to share the photos of Hugh Grant. "This reeks! This totally reeks!" she squealed. She threw off the quilt, jumped up from her seat and showed Charlotte and Abby the screen. "Your mom's on the news. She's telling the whole world we kidnapped a baby and stole her car!"

23 The News is Out

"…a kidnapper and a thief. She's a criminal. She's unstable. She could kill him." Ray singled out three women from the enraged crowd. "You! You! You! Find Charlotte Sutherland and save the boy!"

Nikki looked up from her computer. "Boy? What boy?"

Abby snatched the laptop from Nikki. "Did you see those women? They want to tear us apart."

"Not you," Charlotte said. "Only me."

Nikki turned to Kingsley, slack-jawed, eyes as full as the moon. "Boy? A real live boy?"

Charlotte nodded.

Just as Kingsley had predicted, Nikki was overjoyed. "Yes! Yes! Yes!" Nikki jumped up from her seat and howled like a hungry coyote invited to Thanksgiving dinner. "A boy! A boy! We've finally got a boy!" She danced around the campfire, laughing and cheering, then quickly kneeled beside Charlotte and pulled at Kingsley's blanket. "Prove it!"

"No!" Charlotte said. She pushed Nikki away, much to Kingsley's relief.

Abby tapped the image on the screen. It was of a multistory glass-and-brick building. "That's not the medical center. Mom's not in Charlottesville. We need to see this from the beginning." She hit a button and the glass-and-brick building sparkled in the late-afternoon sun. The crowd wasn't enraged. Not yet. A thirty-something-year-old professional woman with brown hair and glasses stood in front of the building, talking into a microphone. Odelle stood beside her as tense as a clinched fist.

"I'm in front of the Jones Institute in Norfolk, Virginia, waiting for Dr. Miles-Johnson, hoping to unravel the mystery of the boy born last week and her involvement in the creation of the male embryo," the woman said into the microphone. "With me today is Odelle Holland. Chief Holland is in charge of security at the medical center in Charlottesville where the boy was born. Chief Holland, my understanding is that the boy showed no signs of the Y-Chromosome Linked Tumors Syndrome. Can you confirm this?" The reporter jabbed the microphone at Odelle.

Odelle answered coldly. "I'm not a doctor."

The crowd around the building was growing. Women were shouting and begging. They wanted Dr. Miles-Johnson to come out and give them sons.

The reporter talked into the microphone, raising her voice to be heard over the crowd. "Can you tell us anything about his health?" She moved the microphone toward Odelle.

"No."

The reporter kept punching. "Then can you tell us why security around the boy was so ineffective? The first healthy boy born in almost half a century is kidnapped under your watch, and you have no idea where he is? How could this happen?"

Ray butted between the reporter and Odelle. "Security at the medical center is impeccable! The boy would still be there if not for an intolerable breach of ethics by one of our doctors."

"What's the name of the doctor?" the reporter asked. "How was she involved with his kidnapping?"

Odelle stepped in. "All I can tell you is that the physician in question has been terminated from her position, and we've initiated protocols to revoke her medical license. Currently she is in police custody."

"If you can't tell us her name or her involvement, can you explain the penalty for kidnapping?"

"Any penalty beyond losing her position is for the courts to decide," Odelle said. "However, under current Virginia statutes, the maximum prison time for kidnapping is fifty years."

"Fifty years!" Nikki stopped dancing around. "Is she talking about Dr. Cama? What about us? What if we're charged with kidnapping?"

Kingsley's heart ached. He imagined Bapsi shivering on a hard cot with a thick-necked guard slapping a nightstick against the bars of her cell. He'd seen that in movies. Thick-necked guards with nightsticks, but usually the guards were men, and so were the prisoners.

A short doctor wearing a white lab coat toddled slowly out the front door of the glass-and-brick building. She had cropped, gray hair and a disproportionately long chin. The crowd exploded:

"Clone my grandfather!"

"Bring back my son!"

"Please, I want a husband!"

The reporter left Ray and Odelle and rushed to the short doctor. "Dr. Miles-Johnson!" she jabbed the microphone at her, "Did you create the male embryo? Have you cured The Collapse? Do you realize cloning a dead person is illegal?"

"Quiet!" Dr. Miles-Johnson shouted at the crowd. "I can't hear myself think." She turned to the reporter. "It's been a madhouse here ever since the news about that boy. I swear it'd be easier if they came at me with bats and guns. All this whining is killing me."

The reporter turned to the camera. "I'm speaking with Dr. Miles-Johnson to discover—"

The short doctor cut her off. "Of course I know cloning a dead person is illegal. The whole world knows it's illegal. You want the truth? I'll tell you the truth." She nervously fiddled with the buttons of her lab coat. "I did nothing wrong and neither did Charlotte. I've known the Sutherlands for years. We're related."

"Related?"

Dr. Miles-Johnson nodded, "My aunt on my mother's side was married to Charlotte's great-uncle or something like that. I can't remember, exactly."

The crowd moved like an amoeba, calling the doctor by name, begging for her help. Dr. Miles-Johnson called back. "I didn't clone the boy. I don't know anything. Go away and leave me alone." Ray said something that the microphone didn't pick up, and the crowd stretched toward her. Dr. Miles-Johnson returned to the reporter. "Charlotte didn't know she was pregnant with a boy, and neither did I."

"Didn't you tell the authorities that you created the embryo?"

Dr. Miles-Johnson blinked repeatedly and rubbed her hands against the pockets of her white lab coat. "Um, yes. Years ago, when Charlotte first tried to get pregnant. I created Charlotte's clone. It didn't take. Like I said, that was years ago. I didn't have anything to do with creating that boy." She wiped the corners of her mouth and nervously swallowed. "The issue is money, you know. Only the rich can afford children nowadays. Quite a change from the old days. Used to be the poor had twelve children to a family because they couldn't afford birth control while the rich had one or two because they could. Now, it's the other way around. The poor don't have any children at all. Except for Charlotte, I mean. She's certainly not rich." The old doctor blinked repeatedly and rubbed her eyes. She pointed at Ray. "Isn't that the famous Dr. Ray Fells? Creator of the Rotifer Project?"

"Yes," the reporter answered.

Dr. Miles-Johnson's eyes narrowed. The sun was setting and orange hues bounced off the glass-and-brick building. "I met her mother last year. Very interesting woman."

"Are you suggesting that Dr. Fells was involved in cloning the boy?"

Dr. Miles-Johnson recoiled. "No, not at all."

The reporter pressed further. "Since no one is claiming responsibility, why, in your opinion, was this particular male embryo created? And equally curious, why, of all the women in the world, was he implanted in Charlotte Sutherland?"

Dr. Miles-Johnson pulled a cloth handkerchief from her coat pocket and wiped perspiration from her upper lip. "I was thirty-six-years old when The Collapse began. Norfolk was full of sailors back then. You couldn't throw a stick without hitting a man in uniform. The Collapse hit, and it didn't matter who you were. Rich or poor, black or white. Nothing mattered for a long time. People starved while cargo ships full of rotting food drifted in the middle of the ocean. Horrible times. Is the idea of a generous soul secretly trying to bring back men really all that insane? Doesn't everyone deserve the right to have a child? Not just the rich?"

Before the reporter could reply, Ray pushed Dr. Miles-Johnson aside and roared into the microphone, "Charlotte Sutherland kidnapped the boy and two teenaged girls, Nikki Shao and my daughter, Abby Fells. She stole my car. A maroon Pegasus, license plate R0TI4. Charlotte Sutherland is a kidnapper and a thief." The crowd erupted and cursed Charlotte's name, some almost foaming at the mouth. "She's a criminal," Ray said, "She's mentally unstable. She could kill him." Ray pointed at three particularly vicious-looking women. "You! You! You! Find Charlotte Sutherland and save the boy!"

Screams from the crowd:

"Arrest Charlotte Sutherland!"

"Throw her in jail!"

A woman fell to her knees and clasped her hands. "Please! Please! She doesn't deserve a son but I do! Give me that baby! I'm not a criminal. I'm not insane. Let me be his mother. Please! Please!"

Odelle raised her hands and tried to reason with the crowd. "If you see the car or know the location of Ms. Sutherland, call the police. Don't approach her; don't try to take the infant from—"

Ray jumped in. "Take the baby! Don't wait for the police!" She drew the crowd in. "Listen to me. My name is Dr. Ray Fells, Director of Genetic Research and Reproduction. If you want a baby, I can help you. But you have to help me first. Find Charlotte Sutherland!"

The crowd salivated.

"Find her!"

"Kill her!"

"Hold on," Odelle said. "She's not dangerous. Don't go chasing—"

Ray wouldn't let go. "Yes, DO go chasing after her! Find that boy. Your future depends on it."

Charlotte was incensed. "Criminal? Unstable? I'm his mother!"

Nikki, on the other hand, wasn't watching the screen at all. She was mesmerized by Kingsley. She poked his round tummy and stuck out her tongue at him. He stuck his tongue out at her, which delighted Nikki. "Hey, did you see that? Did you see what he did? I knew boys would like me."

"It doesn't make any sense," Abby said.

"Yeah, it does," Nikki said. "Being a bitch is what your mom does best."

"Mom doesn't want to rescue him," Abby said. "She doesn't want men back at all. I don't know why she's in Norfolk. Odelle has to search for him; it's her job, but not Mom's."

Charlotte abruptly stood and ended the conversation. "He needs to eat, and I'm tired. I'm going to bed." She headed for the tent.

Kingsley feared for Charlotte. Feared what that angry crowd would do to her. He shivered as Charlotte carried him and the sleeping bag away from the warm fire. He could still see Abby and Nikki, heads together, illuminated by the glow of the computer screen.

"I don't know why you want men back either, Nik," Abby said. "Do you think we'd be sitting here in the dark, in the middle of nowhere, if men were around? Three women and a baby? You've seen the movies. You've read the history books. We'd be cowering behind locked doors, afraid of being attacked."

"I wouldn't be here at all if I had a man," Nikki said.

"Are you telling me that if some guy appeared in front of you right now, you'd let him stick his thing in you? It's disgusting!"

"Not to me!" Nikki cried. She covered her face and ran from the fire. She left Abby and hurried past Charlotte and Kingsley and climbed into the tent ahead of them. The tent was dimly lit by the full moon. Kingsley could barely see Nikki sitting in the corner, but he could hear her. Sobbing and sniffing, her head was down and her arms were wrapped around her knees. Kingsley had felt so many emotions over the past few days. From despair over learning of Amanda's death, to shock when he realized he'd died in the tunnel, to joy the moment they escaped the medical center, to laughing when Nikki introduced him to Shelia. He wished he could cry in the corner with Nikki, with his head down and his arms wrapped around his knees.

Charlotte slipped out of her shoes, crawled into her sleeping bag and nursed him. Despite hearing Nikki's tears, despite thinking about Ray and the angry crowd screaming for Charlotte's arrest, Kingsley felt safe in her arms.

Abby came into the tent carrying two sleeping bags; she offered one to Nikki. "Hey, Nik" she whispered. "I'm sorry for what I said. I'm trying to save the baby too, aren't I?"

"It's not that," Nikki said, sniffling, "I used to dream about my life when The Collapse ended. I dreamed I'd have a boyfriend, and I'd get married and everything would be perfect. But look at him. He's just a baby. By the time he's my age I'll be, like, thirty years old. Practically ancient. He'll have his pick of girlfriends. He won't want me." She wiped her nose with the edge of the sleeping bag. "It was easier when it was just a fantasy. Now I know for a fact that I'm going to be alone my whole life."

"You're not alone, Nik," Abby said, scooting close. "You'll always have me and Sandy."

Kingsley had never been camping before, not with Joyce or his dad, not even with Amanda. A light wind rustled trees and whispered in the distance. He felt the solid earth under him and Charlotte's slow, steady breath beside him. He fell asleep comforted by the earth and the cool, clean air.

Kingsley woke at daybreak to a sound outside the tent—the crunching of broken twigs or dried leaves. The roof of the tent was covered with dew and pine needles, and the inside smelled of sweat and dried milk. Charlotte was still asleep next to him. Nikki was asleep in her sleeping bag, Abby in hers. The crunching stopped, and was replaced by a low rumble, almost like a moan. The walls of the tent moved.

"Something's out there!" he yelled. "Wake up, something's out there!" A black nose and bright-red eyes poked through the entrance. "A monster!" he cried. "There's a monster outside the tent!"

Nikki shot up and screamed.

The red-eyed monster quickly backed out of the tent.

Abby plugged her ears. "Stop screaming, Nik! You're worse than the baby. It's just one of Mom's deer."

Kingsley and Nikki quieted down. Abby was right. Kingsley caught a glimpse of the deer's white tail as it scampered away. Abby grumbled and threw back her sleeping bag. "Probably the last sunrise I'll ever see." She slipped on her soccer shoes and wrapped her sleeping bag around her like a cloak. "Probably spend the rest of my life in jail," she said as she climbed out of the tent. "I'll never see Sandy again, and it's all your fault."

Charlotte rose up on her elbows and Nikki plopped back down, pulling her sleeping bag up to her neck. "Don't pay any attention to her. She's always a grump in the morning," Nikki said. "Actually, she's always a grump all the time. Sandy's the only person who'll put up with her."

Charlotte scooted out of the warm sleeping bag and slipped on her shoes. She left Kingsley with Nikki as she climbed out of the tent. She hurried back moments later with a clean diaper. Nikki watched as Charlotte changed Kingsley's diaper, much to Kingsley's embarrassment. Nikki stared at him, transfixed, like he was a magic lamp and she was waiting for a genie to pop out. He wished she'd go help Abby build a fire or fix breakfast or whatever Abby was doing. He soon smelled smoke and heard Abby cursing and rattling pots and pans.

Charlotte carried Kingsley out of the tent. Abby had started a fire and was boiling water. "This is all I could find," she said as she handed Charlotte a cup of hot tea.

"Tea's fine," Charlotte said. She took a sip and smacked her lips. "Thanks." She settled into one of the wicker chairs, Kingsley on her lap. The campsite looked so different in the daylight. So simple. A shed, a tent, a round fire pit and a gravel driveway surrounded by miles of dense forest. No one else in sight. Abby sat in the chair opposite them, her hands wrapped around her steaming cup of tea.

Charlotte looked in the direction of the long-gone deer. "Your mother really is a genius," she said. "The Rotifer Project. That's the name, isn't it?"

Abby gave Charlotte a terse nod.

"I spoke with a woman at the hospital who had a baby with red eyes," Charlotte said. "She told me the Rotifer Project makes males, um, what's that word she used?"

"Superfluous," Abby said. "The Rotifer Project makes males superfluous. She probably heard that from my mother. Mom says that males only had one productive function and that was as sperm donors. Since rotifer genes give females the ability to reproduce asexually, Mom says males no longer have any value."

Kingsley wrinkled his nose. He could think of a bunch of things guys were good at. Playing video games and fishing and, um.... Well, that's what he and his dad were good at.

"What's a rotifer?" Charlotte asked.

"They're small invertebrates," Abby said. "Almost microscopic. They live in ponds."

"What's so special about them?"

Abby kicked off her cleats and crossed her legs like The Buddha. "Most complex, multi-celled animals reproduce sexually. Two copies of chromosomes from two parents mean greater genetic variation. That's why cloning isn't sustainable generation after generation. No genetic variation. You're a clone, right?" Charlotte nodded. "Me too," Abby said.

Nikki scurried shoeless out of the tent and jumped into Abby's lap, almost spilling her tea. Abby didn't yell at her. She didn't even complain, which surprised Kingsley. She wrapped her arms around Nikki and calmly explained the technicalities of her mother's research. "With cloning, there's no male infusing his DNA. After a few generations, this lack of diversity undermines the clones' immune system. It's insane to think cloning could repopulate the earth. There just aren't enough facilities or enough scientists. Rotifers are unique. Even though they reproduce asexually, they are able to create genetic diversity. Guess how?"

"I have no idea," Charlotte said, with the greatest sincerity.

"There are several species of rotifers, but the one Mom uses are called bdelloid rotifers. They look like inchworms and have the most amazing system of reproduction. They actually capture bits of DNA from other organisms and assimilate these bits into their own genetic code." Abby sipped her tea and appeared quite pleased at Charlotte's shocked expression. "Plants, animals, even bacteria. This keeps each generation unique."

"I've never heard of such a thing."

"Scientists call them *gene thieves*," Abby said.

"Why do all the animals your mother makes have red eyes? Even that little baby I saw in the hospital had red eyes."

Abby shrugged. "Rotifers have red eyes, so I guess everything with their genetic code will have red eyes, too, at least until Mom figures out how to turn their eyes another color."

"The seagull," Kingsley said. "Ask about the seagull."

"What about that seagull?" Nikki asked, as if she'd read Kingsley's mind. "How did it know to attack those guards?"

"I don't know why the gull helped us get away, but I do know that Mom's animals aren't like animals before The Collapse. The rotifer gene picks up DNA from other organisms, and the only organism around when that bird was made was Mom."

"Eww," Nikki squealed. "So those deer and that seagull have a little bit of your mom in them?" Abby nodded, and Nikki cringed. "Gross."

Abby pushed Nikki off her lap. "Get your shoes on, we're leaving."

24 Who is He?

The tent was still up, the sleeping bags scattered. The girls hadn't even bothered to close the shed doors. At least Abby had the foresight to throw a bucket of water on the morning campfire before they left.

"What about breakfast?" Nikki asked, as she climbed into the back seat of the Pegasus. "I'm starving."

Charlotte was about to sit beside Nikki in the back when Nikki stopped her. She reached for Kingsley. "I'll hold him if you want to sit up front." Charlotte hesitated. "Please," Nikki said. "You had him all night. I want a turn."

Charlotte gratefully handed Kingsley to Nikki, "Thanks. I could use a break." She didn't get into the Pegasus, not right away. She ran her fingers along the sleek, polished exterior of the maroon car. "Beautiful construction. Lightweight, low-aerodynamic drag."

"All I know is that it doesn't need gasoline," Abby said. "Mom insisted on buying a car that didn't need anything from Grandmother's oil wells."

"I believe it," Charlotte said. "I saw the hydrogen fuel cell when I opened the hood." She slipped into the front passenger seat and tapped the ceiling. "Solar cells on the roof. Smart, and lucky for us. They would have found us if we'd had to stop for gas." She ran her fingers along the doorframe. "This metal is so strong yet so light; it doesn't feel like normal steel. I wish I could have seen it built."

"I think you love Dr. Fells' car almost as much as you love this baby,"

Nikki said. She nuzzled Kingsley's face and Kingsley laughed. Nikki's straight black hair tickled his neck. *Her hair!* He couldn't take his eyes off her hair. It looked so tasty, like a licorice waterfall. He felt an overwhelming desire to put her hair in his mouth. He reached out and intertwined a few strands in his fingers. He put them in his mouth and felt an odd rush of accomplishment.

"What are you going to name him?" Abby asked, as she started the engine.

"I'm thinking of—"

"Oh! Oh! I know the perfect name," Nikki said. "Adam. Call him Adam. You know, like the first man."

"I like the name Sylvester," Abby said.

"Sylvester Sutherland?" Nikki cringed. "That's horrible."

Charlotte laughed. Kingsley puckered his lips, spitting out Nikki's hair. He didn't like the name Sylvester either. "My grandfather's name was Andrés, so I might call him Andrés, or maybe Andrew," Charlotte said. "My mother wrote a lot about her father in her diary. He was a good man."

Kingsley smiled. He was indeed a good man and Andrew was a good name.

Abby headed east on dusty back roads. She winced at the bright rising sun. As usual, Nikki chattered nonstop as she played with Kingsley in the back seat. "The Collapse was really dumb," she said. "I saw an old movie about a giant meteor hitting the earth. The government froze all the people, and then blasted them into space. A giant meteor, that's a cool way to die. Not from too much plastic and pesticides. That's just pathetic. I'd be embarrassed if I lived back then."

Kingsley agreed. Captain America could have stopped a giant meteor, especially with Superman's help, but all the superheroes in the world couldn't pick up the billions of pieces of plastic people dumped in the oceans. Fish ate the plastic and the people ate the fish. No wonder all the men were dead. Kingsley looked out the window. He'd seen the smart gull and the scary deer, but no other animals. Not even flies or ants. He thought about Snowball, his neighbor's cat back in New Orleans, and about Amanda's horses. A world without animals was a dreary place.

They passed fallow farms and lifeless towns, shops, schools and libraries. All abandoned, even the McDonald's. They approached an old country church with a *Free Soup* sign in front. Whiffs of white smoke rose from behind the church. "Can we stop?" Nikki asked.

"Might be the only food we find 'til Hampton," Charlotte said.

Abby was reluctant to pull over.

"I'm starving," Nikki whined. "If I don't get food soon, I'll faint."

Abby rolled her eyes and found a secluded spot behind a cluster of unruly rhododendrons. She parked the Pegasus.

Nikki handed Kingsley to Charlotte and hopped out of the car. Abby got out too, but Charlotte stayed inside. A half-dozen or so bedraggled women were walking along the crumbling road to the dilapidated church.

"I, um, I don't know about this," Charlotte said. "It's Sunday morning. They might expect us to stay for church service."

"Dressed like this?" Nikki pulled at her dirty uniform. "We'd stink up the pews." She laughed and nudged Abby. "Pews. Ha! We'd stink up the pews. Get it? "

"Whatever," Abby said and headed toward the church. "You coming?" she asked Charlotte.

"No one's looking for two girls traveling alone," Charlotte said. "They're looking for me and my baby. Just bring me back some soup."

The girls left and Charlotte waited in the Pegasus, Kingsley on her lap. "We'll be in Hampton soon and you'll meet Nanna," she said.

Kingsley's life would be very different living with Charlotte than it was with Joyce. The only thing he'd learned from Joyce was how to steal. His father taught him how to fish, but he also taught him how to give up. Charlotte never gave up. She knew how to repair pumps and fix cars. And he had Abby and Nikki, too. Abby was smart and Nikki was funny. Both knew how to play soccer. Kingsley felt hopeful about his future. He'd learn more about how to be an honorable man now that men were gone than he'd ever learned when they were still around.

Minutes passed and more rag-tag women arrived; the soup line wrapped around the church. "What's taking them so long?" Charlotte grumbled. "I bet those silly girls have forgotten all about me." Charlotte got out of the car, Kingsley in her arms. "What do you think, *Niño?* Do I stay here and starve, or risk being caught?"

Kingsley wanted to stay with the car. His stomach was full and his diaper was clean. But the only thing Charlotte had eaten that day was a cup of weak tea. Charlotte quietly closed the car door and carried Kingsley to the church. She followed the line of wretched-looking women and the tempting aroma of soup. On a gravel parking lot behind the church, a rough-looking woman wearing bib overalls stirred a black cauldron over an open flame. She used a long rowing paddle, her sleeves rolled up revealing solid biceps. Other women, much slighter, served the soup. The half-starved women in line accepted their soup with grateful prayers and murmurs of thanks.

Abby and Nikki weren't in line. Charlotte sighed and hurried to the entrance of the church. She scanned the horizon. No sign of the girls. "Where could they be?" She climbed the rotting front steps of the church, careful of the loose boards.

The girls were wandering inside the gloomy sanctuary, if it could still be called a sanctuary. Paintings with price tags hung next to stained glass windows etched with images of Jesus dressed in long robes, holding two lambs. Nikki was inspecting a series of nature paintings while Abby was staring into a decorative mirror. Charlotte shifted Kingsley to one hip. "I've been searching all over for you two." Her voice echoed in every corner of the cavernous sanctuary, but neither girl stopped what they were doing.

Nikki checked the price tag on one of the nature paintings. "Why do they bother? Who's going to buy any of this stuff? We're the only people here with any money."

Abby was still at the mirror. She smoothed her arched eyebrows and fluffed her blonde hair. "Maybe they just want to be unique, not copies of someone else," she said.

Charlotte stomped her foot, the sound reverberating among the empty pews. "I thought you were hungry. We won't get any soup unless we get in line now."

"Yeah, we know," Nikki said. "First you've got to see this." She beckoned Charlotte to a painting behind the lectern. Three women dressed in black and red, their hair bristling like serpents, carrying icy blue whips and hot pink torches, entitled The Furies. Nikki snickered and pointed at the leader of the furies. "Hey, Abby, isn't that your mom?"

Abby was still staring into the mirror. "Is that how I look to you?"

Nikki giggled, and Charlotte grabbed Nikki's arm. "Come on, before the soup's all gone."

Charlotte was almost out of the sanctuary when Kingsley started kicking his feet. "Look! Look!" he said. It was Mrs. Sutherland's poem. It wasn't calligraphied and it wasn't framed in gold like the one that hung in Mrs. Sutherland's never-used library, but Kingsley still recognized the words.

Charlotte recognized it, too. "Nanna's sonnet." She reached out and caressed the simple canvas and painted words.

"What?" Nikki asked.

"My great-grandmother calligraphied this sonnet, but hers is in a golden frame. Nanna has it now. She claims it was the only thing Joyce didn't steal." Charlotte closed her eyes and recited:

"They that have the pow'r to hurt, and will do none,
That do not do the thing they most do show,
Who moving others, are themselves as stone,
Unmoved, cold, and to temptation slow,
They rightly do inherit heaven's graces,
And husband nature's riches from expense;
They are the lords and owners of their faces,
Others but stewards of their excellence.
The summer's flow'r is to the summer sweet,
Though to itself it only live and die,
But if that flow'r with base infection meet,
The basest weed outbraves his dignity:
For sweetest things turn sourest by their deeds;
Lilies that fester smell far worse than weeds."

Charlotte opened her eyes. "Shakespeare," she said with pride. She left the church and Nikki followed.

"Who's Joyce?" Nikki asked.

"Joyce Smith," Charlotte said. "She robbed my grandmother before The Collapse. She's why I'm here. She may have murdered my great-grandmother."

"Murdered," Nikki repeated with a shudder. "That reeks." She looked back at Abby, who was still in the vestibule, apparently rereading the poem. "Come on, Abby. We're getting in line." Nikki turned back to Charlotte.

"What does the poem mean?"

"I'm not an expert on Shakespeare," Charlotte said. "But I think—"

Abby caught up with them and answered Nikki's question, her voice tearful. "It means that good people who do bad things are worse than bad people." She covered her face and bolted past Nikki and Charlotte.

"Why's she upset?" Nikki asked.

Abby was already in the soup line, her arms crossed and her head bent. Kingsley was struck by how much Abby reminded him of Amanda, especially when she was sad. Nikki wrapped her arm over Abby's shoulder. "Is this because of that stupid painting? I didn't mean what I said about your mom."

Abby shook her head, not looking up. "It's not the painting. It's my family. Grandmother. Mom. Me." She sniffed and wiped her nose with the bottom of her jersey. "It's like that poem's written about us. Lilies that fester are worse than weeds."

Charlotte took Abby's hand. "I owe you everything, Abby. My freedom, my son's freedom, maybe even our lives."

Abby gave Charlotte a grateful nod. "Yeah, well, I suppose."

The line of worn-out women inched forward until it was Charlotte's turn. The strong woman stirring the cauldron stared at Kingsley as another ladled the soup into Charlotte's bowl. Kingsley heard several of the women in line whispering. His sensitive ears heard the word "boy" and he knew they were talking about him.

He had to warn Charlotte. "It's not safe. They know I'm here," he said, but Charlotte didn't react beyond patting his back. It was so frustrating not being understood. After they'd all gotten their soup, Charlotte and the girls carried their bowls to the crumbling front steps of the church. Kingsley agonized. "This isn't a picnic! We've got to get out of here!" He waved his arms, trying to get their attention. All they did was smile at him. Nikki started singing a song she said was from her favorite band, Phillips-Head Screwdrivers.

I'm cheap and easy. No one respects me.
I'm inside you. You're inside me.
Everywhere, everywhere, not a drop to drink
You love me, I don't know you.

You poison me, I'll kill you.
Everywhere, everywhere, not a drop to drink

"The song's called *Aqua City Blues*," Nikki said. She coaxed Abby to join in. They sang and swayed their feet to the rhythm, until Charlotte suddenly shushed them.

"Did you hear that?" She stood up, holding Kingsley tight.

"Hear what?"

"Someone said my name. *Charlotte Sutherland.*"

"I don't hear anything," Nikki said.

"Listen," Charlotte said. Kingsley listened. He heard it, too, *Charlotte Sutherland,* from the side of the church. "There it is again," Charlotte said.

Abby quickly stood up. "Someone's coming."

Nikki dropped her soup and scrambled to her feet. "Now that you mention it."

Six women walked toward them. The strong woman who'd stirred the cauldron led the pack, carrying the paddle over her shoulder like an axe. She swung the paddle off her shoulder and pointed it at Kingsley. "You kidnapped that baby!"

"No, we didn't," Abby said. "That's her baby."

"That's not what the news says. It says you kidnapped a boy! A boy!"

The other women shook their fists. "Kidnappers!" "Thieves!"

A piece of broken asphalt hit Nikki on the side of the face. "Ouch!"

Abby rushed to Nikki's side. "We haven't done anything!" Abby yelled. "We're not kidnappers! We're just on our way home. We were hungry and wanted some soup."

The strong woman carrying the paddle didn't back down. "That's not what I heard," she said. "I heard you're crazy and that he'll die if he stays with you. I'm not letting that happen. Give me the boy!" She tried to pull Kingsley out of Charlotte's arms.

Kingsley wailed. "Let me go!"

Charlotte struggled against the woman, pulling Kingsley back. Other women stepped in, trying to take him.

Abby grabbed a loose board from the church steps and held it like a baseball bat. "Back off!" She yelled at the women. She called to Charlotte and Nikki, "Go get the car."

Charlotte clutched Kingsley to her chest and ran, Nikki beside her.

Four enraged women broke from the pack and ran after them. "Give him to me!" One woman screamed. She clawed at Kingsley, almost grabbing his tiny foot. "I want that baby! Give me that boy!"

Kingsley tried to kick the woman away. "She's got my leg!"

Charlotte balled her fist and POW! She punched the woman in the gut.

"Awww!" the woman doubled over.

Another rushed to take her place. She grabbed Kingsley's arm. "My arm!" he screamed. "She's got my arm!"

Abby charged, swinging the board. "Run, Charlotte, run!" The woman ducked and released Kingsley's arm.

Charlotte ran.

Nikki reached the Pegasus first. She slipped behind the wheel and started the engine. Charlotte climbed in the back with Kingsley. Abby was still swinging the board wildly, holding back the crowd. Nikki steered the Pegasus toward the church, honking the horn and screaming "Get out of the way!" The women scattered like wet cats and Abby ran for the car. She jumped into the front passenger seat beside Nikki.

"Nikki, do you know how to drive?"

"No!" Nikki said as she erratically steered away from the crowd and back onto the road.

"Hit the brakes," Abby yelled. "Look!"

They were trapped. Both ends of the road were barricaded with old benches and dilapidated picnic tables, laid on their side. "This reeks! This totally reeks!" Nikki said.

Three crazed women charged the Pegasus, clawing at the locked doors and banging on the closed windows. "Give me the boy! Give me the boy!" they shouted. The strong woman with the paddle followed close, ready to smash the window.

Nikki screamed. "They're going to break the glass!"

"Switch places with me," Abby said. She grabbed the wheel and pushed Nikki aside. She squared her shoulders and hardened her gaze. "Buckle up!"

Charlotte buckled and locked her arms around Kingsley. Kingsley held his breath as Abby hit the accelerator. Faster and faster, they raced toward the barricade. BAM! They hit the barricade like a sleek maroon battering ram. Splinters and shards of old wooden tables and benches flew into pieces.

Some of the women ran after them but couldn't keep up. Once they were about a mile away, Charlotte relaxed. She pounded Abby on the back. "Thanks, kid. That's the second time you've saved us."

Kingsley nursed until he fell asleep, but his dreams gave him no peace. The women chasing him morphed into red-eyed monsters with arms thick and hairy like poison ivy vines and five-inch thorns instead of fingers. They grabbed his legs and wrapped their vines around his neck. He jumped in his sleep, trying to get away.

Charlotte gently rocked him until he woke to the sound of a train whistle. They were in Hampton. Kingsley looked around. He wasn't being chased. He was safe in the back seat, in Charlotte's arms.

"Is he all right?" Nikki asked. "He wasn't hurt when those women grabbed him, was he?"

"I don't think so," Charlotte said. She unwrapped his blanket and showed Nikki his arm and his leg. Neither was bruised. "At first I thought he was hurt because of the way he cried, but now he seems fine."

Nikki reached out and tickled Kingsley's chin, which helped to calm his fears. "He doesn't look like you. Did you ever figure out who's his real mom?"

Charlotte shook her head. "No, but you heard what Dr. Miles-Johnson said. Some generous soul wants to increase the population. Is that so bad? The only thing I've ever wanted was a baby. Now I have one. The more I think about it, I'm lucky he's a boy."

Abby glanced at Charlotte and Kingsley in the rearview mirror. "Why do you say that?"

"From what I've heard, boys love machines," Charlotte said. "They love getting dirty. That's what I do for a living. Machines and dirt. I'll teach him how to pull a pump, repair a motor and drive a backhoe. He'll be dirty all the time."

Nikki cooed at Kingsley. "Sounds like boy heaven."

"We have to be more careful this time," Abby said as they rumbled over the crumbling streets of Hampton. "We won't leave the Pegasus unless we know we're safe." They passed a few cars and pedestrians, and one lone city bus. When they reached Clare's apartment building, a black-and-white police car was parked on the street in front.

Abby quickly turned down a quiet side road. "We have to go someplace else."

"I can't leave Nanna," Charlotte said.

Abby jerked the Pegasus to a full stop and turned to face Charlotte. "Why?"

"Because she's—"

"We almost died back there!" Abby said, exasperated. "I can drop you off here if you want to take your chances with the cops, but I'm not waiting around for you to rescue Nanna, whoever the hell she is."

"She's my grandmother."

Nikki sided with Abby. "Come back for her after the baby's safe."

"No," Charlotte said. "I can't leave her. She's very fragile. I've already left her alone too long."

"Fragile?"

"Nanna lost everything in The Collapse."

"Everyone did!" Abby said.

"Not like Nanna."

Kingsley listened intently as Charlotte described the theft of the Sutherland fortune. "Nanna lived like a queen before The Collapse. I've seen it. She had a chauffeur, stables, a pool, tennis courts, a golf course. Her family founded Sutherland Shipyard and owned oil wells. The woman I told you about, Joyce Smith, she's the one who swindled Nanna out of her inheritance. That's why I came to Charlottesville, to find Joyce and bring her to justice. Maybe even get back some of my family's lost inheritance."

The pieces were coming together for Kingsley. After he'd died, Joyce stole Mrs. Sutherland's fortune. She stole the Sutherland money, stole the Sutherland oil wells, and even stole Marlbank, the Sutherland home. Amanda was still a girl when she was forced to leave the mansion. Clare's senator must have died, too. Just as well, Kingsley thought. He was still bitter over neither Clare nor the senator helping him deal with Jack. Clare and Amanda must have lived together in this rundown apartment as the world fell apart. When Amanda became an adult, she had a baby girl and named her Charlotte. Kingsley could almost see it. She must have been so happy. Amanda cradled Charlotte just as Charlotte now cradled him. It still didn't add up. Why did Amanda kill herself? Why did she jump off the

Monitor-Merrimac Bridge? He was haunted by that question. It didn't make sense. Amanda had so much to live for.

Nikki gawked at Charlotte. "Oil wells? Your family owned oil wells?"

"We can't leave," Charlotte said. "There's an old automobile dealership across the street from Nanna's apartment building. It's a church now. We can hide—"

"Another church?" Nikki cringed. "I don't think I can handle another church."

"You can park in their lot beside the other cars," Charlotte said. "The police won't notice us."

Abby squinted at the automobile-dealership turned church. "You want us to hide in plain sight while you sneak past the police and get your grandmother," Abby said. "That's your plan?"

Charlotte nodded.

Abby grumbled as she put the Pegasus in drive. "This is a bad idea." She drove to the church and parked next to a threadbare Toyota.

Music drifted from the sanctuary. *I sing because I'm happy, I sing because I'm free.*

Abby cut the engine and turned to Charlotte. "Where are we going once you have her?"

"My boss lives in Chesapeake, about an hour away."

"An hour!" Nikki said. "I can't do this for another hour! I'm tired and I want to go home."

"Nikki's right," Abby said. "I'm not driving another hour." She handed Charlotte her cell phone. "Call your boss and tell her to meet us halfway."

Charlotte made the call and returned the phone to Abby. "Wanda will meet us on the south side of the Monster-Merrimack."

"The what?"

"The Monitor-Merrimac Bridge Tunnel," Charlotte said. "Everyone calls it the Monster-Merrimack. It's old and falling apart. The northbound tunnel's closed on account of a leak, so the southbound tunnel is the only one open."

Kingsley shivered. He remembered the tunnel. He remembered the stalled trucks and dead men. He remembered the choking stench and screaming women. He began to whimper.

Charlotte comforted him. "Don't worry, *Niño.* I'll go get Nanna, and we'll all be safe in Chesapeake soon." She handed Kingsley to Nikki. "Take good care of him. If anything happens to me, um—" She stopped. "I don't know what to tell you to do."

"Then don't let anything happen to you, Charlotte," Nikki said.

Charlotte nodded. "Here goes." She'd just started across the street when a white security truck pulled into Clare's parking lot.

Charlotte ran back to the Pegasus. "Damn!"

"Good call," Abby said. "You might be able to get past the police but you won't get past Chief Holland."

They watched as Odelle parked the truck and she and Ray went up the stairs to Clare's apartment.

"Damn!" Charlotte said. "They'll tell her I'm a kidnapper and a thief. It'll kill her."

Abby leaned back in her seat. "What next, Charlotte? What do we do now? Meet with your boss, or wait for Mom and Odelle to leave?"

Charlotte hesitated. She studied the apartment building and the police officer parked on the street. "We wait."

The parking lot was empty except for Odelle's security truck. The only sound was the occasional chatter coming from the police radio. No birds chirped in the crepe-myrtle trees that lined the crumbling sidewalks. No children played on the rusting playground. No dogs barked in the distance. Even Nikki was quiet.

"Let me use your cell phone," Charlotte said to Abby.

"What for?"

"To call Nanna. Maybe I can get her to throw your mom and Chief Holland off my scent."

Abby reluctantly handed Charlotte her phone. "Mom and Odelle aren't stupid," she said as Charlotte punched in Clare's number. "They'll know who's calling."

A shriveled voice answered, "Hello." It didn't sound anything like the voice of beautiful Clare, the woman Kingsley had once had a crush on.

"Nanna," Charlotte said.

"What? Who is this?"

"Nanna, it's me. Take the phone into your bedroom and close the door. I don't want Dr. Fells and Chief Holland to hear."

"Charlotte, I can't understand you. Speak up, dear." The front curtains of Clare's second-story window pulled aside and Odelle's face appeared.

Abby grabbed the phone and quickly hung up before Charlotte could say another word. "Look," she said, but she wasn't pointing at Odelle. She was pointing at something much more ominous. A long black limousine cruised into the entrance of the parking lot. It slowly maneuvered over the crumbling asphalt and parked alongside Odelle's white security truck. Abby cursed. "Now we're stuck. If we try to leave, Grandmother will see us. And I can tell you right now, she's not alone."

"Your grandmother? That's your grandmother's car? She's here?"

Abby nodded.

"She'll help us, won't she?" Charlotte asked. "She was very kind to me when—"

Abby's eyes darkened. "You don't know anything about Lily Fells."

Kingsley's heart pounded. Abby was right. Charlotte knew nothing about Joyce, but Kingsley knew more than anyone. He'd seen what she did to his father. He was afraid for Charlotte, but he was more afraid that Charlotte might stop loving him if she discovered the truth.

The front door of Clare's apartment building flew open and Ray marched out. Kingsley could hear her yelling at the limo to go home and let Odelle find the boy. Joyce didn't get out of the limo. She didn't even roll down her window. Instead, the back door opened and out stepped Phoebe Ann. The giant pointed at Ray and then at the open door of the limousine. Ray backed away. "I'm not going with you!"

Phoebe Ann moved incredibly fast. She grabbed Ray, threw her into the limo, and slammed the door shut. Kingsley was stunned. Ray was little more than a toy doll in Phoebe Ann's hands. The front door of the apartment complex slammed open and Odelle ran out, yelling at Phoebe Ann to release Ray and calling to the police officer for backup. Phoebe Ann braced herself against the limo and pulled something from her jacket. It flashed in the bright afternoon sun—a knife!

Kingsley held his breath. Everyone inside the Pegasus was silent.

The knife flashed again. Odelle reeled backward and clutched her face. Blood dripped through her fingers. She fell to her knees.

"Oh, my God!" Nikki screamed. "Did you see that?"

Abby covered Nikki's mouth. "She'll hear you." They watched in silence as the police officer charged Phoebe Ann. The officer pulled out her nightstick, but Phoebe Ann was too strong. She swatted the nightstick away and grabbed the police officer, pinning her against the hood of the white security truck. Kingsley was too frightened to make a sound. The giant plunged the knife into the officer's stomach, and then drew the blade up and out, as if she were gutting a deer.

"We've got to help them." Charlotte handed Kingsley to Nikki and started to get out of the car.

Kingsley couldn't stay quiet. "No, she's a monster! Don't go! I love you!"

Abby grabbed Charlotte's arm. "Are you crazy?! She'll kill you!" Charlotte hesitated, looking back and forth from Kingsley to the horrific scene across the street. She finally settled back into the car, and Kingsley was once again grateful to Abby.

Phoebe Ann stepped over the police officer and disappeared into the apartment complex. Kingsley couldn't see what she was doing. Odelle staggered to her feet, pressing her hand against her bleeding face. She stumbled to the supine police officer and kneeled in the pool of blood. "Help!" Odelle yelled up at the gloomy windows. "Someone help us! Officer down! Call an ambulance!"

Phoebe Ann returned, carrying Clare in her arms. She opened the limo door, pushed Clare in, and climbed in after her.

"Nanna!" Charlotte gasped. "Abby, call 9-1-1. Nikki, take care of my baby." She jumped out of the car and started across the street.

Abby ran after her. "You won't win," Abby said, grabbing Charlotte's arm. "Not against Grandmother. Even without Phoebe Ann, you wouldn't win. Not this way. You may be younger than Grandmother, you may be stronger, but she's a lot meaner than you are."

"Is that why she took Nanna? To trade for my baby?"

Abby didn't answer.

"Is that why she wants him? So your mom can kill him? So Dr. Barlow can experiment on him?" The limo's engine started, and Charlotte pulled away from Abby. "I've got to save Nanna before they leave."

"No," Abby said. She scrambled to grab Charlotte's arm, again, desperate to stop her. "Don't you know who she is? Isn't it obvious? She's the woman you're looking for, the one who stole your fortune. She changed her name to Lily Fells. It used to be Joyce Smith."

Charlotte was stunned, and Kingsley's heart fell. *Now she knows the truth about me.*

Abby pointed at Kingsley. "That's her son. That's why she wants him. She's the one who paid Dr. Barlow to create him. She's the one who bribed Dr. Miles-Johnson to implant his embryo in you. If you want to trade him for your grandmother, go ahead. But she'll ruin him. She'll turn him into a criminal."

Abby's voice trembled. "Unless Mom gets to him first. You saw her on the news. *Don't call the police! Do take the boy!* That mob almost tore him apart. Mom wants him dead. Don't you see? It's all about the boy. Whoever controls him controls the future. That's why Dr. Cama wanted you to raise him. She wants him to be a normal child. Not the Messiah and not murdered in his crib."

The church service was letting out. Parishioners were heading to their cars and bicycles, gawking at the two young women standing in the street. Questioning what was happening in the apartment complex parking lot. Charlotte finally relented, and she and Abby ran back to the Pegasus. The congregation took little notice. They were too enthralled at the sight of Joyce's shiny, black limousine as it pulled out of the apartment complex—at least until they saw Odelle and the police officer, both covered in blood. A few parishioners stared in disbelief but most ran across the street to help.

"Joyce knows he's here," Charlotte said. She returned to the back seat. She didn't ask Nikki for Kingsley. She didn't even look at him. "That's why she kidnapped Nanna," she grumbled. "She wants to trade Nanna for HIM."

25 Darkness

Charlotte wasn't trembling. She wasn't crying. Her eyes hardened and the corners of her mouth tightened. "You knew who she was, and you didn't tell me! Joyce Smith. The thief! The murderer! I trusted you, Abby! You knew *he* was her son all along and you didn't tell me!"

The way Charlotte spat out the word *he* tore at Kingsley's heart. "Please don't hate me," he cried. "I love you."

Charlotte ignored his cry. She didn't take him from Nikki's arms. She didn't comfort him and kiss his bald head. "I carried *her* son. I gave birth to *her* son. I saved *her* son's life. And you didn't tell me."

"I couldn't," Abby sputtered, sniffing and wiping her eyes. "She's my grandmother. I thought if I helped you get away—" She couldn't finish her sentence.

Nikki glanced back at Charlotte before leaning close to Abby. "How'd you know all of that stuff about Lily and who he is?"

"Mom and Grandmother argue all the time," Abby said. "I hear things."

"Do you think the police officer's dead?" Nikki asked. "Do you think Phoebe Ann killed her?"

Abby gripped the steering wheel. Her white knuckles trembled. "Yes, and she could have killed Odelle."

Charlotte had no patience for Abby's tears. "Don't just sit there. I'll need Wanda's help if I want to rescue Nanna from that monster."

Abby started the engine. "She kidnapped my mom, too!"

238

"One big happy family," Charlotte said, with disgust.

Charlotte gave Abby directions to the interstate, and then opened her old tweed suitcase. Kingsley watched from Nikki's lap as Charlotte pulled out a faded black-and-white composition notebook. Kingsley recognized it. He was with Amanda when she drew the horses on the cover. "Please hold me," he whimpered, trying to reach out his arms to Charlotte.

Charlotte flinched when Kingsley cried but didn't take him from Nikki. Instead, she pulled out the photograph of Amanda, Joyce and Kingsley. The one Amanda had taken in the car when she went with Kingsley and Joyce to his gene-therapy treatment. Kingsley's throat felt like it was filled with hot coals. Charlotte turned the photo over and read the name written on the back. "Kingsley." She looked up at him. "He doesn't look like a king."

They passed miles and miles of abandoned shopping centers. Huge fortresses of concrete, steel, and glass, one right after another, that stood as testament to a bygone era when shopping was more important than living. The ruined stores and the shattered, trash-filled parking lots seemed to go on forever. They drove under a makeshift traffic sign warning that the northbound tunnel was closed because of a leak. Only the southbound tunnel was open. The stench of the dead harbor fouled the air. The water was covered with a thick, slimy film of algae and oil.

Kingsley hated that tunnel. He hated its slick, narrow walls and low ceilings. He hated the fearsome echoes and the muffled sounds. His cries intensified. He was desperate. He wanted Charlotte. Charlotte ignored him. Tears filled her eyes, but she kept studying Amanda's notebook and the old photograph.

Abby's cell phone rang, and everyone jumped. "It's Grandmother." Abby tried to hand the phone to Nikki. "Answer it."

Nikki recoiled. "Are you kidding? I'm not answering that!"

Abby reluctantly answered the phone. "Stop following us," she yelled, "You can't have the baby."

Sounds of a riot came over the phone from inside Joyce's limousine. Shouting and screaming. Ray was cursing at her mother for what happened to Odelle. Clare was begging Joyce not to take her into the tunnel. Joyce yelled over the commotion. "Abby, hon, just a tip for future reference, if you don't want to be found, ditch your cell phone. Now let me speak to Charlotte."

Abby grimly stared ahead and passed the phone back to Charlotte. "She wants to talk to you."

Charlotte snatched the phone and yelled into the receiver. "You already robbed us once, Joyce. Wasn't that enough? Now you kidnap Nanna. You want to trade her for my baby? What if I don't? Will you murder her like you murdered that police officer? Like you murdered Nanna's mother?"

Kingsley recognized Joyce's usual self-satisfied voice, the same smug tone she'd so often use when she talked to Amanda. "Charlotte, hon, you've got it backwards," she said. "I never hurt Leslie, and I'm not going to hurt Clare. All I want is my boy. Listen to me, Charlotte, I can help you. I can help Clare. You can move back into the old Sutherland mansion. Both of you. You can have a cook, a chauffeur, whatever you want. It'll be just like before The Collapse. You're young, Charlotte, you can have more children. I'm a very rich woman. Think of all I can do for you. I'll pay for your next pregnancy. You can even have one of Rachel's red-eyed babies, if you want. All I'm asking is that you tell Abby to pull over. That's all. I'll make sure you have everything you ever wanted. Pull over now and you'll live like a queen."

Waves of memories flooded Kingsley. The Sutherland mansion was more impressive than the grandest plantation along the banks of the Mississippi, with its long wrought-iron fence decorated with brass roses and copper thistles, its arched front gate and curved brick driveway. Every day, Floyd buffed Mrs. Sutherland's sleek black limousine with a soft hand towel. Kingsley didn't know what happened to Floyd after he moved to Lake Monticello. He didn't know what had become of his two crazy aunts, Mavis and Maureen. None of that mattered. All that mattered was Charlotte. What if Charlotte wanted all of this more than she wanted him? What if she wanted a mansion and a chauffeur? What if she wanted to live like a queen? Kingsley may have loved Joyce once, and maybe he still did, but he didn't trust her. He didn't want to live with her. He loved Charlotte. But did she love him?

Charlotte might have answered Joyce if not for Clare's screams. "Please, Joyce, I can't go in that tunnel. Amanda! Amanda! All those dead men. Stop the car. I have to get out of here. I'm going to be sick. Please, Joyce, please let me out—"

"Phoebe Ann," Joyce yelled, "shut her up."

"No! No, please. Stop it! Stop it!"

The screaming stopped.

"Nanna!" Charlotte yelled.

Kingsley started to cry. He tried to reach for Charlotte. "Don't give me back to her. I want you. I can't go back."

"I hear my baby crying," Joyce said. "My baby! Not yours! You don't even know who he is. I'm a very influential woman, Charlotte. Pull over."

"They're right behind us," Abby said. Everyone turned. Joyce's long black limousine was speeding up behind them.

"NO!" Kingsley howled.

"Go to hell!" Charlotte cursed and hung up the phone.

Abby wiped beads of perspiration from her forehead. "Call your boss. Tell her we've got trouble. Tell her to bring help." She revved the accelerator, and the Pegasus sailed ahead, leaving Joyce's black limousine far behind. "This car can outrun anything on wheels but that won't stop her. Grandmother never gives up."

The dark mouth of the tunnel rose before them like the gaping mouth of an angry sea serpent. Kingsley buried his face in Nikki's dirty soccer jersey as Charlotte made her call and handed the phone back to Abby. "Wanda's waiting for us on the other side of the bridge-tunnel. Sarah and Kathy are with her. The northbound tunnel's closed. The southbound isn't much better, so don't go too fast. Stuff's all over the place."

"What sort of stuff?"

"Fallen tiles, blown tires. And most of the lights are out."

"Is it safe?" Nikki asked.

"Doesn't matter," Abby said, as the tunnel swallowed them. "We're in."

Tunnel lights flickered as the Pegasus rumbled over fallen ceiling tiles. Behind them, the limousine grew closer. Kingsley couldn't watch. He closed his eyes tight, holding desperately onto to Nikki's dirty soccer shirt. "She's coming," he cried, trying to bury his head. "She's coming, and no one can stop her."

He could hear Charlotte shouting from the back seat, "Watch out for dumped cars, Abby, get in the left lane, quick." He could hear Abby breathing hard and cursing every time she had to maneuver around the cars, trucks and motorcycles abandoned by long-dead drivers. He could hear Nikki fretfully murmuring, "This reeks, this totally reeks," over and over.

Suddenly all the shouting and muttering was drowned out by a loud screech of metal against metal, like a freight train coming to a stop. Kingsley opened his eyes and looked out the rear window. The limousine was shrinking in the distance.

"They crashed!" Nikki said. "Did you see that? They crashed!"

"Yeah, I saw it," Abby said. She wiped perspiration off her upper lip and kept a steady speed.

"We have to go back!" Charlotte said. "We have to help them."

"Are you insane?" Nikki said. "Farty Ann's in there. She'll kill us."

"So's Nanna," Charlotte insisted.

The headlights of the limousine started growing, again. "They're still coming," Abby said. "I can see them. They didn't wreck. They only scraped the side of the tunnel. We have to figure out a way to stop them."

The darkness intensified the further down they went. Kingsley could barely see Nikki. He couldn't see Charlotte at all, but he could smell her sweet, milky aroma. He squirmed and cried in Nikki's arms.

"I think he's hungry or something," Nikki said. She turned on the overhead light and tried to hand Kingsley back to Charlotte, but Charlotte wouldn't take him. "Listen, Charlotte," Nikki said. "Lily might be his biological mother but you're his real mom. If you don't believe me, believe Dr. Cama. She wanted you to raise him. Remember?"

Tears lingered in the corners of Charlotte's eyes but refused to fall.

Nikki wouldn't give up. "If you don't believe Dr. Cama, believe in yourself. Remember what you said about being lucky to have a boy? That hasn't changed. You're still lucky. You're a good person. Smart and brave. You fixed that water system in Fork Union. You saved him from that crowd of crazy women this morning. He's a sweet baby, Charlotte. None of what Lily, um," she stumbled over which name to use. "I mean, what Joyce did is his fault." She offered Kingsley again. "Please, Charlotte, he needs you."

Charlotte took one last look at the photograph of Amanda, Joyce and Kingsley. She carefully tucked the photo into Amanda's black-and-white notebook and stored it in her old, tattered suitcase. She took a deep breath. "Thank you, Nikki," she whispered, her voice breaking. She took Kingsley into her arms, nuzzling him close. "You're my baby. You'll always be my baby."

Kingsley melted. He stopped hurting. He stopped crying. He was still in the tunnel, the same tunnel he'd died in forty years ago, still chased by Joyce and her murderous bodyguard, but at least he had Charlotte. She gave him the courage to stop crying and the strength to face whatever happened next.

"I have an idea," Abby said. "The other tunnel is flooded, right?"

Charlotte nodded. "It closed ten years ago because of a leak."

"So if we block this tunnel, they can't get across. Grandmother couldn't follow you to Chesapeake."

"They'd have to drive up to Norfolk or take the James River Bridge. Both are miles away."

"And your boss is meeting us on the other side of the tunnel?"

"Yeah," Charlotte said. "Wanda's waiting for us."

"Good," Abby said. She slowed the Pegasus as they reached the deepest point of the tunnel, and then wheeled the car sideways. She turned off the engine, leaving all the lights on—both the interior lights and headlights. "Get out of the car!" she ordered. "Hurry!" Abby leaped out, opened the trunk and pulled out a tire iron. She pointed toward the exit. "Go," she said, "Go find your boss, Charlotte. I'll catch up."

Nikki gawked at Abby. "What are you doing? You're not going to fight Farty Ann, are you?"

"Don't be stupid, Nikki," Abby said. She started swinging the tire iron. Glass cracked as she hit the windows. She hit them again and again until they shattered.

"Then what are you doing? Why wreck the car?"

"I'm blocking the tunnel," Abby said, breathing hard as she pounded the hood of the Pegasus. "I have to make sure the car won't start. Mom has keys; she'll move it."

Charlotte winced with each blow. "You're just hitting the body. If you want the car inoperable, you should open the hood and crack the radiator."

Abby opened the hood and jammed the tire iron into the radiator.

"I can't watch," Charlotte said, turning away. "That's the most beautiful machine I've ever seen." Holding her tweed suitcase, she started up the bleak incline to the tunnel exit; Kingsley lodged snugly in her other arm. "Come on, Nikki. Wanda's waiting."

Nikki followed. "How am I getting back home?" she asked. "My mom'll go berserk if she has to drive all the way to Chesapeake to pick me up."

Behind them, Abby was still pounding the radiator. *Clang! Clang! Clang!* ricocheted off the tunnel walls.

"That's good enough, Abby," Charlotte called back. "Your grandmother will be here any second. Move away from the car."

Abby threw the tire iron aside. She'd barely taken a step when a growing rumble and brightening headlights filled the dark tunnel. The floor vibrated as the limousine roared toward them louder and louder.

"Get away from the car!" Charlotte yelled.

Tires squealed and Kingsley could almost see the terrified eyes of the limo driver as she hit the brakes. He could almost hear her shrieks as the speeding limousine plowed into the side of the Pegasus, spinning both cars forward, rolling the limousine on its side. Abby was fast, but not fast enough. She was thrown against the concrete wall of the tunnel.

"Abby!" Nikki screamed. She ran back to Abby. Charlotte quickly joined her, Kingsley in her arms. Nikki stood over Abby, "She's dead! She's dead!"

Kingsley could feel the heat radiating from the mangled cars. They'd come close to pinning Abby against the side of the tunnel. Abby's arms were bloodied, her forehead was bruised and her eyes were closed. Charlotte kneeled beside Abby and checked her pulse. "She's alive, but she needs help." Charlotte searched Abby's pockets for her cell phone. No signal. "Damn! It won't work in the tunnel!"

Nikki was frantic. "What do we do? What do we do?"

Charlotte shoved the phone in Nikki's hand. "Go get Wanda. She's waiting for us. She can take Abby to the hospital. And call the police."

Nikki hesitated. "What does she look like?"

Exasperated, Charlotte pushed Nikki toward the exit. "She's in the truck with two other women. Now go! Run, Nikki, run!!"

Nikki raced up the dark incline and disappeared from view.

Twisted metal and shards of broken glass littered the dirty tunnel floor. Moans and the sound of metal scraping against metal. Phoebe Ann emerged, her blank, oaken face illuminated by the few remaining unbroken lights. She carried the pistol with pearl handle. Another moan. Another rasp of metal against metal. Joyce climbed out of the wreckage, like an oversized butterfly from a grotesque cocoon. She reached out her hand to Phoebe Ann, who gingerly helped her stand. She smoothed the front of her skirt. "Can you believe it? Barely a wrinkle." She searched the darkness, squinting in the broken light. "My baby. Where's my baby?" She spotted Kingsley. "Give me my boy."

Kingsley clung to Charlotte's denim jumper. He hadn't forgotten about Clare and Ray, still inside the limousine. He hadn't forgotten about the smashed driver buried under the twisted cars. And what of Abby? Bleeding and unconscious on the tunnel floor. None of them mattered to Joyce. Horrible images of Joyce shooting his father and of Phoebe Ann butchering the police officer played in his head. His revulsion grew with every step Joyce took. "My boy," she cooed, "my precious boy."

"Abby's hurt," Charlotte said, clutching Kingsley. "Nikki's gone to get help."

Joyce dismissed Abby without a glance. "She'll be fine."

"She's your granddaughter!"

"She's a clone," Joyce said. "Clones aren't real. They're just fancy experiments, no better than Rachel's red-eyed freaks. He's my son. He's family. He's all that matters."

Joyce had once been a kind woman, a loving mother and a good wife. But that was years ago, before the *Deepwater Horizon* explosion in the Gulf. Before the oil spill cost her husband his livelihood, and before all the other oil spills and all the other greed and all the other neglect caused The Collapse. Kingsley didn't know how she'd become this rich and powerful woman who needed an armed bodyguard, but he could imagine. She bullied everyone just like she was trying to bully Charlotte now. But Charlotte didn't back away. She didn't release Kingsley to Joyce.

"I want to see Nanna," Charlotte said.

Joyce nodded at the wrecked limo. "Go ahead. Clare's somewhere in that mess. You can see her after you give me my boy."

"He's not your son, Joyce," Charlotte said. "Not anymore."

Joyce sighed deeply and motioned to Phoebe Ann. "Remind Charlotte who has the gun, hon," she said. "Her memory ain't too good."

Phoebe Ann moved to stand beside Joyce and pointed the pistol at Charlotte.

Charlotte remained defiant. "I'm not afraid of you."

Kingsley could hear Charlotte's heart pounding. He could feel the tension in her muscles. He stared at Joyce, at Phoebe Ann and at the gun. If I were a man I would grab the gun. I would wrestle it away from that brute. I'd protect Charlotte and carry Abby to the hospital just like Captain America. I'd be a hero.

But Kingsley wasn't a hero. He wasn't even a man. Not yet. All he could do was cry.

Joyce reacted immediately to Kingsley's cries. She placed her hand on the muzzle and lowered Phoebe Ann's aim, and Kingsley stopped crying. He had a revelation. He had made her lower the gun. Maybe he could be a hero! All he had to do was cry every time she threatened Charlotte. He wasn't afraid anymore. He was determined.

Joyce shook her head, confounded by the situation. "I've done everything I can do. I've offered to give you the old Sutherland mansion. I've offered to pay for your next pregnancy. You would've had a good life, Charlotte." She stroked Kingsley's soft pink cheek. "Kingsley's a very special boy. Smart as a whip, knew his ABC's before he started school."

"I saw what happened to that police officer," Charlotte said. "You're a murderer and a thief. You're not fit to be his mother."

Joyce reached out and brushed a stray black hair away from Charlotte's brow. "So much like Amanda," she said. "I could tell you the truth about what happened to the Sutherlands, not the nonsense Clare spews."

Charlotte's body shift was slight, but Kingsley could feel it. Joyce had touched a deep hunger.

"It takes a lot of suffering for a strong girl like Amanda to throw herself off a bridge," Joyce said. "I know that for a fact. Clare deserted Amanda when she was just a child. Abandoned her and Andrés and married that idiot Senator Steele who closed down the EPA." She sniffed hard and spat on the floor. "He didn't do a damn thing to stop The Collapse. Clare left me to raise Amanda and take care of poor old Mrs. Sutherland all by myself. Did she tell you about that?"

"Nanna never talks about my mother."

"Yeah, I believe that," Joyce scoffed. "Clare has a lot to be ashamed of.

Did she tell you that Amanda had to fend off a pack of monsters, led by Clare's own brother, Jack Sutherland?"

"Her brother?" Charlotte said. "She never told me she had a brother."

"Don't look so shocked. The Sutherlands were rich but they were trash. Most of them, at least. I cared deeply for Mrs. Sutherland, and my son was good friends with Amanda, but you already know that. What you don't know is that we're related. Clare's brother is Rachel's dad. Did Clare tell you that?"

Charlotte barely shook her head. "No," she whispered. Comprehension filled her face and she glanced at Abby, still on the floor of the tunnel. "I didn't know, but Abby did."

"Not my choice, that's for sure. I was raped by that monster."

Kingsley was shocked to hear Joyce say that word, *rape*. His emotions were in an uproar. His feelings toward Joyce softened, and his hatred of Jack surfaced once again, like a rotten corpse in a dead ocean.

"Good God Almighty, Charlotte. The stories I could tell you. It feels like yesterday I was rushing back from the hospital during a hurricane to check on Mrs. Sutherland and Amanda. My sweet Kingsley was sick with that disease. Clare wasn't at the mansion, of course. The senator wasn't there, either, even though they were married by then. No one was there 'cept Amanda, poor old Mrs. Sutherland and Clare's monster of a brother, Jack. Two other convicts were with him. One of them broke Amanda's arm. Did Clare tell you that?"

"Broke her arm!" Charlotte repeated, shocked.

"Clare painted a rosy picture of life at the Sutherland mansion, didn't she? Maybe it was rosy for her, with her fancy cars and fancy horses, but not for me. I was just a servant. Not worth protecting. I was raped and beaten and pretty much left to die. I paid a dear price for my loyalty to the Sutherlands. A dear price indeed."

Joyce's hand floated to caress Kingsley. "The Sutherlands owe me. Not the other way around. Look at him. Hazel eyes, light skin. He doesn't look like you at all. Can't you see? He's my baby." She wrapped her hands around Kingsley. "He's my son, Charlotte. Not yours. I deserve him after all I've been through. I was married to his father. My parents are his grandparents. You want to see Clare again, don't you?"

Charlotte trembled. "Yes."

"Then let go," Joyce hissed, and she carefully lifted Kingsley out of Charlotte's arms.

Charlotte didn't struggle. "My baby," she whispered as she let Kingsley go. She clutched her hands to her mouth. "My baby."

Kingsley, however, knew the whole truth. His feelings may have softened, but he'd not forgotten. He knew that his mother had swindled Mrs. Sutherland, and that she'd murdered his father. Her two drug-addled sisters were at the mansion with Jack and his henchmen and they did nothing to protect Mrs. Sutherland or Amanda.

As Joyce gloated, a stirring had come from the wreckage. That was why Kingsley didn't cry when Joyce took him from Charlotte. Not yet. He had to be strategic. He had to use his cries wisely, so he held back his tears and waited.

Metal creaked against metal as Ray Fells climbed out of the shadows into the dim light of the tunnel. Joyce didn't see Ray. Neither did Charlotte. But Kingsley saw her. She silently picked up the tire iron Abby had used to wreck the Pegasus. She crept behind Phoebe Ann, holding the tire iron like a sword, ready to strike. No one else saw her. Not Joyce, not Charlotte, not even Phoebe Ann. Only Kingsley.

Kingsley had already discovered the power of his cries. Everyone tensed when he cried. Everyone became more alert. Now he had to make a choice. If he cried, Phoebe Ann would turn and see Ray, and that would be the end of it. He'd go home with Joyce. But if he stayed quiet, what would happen? Would Ray disarm Phoebe Ann? Would she grab the gun? And what would happen after that? Would Ray give him back to Charlotte? Ray was his half-sister. She was Amanda's cousin. Even if both of her parents—Jack Sutherland and Joyce Smith—were criminals, Kingsley had seen a glimmer of good in her. She was kind to animals and she was Abby's mother. Abby had saved him. Maybe Ray would, too. Kingsley decided to trust Ray. He decided to stay quiet.

Ray stood behind Phoebe Ann and swung the tire iron with all her strength, grunting from the effort.

"Braaugh!" Phoebe Ann screamed, falling to her knees. She hit the ground and pulled the trigger.

The bullet ricocheted off the floor and reverberated off the tunnel walls. Joyce screamed and clutched her thigh, almost dropping Kingsley. The bullet had nicked the top of her leg, just above her knee. Charlotte ran for her baby.

"Stop!" Ray shouted. She'd pulled the gun out of Phoebe Ann's hand and pointed it at Charlotte.

Joyce pulled her skirt aside. Blood was trickling down her shin. "Have you lost your mind? Goddamn it, Rachel! Look what you did!"

Ray shifted the pearl-handled pistol and aimed it at Joyce.

"Put that thing away!" Joyce yelled. "I could've dropped Kingsley."

Ray's aim didn't waiver.

Joyce released her skirt. She smiled at Ray. "What'cha gonna do, Rachel, kill me?" Her voice was as warm as a New Orleans summer.

"No," Ray said. She shifted the gun ever so slightly and aimed it at Kingsley. "I'm going to kill *him*."

26 Family

Kingsley had died in the tunnel once, and now he faced dying in it again. He tried to control his tongue and lips, tried to sculpt his mouth to form actual words and sentences. "I'm your brother. I'm not like Jack Sutherland. Let me live and you'll see. We're family." But all that came out were cries.

Both Joyce and Charlotte reacted immediately. Joyce shifted Kingsley away from Ray and Charlotte lunged for the pistol.

"Stop!" Ray said. Her hand trembled as she shuddered the gun back and forth between Charlotte and Joyce. "Move again and I'll...I'll shoot all three of you."

Joyce tried to reason with Ray. "Rachel, hon, that gun's over forty years old. It belonged to my shit-drunk dad and Lord knows the last time it's been cleaned. Could go off by accident. Give it to me and all will be forgiven."

Ray grasped the pistol with both hands, steadying her tremor. "I did everything for you. I became what you couldn't. Educated. Respected. I even gave you a granddaughter." She glanced at Abby, still crumbled on the cold tunnel floor. Her eyes filled with tears. "But it wasn't enough. It was never enough. You had to bring *him* into this world. Then you killed the only person who ever really loved me."

"Odelle's not dead," Joyce said. "You can still have a life together, Rachel."

"Don't lie to me! I know how much you've wanted to get rid of Odelle.

250

You didn't want her finding out what you and Barlow were cooking up."
Ray pulled back the hammer. The click echoed in the dank tunnel. "She was
the only person in the world who loved me, and now she's dead." Ray
sniffed and wiped her tears with her sleeve. "And don't call me Rachel!"

Kingsley could hear Joyce's heart beating. He could feel her breath. She
closed her eyes. "My baby. My sweet baby." She rubbed her cheek against
his smooth bald head and kissed his forehead. He could feel the ache in her,
as she did the most honorable thing she'd ever done. And the most
difficult. She handed Kingsley to Charlotte. "Take him." She pointed
toward the exit. "Go."

Charlotte didn't hesitate. She took Kingsley and moved away from Ray.

Joyce stepped forward until the barrel of Ray's cocked gun was touching
her chest. "If you want to kill somebody, Rache—" She nervously wiped
the corners of her mouth. "If you want to kill somebody, Ray, kill me. Not
my son."

Ray's eyes were cold. "Why should I kill you, Mother?"

"Because I deserve it," she said. "I shot Kingsley's father for no good
reason. And, yes, I admit it, I stole from the Sutherlands. I stole everything
they owned, but I had to, Kingsley was dying. The Sutherland money kept
Joan Barlow's research going." Joyce gingerly reached out and gently
stroked Ray's cheek. "What would you do to save your child? Kill me, Ray.
Not my boy. He never did anything wrong. He was only fourteen when he
died."

Ray took an abrupt step back, as if Joyce's caress was a slap. "He'll grow
up," she said. "He'll destroy everything, just like men did—"

"You blame men for The Collapse?" Joyce scoffed. She wiped her eyes
and squared her shoulders. The old Joyce Smith was back. Kingsley could
see it in the way she stood. The tough, vulgar, New Orleans Joyce Smith
who never begged for anything was back. "Don't be stupid," she snapped.
"Everybody was responsible, women as much as men, maybe even more.
We're the ones who wanted big houses and fancy cars. We're the ones who
wore fur coats and diamond earrings. Most men I knew could've lived in a
cave and been just as happy. It's the women who wanted spotless apples,
sparkling toilets, and every piece of worthless shit in the whole wide world
double-wrapped in plastic. Clare was the worst. Spoiled rotten. She had
everything but still wanted more." Joyce turned to Charlotte.

"But your momma knew. Amanda was a smart girl. She knew we were messing up the planet. Some she learned from her father, some she figured out on her own. She was a good girl, too. Tried to save my Kingsley. Wanted him to have the best doctors in the world."

Kingsley felt a rush of pride for his beloved Amanda, and a tugging at his heart for Joyce. He couldn't help it. She was his mother and he loved her. He just didn't want to live with her ever again.

"I'm not saying men were all good, your father's proof of that, Ray, but they weren't all bad either." Joyce winced. Blood was trickling from where the bullet grazed her leg. "Damn, that hurts."

Ray still hadn't lowered the pistol, so Joyce took another tack. Her voice hardened. "What are you really worried about, Rachel? Your career? Your legacy? All your work creating those red-eyed freaks won't be worth a plug-nickel if making babies returns to the good ole days. Believe me, sex is a lot more fun than sequencing DNA."

Ray's eyes narrowed. "I'm a doctor."

"You control who'll be born. Not many would abdicate being a god."

"Don't be profane."

The tension was unbearable. Kingsley didn't know whether to cry or scream. He heard a cough echoing through the tunnel. It was Abby. She was awake, barely.

"Grandmother's right," she said, struggling to speak. "Mom, you told me the world was better now without men because women aren't criminals. Women aren't violent. That's what you said, Mom, and I believed you."

Charlotte kneeled beside Abby, still holding Kingsley. She looked up at Joyce and Ray. "What's wrong with you two? Can't you put your hate aside long enough to save your daughter? Your granddaughter?"

Abby grimaced in pain and worked to catch her breath. "It's like that poem we saw in the church. Good people who do bad things are worse than bad people. Mom, if you shoot that baby, you'll be a murderer. Nothing else you ever do in your entire life will make up for that."

Phoebe Ann hadn't moved since she'd collapsed on the floor. She could be dead, for all Kingsley knew. No one had climbed from the wreckage since Ray. Kingsley wondered about Clare and the driver. Were they alive? He could feel the tension in Charlotte's arms. He couldn't stand the silence. He wanted something to happen.

And it did.

Ray slowly uncocked the gun. "You're right, Abby," she said. She hurried to Abby's side. "You and Odelle are the innocents here." She examined the wounds on Abby's arms and legs. She waved her forefinger in front of Abby's eyes. Abby tried to follow. "You have a concussion."

While Ray and Charlotte were tending to Abby, Joyce kneeled beside Phoebe Ann. "You poor, dumb animal," she said, stroking Phoebe Ann's short black hair like she was a big dog run over by a car, careful of where Ray had bludgeoned her with the tire iron.

"Nikki went to get help," Charlotte told Ray. "My boss is waiting on the other side of the bridge-tunnel. I have to find Nanna."

"Wait," Ray said. "He may be your baby, but he belongs to her, too. She won't give up. You know that, don't you? She'll try to get him back."

"Joyce should be in prison," Charlotte said, glancing at Joyce and the motionless Phoebe Ann. "Not just for what she did to my family, but for what she did to Chief Holland and that police officer."

Ray winced. "You saw the attack?"

Charlotte nodded.

"Was she telling the truth? Is Odelle alive?"

"She was badly injured but, yes, she's alive. She was giving the police officer CPR when we left."

Ray let out a deep sigh and bowed her head. "Thank you."

The tunnel started rumbling. Headlights lit the wreckage. Someone was coming. Kingsley wouldn't feel safe until he was out of the tunnel and away from Joyce's gun, which was now in the pocket of Ray's jacket. The rumbling stopped and a door slammed.

Nikki appeared in the headlights, gawking at the scene: Abby leaning against the tunnel wall and Kingsley safe in Charlotte's arms. Joyce's leg was bloody. Phoebe Ann was out cold on the hard floor. "This reeks!" Nikki said. She ran to Abby. "This totally reeks!"

Another door slammed, and a woman wearing coveralls stepped into the headlights—Wanda Gentry. Two other women came into the headlights, both wearing coveralls. One looked like Wanda's daughter, same ruddy features but younger and thinner. The other had gray hair and wore a faded *Asheville, North Carolina* t-shirt. Wanda carried a flashlight and quickly made her way to Charlotte. She gave Charlotte a hug. "You okay?"

"Nanna's still in the limo," Charlotte said. "I have to get her out."

Charlotte had barely taken a step toward the limo when Ray grabbed the hem of her denim jumper, holding it tight. "Don't go." She shook her head. "That's not something you want to see."

"You wait here," Wanda told Charlotte. "I'll go get Clare." She motioned to the other women. They followed Wanda to the wreckage. "Good thing there's no traffic coming," she said as the three women pried open one of the doors. Wanda's shock was visible. "Shit, what a mess." The other two women backed away from the wreck.

Charlotte started toward the cars.

"Stay there," Wanda said, holding up her hand. "She's right. You don't want to see this." Wanda took off her John Deere cap and her braided ponytail fell out. She wiped her forehead and let out a loud whew as she stepped inside the mangled door. "What was Clare doing?" she called from inside the wreckage, "She's practically on top of the driver."

"She was hysterical," Ray said. "Even Phoebe Ann couldn't control her. She grabbed the steering wheel. That's why we scraped against the wall of the tunnel. I don't know if she grabbed the wheel to stay out of the tunnel or to save Charlotte."

"Nanna?" Charlotte said. "Wanda, what are you saying? Is she hurt?"

Wanda headed back to Charlotte. She wrapped her arms around Charlotte and Kingsley and spoke in a soft whisper, "Clare's dead, Charlotte. Both Clare and the chauffeur died in the crash."

Charlotte started to cry. "Nanna." Wanda pulled her close and let Charlotte cry on her shoulder.

Clare was gone and Kingsley mourned. He mourned for the past and his innocent crush on Clare, the most beautiful woman he'd ever known. He was glad that Charlotte hadn't carried him to the wreckage. He didn't want to see. He didn't want to remember her that way.

"The police should be here soon," Wanda said, gently. "Let them handle this."

Nikki and the other women carried Abby to the back of Wanda's truck. Ray supervised, making sure they were careful with Abby's injured head and neck. Nikki climbed in after them and cradled Abby in her lap. Joyce was still kneeling beside Phoebe Ann. She stood, careful of her injured thigh.

She pulled her skirt aside so it didn't brush against the wound and limped toward Wanda's truck. Wanda left Charlotte and called the other women to help her pick up Phoebe Ann. "Come over here and help me with this here giant," Wanda said. Wanda grabbed Phoebe Ann's shoulders and the other women held her legs.

"No," Ray said. "They're staying here. Both of them."

"Both? Who?" Wanda asked, still holding onto Phoebe Ann.

"My mother and Phoebe Ann," Ray said. "You're not taking them with you."

"Almost everyone here needs a doctor," Wanda said.

"I'm a doctor," Ray said. "They're staying with me until the police arrive."

"I hope you know what you're doing," Wanda said as she gently returned Phoebe Ann's massive shoulders to the tunnel floor and motioned the other women to do the same with her feet.

Ray walked with Charlotte to Wanda's truck and helped her climb into the front passenger seat. "Go. Take the boy. I never want to see him again." With Charlotte securely in the cab of the truck and Kingsley in her arms, Wanda climbed up and took the driver's seat. The other women who'd come with her climbed into the back with Nikki and Abby.

Behind them, Joyce crumpled to the dirty floor of the tunnel. "Kingsley! My boy!"

Kingsley had never seen her like this. It tore at him. She'd loved him with a grit and fire that had brought him back into this world. He owed her his life—twice. The truth was Kingsley wanted them both, Charlotte and Joyce. Both of his mothers. He wanted Abby and Nikki. He wanted Bapsi and his brilliant half-sister, Ray. He wanted his father. But most of all, he wanted Amanda. They were all his family and he wanted every single one.

Joyce looked like a beggar as she sat on the dirty tunnel floor. Her dress torn and bloody, her perfect makeup smeared with tears and sweat. She called to Charlotte and her voice broke. "My son," she said. "His name is Kingsley."

"I know." Charlotte said.

Ray stood beside Charlotte's open door. She nodded at Joyce. "She won't give up," Ray said. "She'll find a way to wiggle out of being arrested this time just like she did before. And after she does, she'll come for him."

"I'll be ready," Charlotte said.

Ray slammed the door shut and went to the back of the truck to check on Abby. She gently stroked Abby's head. "I love you."

"I love you too, Mom."

Wanda started the truck.

"Take care of her, Nikki," Ray's voice echoed through the tunnel. "Be happy, Charlotte. Enjoy your clean air. Your clear water. Your peaceful world. Take him. Raise him. It won't make any difference. Biology is destiny. He'll ruin everything just like he did forty years ago."

Wanda turned the truck around and headed up the incline. Kingsley watched from Charlotte's shoulder. He watched Joyce struggle to her feet. She didn't scream or try to chase him. She didn't go for the gun in Ray's pocket. She stood there as the truck drove away, a determined look in her sharp hazel eyes and a slight smile on her lips.

They left the tunnel and headed down the long bridge to Chesapeake. The calm waters of the Hampton Roads harbor sparkled in the afternoon sun. In the back, Abby's head rested on Nikki's lap. "It figures," Nikki said. "We finally get a guy in the world, and he'll probably grow up to be a criminal."

"Not this boy," Abby said. "Remember, he's my uncle."

"Uncle!" Kingsley repeated. "She called me Uncle. I have a family."

Kingsley thought about his future. Charlotte would teach him how to drive a backhoe. Nikki would teach him how to play soccer. And Abby would teach him everything else. He'd grow up strong and fast and smart. He'd need that if he was going to fulfill the promise he'd made to rescue Bapsi from whatever punishment she faced for helping him escape. He thought of all the people who had sacrificed to save him and he made a solemn vow to honor their efforts. He would take what he'd learned from his past and make the future a better world. He looked up and saw something following them. Something silhouetted against the bright sky.

A large white gull with bright-red eyes.

Acknowledgements

My first thanks goes to my son, Michael O'Neal, for helping me turn my worries into words. He was one of my beta readers and his input was spot on.

Special thanks to David and Jan O'Neal, Elizabeth Mandell, Michael Kaminski, Judy Reigel, Jennifer Kochard, Robert and Sue Jones, Katie Fusco, Robert Boyle, Pam Evans, Delnavaz Sanjana, and Julie Baird. You were there when I needed you!

I thank the wonderful Janet Macarthur for saving my life. Maintaining a teenager's point of view in a novel can be tricky. Many thanks to my niece Jenai Macarthur for keeping it real. Thanks to Milton and Carolyn Jones for their wisdom.

I thank my creative writing and poetry teachers at WriterHouse in Charlottesville, especially David Ronka whose "necessary and sufficient" mantra pushed me to improve.

It was in David Ronka's classes that I met the talented writers of BACCA Literary (http://baccaliterary.com/), Bethany Carlson, Anne Carley, and Claire Elizabeth Cameron, as well as critique group members Michelle Frazier, Cortney Meriwether, Susan Holland, Kelley Libby, and Raennah Lorne. I thank them all for their patience and insights.

Thanks to book group members Deborah Anderson, Diane Bayer, Jan Eckert, Diane Haldane, Lola Heffner, Regina Hissong, Sherrel Hissong, Vicki Heitsch, Vicki Krauss, Saundra Larson, Susan Lawrence, Cathy Leitner, Kathy Marchal, June Nabors, Cynthia Page, Sally Pettit, Sharon Poff, Sandy Riner, Patty Sensabaugh, Kathy Thompson, Sue Totty, Annette Will, and Jennifer Matthaei for their feedback.

The medical center in *Kingsley* is very loosely based on the University of Virginia Medical Center. I thank Dr. Leigh Cantrell, Nurse Peggy Scott, and Social Worker Bridget Peterson-Fennel, as well as Dr. Louisa Hann for their care and encouragement.

"*. . . the ability of environmental factors to act on gonadal development has been* *shown to cause the epigenetic transgenerational inheritance of disease . . ."* Skinner Laboratory http://skinner.wsu.edu/research.html.

Above is a quote from one of the many articles I used to link environmental pollutants and disease to create The Collapse. I thank the brilliant work of Dr. Michael K. Skinner and the Skinner Laboratory at Washington State University for their research on Epigenetic Transgenerational Inheritance. I thank PRI Science Friday correspondent Ira Flatow for his segment on rotifers. I thank the University of Virginia Department of Neuroscience for their discovery of the brain – immune system connection. I thank Neurologist Madeline Harrison (another alumni of David Ronka's creative writing class) for her expertise.

Many editors and artists helped prepare *Kingsley* for publication: Aimee Brasseur of JMU, Catherine Adams of Inkslinger Editing LLC, and editor Betsy Ballenger. I thank video director Michael Duni for KINGLEY'S enticing book trailer and graphic artist Mayapriya Long of Bookwrights for her haunting cover design. Coordinating a team of artists, editors, and film makers requires a great coach. I am grateful to Bethany Carlson of The Artists Partner (http://theartistspartner.com/) for her leadership.

Acknowledgments, like stories, should begin and end with those most essential. Without them, *Kingsley* would exist only as a deleted file on a recycled computer. I thank my beloved sister, Elizabeth Brickhouse, for cheering me every step of the way. And, finally, I thank the man who literally supported me as I wrote *Kingsley*, my husband, Don O'Neal. I love you, Don. Forever.

About the Author

Carolyn O'Neal is an Environmentalist and a Storyteller. Her eco-fiction SILENT GRACE won The Hook's 2013 Short Story contest, judged by bestselling author John Grisham. She volunteers for the Chesapeake Bay Foundation and the Virginia Oyster Shell Recycling Program. Carolyn was born three blocks from the Chesapeake Bay in Norfolk, Virginia. She currently resides in Charlottesville, Virginia.

AuthorCarolynONeal.com

Facebook.com/AuthorCarolynONeal

AuthorCarolynONeal@gmail.com

Made in the USA
Charleston, SC
23 February 2016